NEGIMA!

Ken Akamatsu

TRANSLATED BY

Hajime Honda

ADAPTED BY

Peter David and Kathleen O'Shea David

LETTERED BY

Studio Cutie

DEL REY

BALLANTINE BOOKS • NEW YORK

A Word from the Author

Hi, this is Ken Akamatsu. It's been a while.

After taking over a year off after *Love Hina*, I have returned to work with my new serial, *Magister Negi Magi*! I hope you enjoy it.

The protagonist of *Negima!*, Negi, is cute, smart and talented—the kind of protagonist you'd never find in my previous manga! Ironically enough, though, top student personalities like him don't usually stand out (ha ha)!

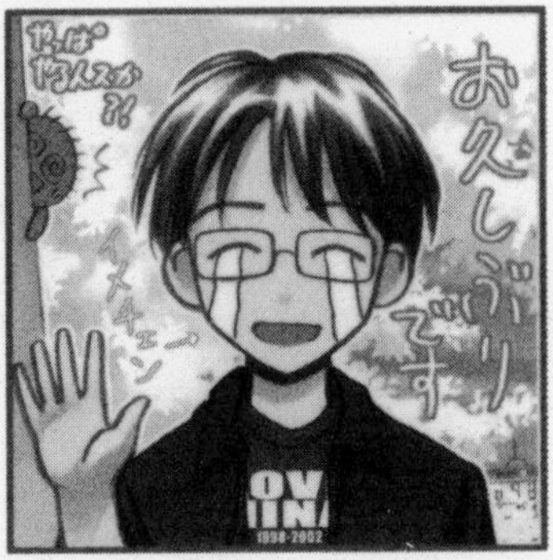
お久しぶりです

It's been so long.

So, are you gonna take the plunge!?

The 31 beautiful girls in his class all have unique personalities, each with her share of trials and tribulations. (Actually, some of them aren't even human. . . .) Maybe they're the real protagonists of *Negima!*?

So let's take our time and watch over Negi as he grows up.

Ken Akamatsu
http://www.ailove.net

Translator—Hajime Honda
Adaptors—Peter David and Kathleen O'Shea David
Lettering—Studio Cutie
Cover Design—David Stevenson

A Del Rey® Book
Published by The Random House Publishing Group

Published in the United States by Del Rey Books, an imprint of The Random House Publishing Group, a division of Random House, Inc., New York, and simultaneously in Canada by Random House of Canada Limited, Toronto. First published in serial form by Shonen Magazine Comics and subsequently published in book form by Kodansha, Ltd., Tokyo in 2003. Copyright © 2003 by Ken Akamatsu.

Del Rey is a registered trademark and the Del Rey colophon is a trademark of Random House, Inc.

www.delreymanga.com

Library of Congress Control Number: 2004090830

ISBN 0-345-47046-X

Manufactured in the United States of America

First Edition: May 2004

19 18 17 16 15 14 13 12

Honorifics

Throughout the Del Rey Manga books, you will find Japanese honorifics left intact in the translations. For those not familiar with how the Japanese use honorifics, and more important, how they differ from American honorifics, we present this brief overview.

Politeness has always been a critical facet of Japanese culture. Ever since the feudal era, when Japan was a highly stratified society, use of honorifics—which can be defined as polite speech that indicates relationship or status—has played an essential role in the Japanese language. When addressing someone in Japanese, an honorific usually takes the form of a suffix attached to one's name (example: "Asuna-san"), or as a title at the end of one's name or in place of the name itself (example: "Negi-sensei," or simply "Sensei!").

Honorifics can be expressions of respect or endearment. In the context of manga and anime, honorifics give insight into the nature of the relationship between characters. Many translations into English leave out these important honorifics, and therefore distort the "feel" of the original Japanese. Because Japanese honorifics contain nuances that English honorifics lack, it is our policy at Del Rey not to translate them. Here, instead, is a guide to some of the honorifics you may encounter in Del Rey Manga.

-*san*: This is the most common honorific, and is equivalent to Mr., Miss, Ms., Mrs., etc. It is the all-purpose honorific and can be used in any situation where politeness is required.

-*sama*: This is one level higher than *san*. It is used to confer great respect.

-*dono*: This comes from the word *tono*, which means *lord*. It is an even higher level than *sama*, and confers utmost respect.

-*kun*: This suffix is used at the end of boys' names to express familiarity or endearment. It is also sometimes used by men among friends, or when addressing someone younger or of a lower station.

-*chan*: This is used to express endearment, mostly toward girls. It is also used for little boys, pets, and even among lovers. It gives a sense of childish cuteness.

Sempai: This title suggests that the addressee is one's "senior" in a group or organization. It is most often used in a school setting, where underclassmen refer to their upperclassmen as "sempai." It can also be used in the workplace, such as when a newer employee addresses an employee who has seniority in the company.

Kohai: This is the opposite of *sempai*, and is used toward underclassmen in school or newcomers in the workplace. It connotes that the addressee is of lower station.

Sensei: Literally meaning "one who has come before," this title is used for teachers, doctors, or masters of any profession or art.

-[blank]: Usually forgotten in these lists, but perhaps the most significant difference between Japanese and English. The lack of honorific means that the speaker has permission to address the person in a very intimate way. Usually, only family, spouses, or very close friends have this kind of permission. Known as *yobisute*, it can be gratifying when someone who has earned the intimacy starts to call one by one's name without an honorific. But when that intimacy hasn't been earned, it can also be very insulting.

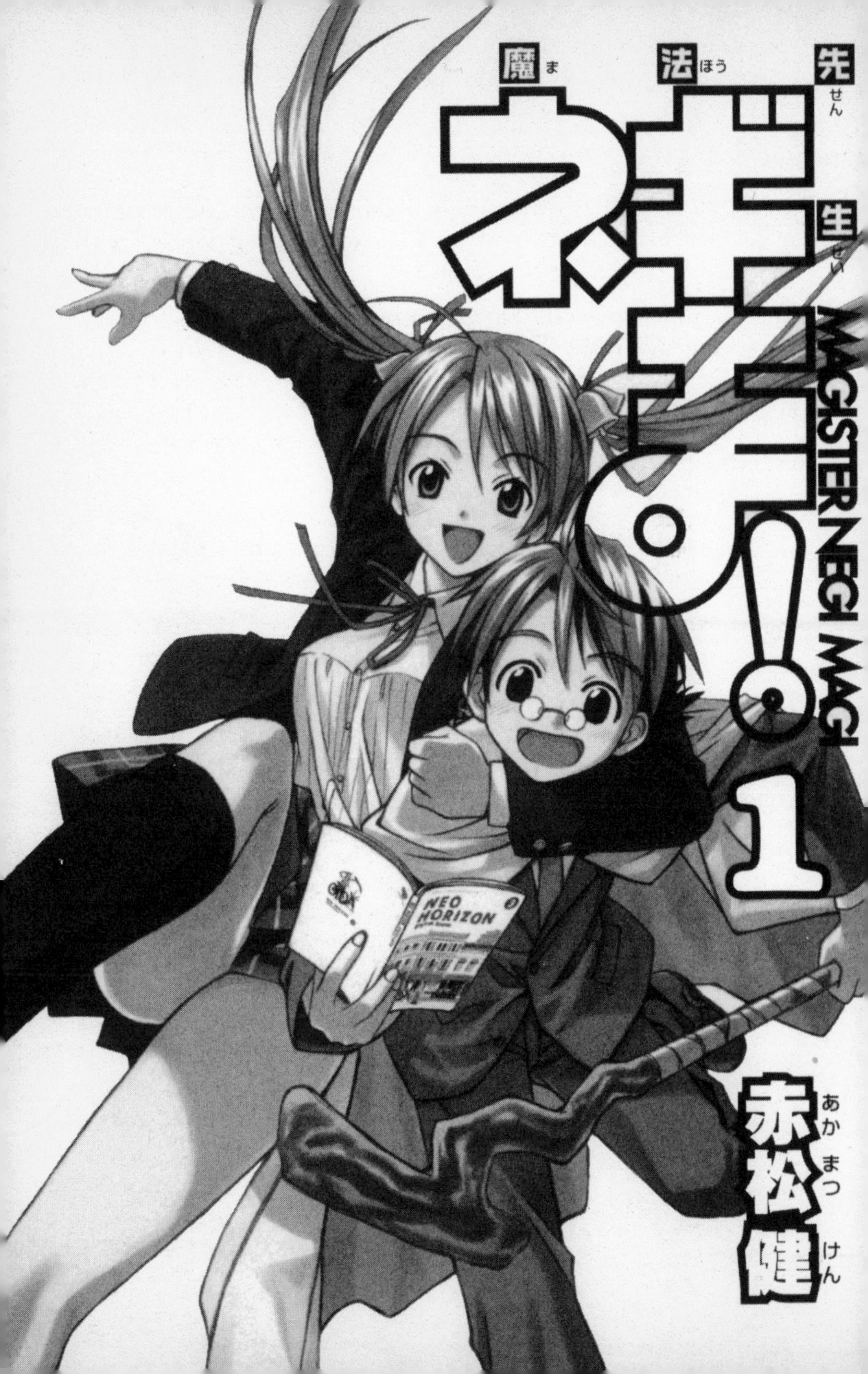

魔法先生ネギま！
MAGISTER NEGI MAGI
1
赤松健
NEO HORIZON

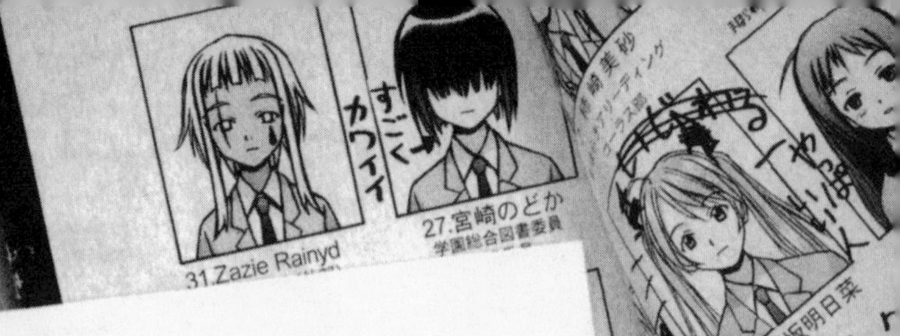

31.Zazie Rainyd
すごくカワイイ
27.宮崎のどか
8. 神楽坂明日菜

Contents

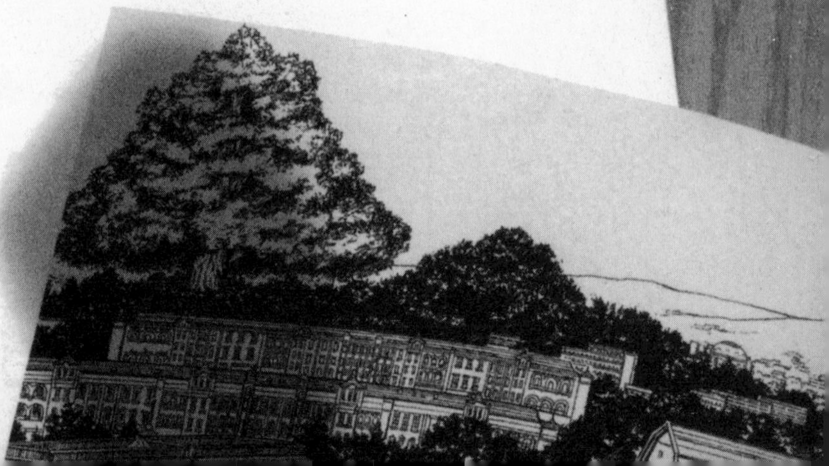

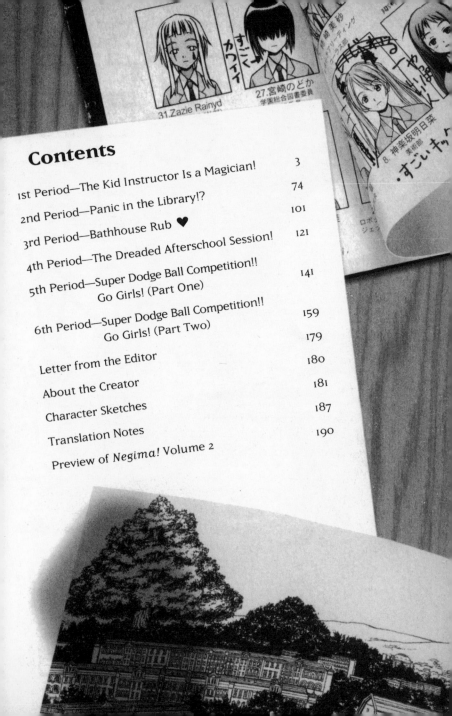

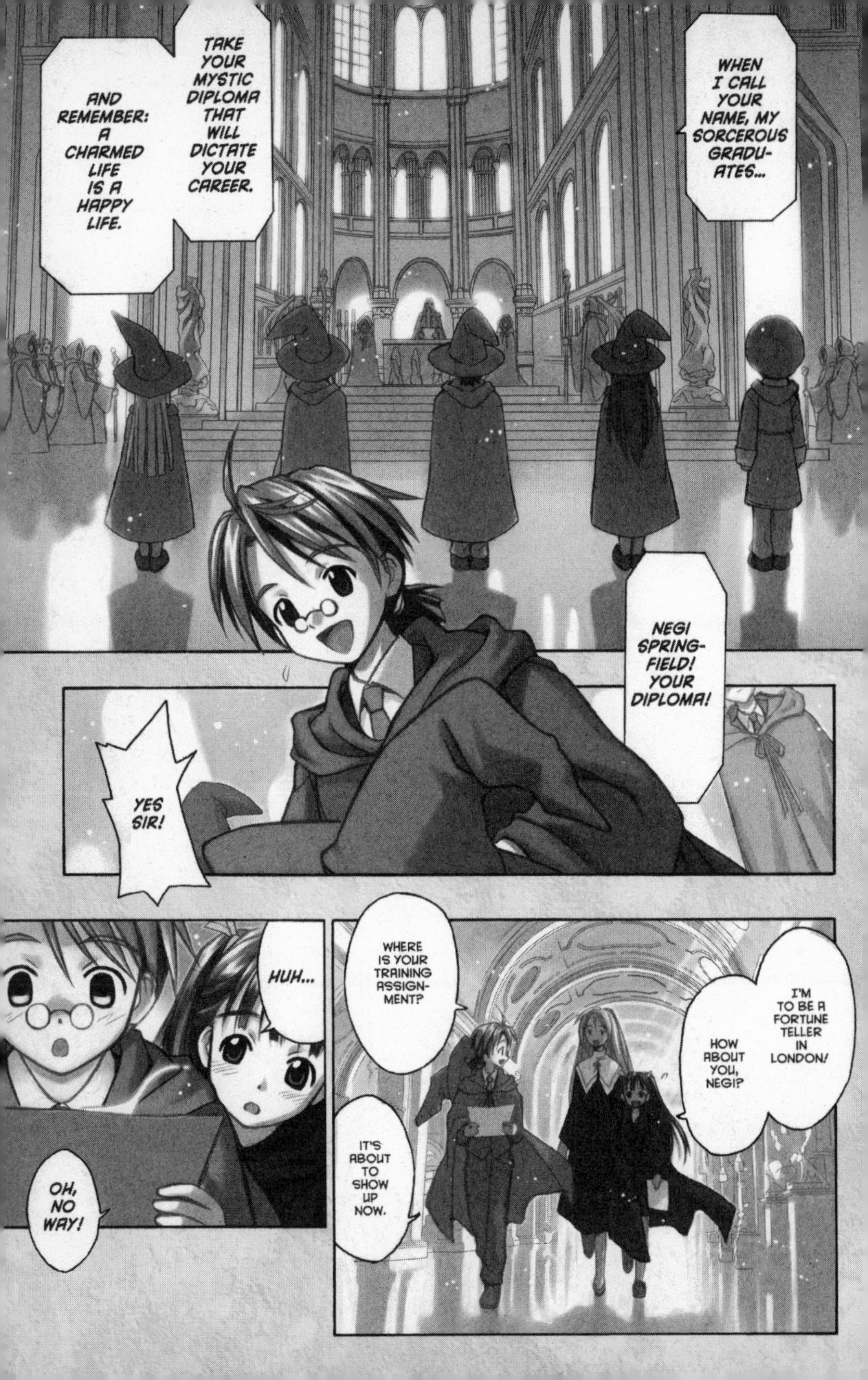
WHEN I CALL YOUR NAME, MY SORCEROUS GRADU-ATES...
TAKE YOUR MYSTIC DIPLOMA THAT WILL DICTATE YOUR CAREER.
AND REMEMBER: A CHARMED LIFE IS A HAPPY LIFE.
NEGI SPRING-FIELD! YOUR DIPLOMA!
YES SIR!
WHERE IS YOUR TRAINING ASSIGN-MENT?
I'M TO BE A FORTUNE TELLER IN LONDON!
HOW ABOUT YOU, NEGI?
IT'S ABOUT TO SHOW UP NOW.
HUH...
OH, NO WAY!

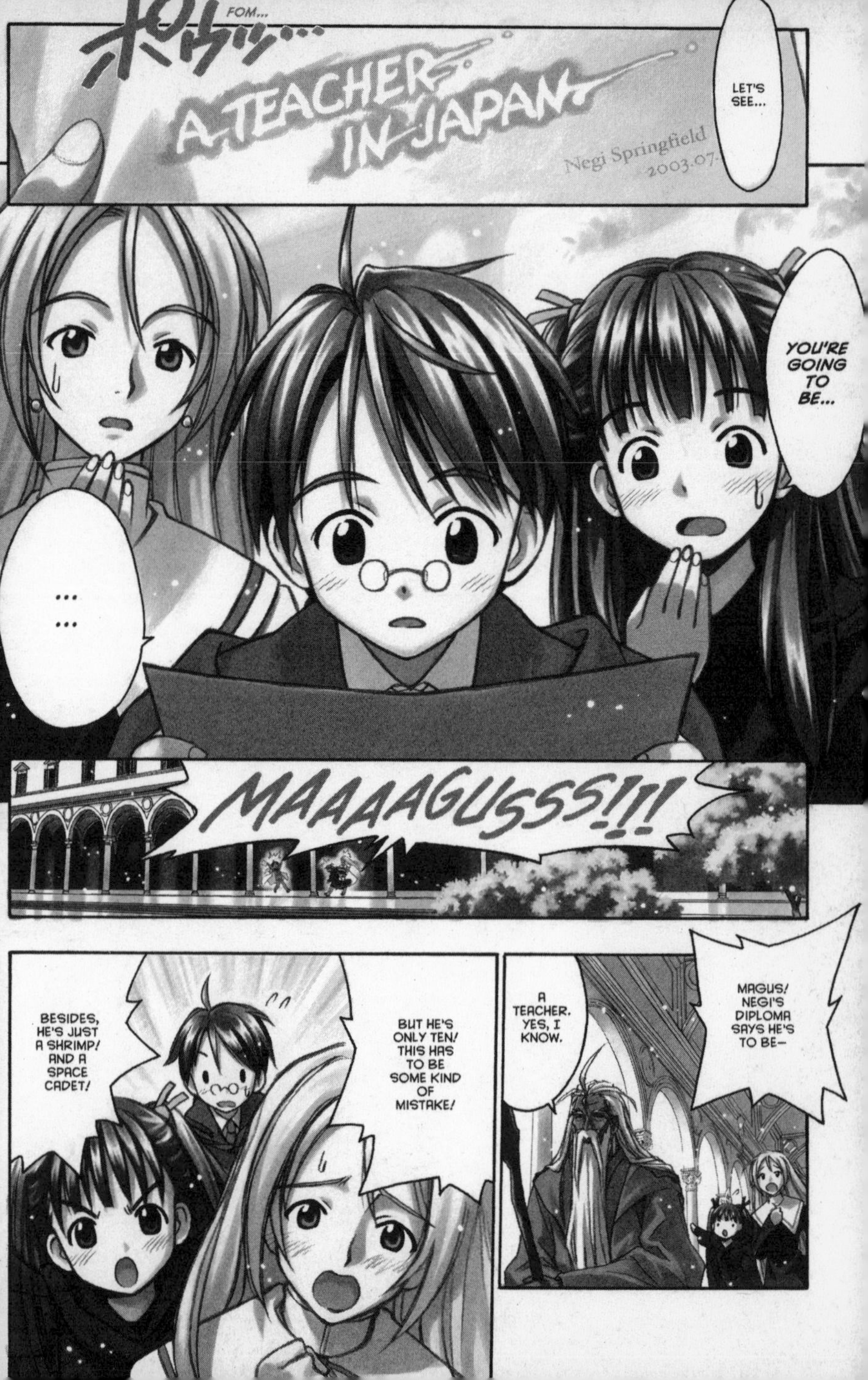
LET'S SEE...
FOM...
A TEACHER IN JAPAN
Negi Springfield
2003.07.
YOU'RE GOING TO BE...
...
...
MAAAAGUSSS!!!
MAGUS! NEGI'S DIPLOMA SAYS HE'S TO BE—
A TEACHER. YES, I KNOW.
BUT HE'S ONLY TEN! THIS HAS TO BE SOME KIND OF MISTAKE!
BESIDES, HE'S JUST A SHRIMP! AND A SPACE CADET!

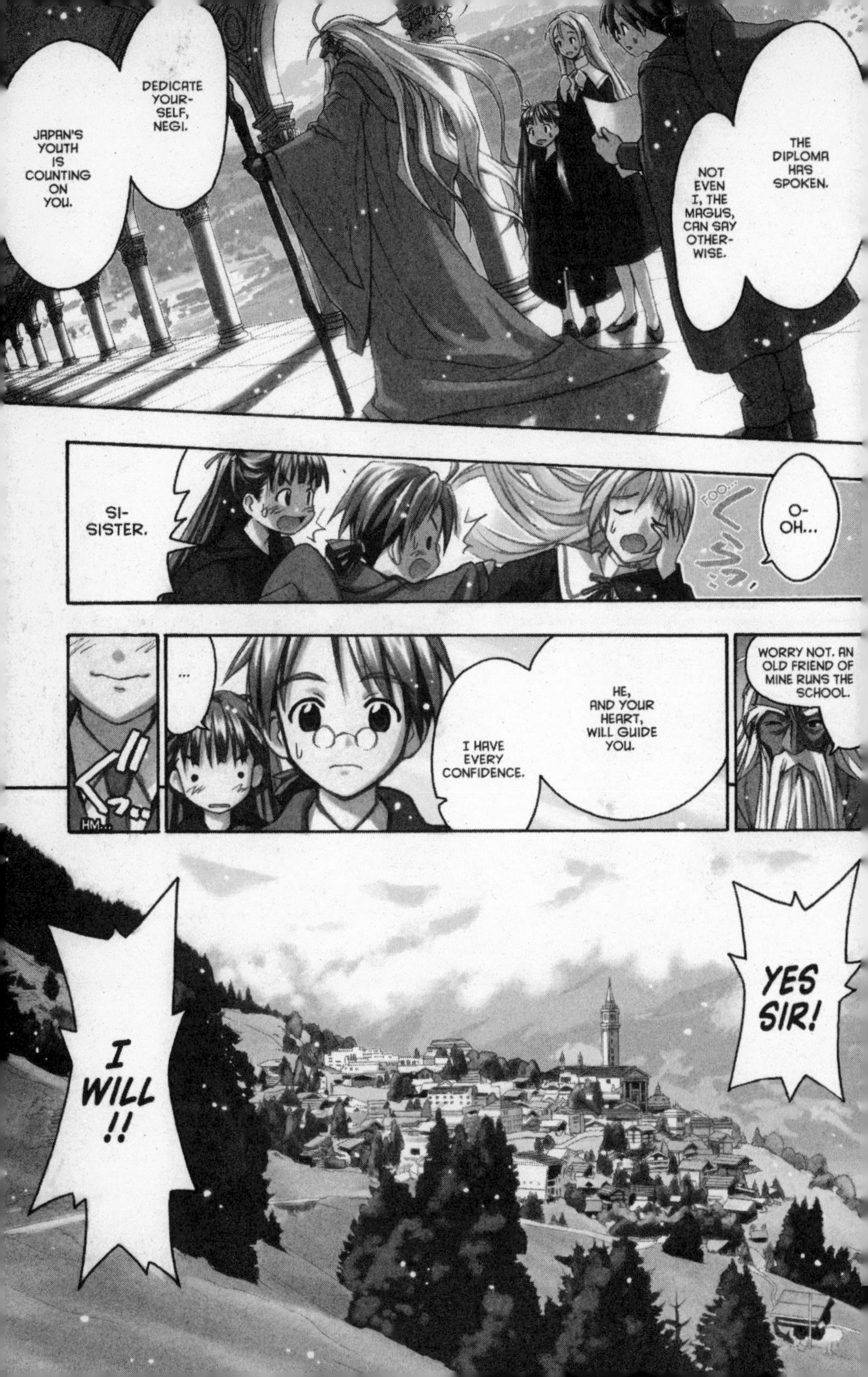
THE DIPLOMA HAS SPOKEN.
NOT EVEN I, THE MAGUS, CAN SAY OTHERWISE.
DEDICATE YOURSELF, NEGI.
JAPAN'S YOUTH IS COUNTING ON YOU.
O-OH...
FOO...
SI-SISTER.
WORRY NOT. AN OLD FRIEND OF MINE RUNS THE SCHOOL.
HE, AND YOUR HEART, WILL GUIDE YOU.
I HAVE EVERY CONFIDENCE.
...
HM...
YES SIR!
I WILL!!

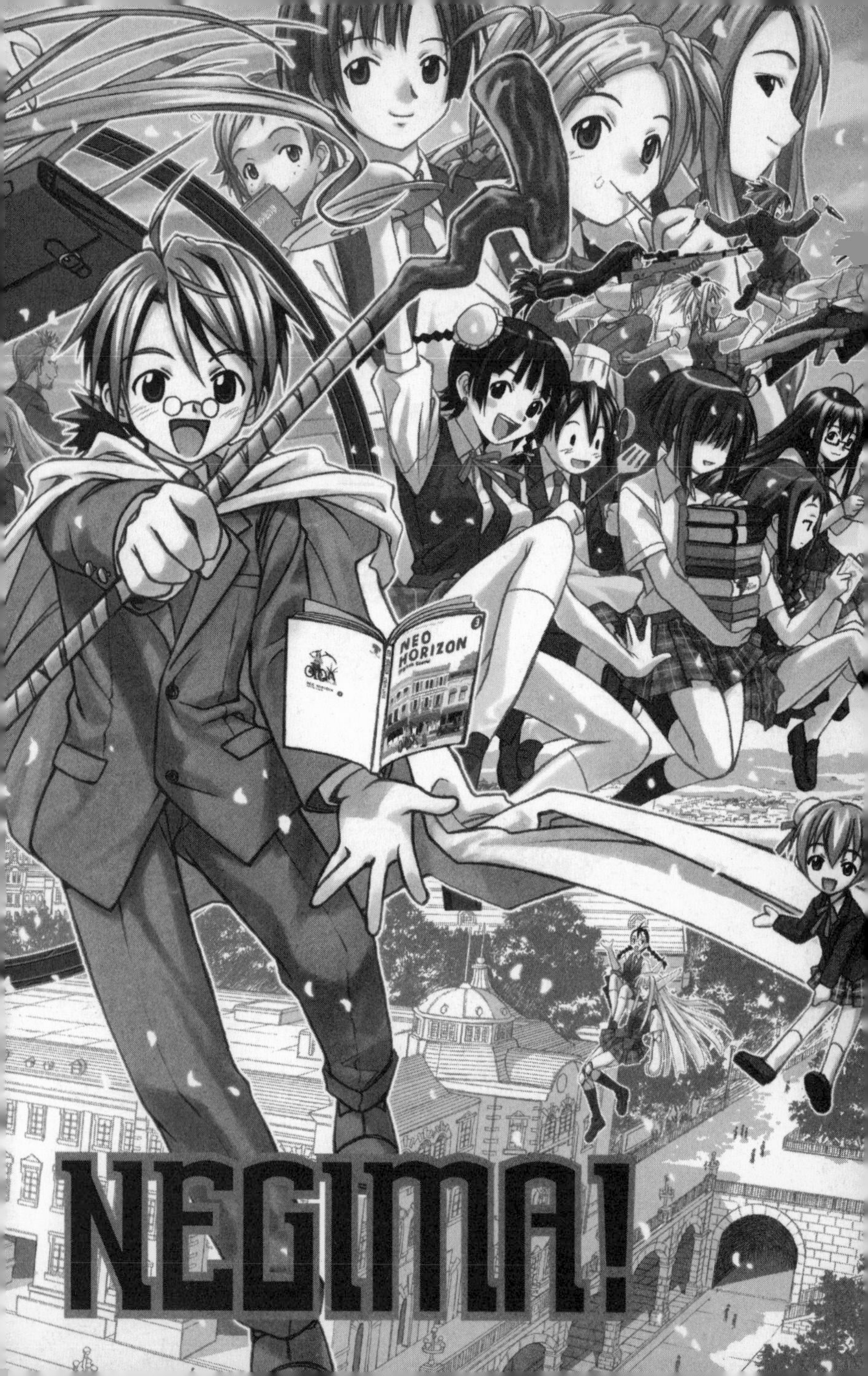
NEO HORIZON
3
NEGIMA!

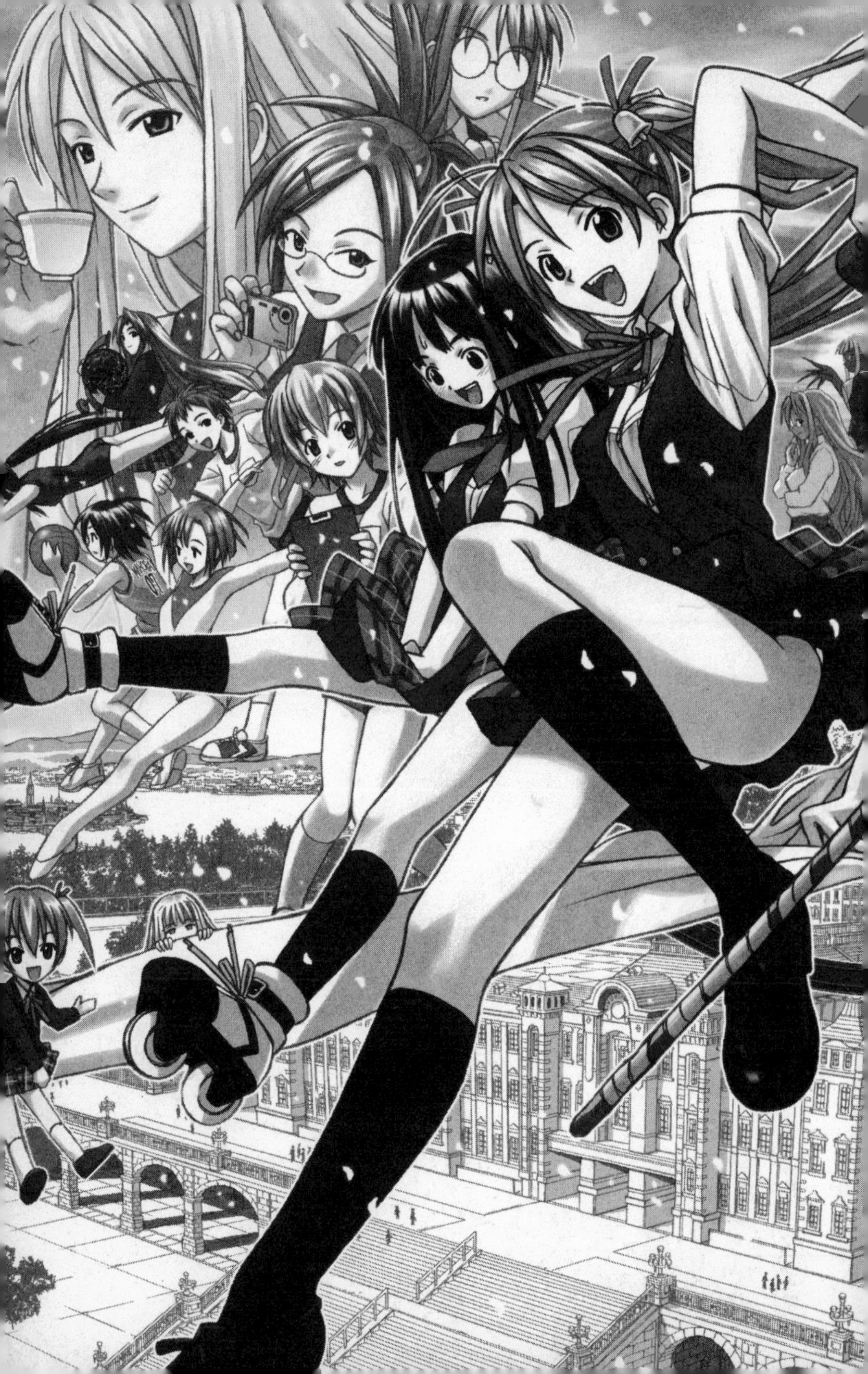

MAHORA
NEGIMA!

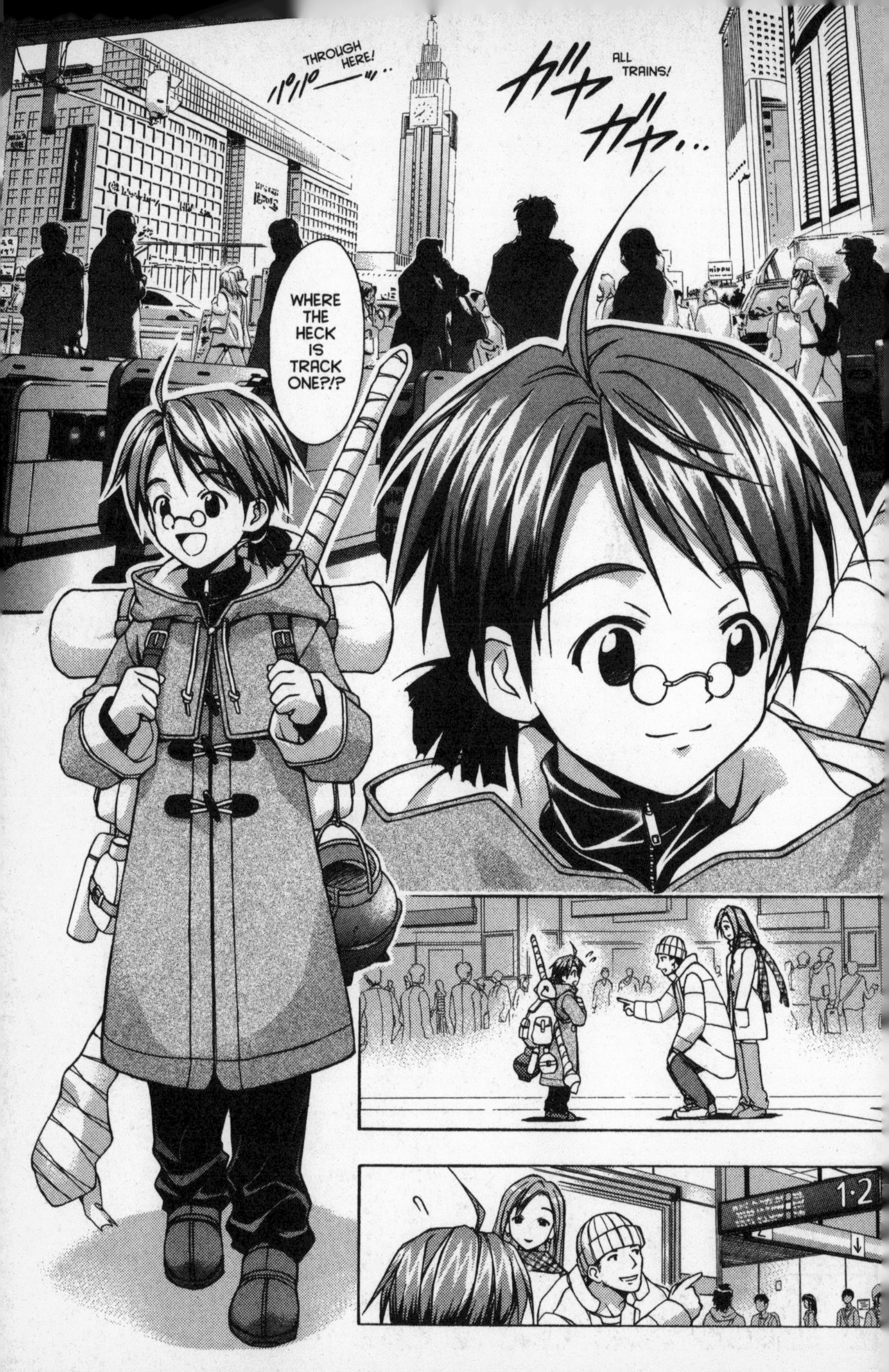

ALL TRAINS!
ガヤ ガヤ…
THROUGH HERE!
WHERE THE HECK IS TRACK ONE?!?
1·2

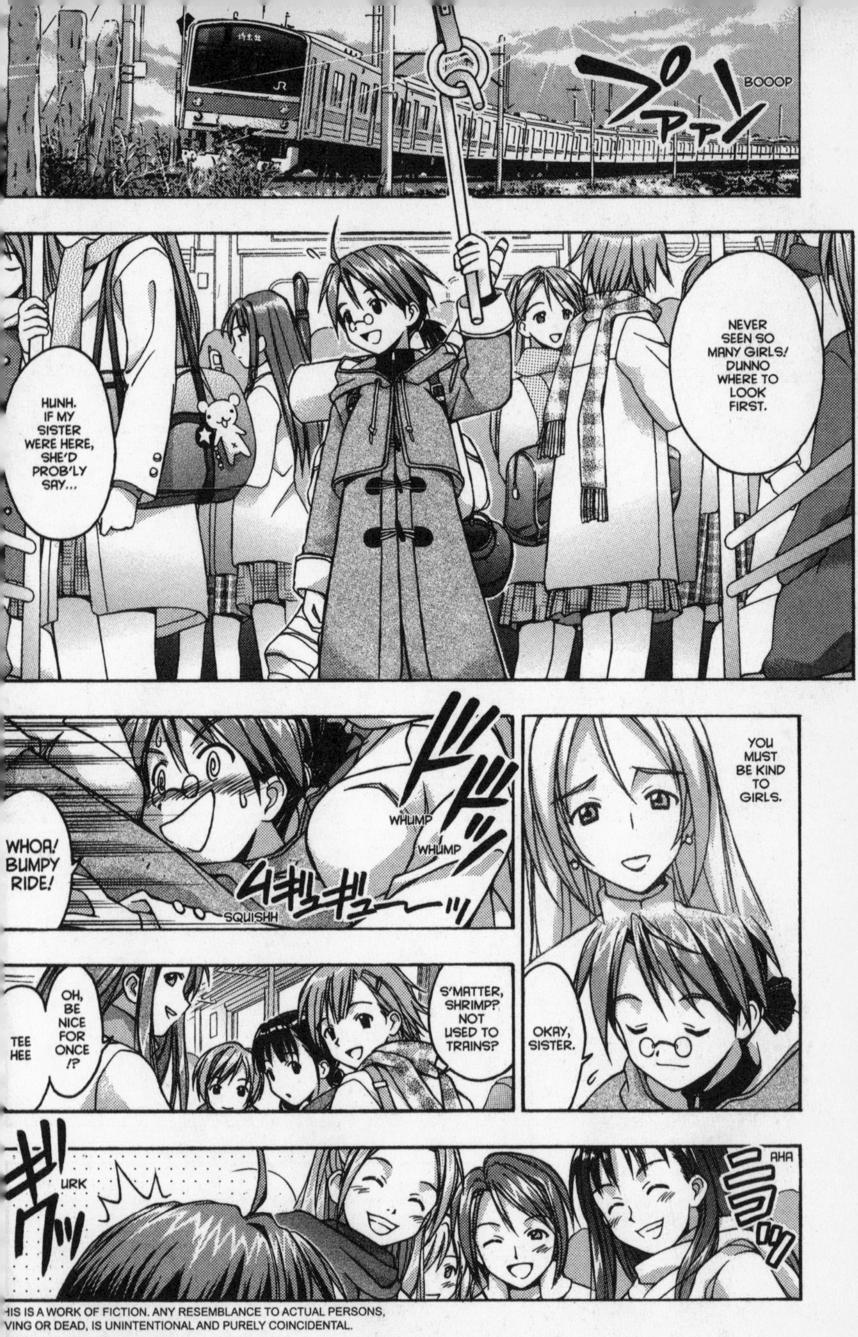
BOOOP
NEVER SEEN SO MANY GIRLS! DUNNO WHERE TO LOOK FIRST.
HUNH. IF MY SISTER WERE HERE, SHE'D PROB'LY SAY...
YOU MUST BE KIND TO GIRLS.
OKAY, SISTER.
WHUMP
WHUMP
SQUISHH
WHOA! BUMPY RIDE!
S'MATTER, SHRIMP? NOT USED TO TRAINS?
OH, BE NICE FOR ONCE!?
TEE HEE
AHA
URK

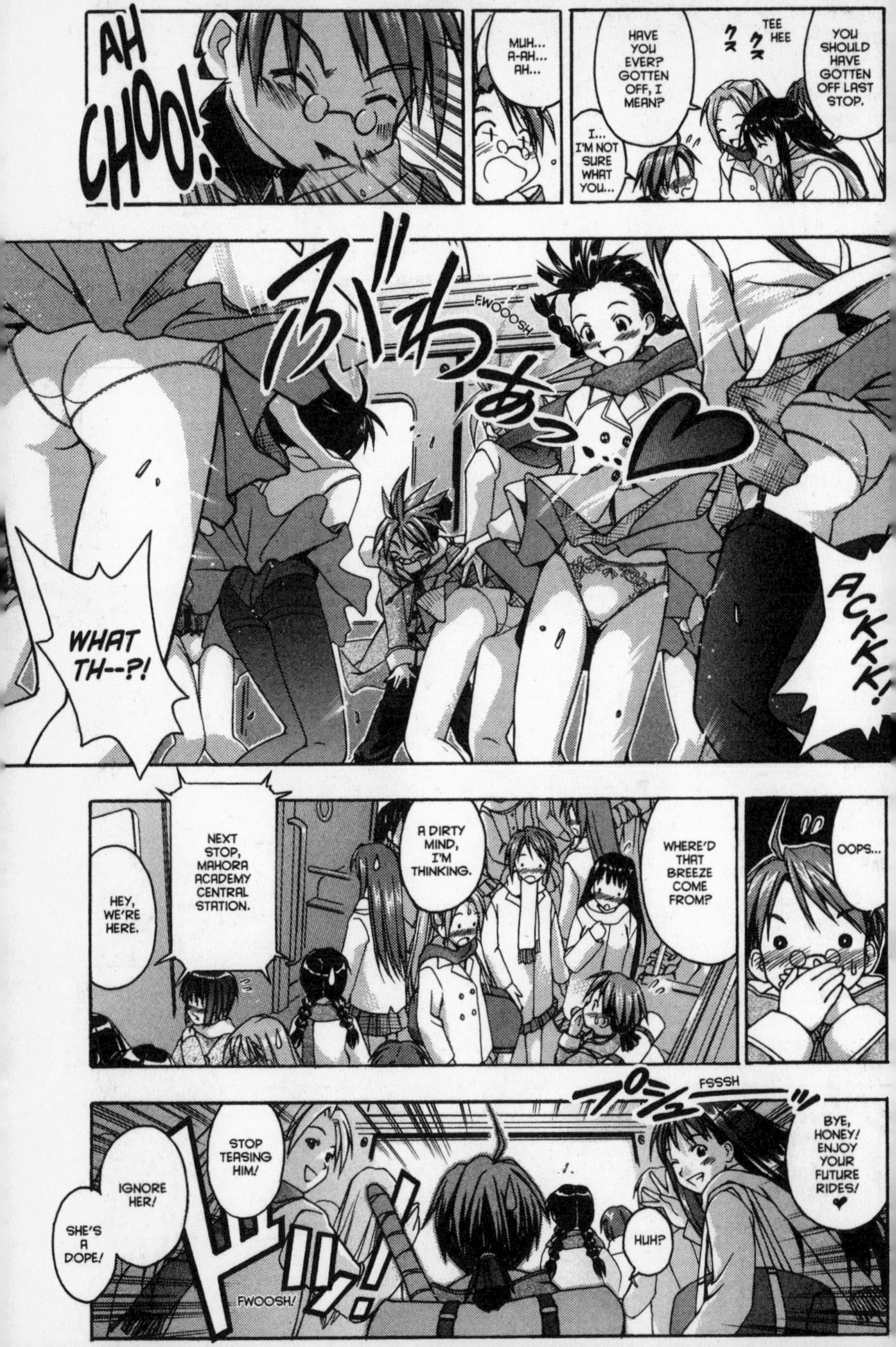

YOU SHOULD HAVE GOTTEN OFF LAST STOP.
TEE HEE
クス クス
HAVE YOU EVER? GOTTEN OFF, I MEAN?
I... I'M NOT SURE WHAT YOU...
MUH... A-AH... AH...
AH CHOO!
ぶわあっ
FWOOOSH
ACKKK!
WHAT TH--?!
OOPS...
WHERE'D THAT BREEZE COME FROM?
A DIRTY MIND, I'M THINKING.
NEXT STOP, MAHORA ACADEMY CENTRAL STATION.
HEY, WE'RE HERE.
プシューッ
FSSSH
BYE, HONEY! ENJOY YOUR FUTURE RIDES! ❤
HUH?
STOP TEASING HIM!
IGNORE HER!
SHE'S A DOPE!
FWOOSH!

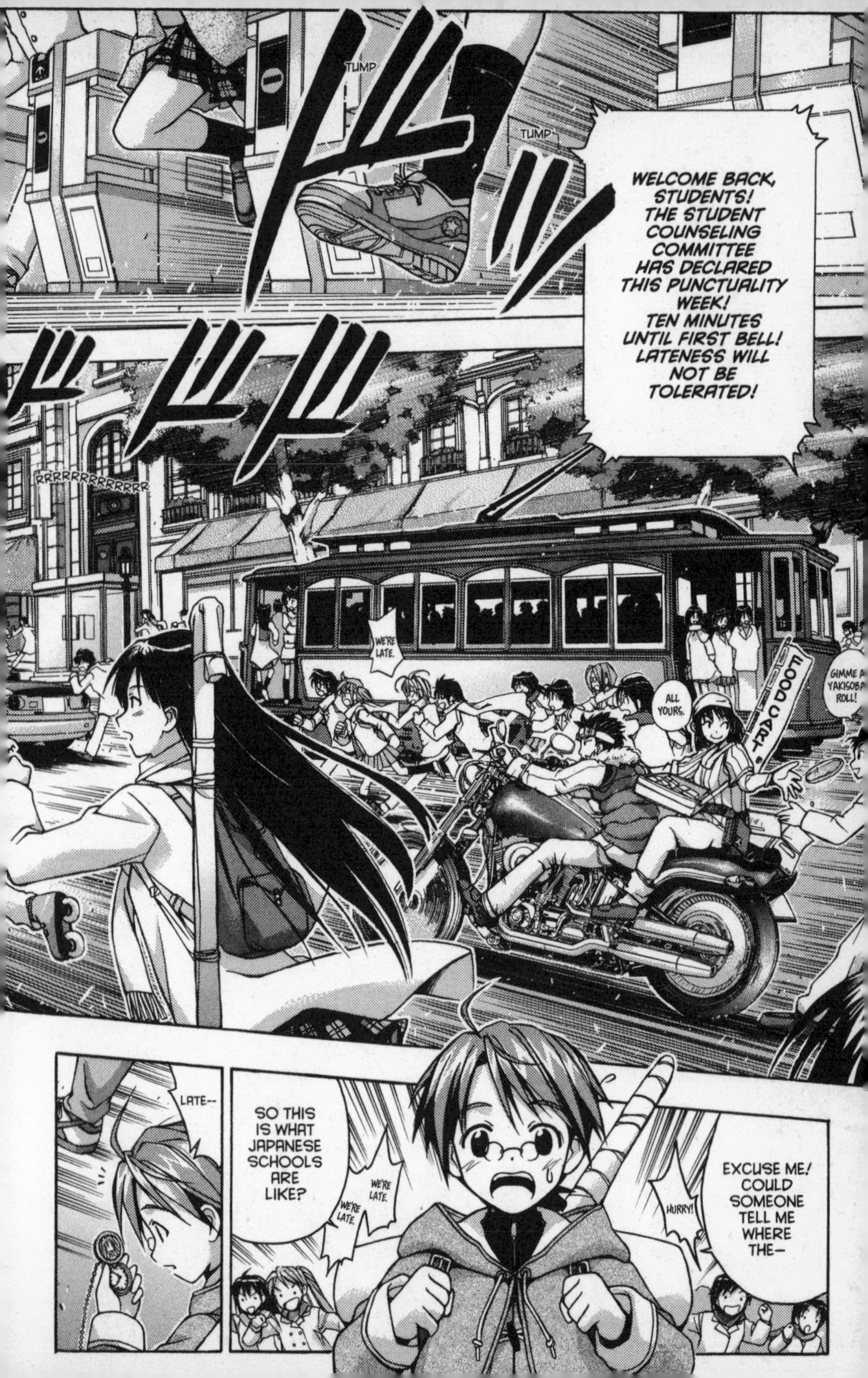
TUMP
TUMP
WELCOME BACK, STUDENTS! THE STUDENT COUNSELING COMMITTEE HAS DECLARED THIS PUNCTUALITY WEEK! TEN MINUTES UNTIL FIRST BELL! LATENESS WILL NOT BE TOLERATED!
GIMME A YAKISOBA ROLL!
ALL YOURS.
FOOD CART
WE'RE LATE.
RRRRRRRRRRRRR
EXCUSE ME! COULD SOMEONE TELL ME WHERE THE—
HURRY!
SO THIS IS WHAT JAPANESE SCHOOLS ARE LIKE?
WE'RE LATE.
WE'RE LATE.
LATE--

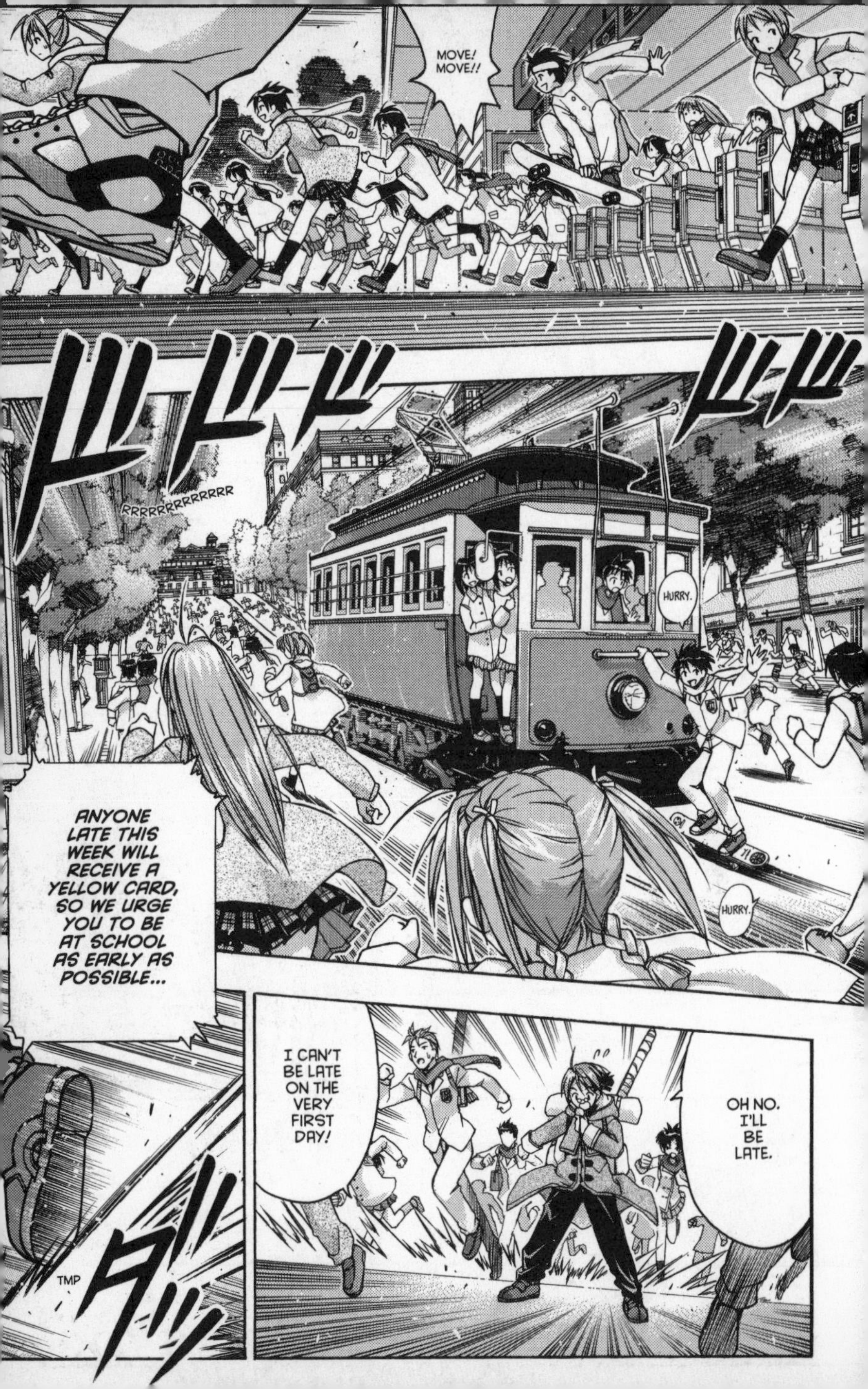
MOVE! MOVE!!
HURRY.
RRRRRRRRRRRR
HURRY.
ANYONE LATE THIS WEEK WILL RECEIVE A YELLOW CARD, SO WE URGE YOU TO BE AT SCHOOL AS EARLY AS POSSIBLE...
OH NO. I'LL BE LATE.
I CAN'T BE LATE ON THE VERY FIRST DAY!
TMP

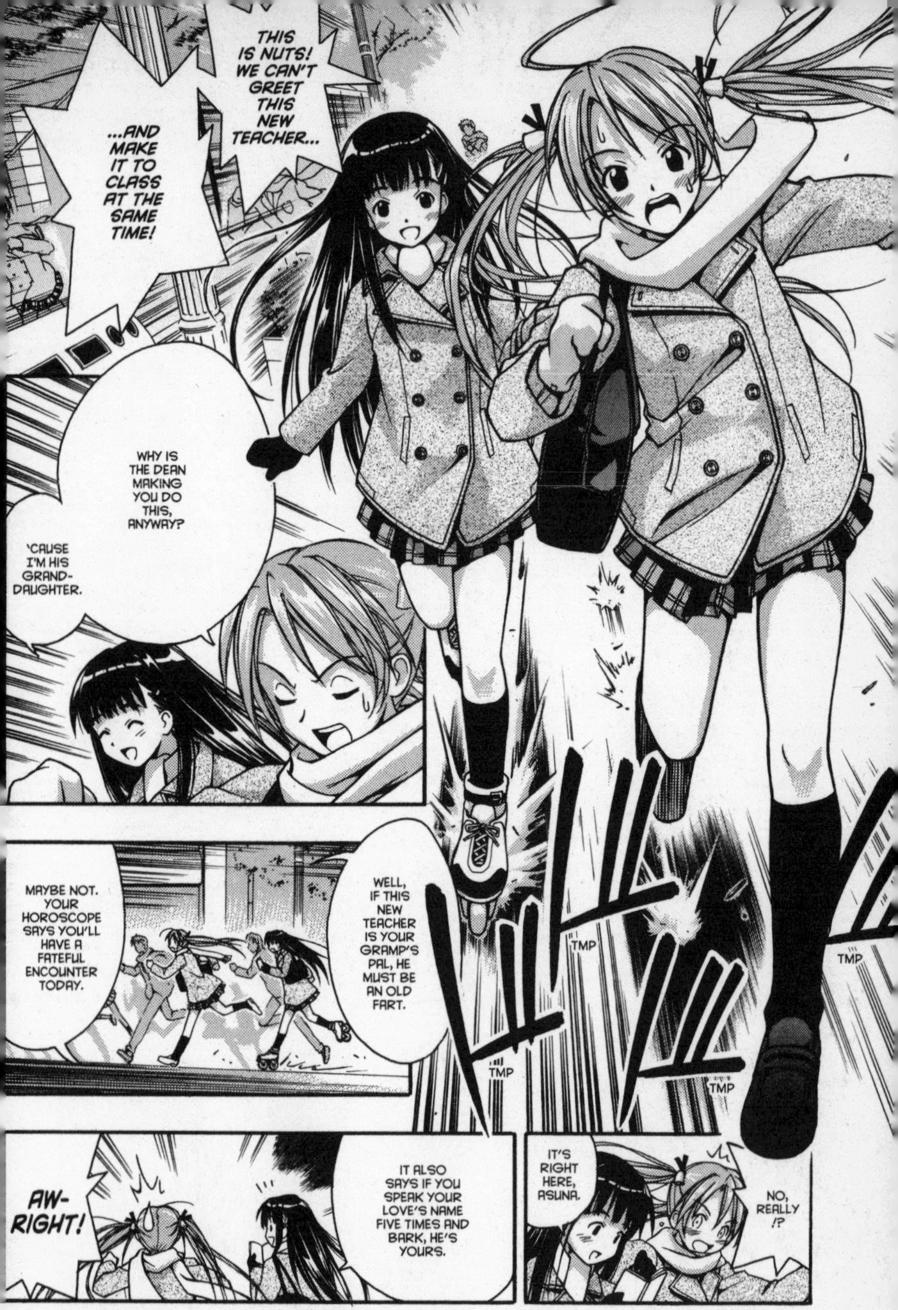
THIS IS NUTS! WE CAN'T GREET THIS NEW TEACHER...
...AND MAKE IT TO CLASS AT THE SAME TIME!
WHY IS THE DEAN MAKING YOU DO THIS, ANYWAY?
'CAUSE I'M HIS GRAND-DAUGHTER.
TMP
TMP
TMP
TMP
WELL, IF THIS NEW TEACHER IS YOUR GRAMP'S PAL, HE MUST BE AN OLD FART.
MAYBE NOT. YOUR HOROSCOPE SAYS YOU'LL HAVE A FATEFUL ENCOUNTER TODAY.
NO, REALLY !?
IT'S RIGHT HERE, ASUNA.
IT ALSO SAYS IF YOU SPEAK YOUR LOVE'S NAME FIVE TIMES AND BARK, HE'S YOURS.
AW-RIGHT!

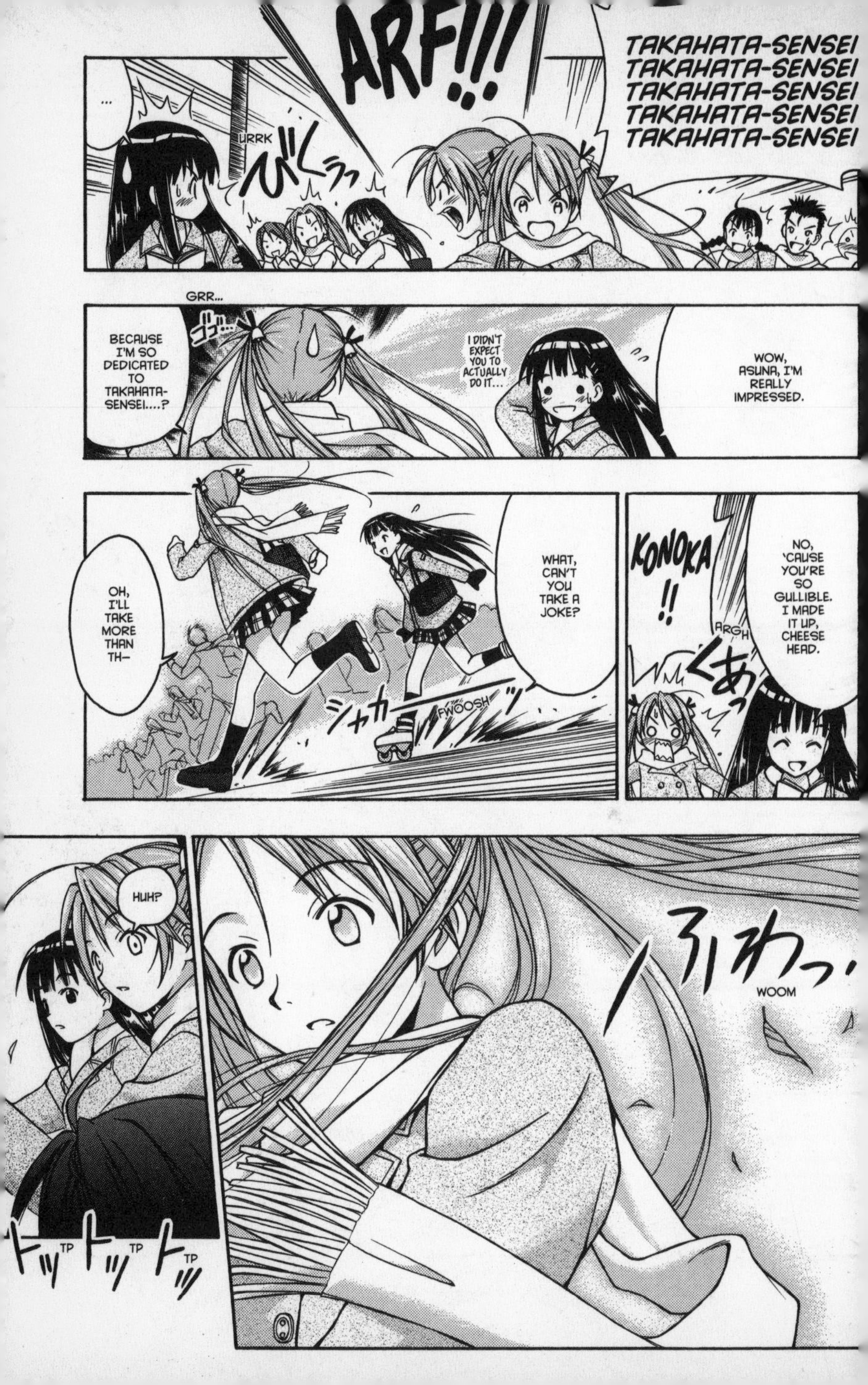

TAKAHATA-SENSEI
TAKAHATA-SENSEI
TAKAHATA-SENSEI
TAKAHATA-SENSEI
TAKAHATA-SENSEI
ARF!!!
URRK
...
WOW, ASUNA, I'M REALLY IMPRESSED.
I DIDN'T EXPECT YOU TO ACTUALLY DO IT...
GRR...
BECAUSE I'M SO DEDICATED TO TAKAHATA-SENSEI....?
NO, 'CAUSE YOU'RE SO GULLIBLE. I MADE IT UP, CHEESE HEAD.
KONOKA!!
ARGH
WHAT, CAN'T YOU TAKE A JOKE?
FWOOSH
OH, I'LL TAKE MORE THAN TH—
WOOM
HUH?
TP
TP
TP

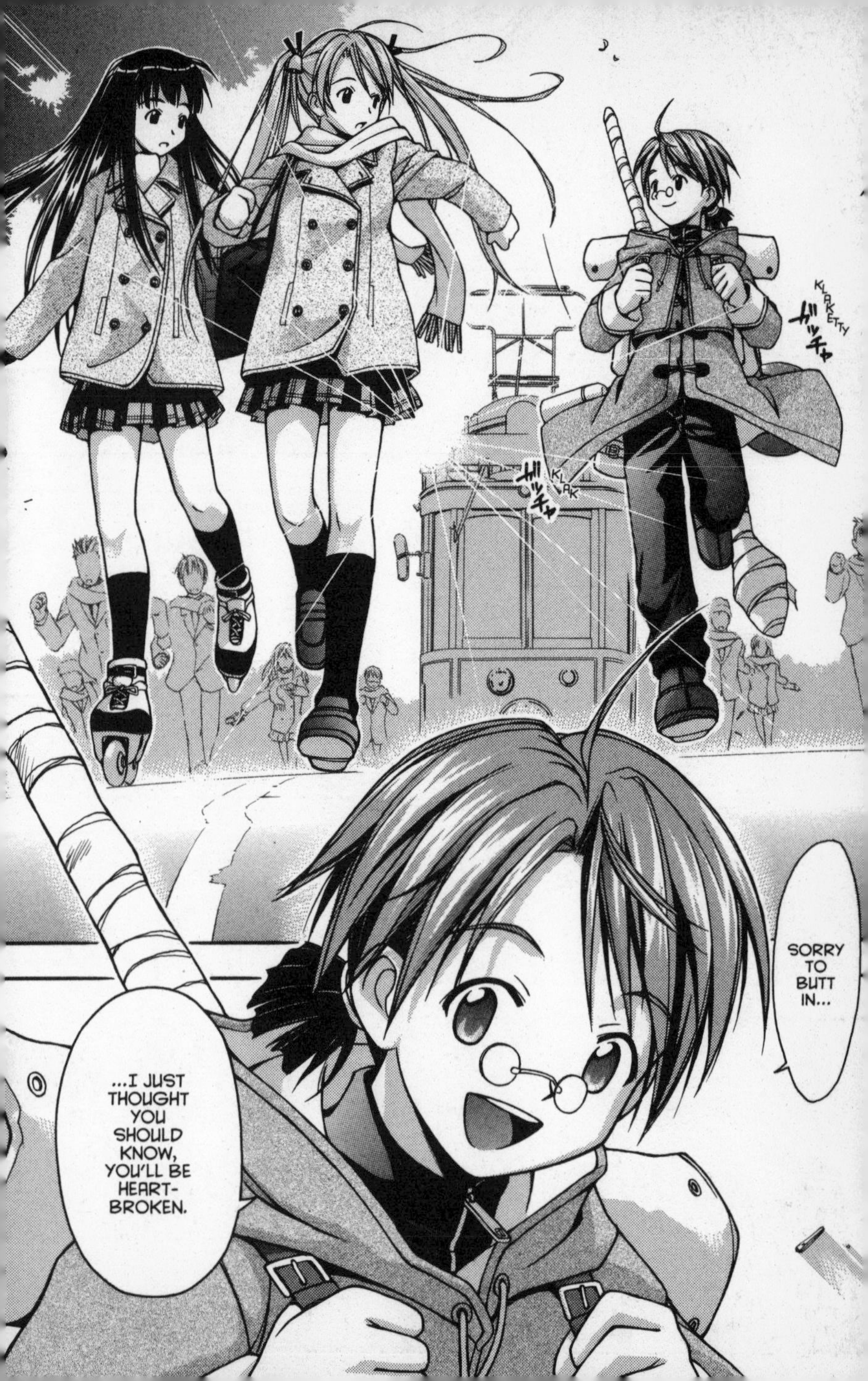
KLAKETTY
ガッチャ
KLAK
ガッチャ
SORRY TO BUTT IN...
...I JUST THOUGHT YOU SHOULD KNOW, YOU'LL BE HEART-BROKEN.

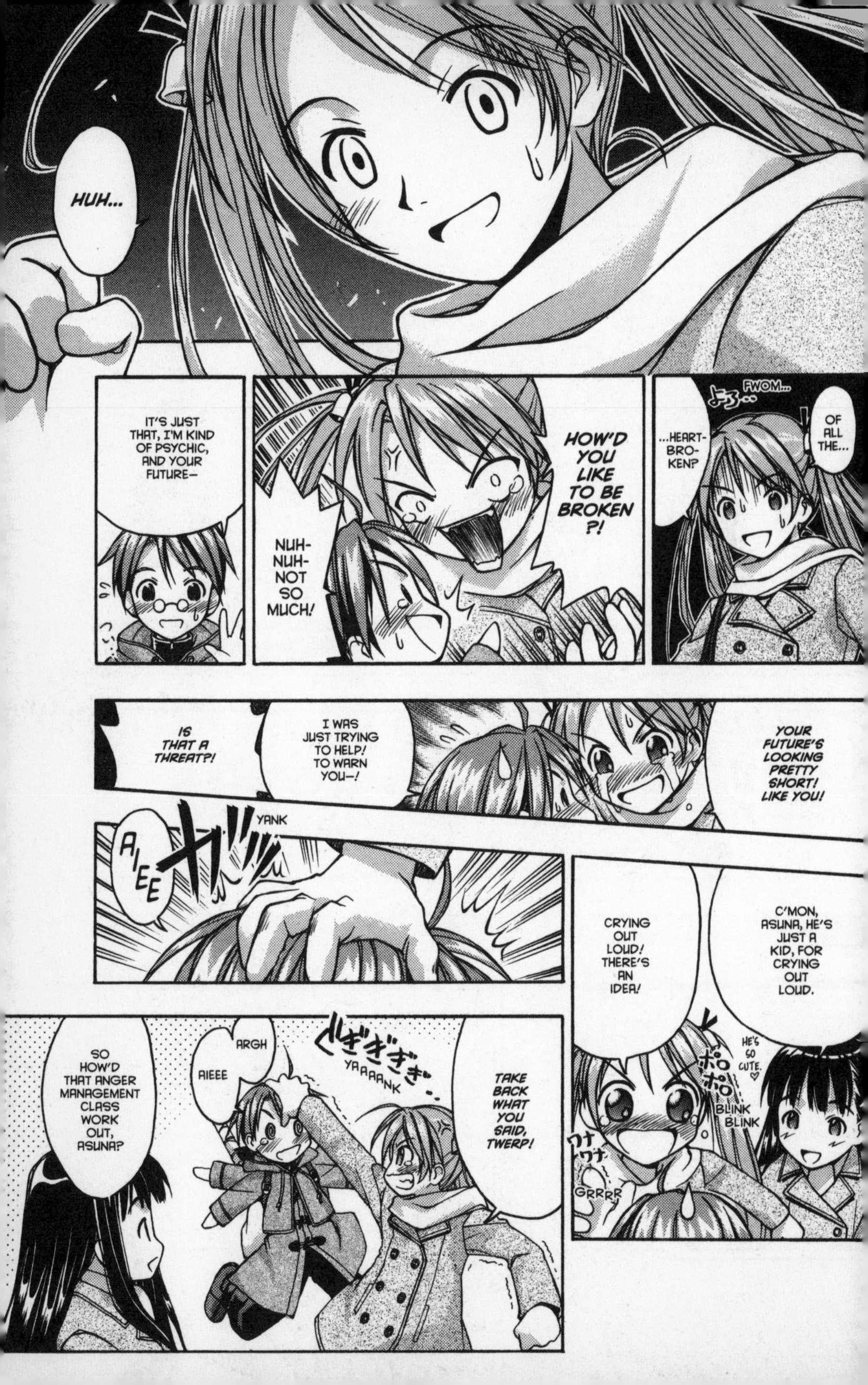
HUH...
OF ALL THE...
FWOM...
...HEART-BROKEN?
HOW'D YOU LIKE TO BE BROKEN?!
NUH-NUH-NOT SO MUCH!
IT'S JUST THAT, I'M KIND OF PSYCHIC, AND YOUR FUTURE—
YOUR FUTURE'S LOOKING PRETTY SHORT! LIKE YOU!
I WAS JUST TRYING TO HELP! TO WARN YOU—!
IS THAT A THREAT?!
C'MON, ASUNA, HE'S JUST A KID, FOR CRYING OUT LOUD.
CRYING OUT LOUD! THERE'S AN IDEA!
HE'S SO CUTE.
BLINK BLINK
GRRRR
YANK
AIEE
TAKE BACK WHAT YOU SAID, TWERP!
YAAAAANK
ARGH
AIEEE
SO HOW'D THAT ANGER MANAGEMENT CLASS WORK OUT, ASUNA?

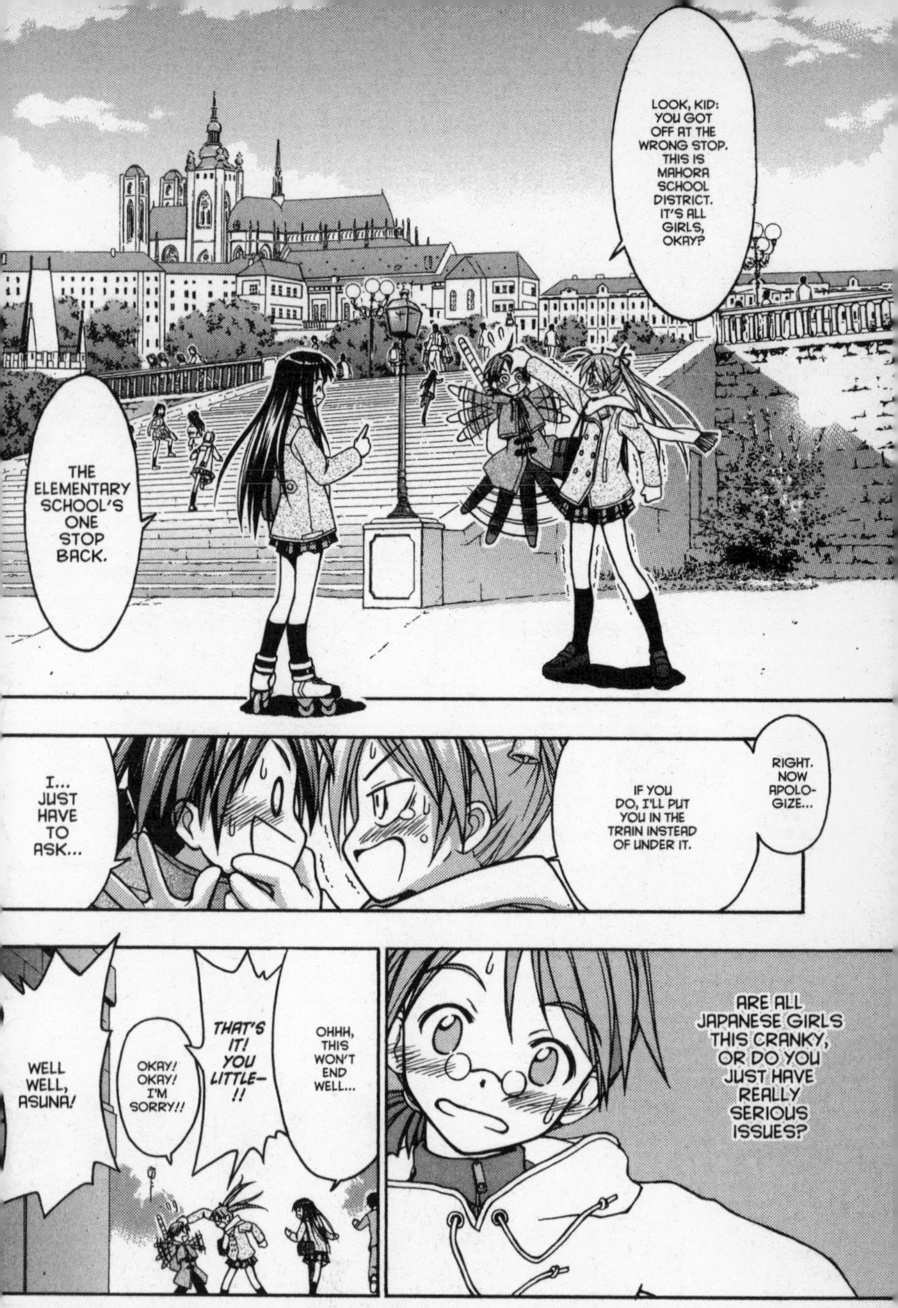
LOOK, KID: YOU GOT OFF AT THE WRONG STOP. THIS IS MAHORA SCHOOL DISTRICT. IT'S ALL GIRLS, OKAY?
THE ELEMENTARY SCHOOL'S ONE STOP BACK.
RIGHT. NOW APOLOGIZE...
IF YOU DO, I'LL PUT YOU IN THE TRAIN INSTEAD OF UNDER IT.
I... JUST HAVE TO ASK...
ARE ALL JAPANESE GIRLS THIS CRANKY, OR DO YOU JUST HAVE REALLY SERIOUS ISSUES?
OHHH, THIS WON'T END WELL...
THAT'S IT! YOU LITTLE—!!
OKAY! OKAY! I'M SORRY!!
WELL WELL, ASUNA!

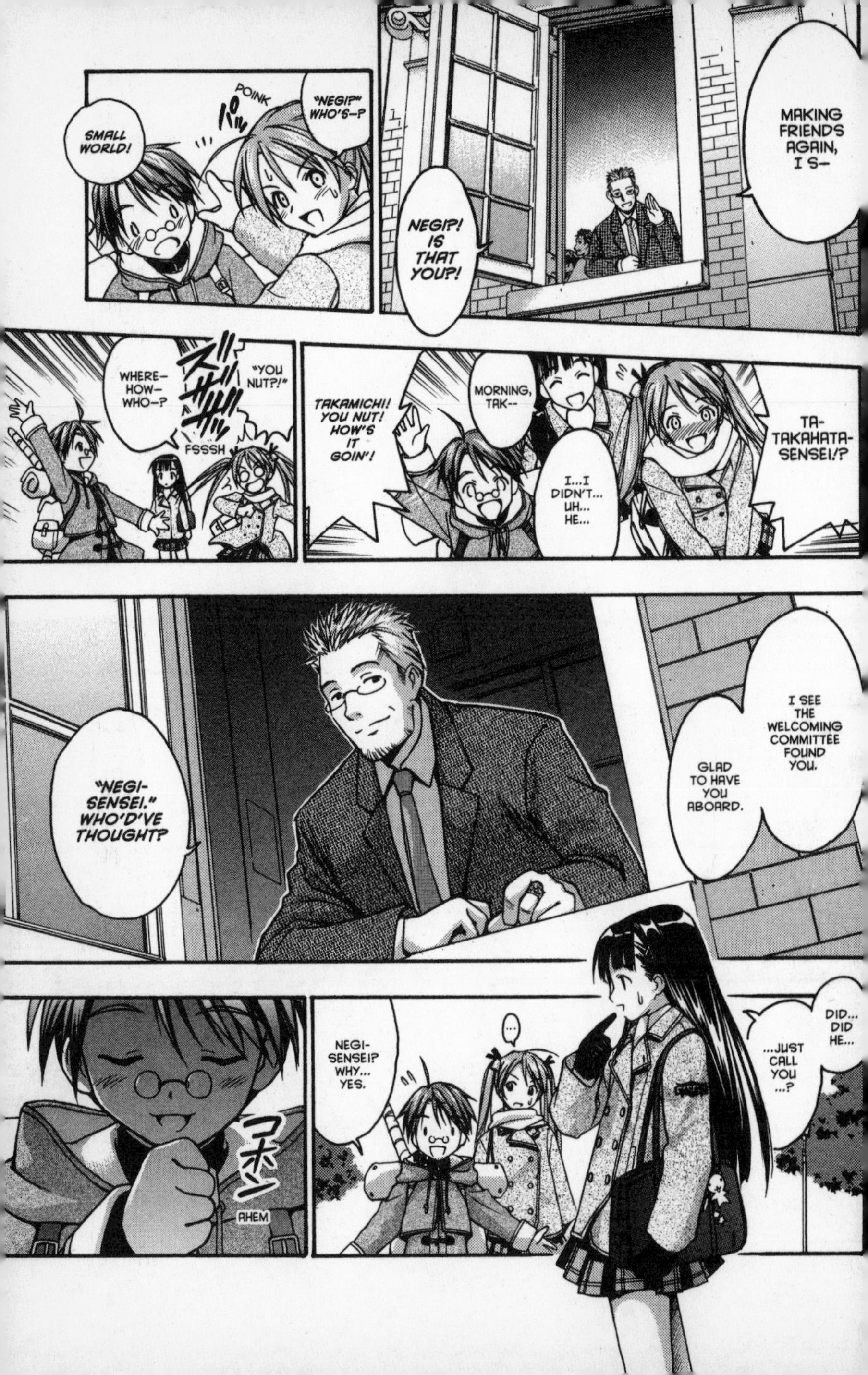
MAKING FRIENDS AGAIN, I S—
NEGI?! IS THAT YOU?!
"NEGI?" WHO'S—?
POINK
パッ
SMALL WORLD!
TA-TAKAHATA-SENSEI!?
I...I DIDN'T... UH... HE...
MORNING, TAK--
TAKAMICHI! YOU NUT! HOW'S IT GOIN'!
"YOU NUT?!"
FSSSH
WHERE-HOW-WHO-?
I SEE THE WELCOMING COMMITTEE FOUND YOU.
GLAD TO HAVE YOU ABOARD.
"NEGI-SENSEI." WHO'D'VE THOUGHT?
DID... DID HE...
...JUST CALL YOU ...?
...
NEGI-SENSEI? WHY... YES.
コホン
AHEM

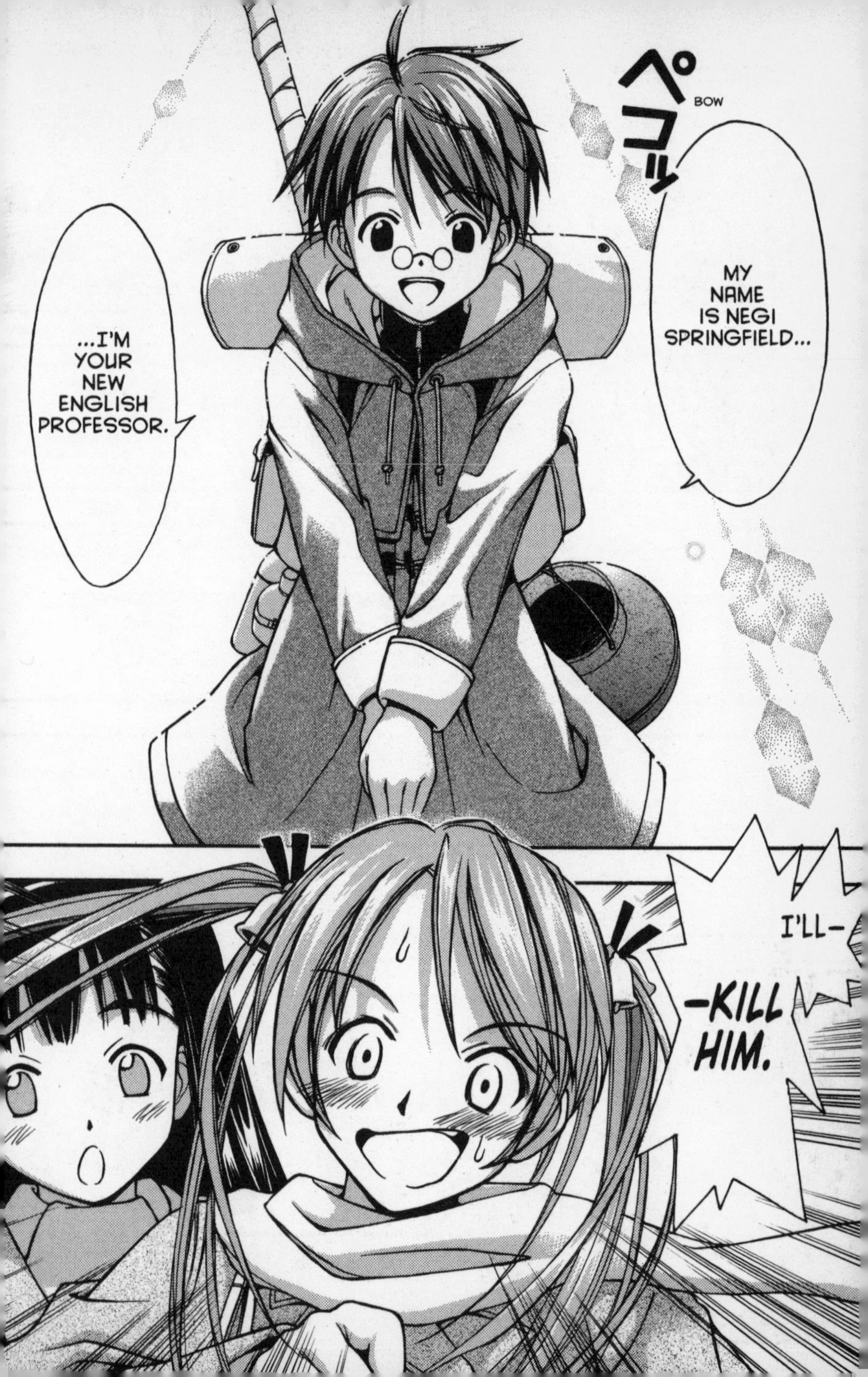
ペコッ
BOW
MY NAME IS NEGI SPRINGFIELD...
...I'M YOUR NEW ENGLISH PROFESSOR.
I'LL-
-KILL HIM.

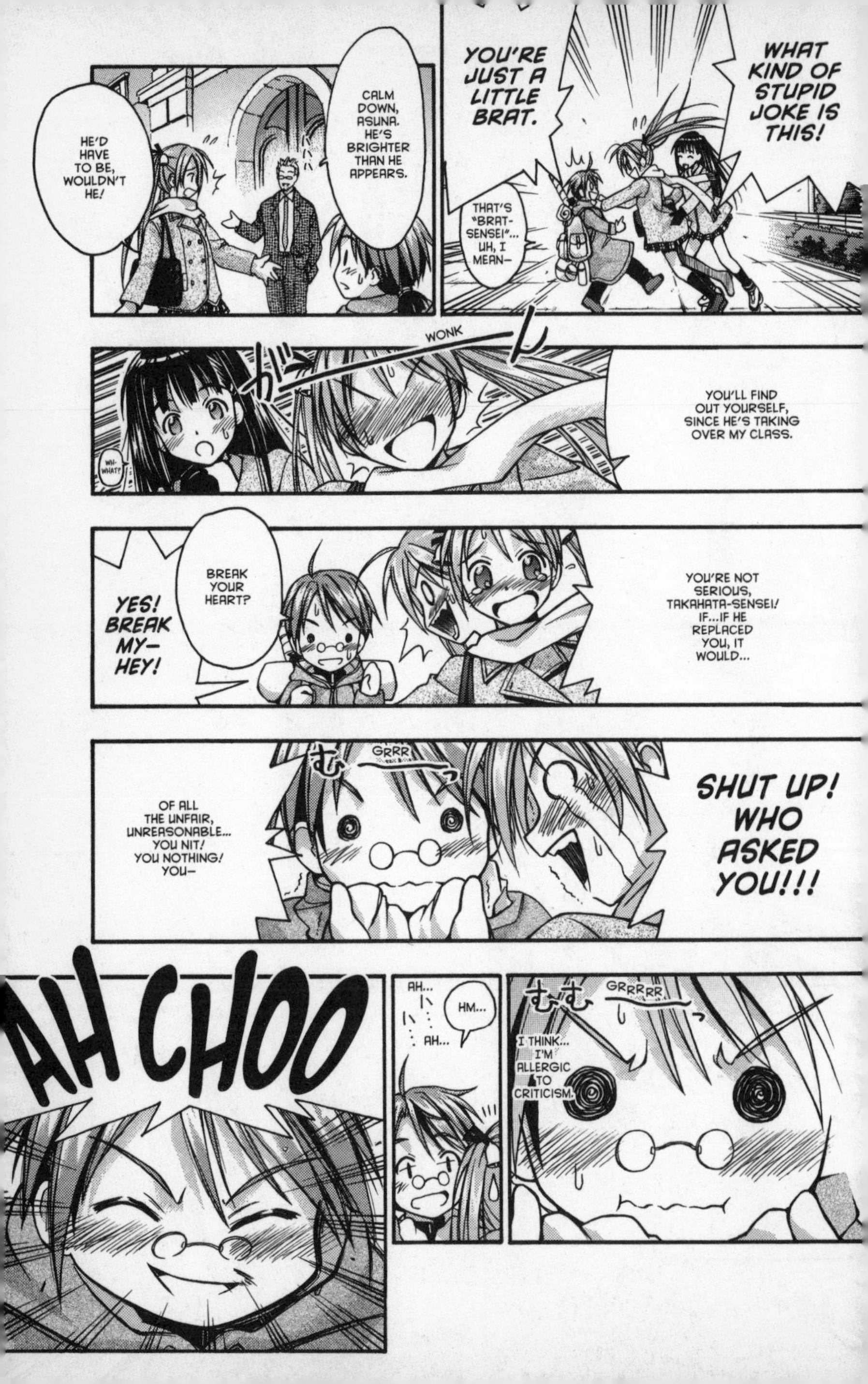
WHAT KIND OF STUPID JOKE IS THIS!
YOU'RE JUST A LITTLE BRAT.
THAT'S "BRAT-SENSEI"... UH, I MEAN—
CALM DOWN, ASUNA. HE'S BRIGHTER THAN HE APPEARS.
HE'D HAVE TO BE, WOULDN'T HE!
YOU'LL FIND OUT YOURSELF, SINCE HE'S TAKING OVER MY CLASS.
WONK
WH-WHAT?
YOU'RE NOT SERIOUS, TAKAHATA-SENSEI! IF...IF HE REPLACED YOU, IT WOULD...
BREAK YOUR HEART?
YES! BREAK MY— HEY!
SHUT UP! WHO ASKED YOU!!!
GRRR
OF ALL THE UNFAIR, UNREASONABLE... YOU NIT! YOU NOTHING! YOU—
GRRRRR
I THINK... I'M ALLERGIC TO CRITICISM.
HM...
AH... AH...
AH CHOO

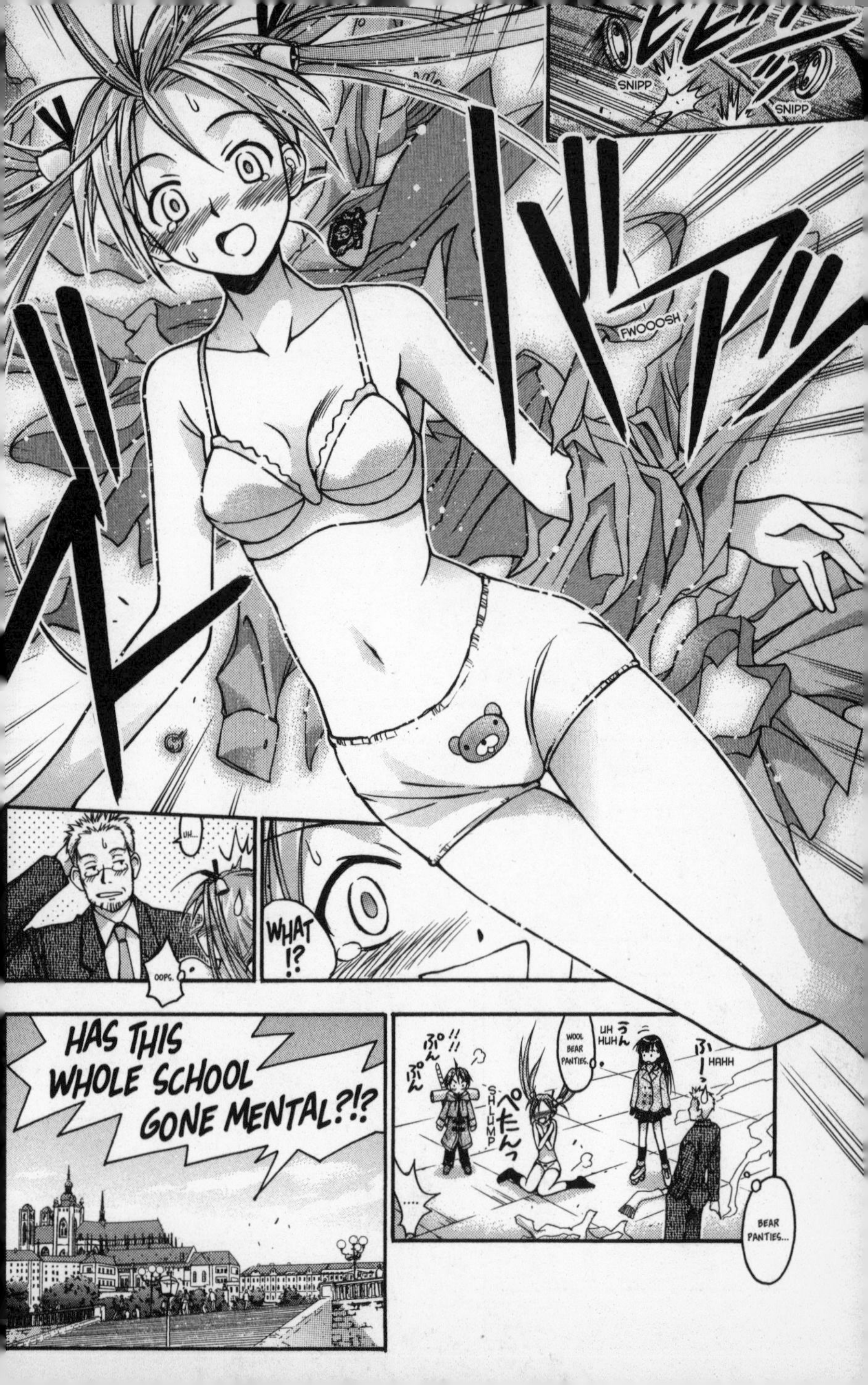
SNIPP
SNIPP
FWOOOSH
WHAT!?
UH...
OOPS.
HAHH
UH HUH
WOOL BEAR PANTIES...
SHLUMP
BEAR PANTIES...
...
HAS THIS WHOLE SCHOOL GONE MENTAL?!?

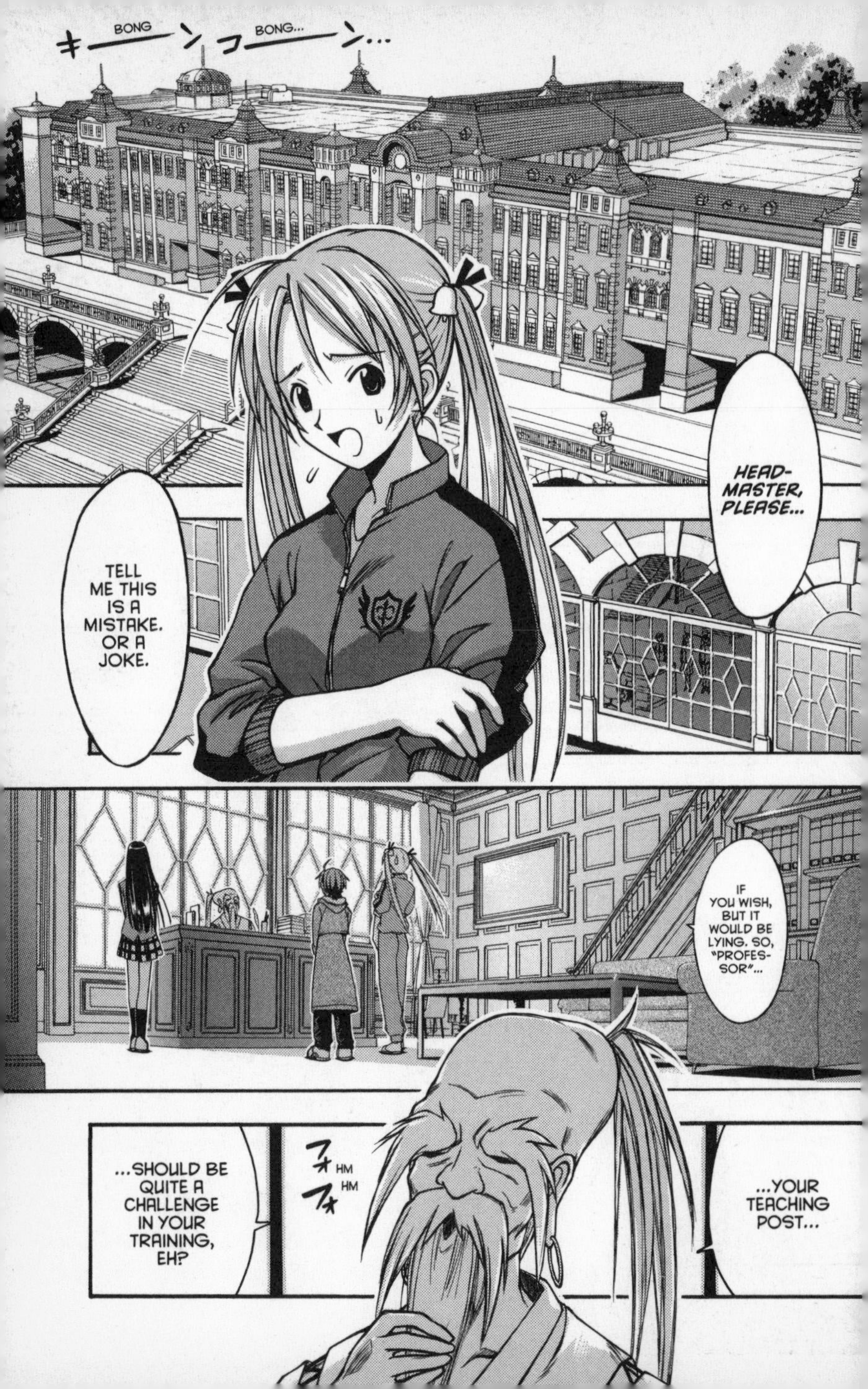
キーンコーン…
BONG BONG…
HEAD-MASTER, PLEASE…
TELL ME THIS IS A MISTAKE. OR A JOKE.
IF YOU WISH, BUT IT WOULD BE LYING. SO, "PROFESSOR"…
…YOUR TEACHING POST…
フォ HM フォ HM
…SHOULD BE QUITE A CHALLENGE IN YOUR TRAINING, EH?

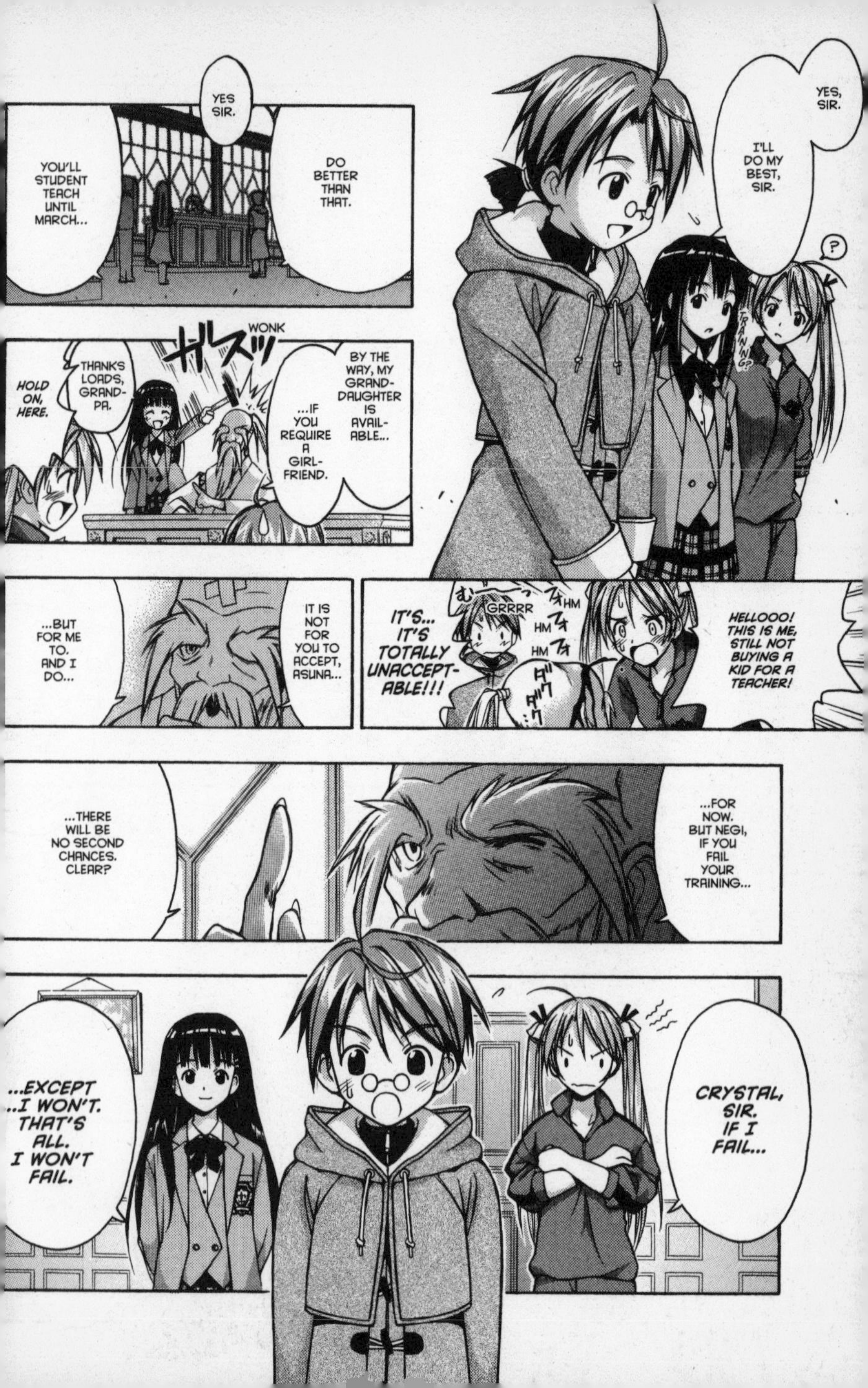
YES, SIR.
I'LL DO MY BEST, SIR.
?
TRAINING?
YES SIR.
DO BETTER THAN THAT.
YOU'LL STUDENT TEACH UNTIL MARCH...
BY THE WAY, MY GRAND-DAUGHTER IS AVAIL-ABLE...
...IF YOU REQUIRE A GIRL-FRIEND.
WONK
THANKS LOADS, GRAND-PA.
HOLD ON, HERE.
HELLOOO! THIS IS ME, STILL NOT BUYING A KID FOR A TEACHER!
HM
HM
HM
GRRRR
IT'S... IT'S TOTALLY UNACCEPT-ABLE!!!
IT IS NOT FOR YOU TO ACCEPT, ASUNA...
...BUT FOR ME TO. AND I DO...
...FOR NOW. BUT NEGI, IF YOU FAIL YOUR TRAINING...
...THERE WILL BE NO SECOND CHANCES. CLEAR?
CRYSTAL, SIR. IF I FAIL...
...EXCEPT ...I WON'T. THAT'S ALL. I WON'T FAIL.

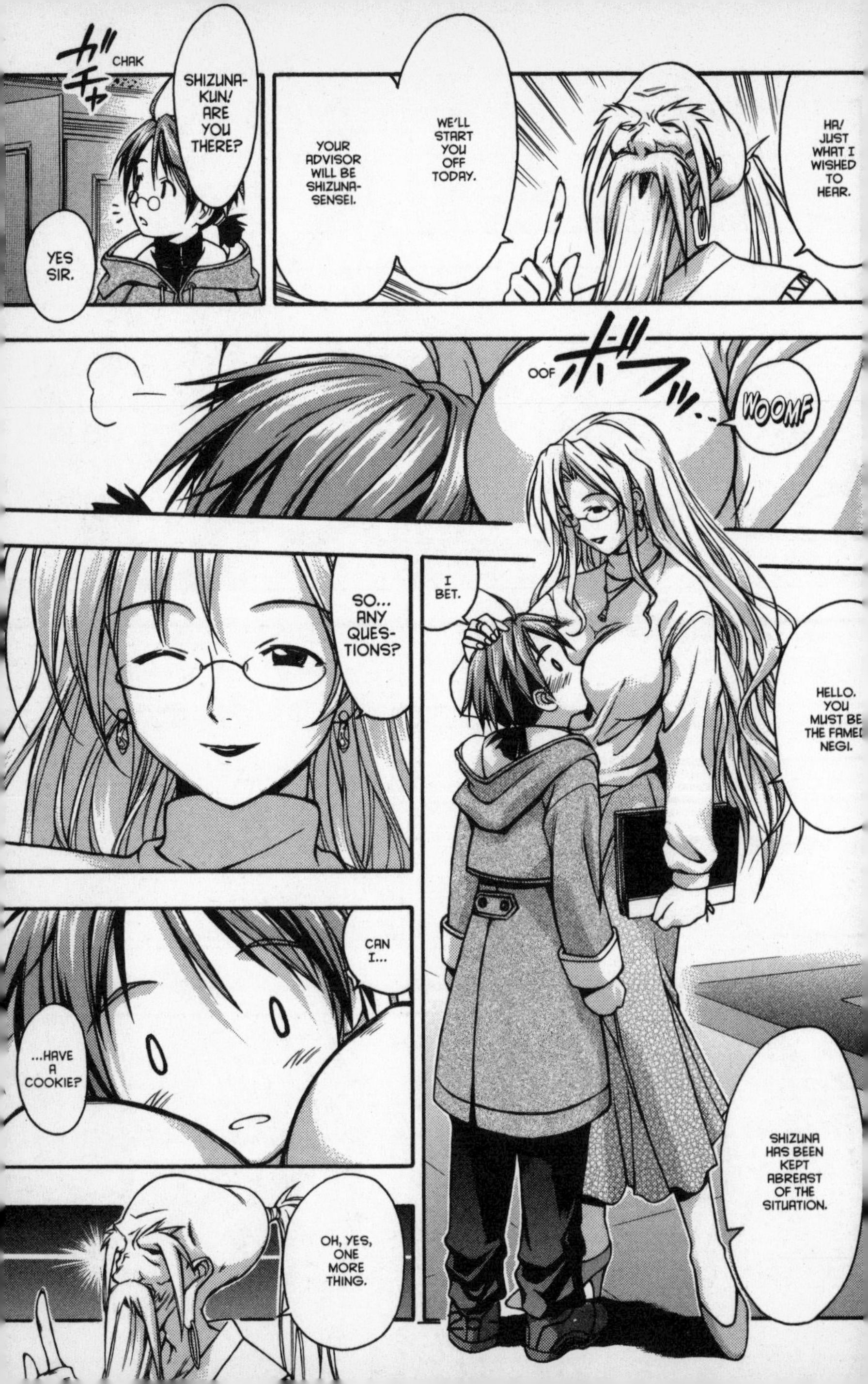
HA! JUST WHAT I WISHED TO HEAR.
WE'LL START YOU OFF TODAY.
YOUR ADVISOR WILL BE SHIZUNA-SENSEI.
ガチャ
CHAK
SHIZUNA-KUN! ARE YOU THERE?
YES SIR.
WOOMF
ボフッ...
OOF
HELLO. YOU MUST BE THE FAMED NEGI.
I BET.
SHIZUNA HAS BEEN KEPT ABREAST OF THE SITUATION.
SO... ANY QUESTIONS?
CAN I...
...HAVE A COOKIE?
OH, YES, ONE MORE THING.

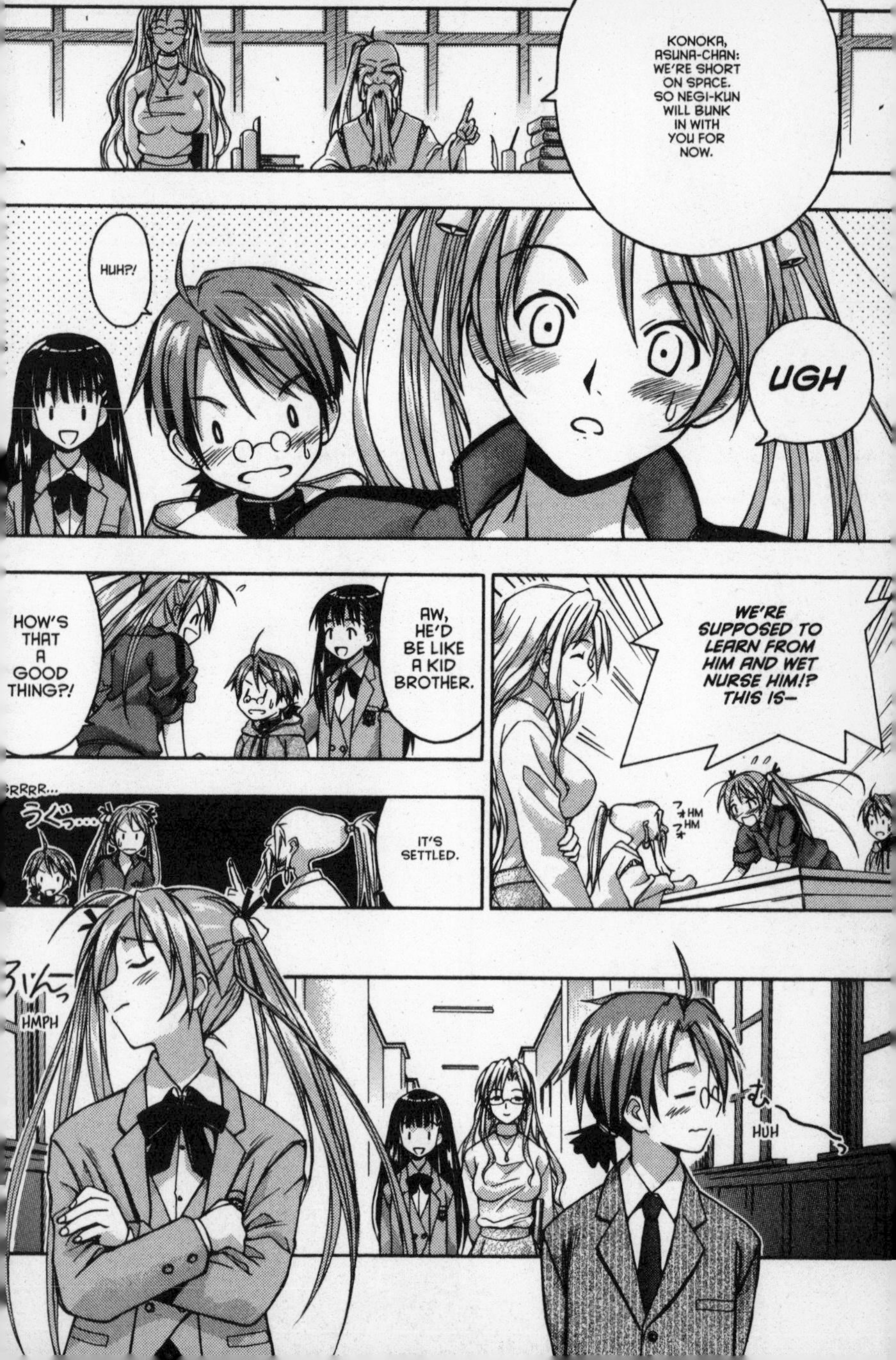
KONOKA, ASUNA-CHAN: WE'RE SHORT ON SPACE. SO NEGI-KUN WILL BUNK IN WITH YOU FOR NOW.
UGH
HUH?!
WE'RE SUPPOSED TO LEARN FROM HIM AND WET NURSE HIM!? THIS IS—
HM HM
AW, HE'D BE LIKE A KID BROTHER.
HOW'S THAT A GOOD THING?!
IT'S SETTLED.
うぐっ…
RRRRR...
HUH
HMPH

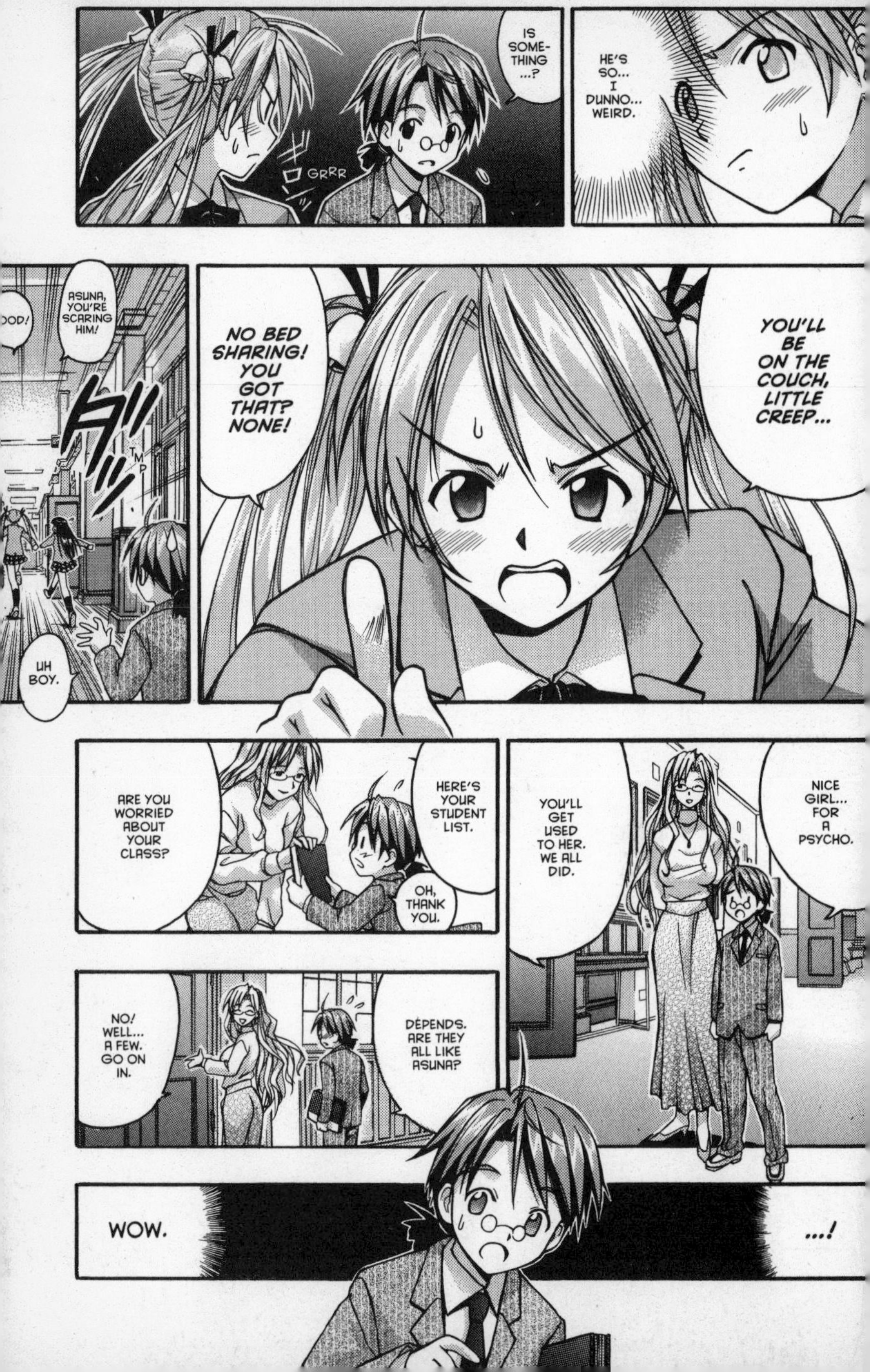
HE'S SO... I DUNNO... WEIRD.
IS SOME-THING ...?
GRRR
YOU'LL BE ON THE COUCH, LITTLE CREEP...
NO BED SHARING! YOU GOT THAT? NONE!
ASUNA, YOU'RE SCARING HIM!
TMP
UH BOY.
NICE GIRL... FOR A PSYCHO.
YOU'LL GET USED TO HER. WE ALL DID.
HERE'S YOUR STUDENT LIST.
ARE YOU WORRIED ABOUT YOUR CLASS?
OH, THANK YOU.
DEPENDS. ARE THEY ALL LIKE ASUNA?
NO! WELL... A FEW. GO ON IN.
...!
WOW.

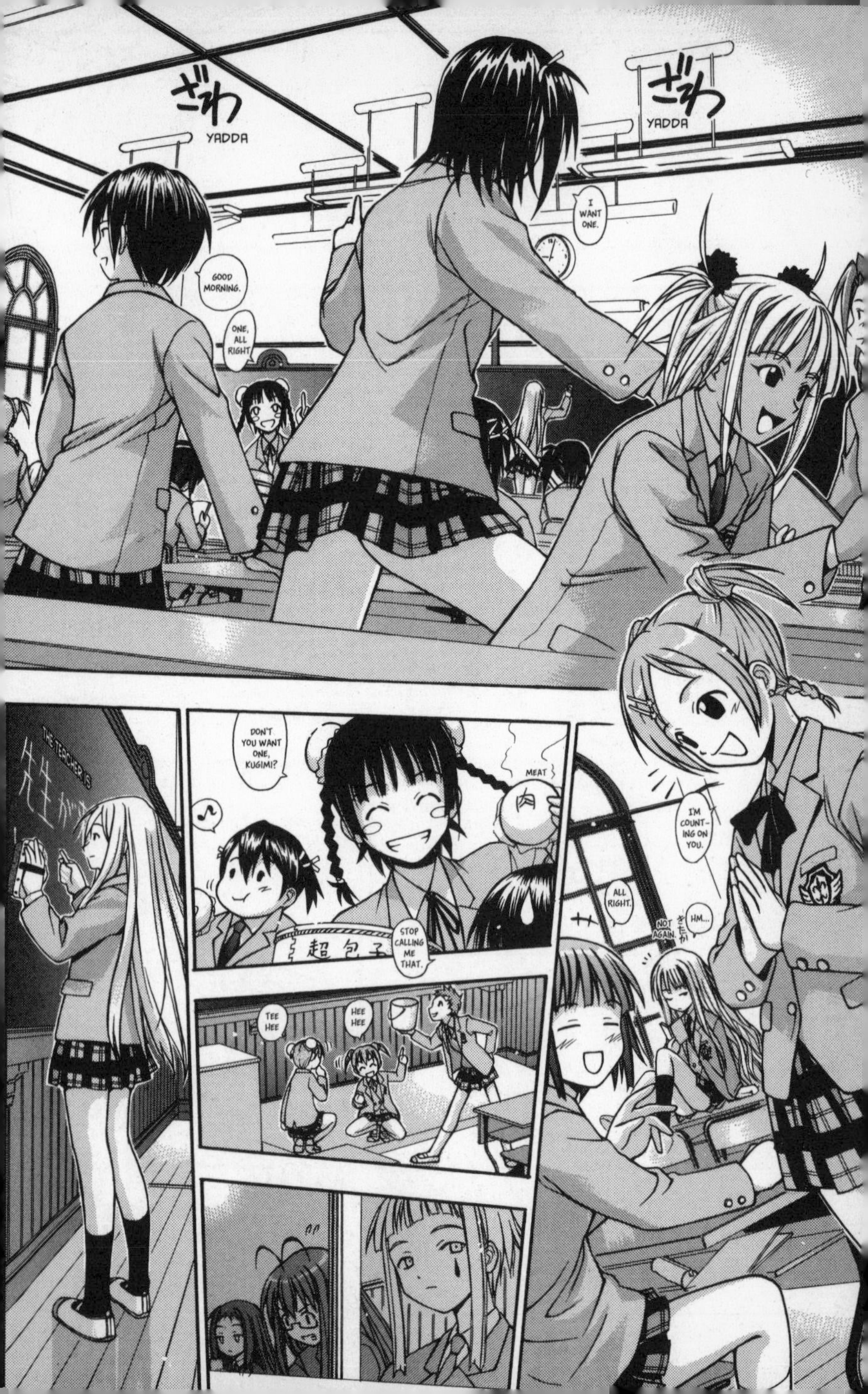
ざわ
YADDA
ざわ
YADDA
I WANT ONE.
GOOD MORNING.
ONE, ALL RIGHT.
I'M COUNTING ON YOU.
HM...
ALL RIGHT.
NOT AGAIN.
MEAT
肉
DON'T YOU WANT ONE, KUGIMI?
STOP CALLING ME THAT.
超包子
HEE HEE
TEE HEE
THE TEACHER IS
先生が

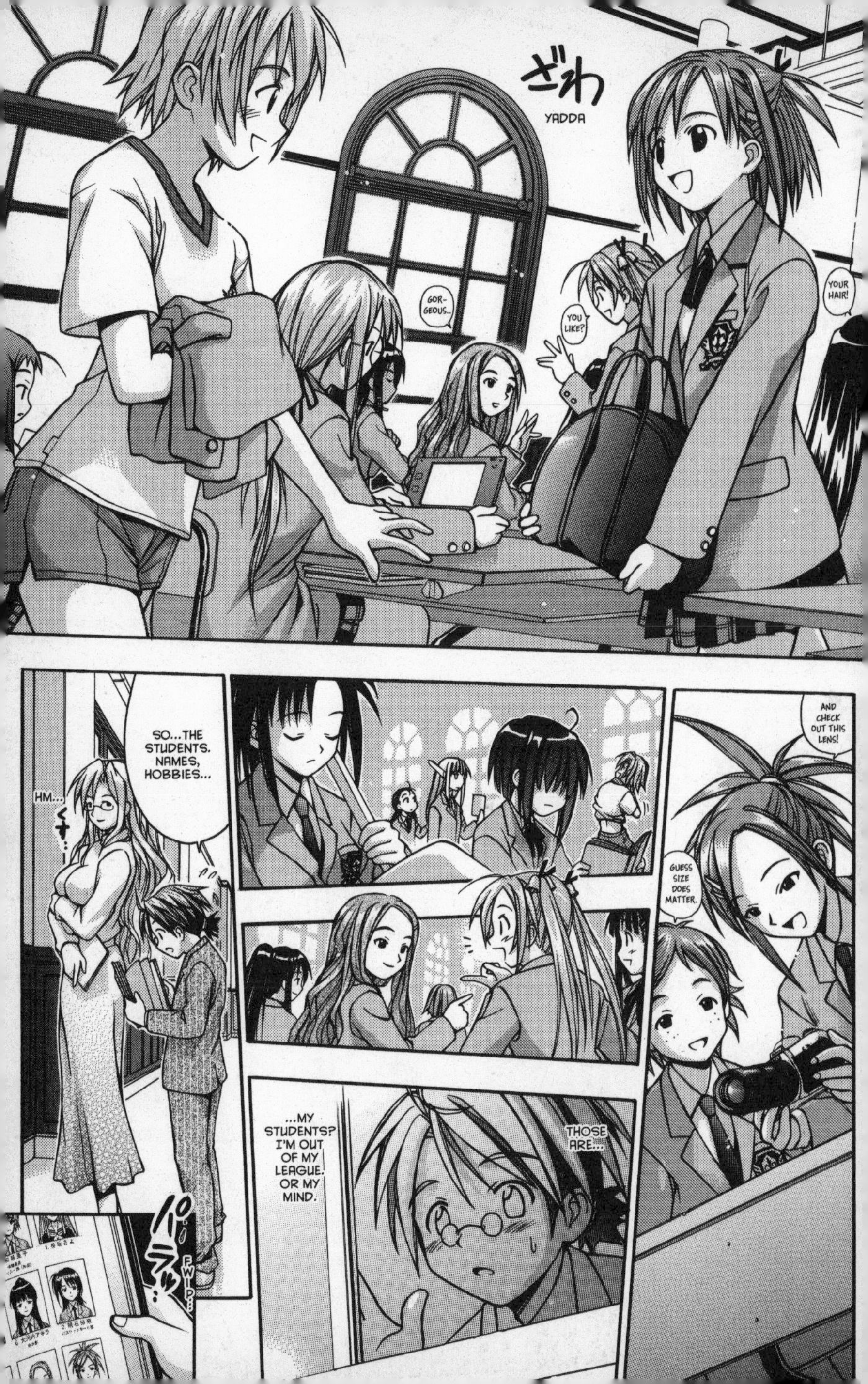

ざわ
YADDA
YOUR HAIR!
YOU LIKE?
GOR-GEOUS...
AND CHECK OUT THIS LENS!
GUESS SIZE DOES MATTER.
THOSE ARE...
...MY STUDENTS? I'M OUT OF MY LEAGUE. OR MY MIND.
SO...THE STUDENTS. NAMES, HOBBIES...
HM...
FWIP...

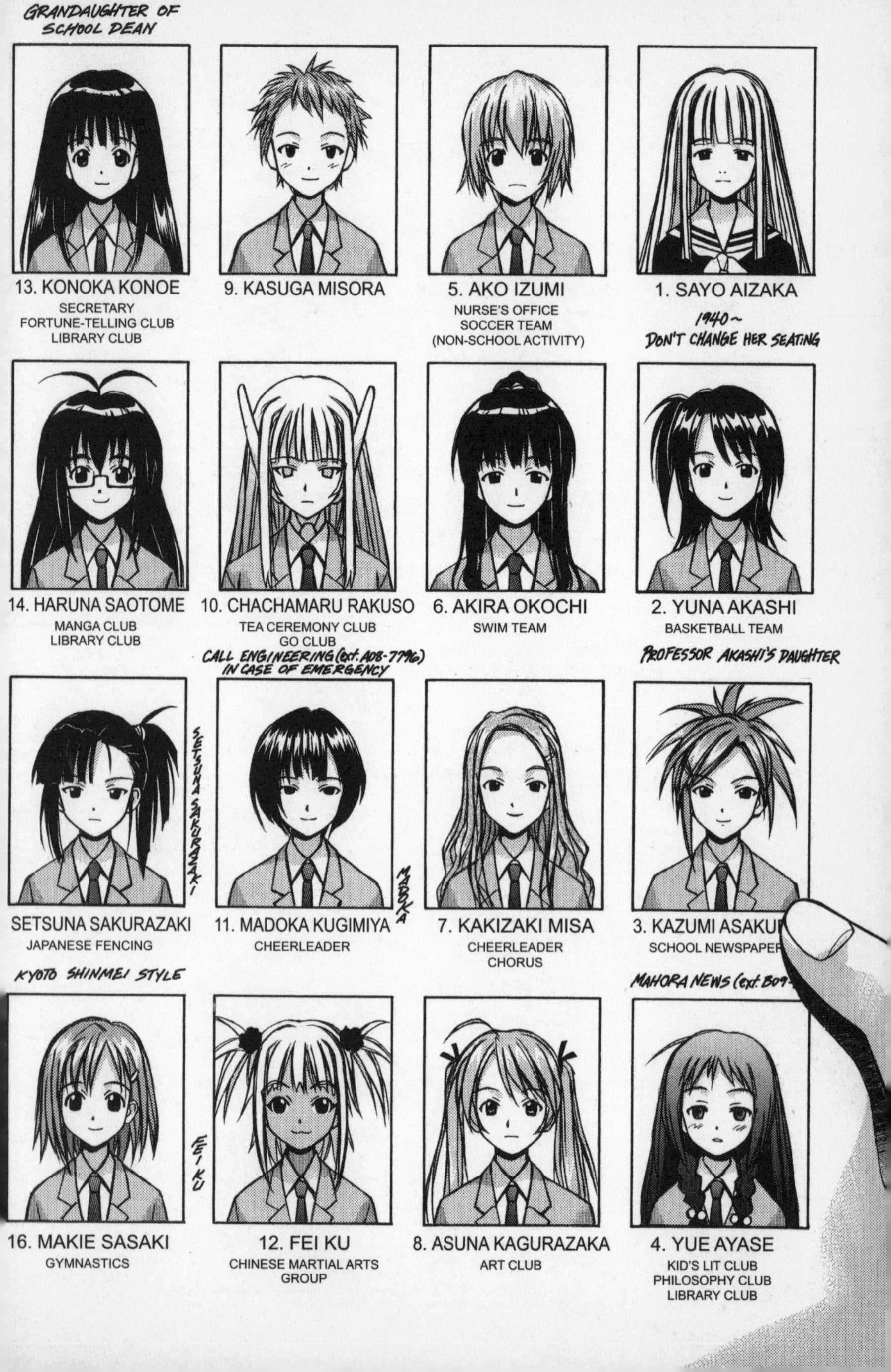
GRANDAUGHTER OF SCHOOL DEAN
1. SAYO AIZAKA
1940~
DON'T CHANGE HER SEATING
5. AKO IZUMI
NURSE'S OFFICE
SOCCER TEAM
(NON-SCHOOL ACTIVITY)
9. KASUGA MISORA
13. KONOKA KONOE
SECRETARY
FORTUNE-TELLING CLUB
LIBRARY CLUB
2. YUNA AKASHI
BASKETBALL TEAM
PROFESSOR AKASHI'S DAUGHTER
6. AKIRA OKOCHI
SWIM TEAM
10. CHACHAMARU RAKUSO
TEA CEREMONY CLUB
GO CLUB
CALL ENGINEERING (ext. A08-7796) IN CASE OF EMERGENCY
14. HARUNA SAOTOME
MANGA CLUB
LIBRARY CLUB
3. KAZUMI ASAKU
SCHOOL NEWSPAPE
MAHORA NEWS (ext. B09-
7. KAKIZAKI MISA
CHEERLEADER
CHORUS
MADOKA
11. MADOKA KUGIMIYA
CHEERLEADER
SETSUNA SAKURAZAKI
SETSUNA SAKURAZAKI
JAPANESE FENCING
KYOTO SHINMEI STYLE
4. YUE AYASE
KID'S LIT CLUB
PHILOSOPHY CLUB
LIBRARY CLUB
8. ASUNA KAGURAZAKA
ART CLUB
FEI KU
12. FEI KU
CHINESE MARTIAL ARTS GROUP
16. MAKIE SASAKI
GYMNASTICS

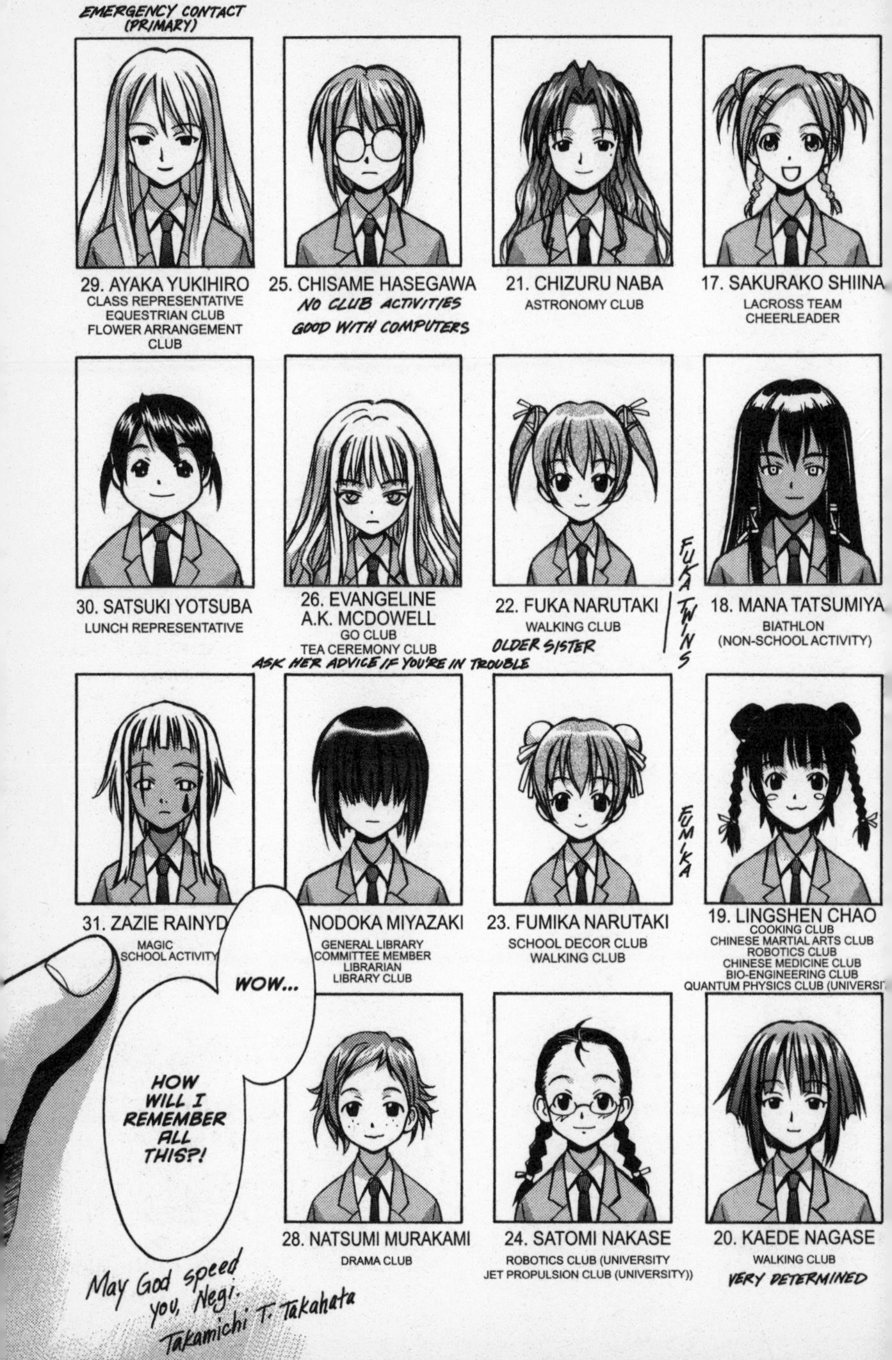
EMERGENCY CONTACT (PRIMARY)
17. SAKURAKO SHIINA
LACROSS TEAM
CHEERLEADER
21. CHIZURU NABA
ASTRONOMY CLUB
25. CHISAME HASEGAWA
NO CLUB ACTIVITIES
GOOD WITH COMPUTERS
29. AYAKA YUKIHIRO
CLASS REPRESENTATIVE
EQUESTRIAN CLUB
FLOWER ARRANGEMENT CLUB
18. MANA TATSUMIYA
BIATHLON
(NON-SCHOOL ACTIVITY)
FUKA TWINS
22. FUKA NARUTAKI
WALKING CLUB
OLDER SISTER
26. EVANGELINE A.K. MCDOWELL
GO CLUB
TEA CEREMONY CLUB
ASK HER ADVICE IF YOU'RE IN TROUBLE
30. SATSUKI YOTSUBA
LUNCH REPRESENTATIVE
19. LINGSHEN CHAO
COOKING CLUB
CHINESE MARTIAL ARTS CLUB
ROBOTICS CLUB
CHINESE MEDICINE CLUB
BIO-ENGINEERING CLUB
QUANTUM PHYSICS CLUB (UNIVERSI
FUMIKA
23. FUMIKA NARUTAKI
SCHOOL DECOR CLUB
WALKING CLUB
NODOKA MIYAZAKI
GENERAL LIBRARY COMMITTEE MEMBER
LIBRARIAN
LIBRARY CLUB
31. ZAZIE RAINYD
MAGIC
SCHOOL ACTIVITY
WOW...
20. KAEDE NAGASE
WALKING CLUB
VERY DETERMINED
24. SATOMI NAKASE
ROBOTICS CLUB (UNIVERSITY
JET PROPULSION CLUB (UNIVERSITY))
28. NATSUMI MURAKAMI
DRAMA CLUB
HOW WILL I REMEMBER ALL THIS?!
May God speed you, Negi.
Takamichi T. Takahata

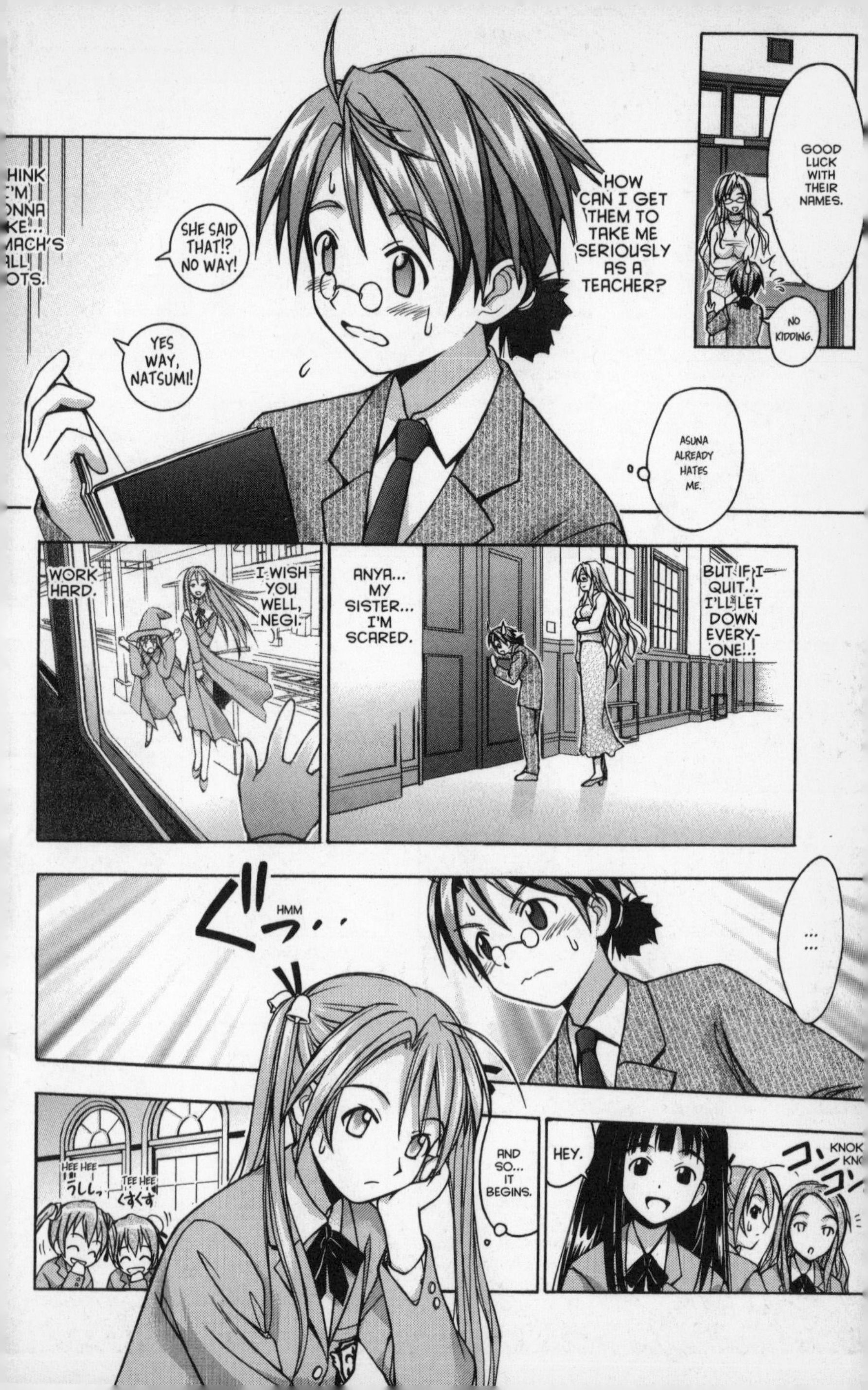
GOOD LUCK WITH THEIR NAMES.
NO KIDDING.
HOW CAN I GET THEM TO TAKE ME SERIOUSLY AS A TEACHER?
SHE SAID THAT!? NO WAY!
YES WAY, NATSUMI!
ASUNA ALREADY HATES ME.
BUT IF I QUIT... I'LL LET DOWN EVERY-ONE...!
ANYA... MY SISTER... I'M SCARED.
I WISH YOU WELL, NEGI.
WORK HARD.
......
HMM
ぐっ...
HEY.
AND SO... IT BEGINS.
TEE HEE くすくす
HEE HEE うしし

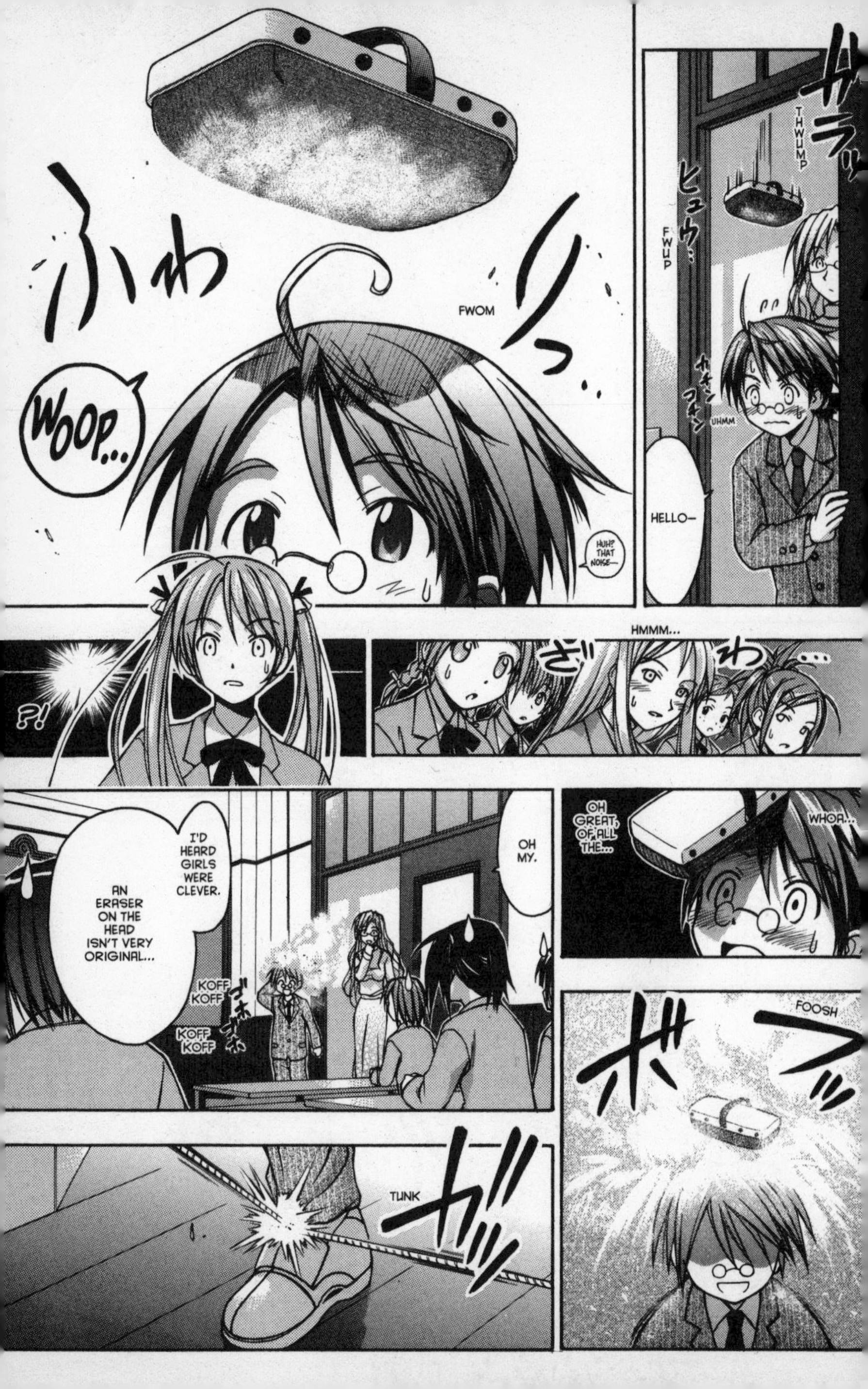
THWUMP
FWUP
UHMM
HELLO—
FWOM
WOOP...
HUH? THAT NOISE—
HMMM...
?!
OH GREAT, OF ALL THE...
WHOA...
FOOSH
OH MY.
I'D HEARD GIRLS WERE CLEVER.
AN ERASER ON THE HEAD ISN'T VERY ORIGINAL...
KOFF KOFF
KOFF KOFF
TUNK

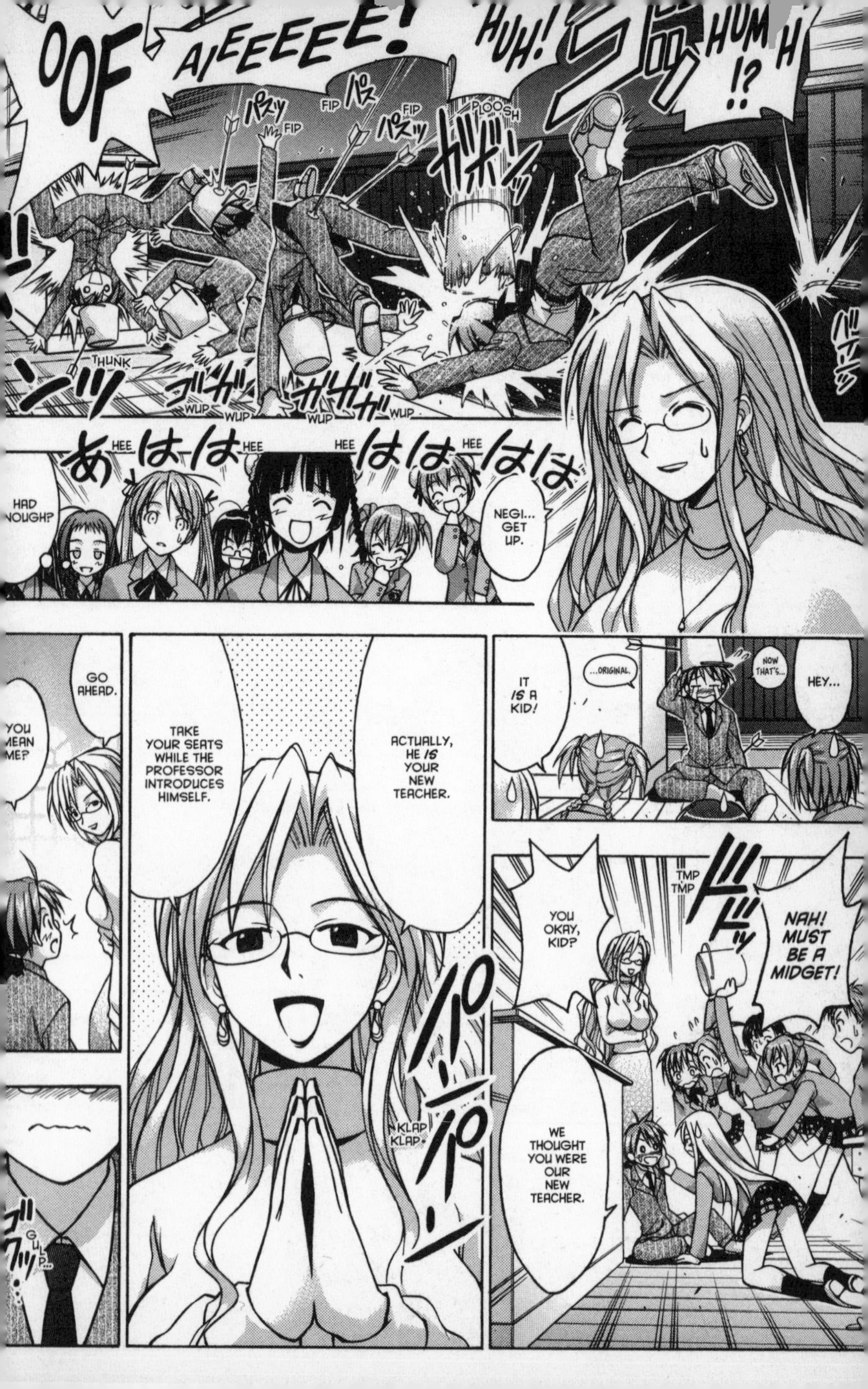
HUM H
!?
HUH!
AIEEEEEE!
OOF
PLOOSH
FIP
FIP
FIP
THUNK
WUP
WUP
WUP
WUP
HEE
HEE
HEE
HEE
NEGI... GET UP.
HAD NOUGH?
HEY...
NOW THAT'S...
...ORIGINAL.
IT IS A KID!
TMP TMP
NAH! MUST BE A MIDGET!
YOU OKAY, KID?
WE THOUGHT YOU WERE OUR NEW TEACHER.
ACTUALLY, HE IS YOUR NEW TEACHER.
TAKE YOUR SEATS WHILE THE PROFESSOR INTRODUCES HIMSELF.
KLAP KLAP
GO AHEAD.
YOU MEAN ME?
GULP...

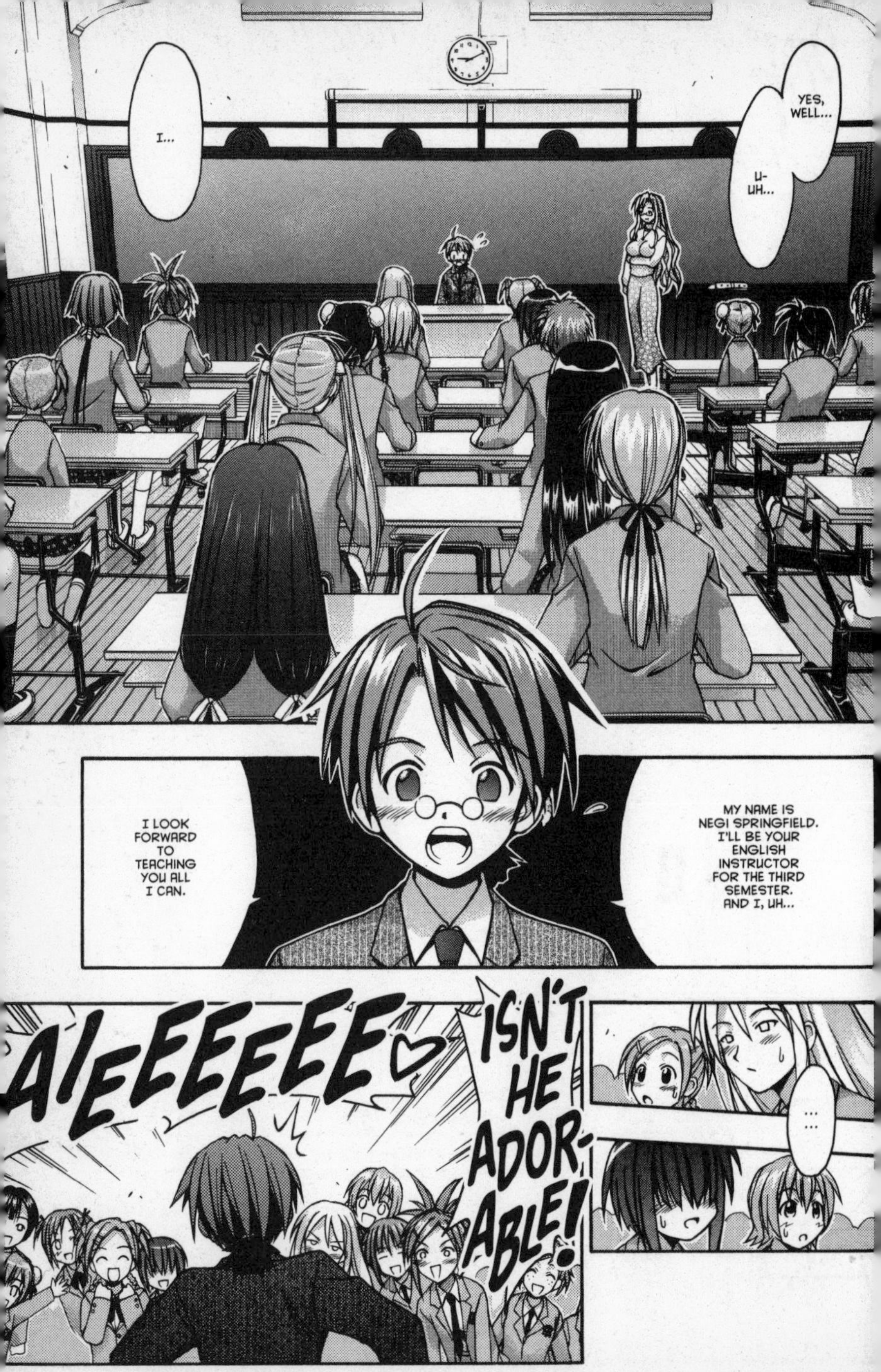
YES, WELL...
U-UH...
I...
MY NAME IS NEGI SPRINGFIELD. I'LL BE YOUR ENGLISH INSTRUCTOR FOR THE THIRD SEMESTER. AND I, UH...
I LOOK FORWARD TO TEACHING YOU ALL I CAN.
......
ISN'T HE ADORABLE!
AIEEEEEEE♡

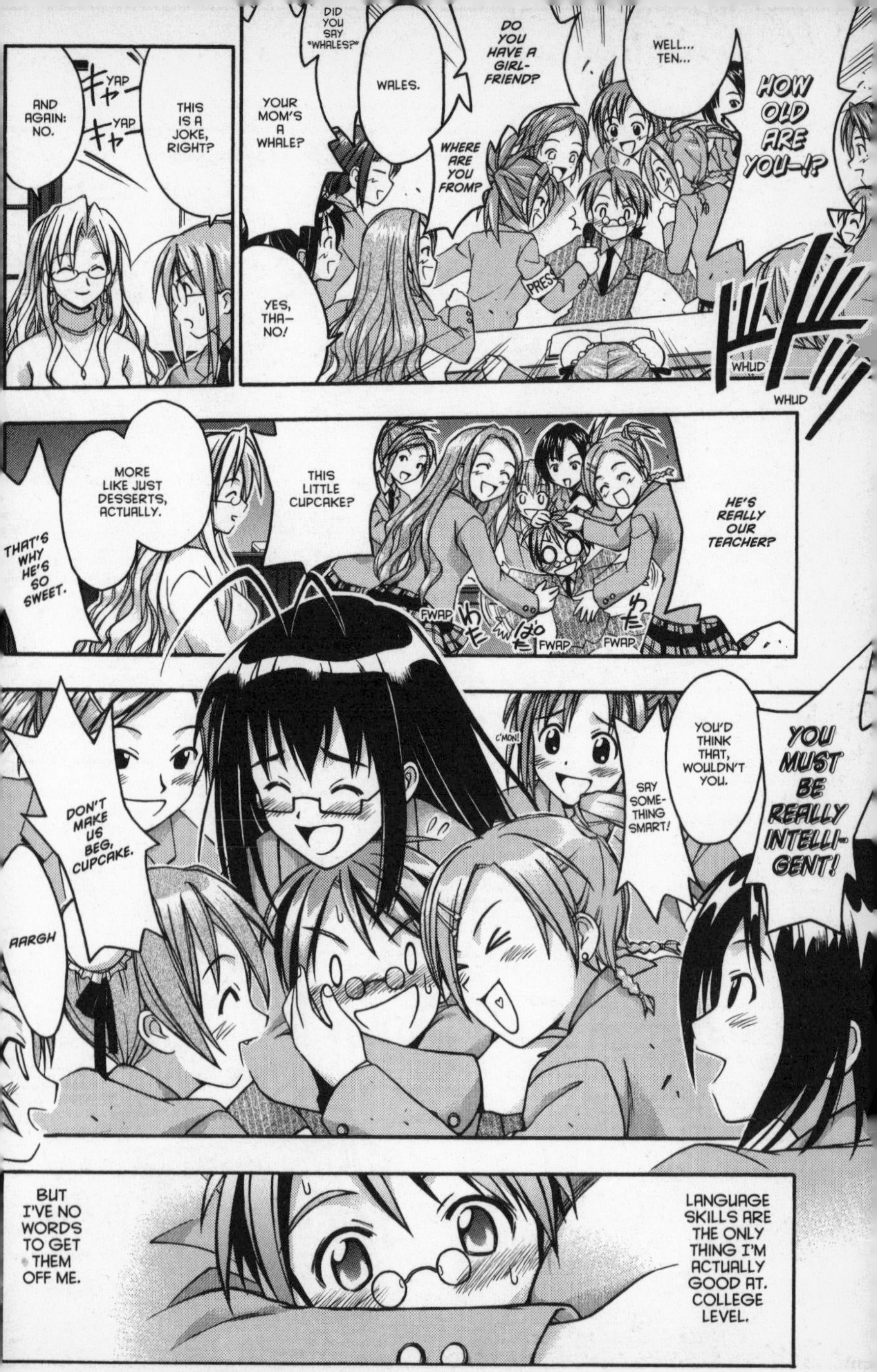
HOW OLD ARE YOU—!?
WELL... TEN...
DO YOU HAVE A GIRL-FRIEND?
WHERE ARE YOU FROM?
WALES.
DID YOU SAY "WHALES?"
YOUR MOM'S A WHALE?
YES, THA— NO!
WHUD
WHUD
THIS IS A JOKE, RIGHT?
YAP
YAP
AND AGAIN: NO.
HE'S REALLY OUR TEACHER?
THIS LITTLE CUPCAKE?
FWAP
FWAP
FWAP
MORE LIKE JUST DESSERTS, ACTUALLY.
THAT'S WHY HE'S SO SWEET.
YOU MUST BE REALLY INTELLI-GENT!
YOU'D THINK THAT, WOULDN'T YOU.
SAY SOME-THING SMART!
C'MON!
DON'T MAKE US BEG, CUPCAKE.
AARGH
LANGUAGE SKILLS ARE THE ONLY THING I'M ACTUALLY GOOD AT. COLLEGE LEVEL.
BUT I'VE NO WORDS TO GET THEM OFF ME.

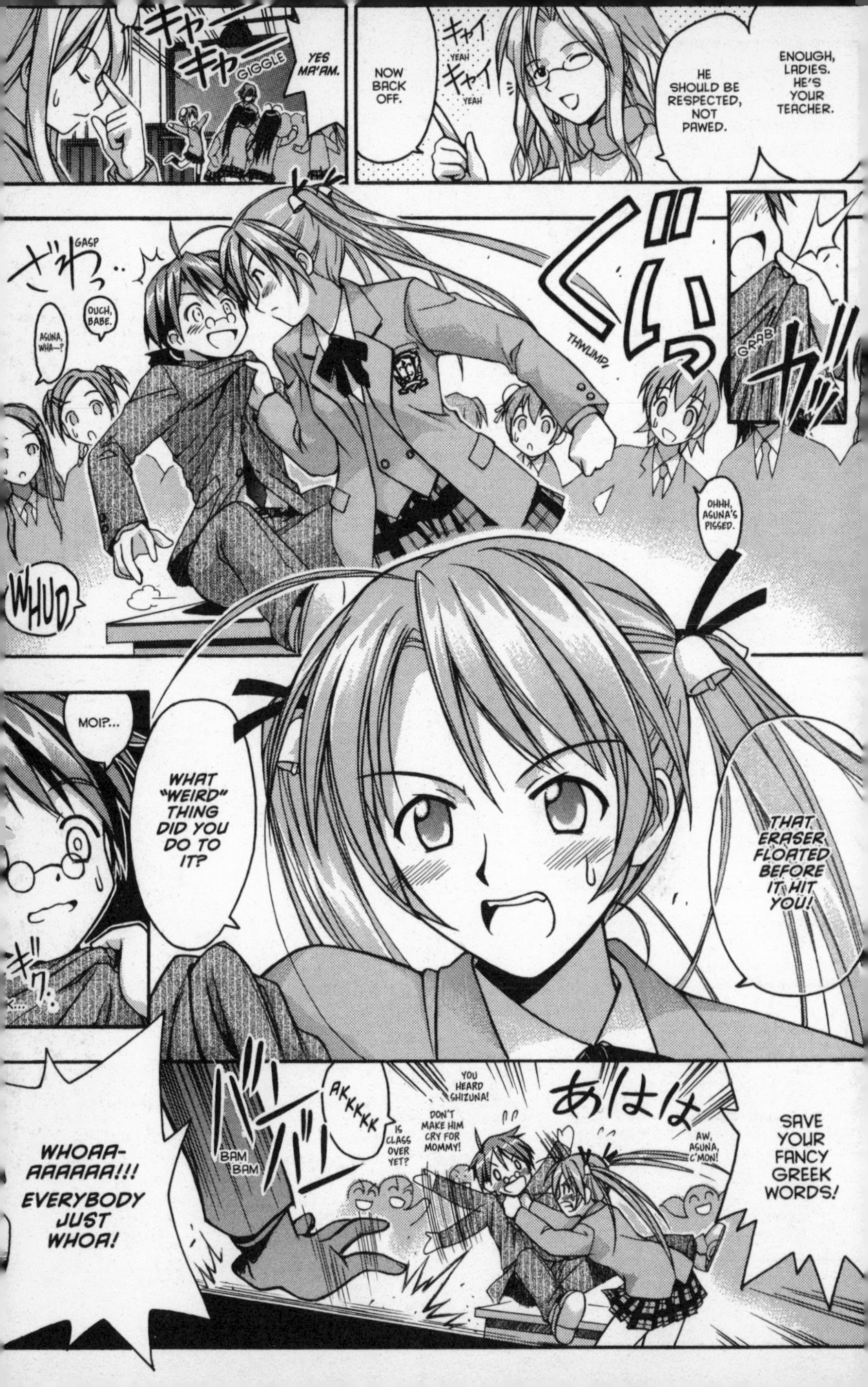
ENOUGH, LADIES. HE'S YOUR TEACHER.
HE SHOULD BE RESPECTED, NOT PAWED.
キャイ YEAH
キャイ YEAH
NOW BACK OFF.
YES MA'AM.
キャー
キャー GIGGLE
グッ GRAB
ぐいっ THWUMP
ざわっ.. GASP
OUCH, BABE.
ASUNA, WHA—?
OHHH, ASUNA'S PISSED.
WHUD
THAT ERASER FLOATED BEFORE IT HIT YOU!
WHAT "WEIRD" THING DID YOU DO TO IT?
MOI?...
ギク
SAVE YOUR FANCY GREEK WORDS!
AW, ASUNA, C'MON!
あはは
YOU HEARD SHIZUNA!
DON'T MAKE HIM CRY FOR MOMMY!
IS CLASS OVER YET?
AKKKKK
バンバン BAM BAM
WHOAA-AAAAAA!!! EVERYBODY JUST WHOA!

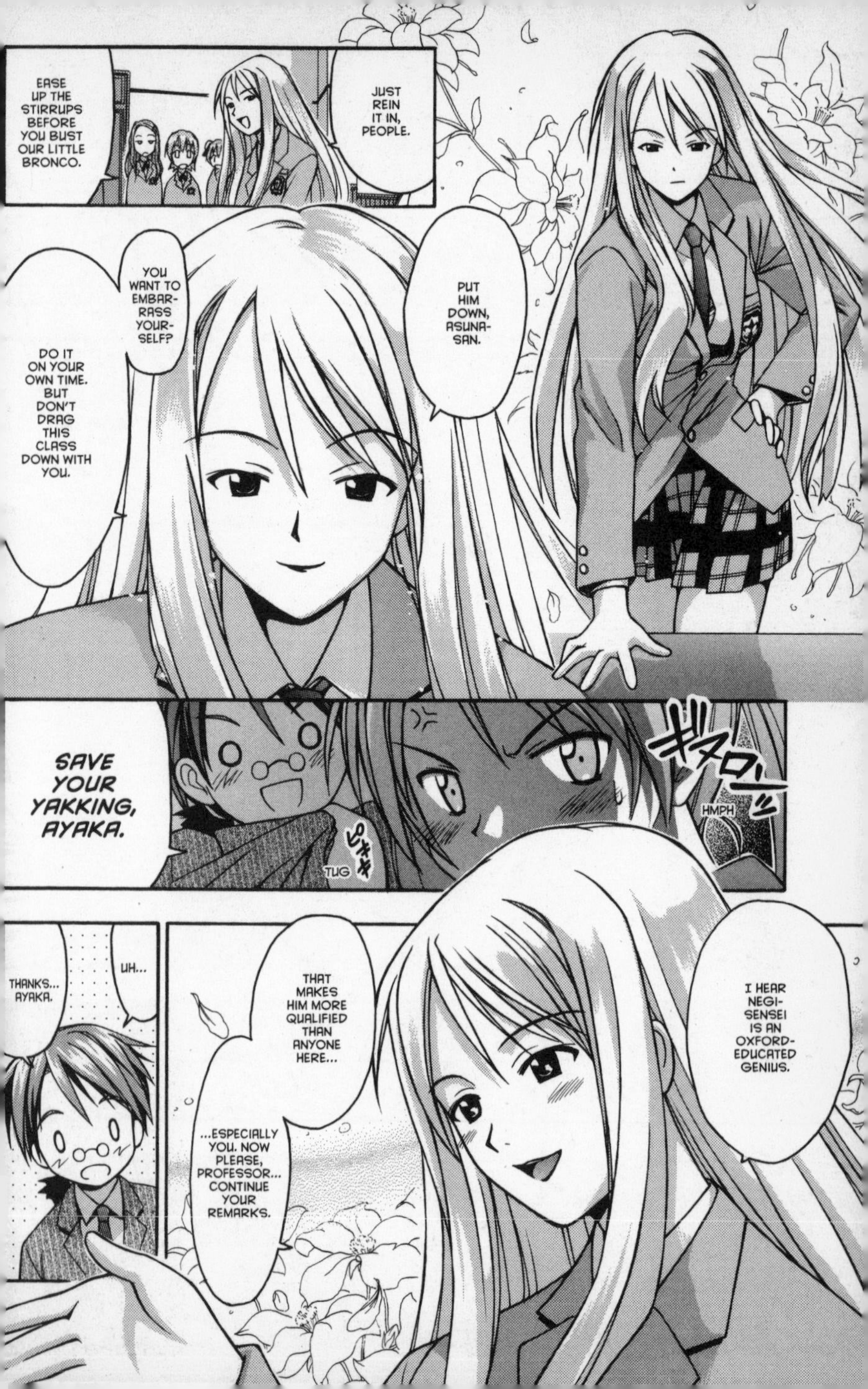
JUST REIN IT IN, PEOPLE.
EASE UP THE STIRRUPS BEFORE YOU BUST OUR LITTLE BRONCO.
PUT HIM DOWN, ASUNA-SAN.
YOU WANT TO EMBARRASS YOURSELF?
DO IT ON YOUR OWN TIME. BUT DON'T DRAG THIS CLASS DOWN WITH YOU.
HMPH
TUG
SAVE YOUR YAKKING, AYAKA.
I HEAR NEGI-SENSEI IS AN OXFORD-EDUCATED GENIUS.
THAT MAKES HIM MORE QUALIFIED THAN ANYONE HERE...
...ESPECIALLY YOU. NOW PLEASE, PROFESSOR... CONTINUE YOUR REMARKS.
UH...
THANKS... AYAKA.

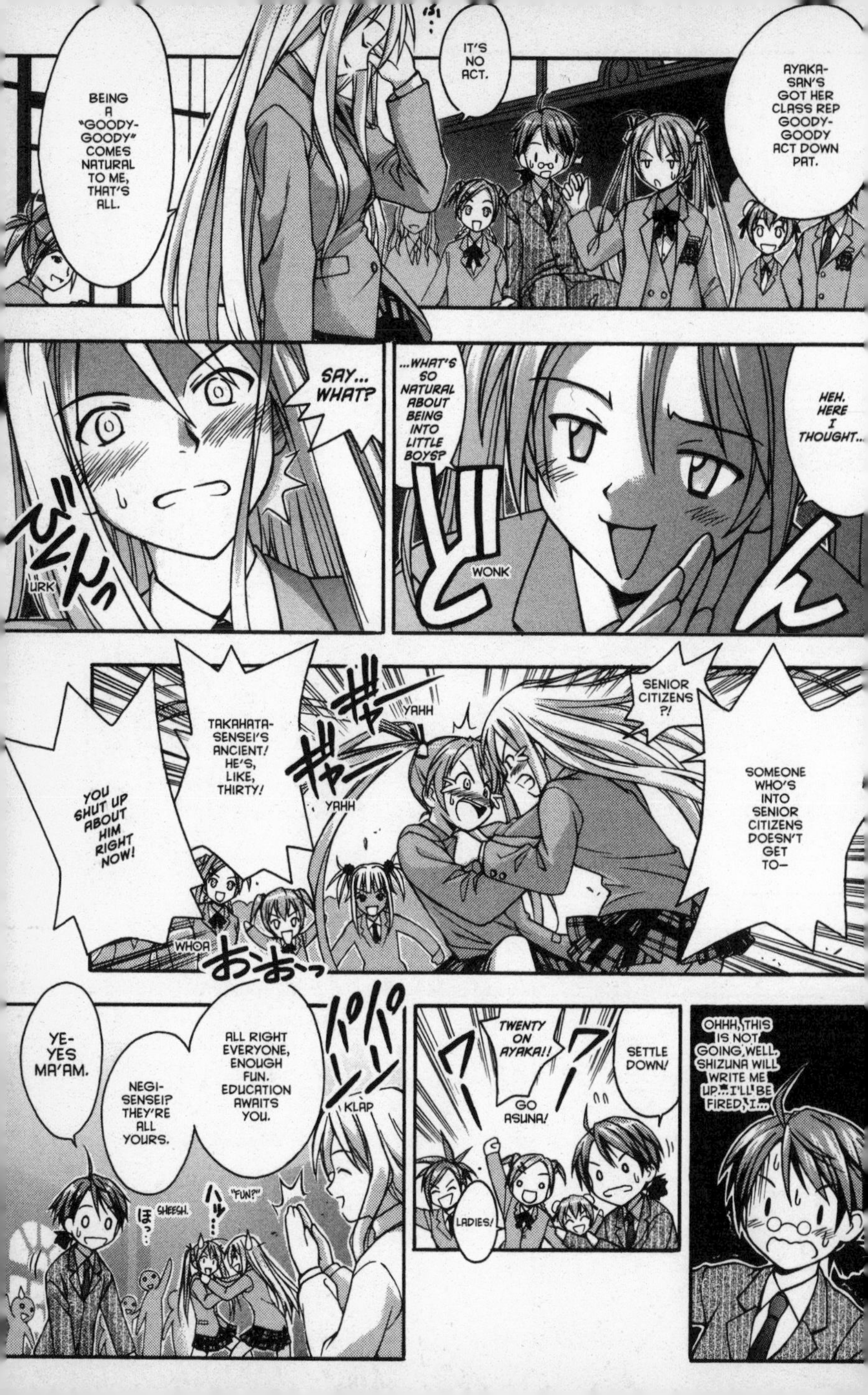
AYAKA-SAN'S GOT HER CLASS REP GOODY-GOODY ACT DOWN PAT.
IT'S NO ACT.
BEING A "GOODY-GOODY" COMES NATURAL TO ME, THAT'S ALL.
HEH. HERE I THOUGHT...
...WHAT'S SO NATURAL ABOUT BEING INTO LITTLE BOYS?
WONK
SAY... WHAT?
URK
SENIOR CITIZENS?!
SOMEONE WHO'S INTO SENIOR CITIZENS DOESN'T GET TO—
YAHH
YAHH
TAKAHATA-SENSEI'S ANCIENT! HE'S, LIKE, THIRTY!
YOU SHUT UP ABOUT HIM RIGHT NOW!
WHOA
OHHH, THIS IS NOT GOING WELL. SHIZUNA WILL WRITE ME UP...I'LL BE FIRED, I...
SETTLE DOWN!
TWENTY ON AYAKA!!
GO ASUNA!
LADIES!
KLAP
ALL RIGHT EVERYONE, ENOUGH FUN. EDUCATION AWAITS YOU.
NEGI-SENSEI? THEY'RE ALL YOURS.
YE-YES MA'AM.
"FUN?"
SHEESH.

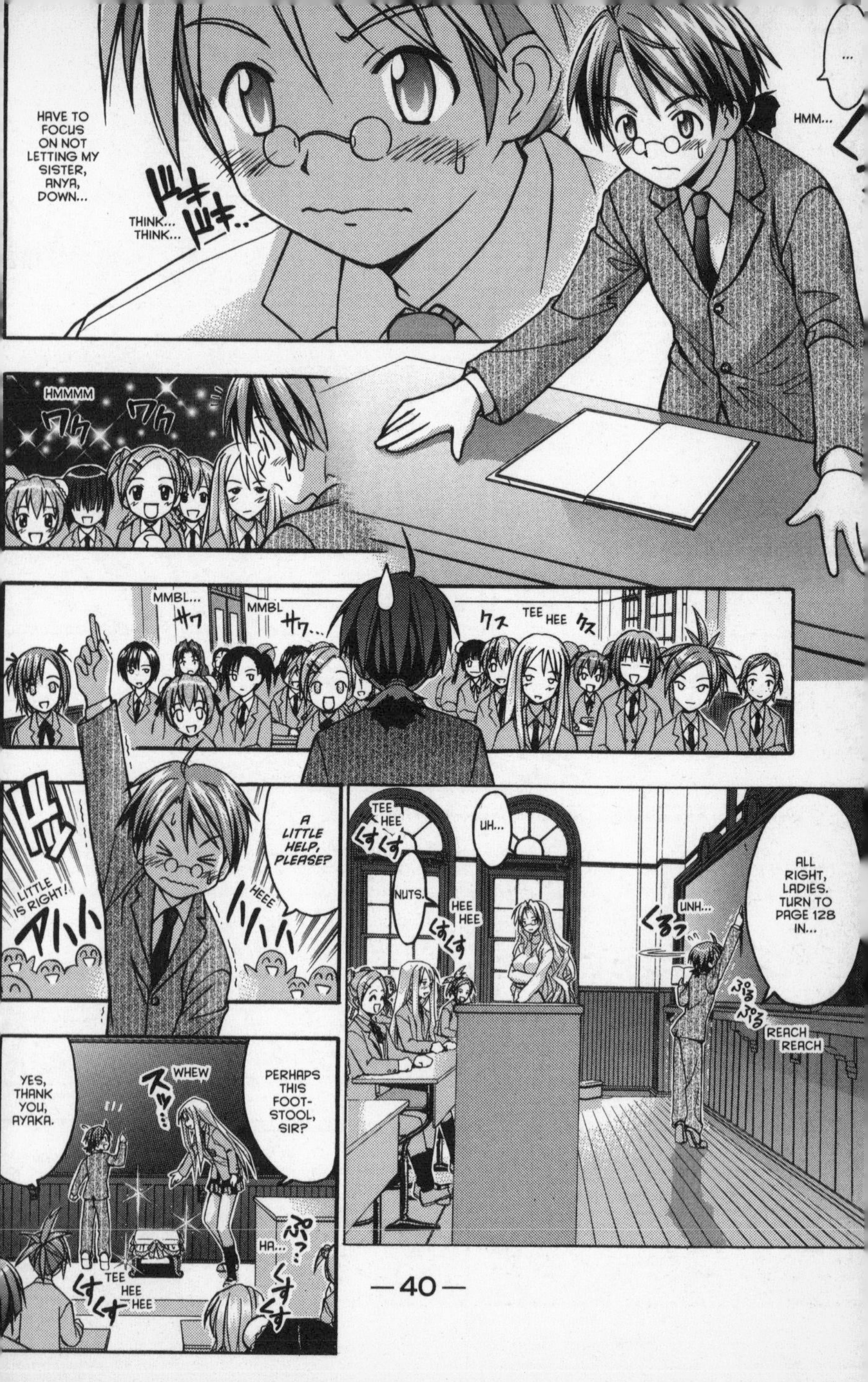
...
HMM...
HAVE TO FOCUS ON NOT LETTING MY SISTER, ANYA, DOWN...
THINK... THINK...
HMMMM
TEE HEE
MMBL...
MMBL
ALL RIGHT, LADIES. TURN TO PAGE 128 IN...
UNH...
REACH REACH
UH...
HEE HEE
NUTS.
TEE HEE
A LITTLE HELP, PLEASE?
HEEE
LITTLE IS RIGHT!
PERHAPS THIS FOOT-STOOL, SIR?
WHEW
YES, THANK YOU, AYAKA.
HA...
TEE HEE HEE

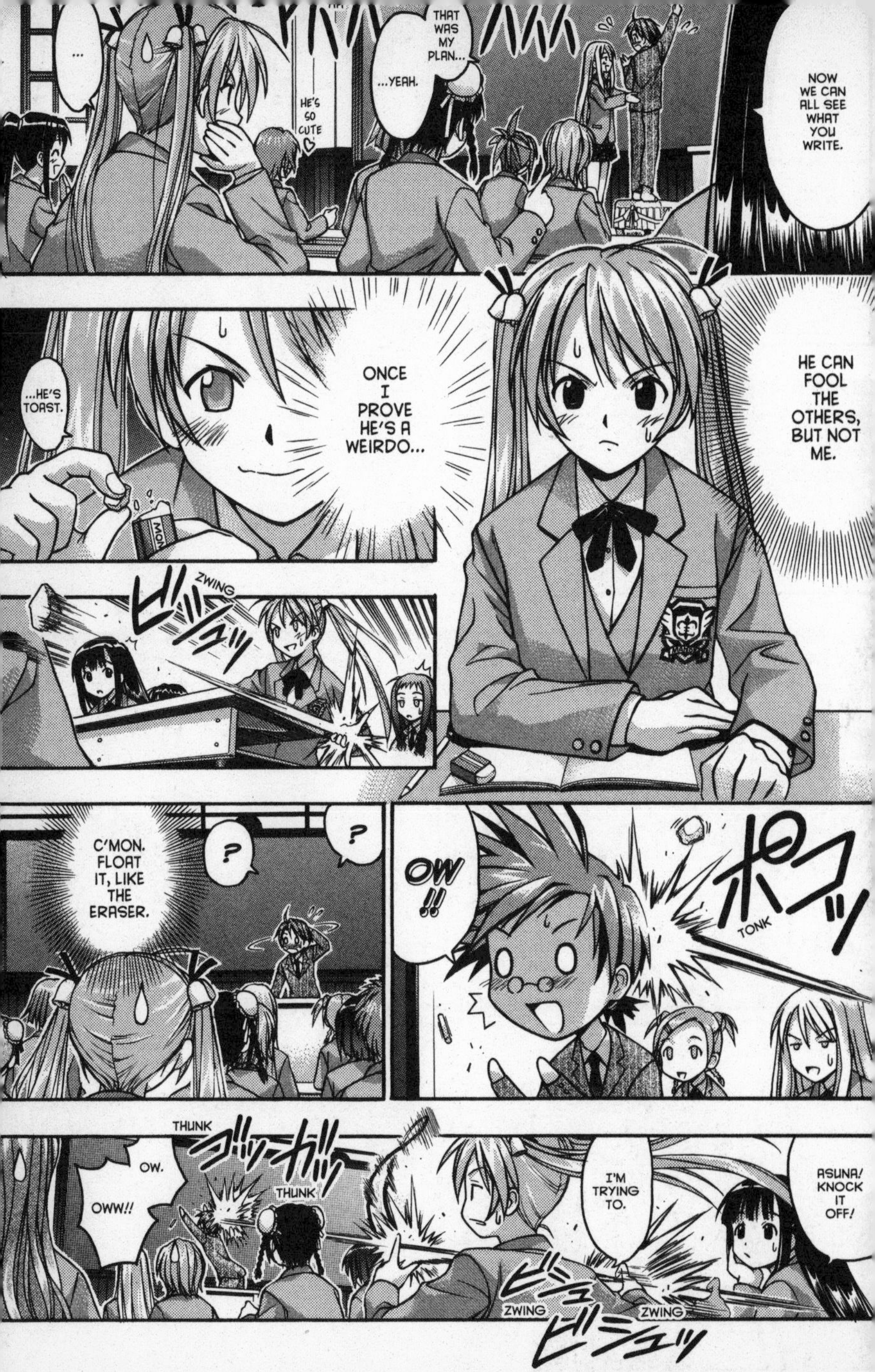
NOW WE CAN ALL SEE WHAT YOU WRITE.
THAT WAS MY PLAN...
...YEAH.
HE'S SO CUTE ♡
...
HE CAN FOOL THE OTHERS, BUT NOT ME.
ONCE I PROVE HE'S A WEIRDO...
...HE'S TOAST.
ZWING
TONK
OW!!
?
?
C'MON. FLOAT IT, LIKE THE ERASER.
ASUNA! KNOCK IT OFF!
I'M TRYING TO.
ZWING
ZWING
THUNK
THUNK
OW.
OWW!!

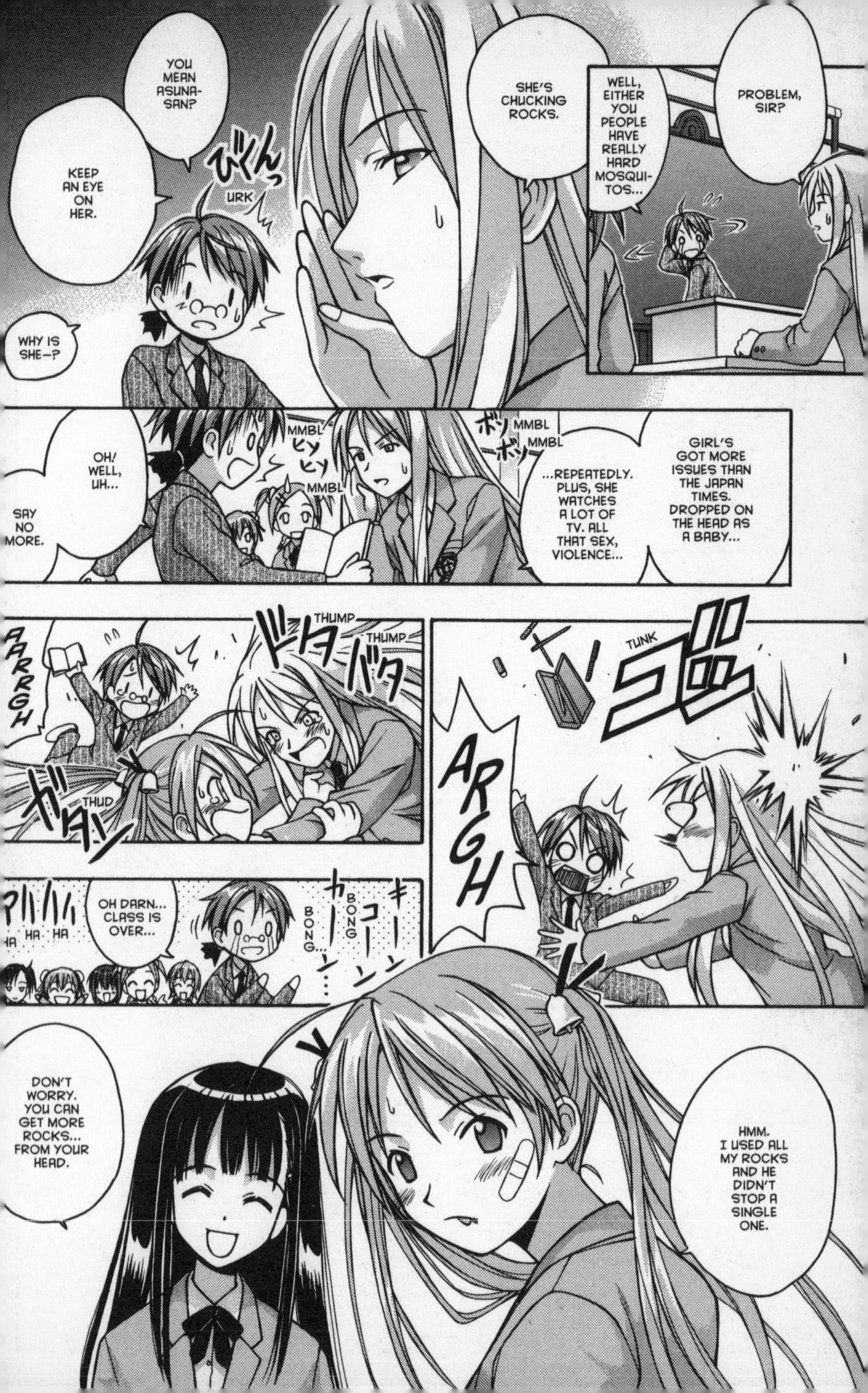
PROBLEM, SIR?
WELL, EITHER YOU PEOPLE HAVE REALLY HARD MOSQUITOS...
SHE'S CHUCKING ROCKS.
YOU MEAN ASUNA-SAN?
びくんっ
URK
KEEP AN EYE ON HER.
WHY IS SHE—?
GIRL'S GOT MORE ISSUES THAN THE JAPAN TIMES. DROPPED ON THE HEAD AS A BABY...
...REPEATEDLY. PLUS, SHE WATCHES A LOT OF TV. ALL THAT SEX, VIOLENCE...
MMBL
MMBL
MMBL
MMBL
OH! WELL, UH...
SAY NO MORE.
TUNK
ARGH
ドタバタ
THUMP
THUMP
AARRGH
ガタン
THUD
BONG
BONG
BONG...
OH DARN... CLASS IS OVER...
HA
HA
HA
HMM. I USED ALL MY ROCKS AND HE DIDN'T STOP A SINGLE ONE.
DON'T WORRY. YOU CAN GET MORE ROCKS... FROM YOUR HEAD.

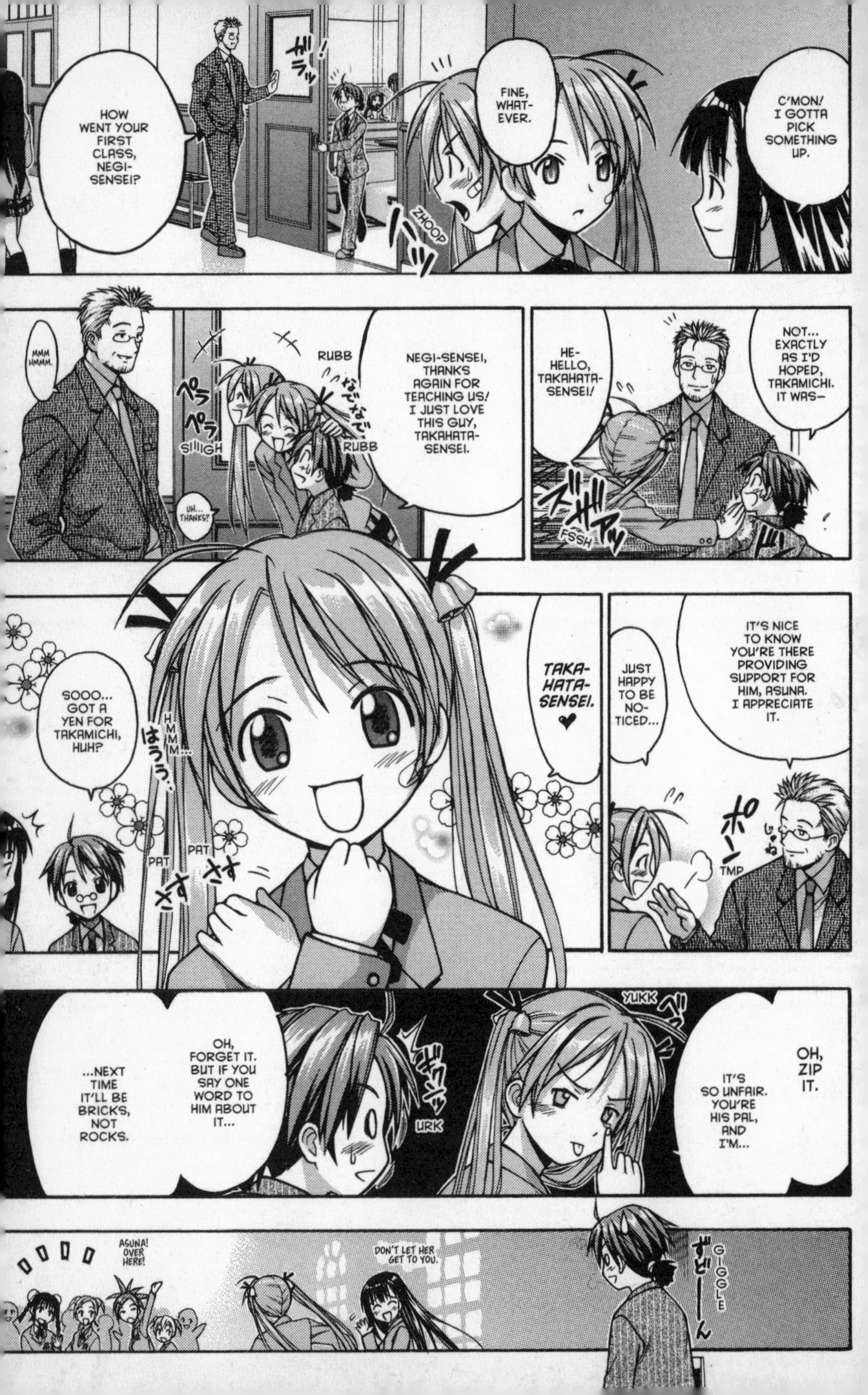
C'MON! I GOTTA PICK SOMETHING UP.
FINE, WHATEVER.
ZHOOP
ガラッ!
HOW WENT YOUR FIRST CLASS, NEGI-SENSEI?
NOT... EXACTLY AS I'D HOPED, TAKAMICHI. IT WAS—
HE-HELLO, TAKAHATA-SENSEI!
ズザァッ
FSSH
NEGI-SENSEI, THANKS AGAIN FOR TEACHING US! I JUST LOVE THIS GUY, TAKAHATA-SENSEI.
RUBB
なでなで
RUBB
ペラペラ
SIIIGH
UH... THANKS?
MMM HMMM.
IT'S NICE TO KNOW YOU'RE THERE PROVIDING SUPPORT FOR HIM, ASUNA. I APPRECIATE IT.
ポン
TMP
JUST HAPPY TO BE NOTICED...
TAKAHATA-SENSEI. ❤
SOOO... GOT A YEN FOR TAKAMICHI, HUH?
はうう
HMMM...
さすさす
PAT PAT
OH, ZIP IT.
IT'S SO UNFAIR. YOU'RE HIS PAL, AND I'M...
YUKK
URK
OH, FORGET IT. BUT IF YOU SAY ONE WORD TO HIM ABOUT IT...
...NEXT TIME IT'LL BE BRICKS, NOT ROCKS.
ずど～ん
GIGGLE
DON'T LET HER GET TO YOU.
ASUNA! OVER HERE!

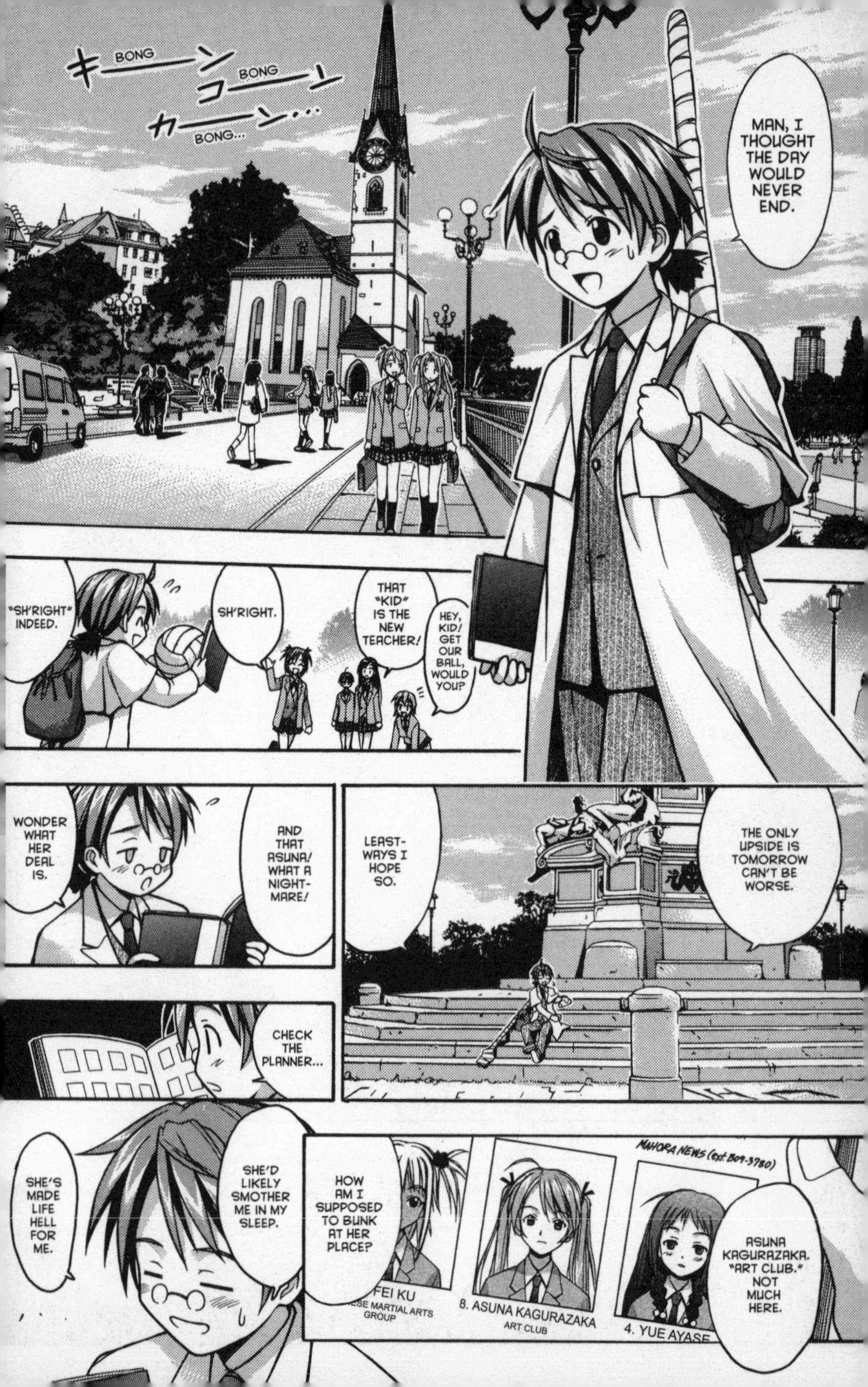
キーンコーンカーン…
BONG BONG BONG...
MAN, I THOUGHT THE DAY WOULD NEVER END.
HEY, KID! GET OUR BALL, WOULD YOU?
THAT "KID" IS THE NEW TEACHER!
SH'RIGHT.
"SH'RIGHT" INDEED.
THE ONLY UPSIDE IS TOMORROW CAN'T BE WORSE.
LEAST-WAYS I HOPE SO.
AND THAT ASUNA! WHAT A NIGHTMARE!
WONDER WHAT HER DEAL IS.
CHECK THE PLANNER...
MAHORA NEWS (ext. 809-3780)
ASUNA KAGURAZAKA. "ART CLUB." NOT MUCH HERE.
4. YUE AYASE
8. ASUNA KAGURAZAKA
ART CLUB
FEI KU
HOW AM I SUPPOSED TO BUNK AT HER PLACE?
SHE'D LIKELY SMOTHER ME IN MY SLEEP.
SHE'S MADE LIFE HELL FOR ME.

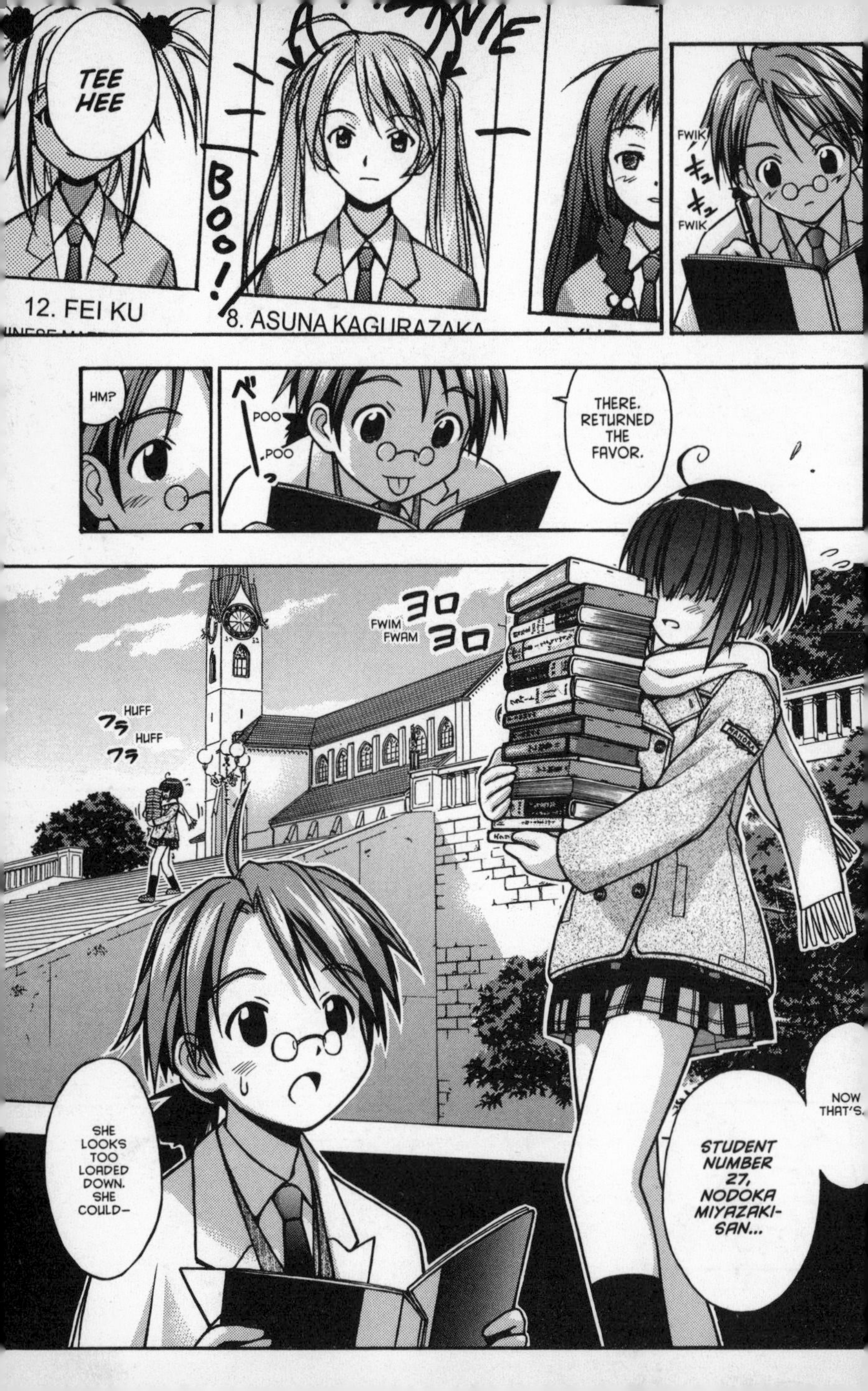
FWIK
キュ
キュ
FWIK
BOO!
8. ASUNA KAGURAZAKA
TEE HEE
12. FEI KU
THERE. RETURNED THE FAVOR.
べー
POO
POO
HM?
NOW THAT'S.
STUDENT NUMBER 27, NODOKA MIYAZAKI-SAN...
ヨロヨロ
FWIM FWAM
フラ
HUFF
フラ
HUFF
SHE LOOKS TOO LOADED DOWN. SHE COULD–

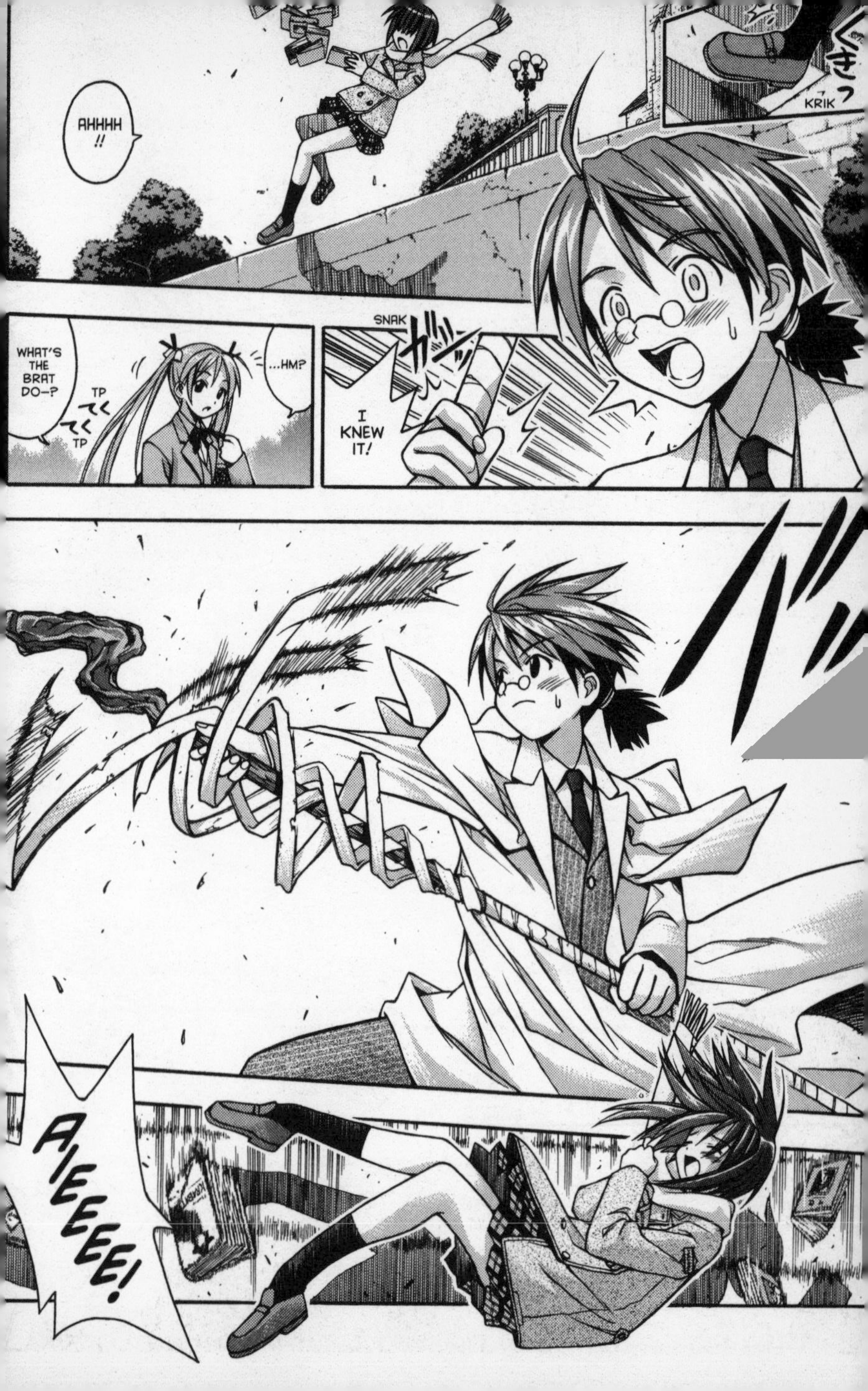
KRIK
AHHHH!!
SNAK
I KNEW IT!
...HM?
WHAT'S THE BRAT DO—?
TP TP
AIEEEE!

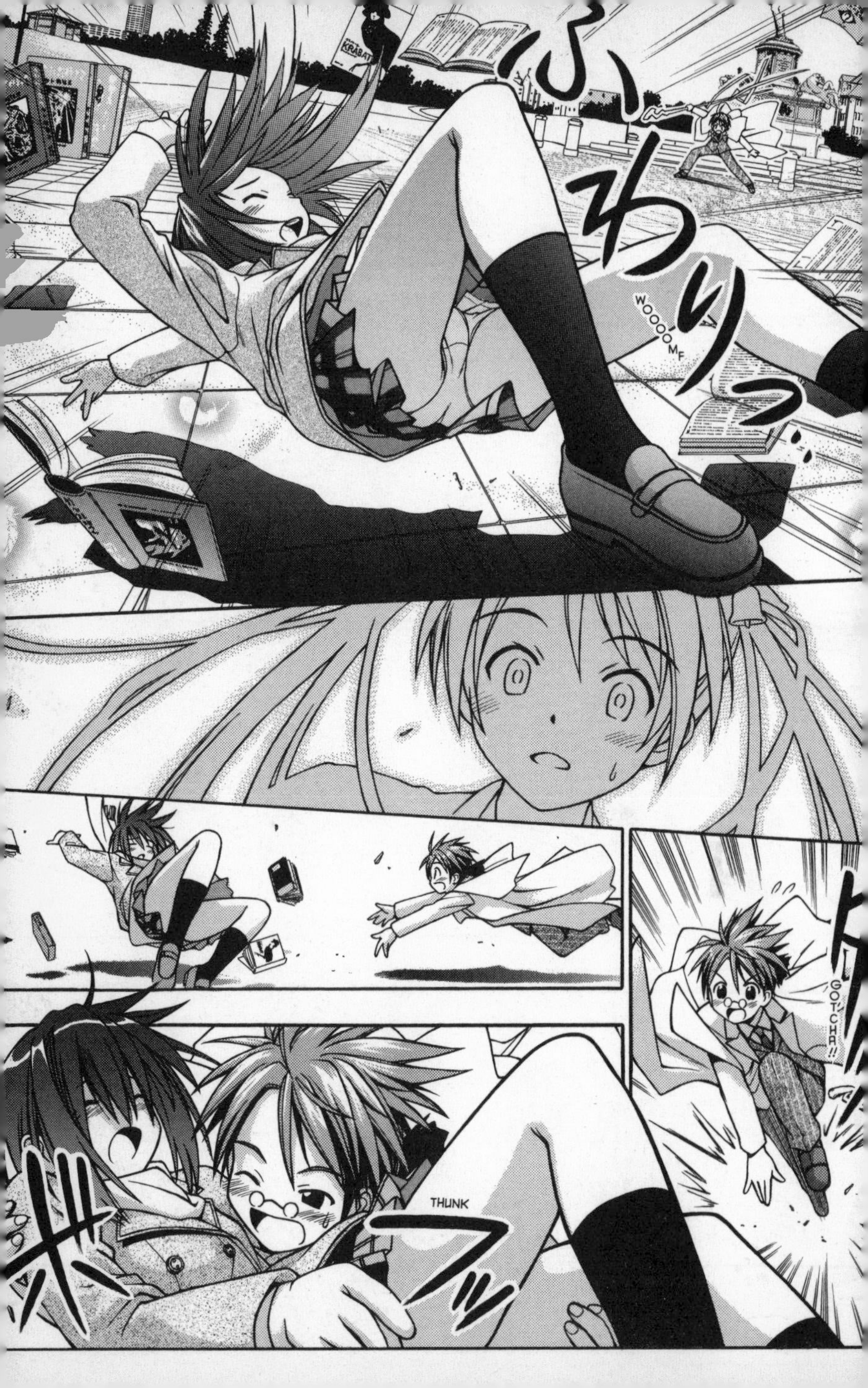
ふわりっ
WOOOOOMF
GOTCHA!!
THUNK

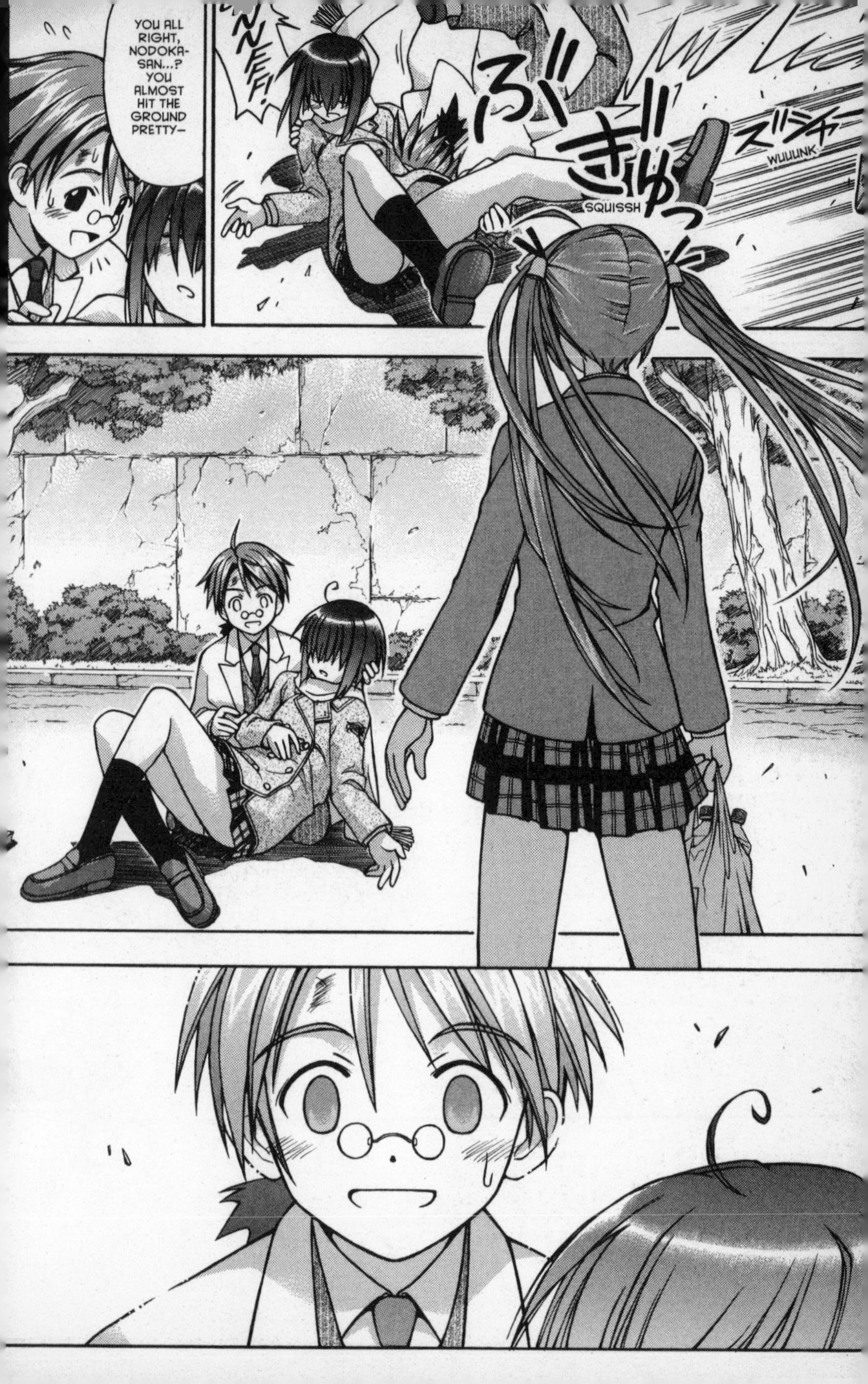
ズシャ
WUUUNK
きゅっ
SQUISSH
NNFF!
YOU ALL RIGHT, NODOKA-SAN...? YOU ALMOST HIT THE GROUND PRETTY—

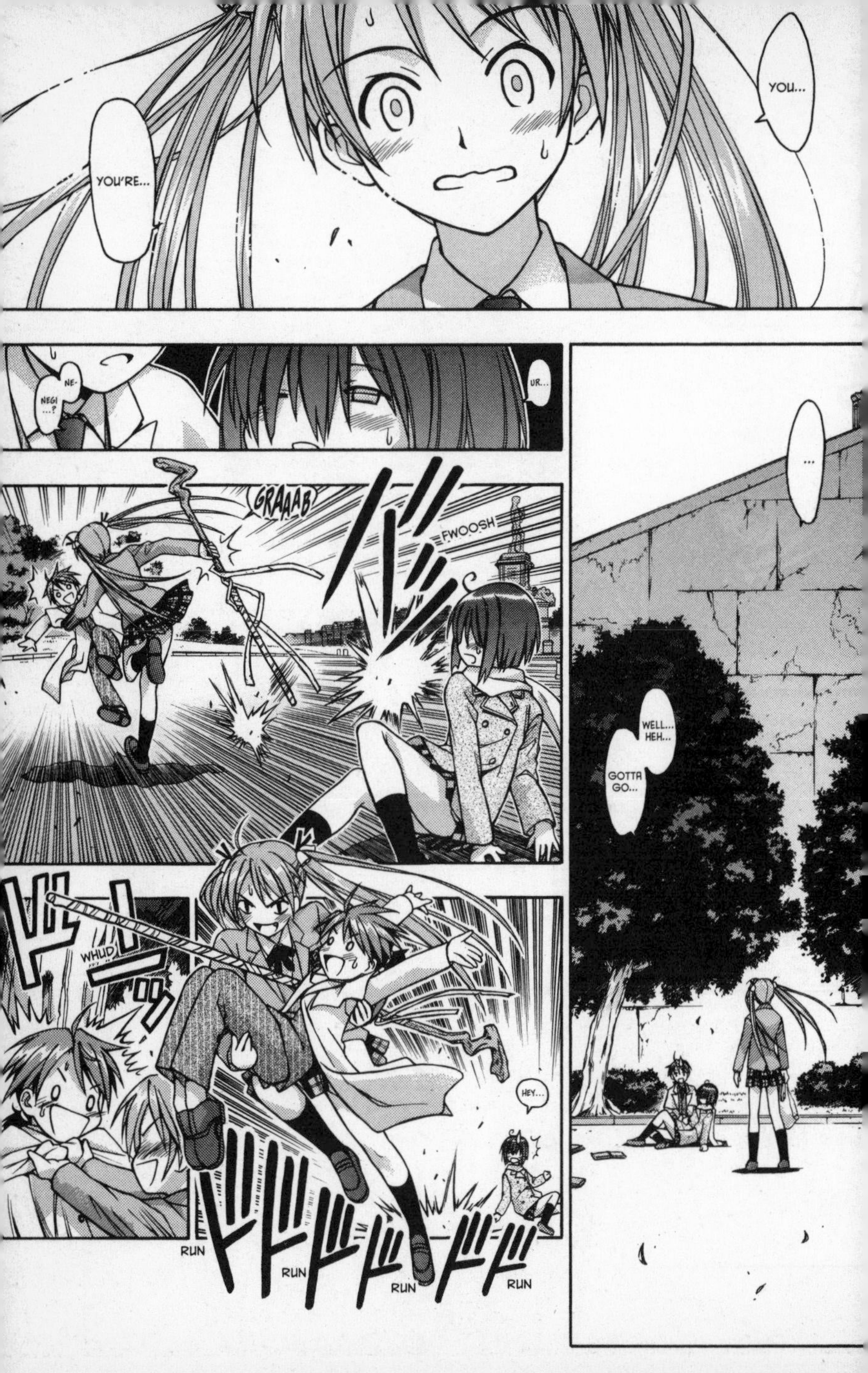
YOU...
YOU'RE...
...
WELL... HEH...
GOTTA GO...
UR...
NE-
NEGI ...?
FWOOSH
GRAAAB
HEY...
WHUD
RUN
RUN
RUN
RUN

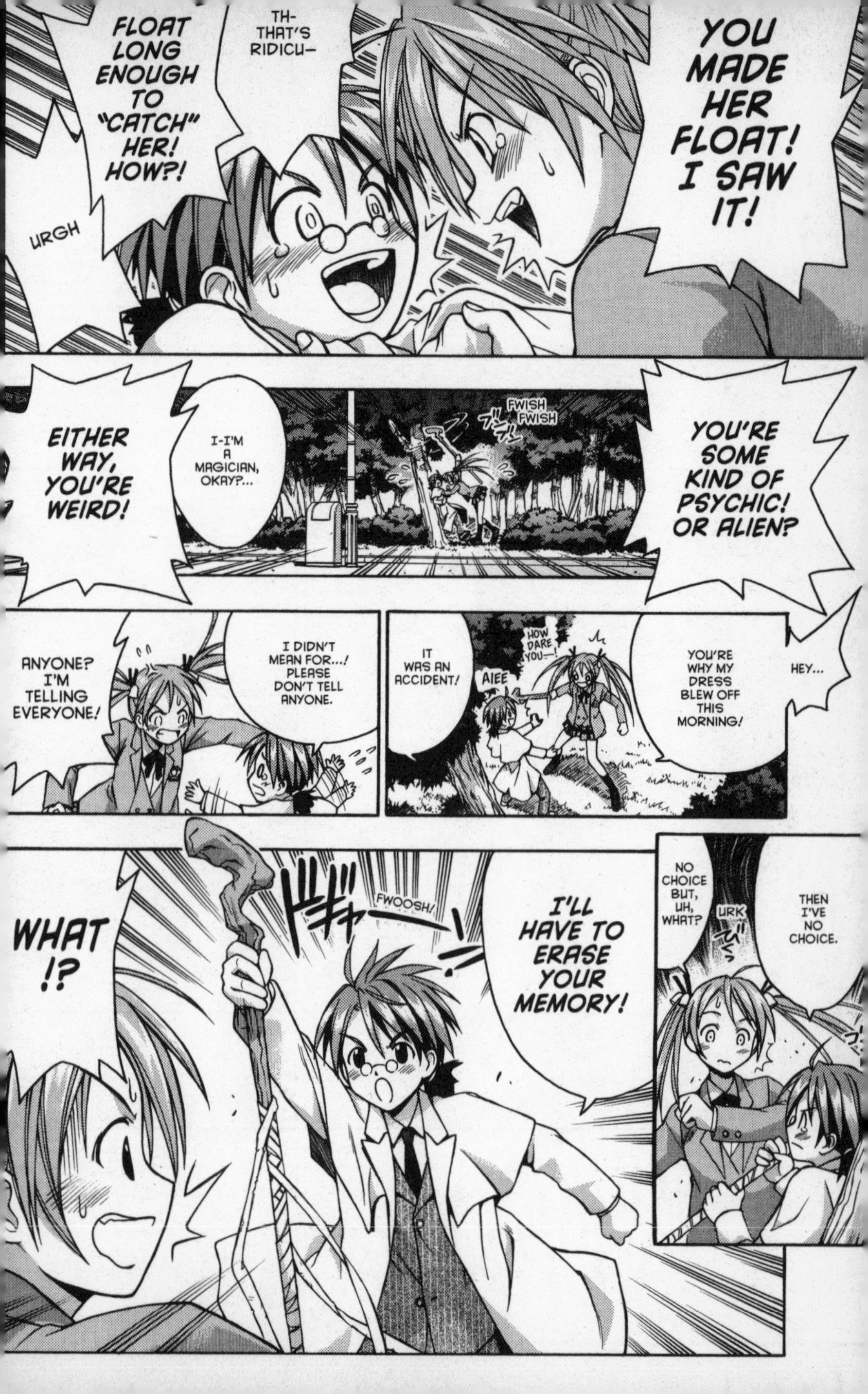
YOU MADE HER FLOAT! I SAW IT!
TH- THAT'S RIDICU—
FLOAT LONG ENOUGH TO "CATCH" HER! HOW?!
URGH
YOU'RE SOME KIND OF PSYCHIC! OR ALIEN?
FWISH FWISH
I-I'M A MAGICIAN, OKAY?...
EITHER WAY, YOU'RE WEIRD!
HEY...
YOU'RE WHY MY DRESS BLEW OFF THIS MORNING!
HOW DARE YOU—!
AIEE
IT WAS AN ACCIDENT!
I DIDN'T MEAN FOR...! PLEASE DON'T TELL ANYONE.
ANYONE? I'M TELLING EVERYONE!
THEN I'VE NO CHOICE.
URK
NO CHOICE BUT, UH, WHAT?
I'LL HAVE TO ERASE YOUR MEMORY!
FWOOSH!
WHAT!?

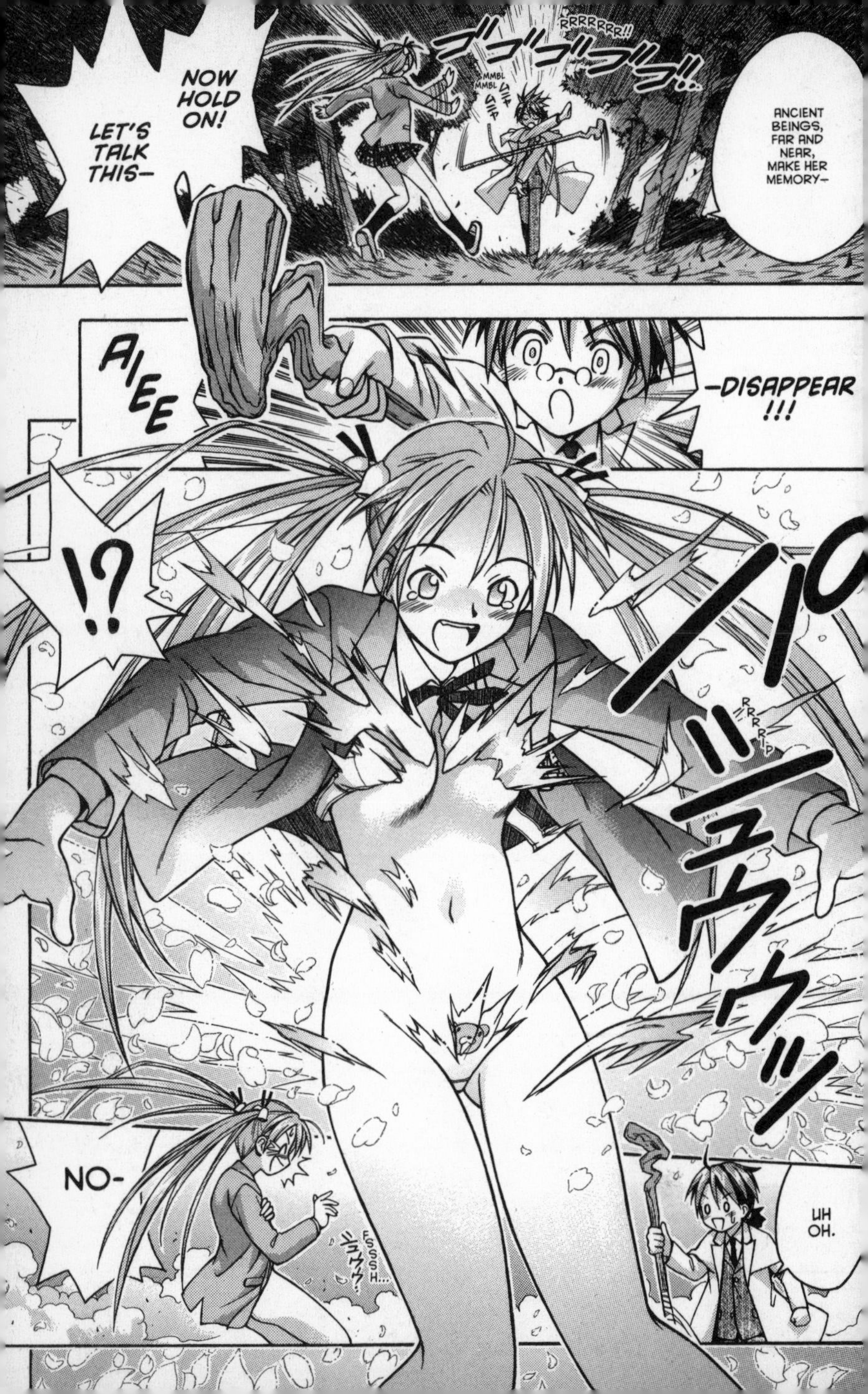
ANCIENT BEINGS, FAR AND NEAR, MAKE HER MEMORY—
RRRRRRR!!
MMBL MMBL
NOW HOLD ON!
LET'S TALK THIS—
—DISAPPEAR !!!
AIEE
!?
RRRRIP
UH OH.
NO-
FSSSH...

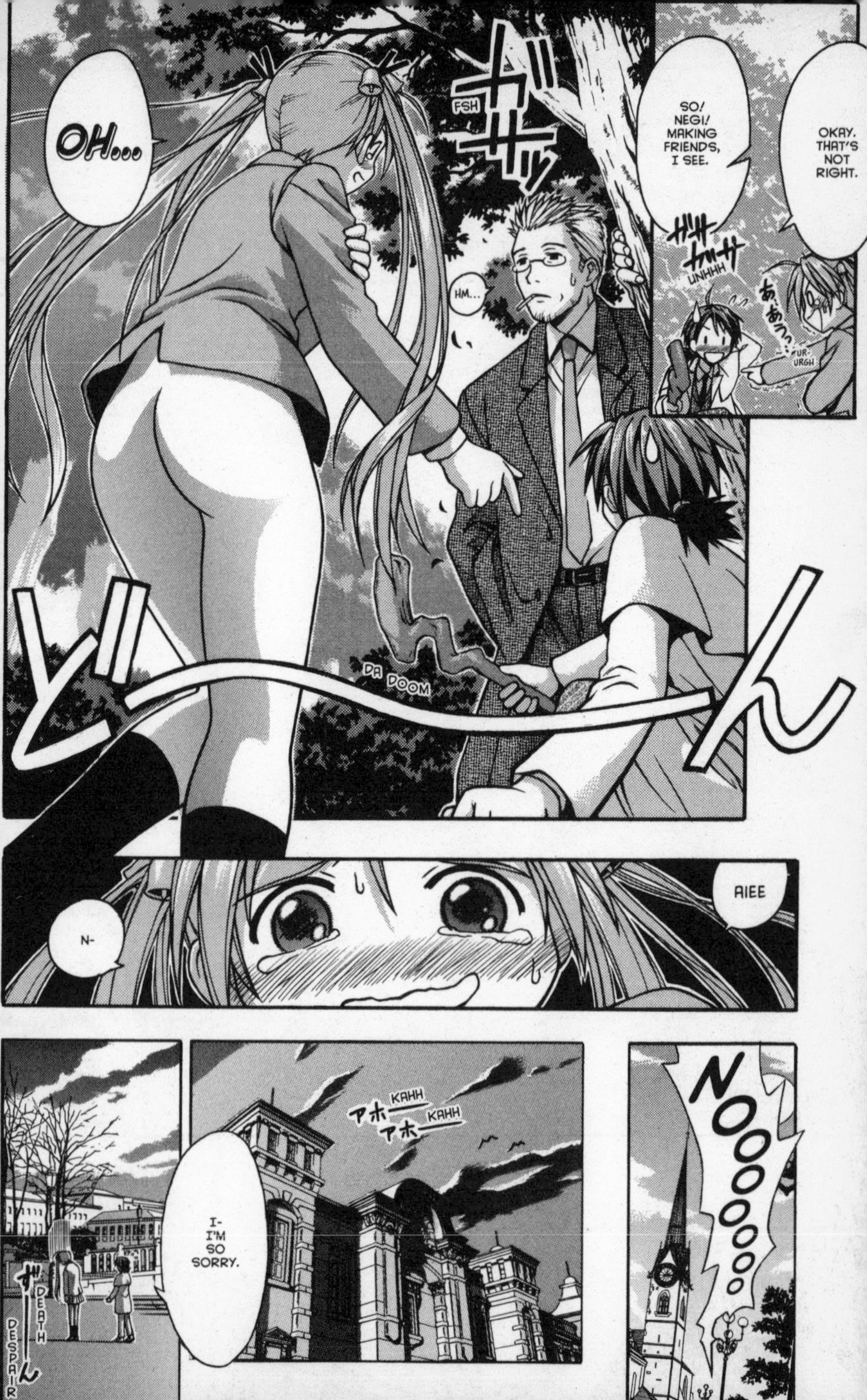
OKAY. THAT'S NOT RIGHT.
SO! NEGI! MAKING FRIENDS, I SEE.
ガサ ガサ
UNHHH
UR- URGH
ガサッ
FSH
OH...
HM...
どーん
DA DOOM
AIEE
N-
NOOOOOOO
アホー KAHH
アホー KAHH
I- I'M SO SORRY.
ずーん
DEATH
DESPAIR

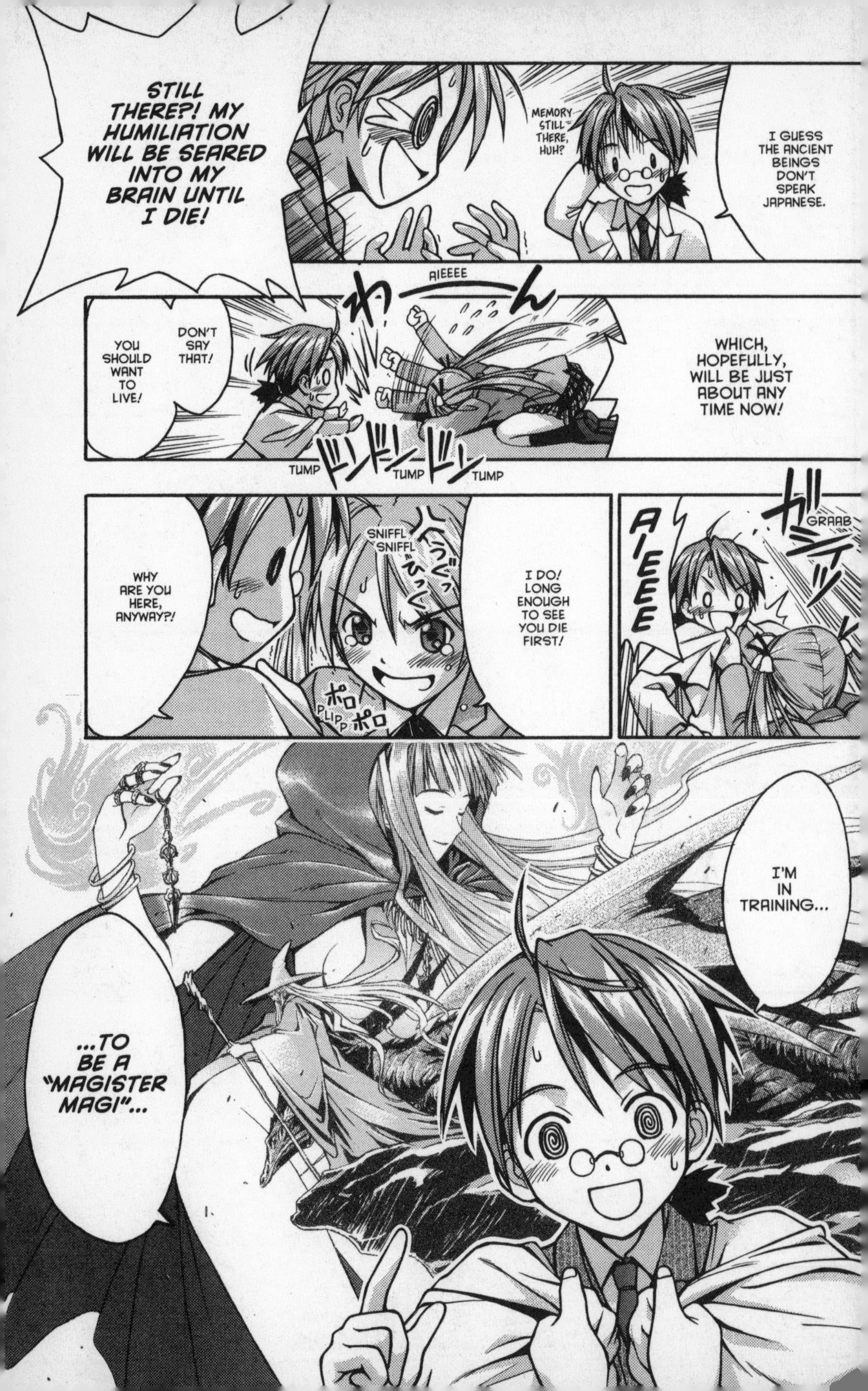
I GUESS THE ANCIENT BEINGS DON'T SPEAK JAPANESE.
MEMORY STILL THERE, HUH?
STILL THERE?! MY HUMILIATION WILL BE SEARED INTO MY BRAIN UNTIL I DIE!
WHICH, HOPEFULLY, WILL BE JUST ABOUT ANY TIME NOW!
わーん
AIEEEE
DON'T SAY THAT!
YOU SHOULD WANT TO LIVE!
TUMP TUMP TUMP
GRAAB
AIEEE
I DO! LONG ENOUGH TO SEE YOU DIE FIRST!
SNIFFL SNIFFL
WHY ARE YOU HERE, ANYWAY?!
ポロポロ
PLIPP
I'M IN TRAINING...
...TO BE A "MAGISTER MAGI"...

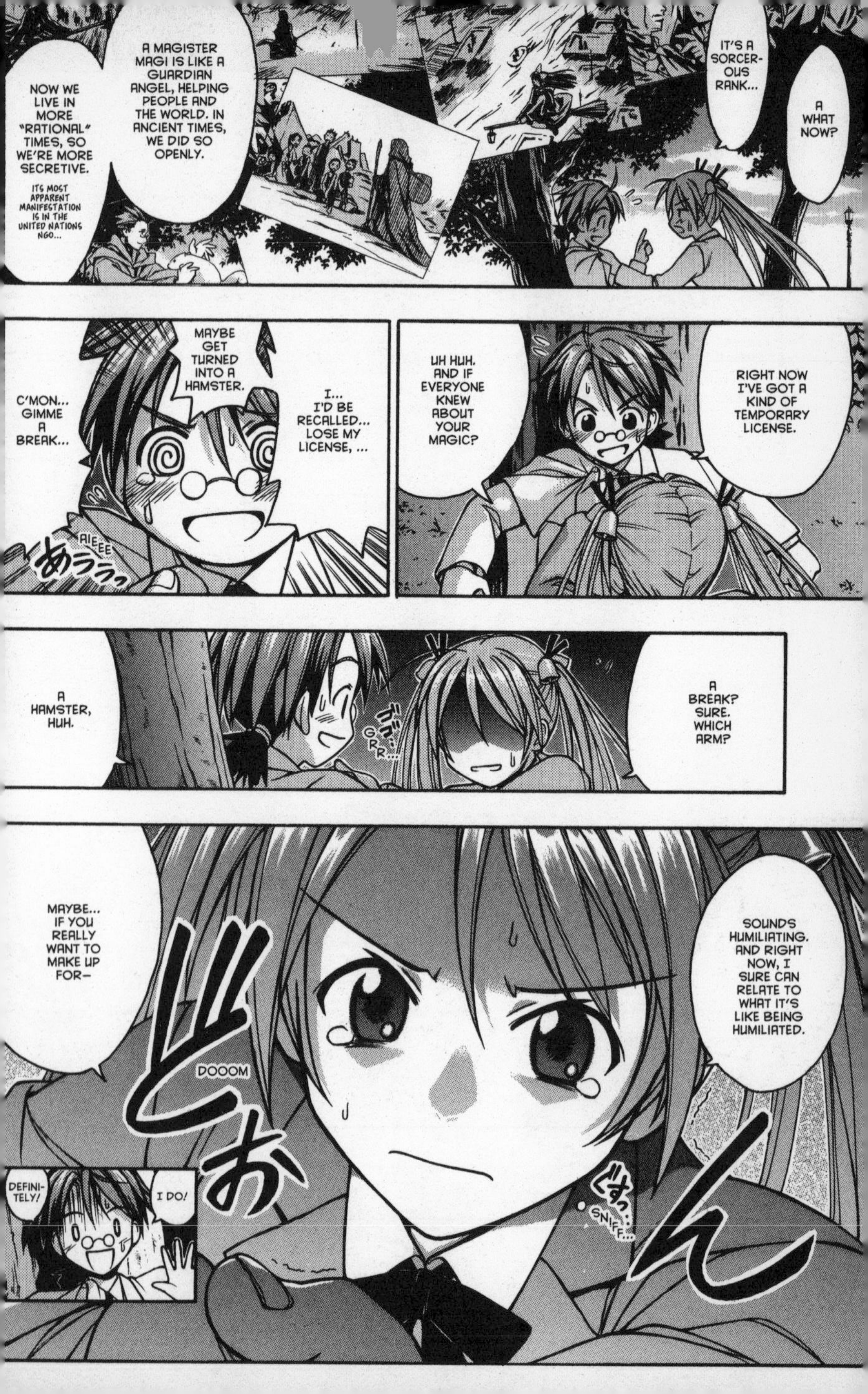
IT'S A SORCEROUS RANK...
A WHAT NOW?
A MAGISTER MAGI IS LIKE A GUARDIAN ANGEL, HELPING PEOPLE AND THE WORLD. IN ANCIENT TIMES, WE DID SO OPENLY.
NOW WE LIVE IN MORE "RATIONAL" TIMES, SO WE'RE MORE SECRETIVE.
ITS MOST APPARENT MANIFESTATION IS IN THE UNITED NATIONS NGO...
RIGHT NOW I'VE GOT A KIND OF TEMPORARY LICENSE.
UH HUH. AND IF EVERYONE KNEW ABOUT YOUR MAGIC?
I... I'D BE RECALLED... LOSE MY LICENSE, ...
MAYBE GET TURNED INTO A HAMSTER.
C'MON... GIMME A BREAK...
あうぅっ AIEEE
A BREAK? SURE. WHICH ARM?
ゴゴ GRR...
A HAMSTER, HUH.
SOUNDS HUMILIATING. AND RIGHT NOW, I SURE CAN RELATE TO WHAT IT'S LIKE BEING HUMILIATED.
MAYBE... IF YOU REALLY WANT TO MAKE UP FOR—
ぐすっ SNIFF...
どぉん DOOOM
I DO!
DEFINITELY!

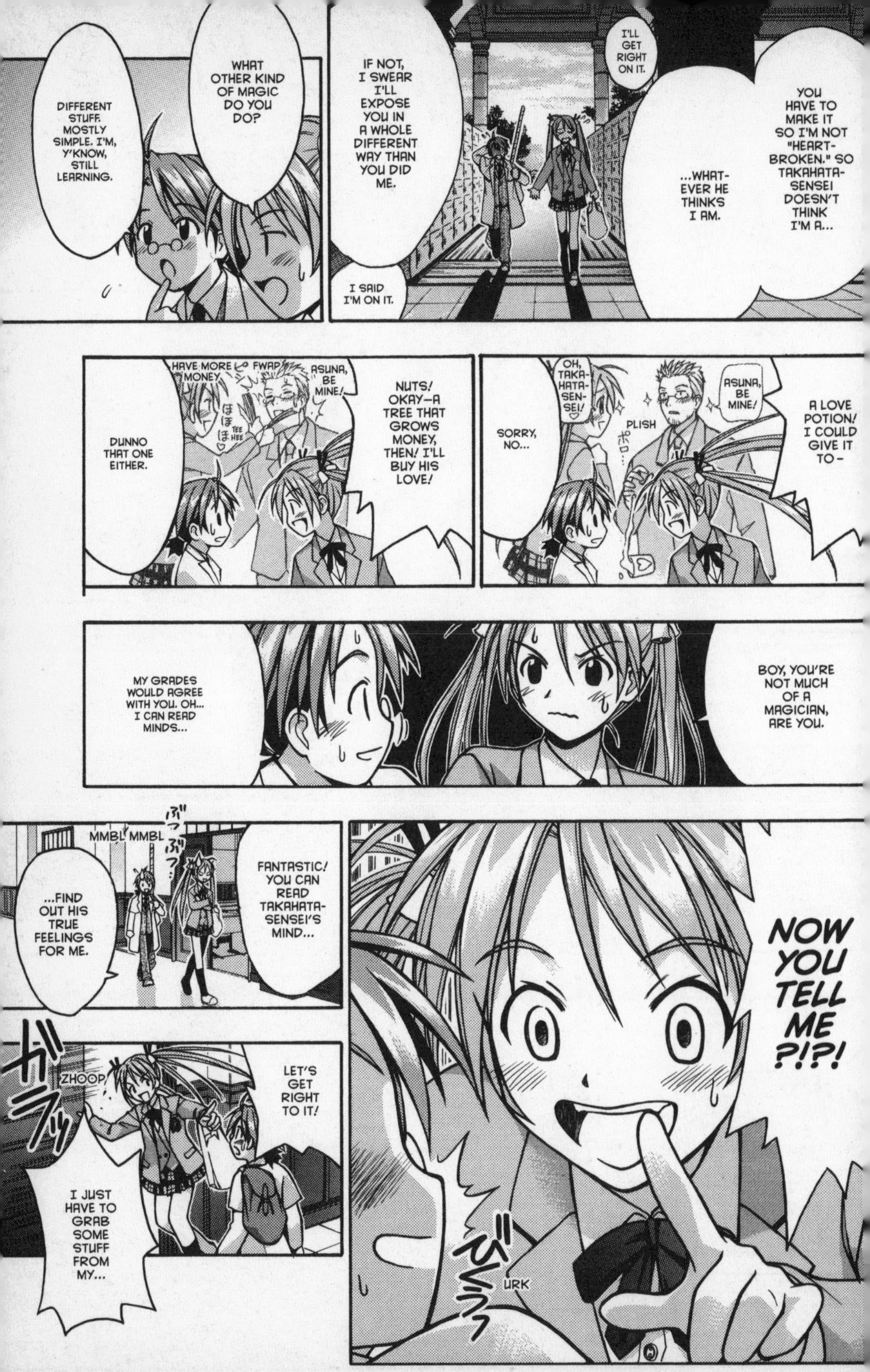
YOU HAVE TO MAKE IT SO I'M NOT "HEART-BROKEN." SO TAKAHATA-SENSEI DOESN'T THINK I'M A...
...WHATEVER HE THINKS I AM.
I'LL GET RIGHT ON IT.
IF NOT, I SWEAR I'LL EXPOSE YOU IN A WHOLE DIFFERENT WAY THAN YOU DID ME.
I SAID I'M ON IT.
WHAT OTHER KIND OF MAGIC DO YOU DO?
DIFFERENT STUFF. MOSTLY SIMPLE. I'M, Y'KNOW, STILL LEARNING.
A LOVE POTION! I COULD GIVE IT TO–
ASUNA, BE MINE!
PLISH
OH, TAKAHATA-SENSEI!
SORRY, NO...
NUTS! OKAY—A TREE THAT GROWS MONEY, THEN! I'LL BUY HIS LOVE!
ASUNA, BE MINE!
FWAP
HAVE MORE MONEY
TEE HEE
DUNNO THAT ONE EITHER.
BOY, YOU'RE NOT MUCH OF A MAGICIAN, ARE YOU.
MY GRADES WOULD AGREE WITH YOU. OH... I CAN READ MINDS...
NOW YOU TELL ME?!?!
URK
FANTASTIC! YOU CAN READ TAKAHATA-SENSEI'S MIND...
MMBL MMBL
...FIND OUT HIS TRUE FEELINGS FOR ME.
LET'S GET RIGHT TO IT!
ZHOOP
I JUST HAVE TO GRAB SOME STUFF FROM MY...

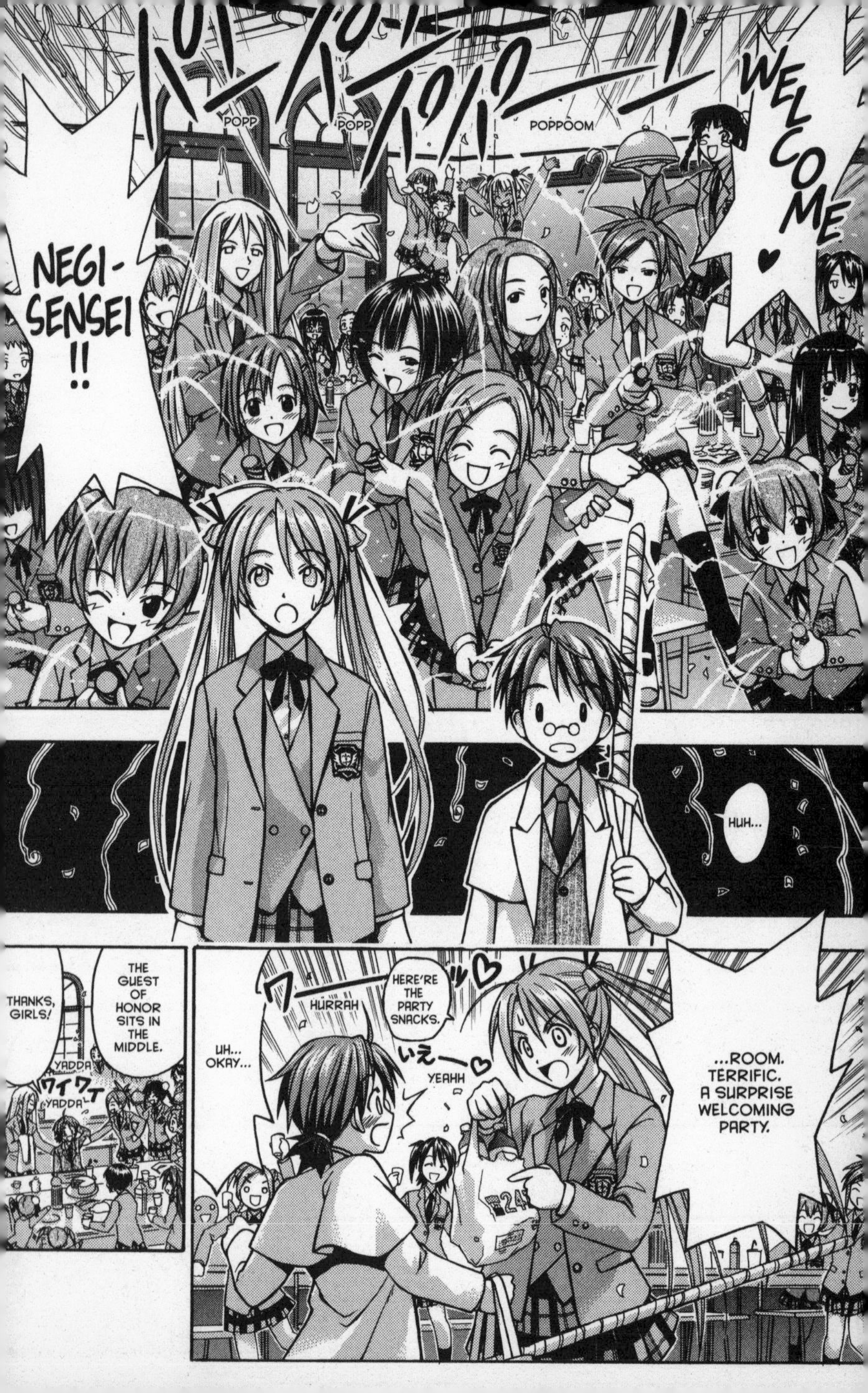
WELCOME ♥
POPPOOM
POPP
POPP
NEGI-SENSEI!!
HUH...
...ROOM. TERRIFIC. A SURPRISE WELCOMING PARTY.
HERE'RE THE PARTY SNACKS.
HURRAH
YEAHH
UH... OKAY...
THE GUEST OF HONOR SITS IN THE MIDDLE.
THANKS, GIRLS!
YADDA
YADDA

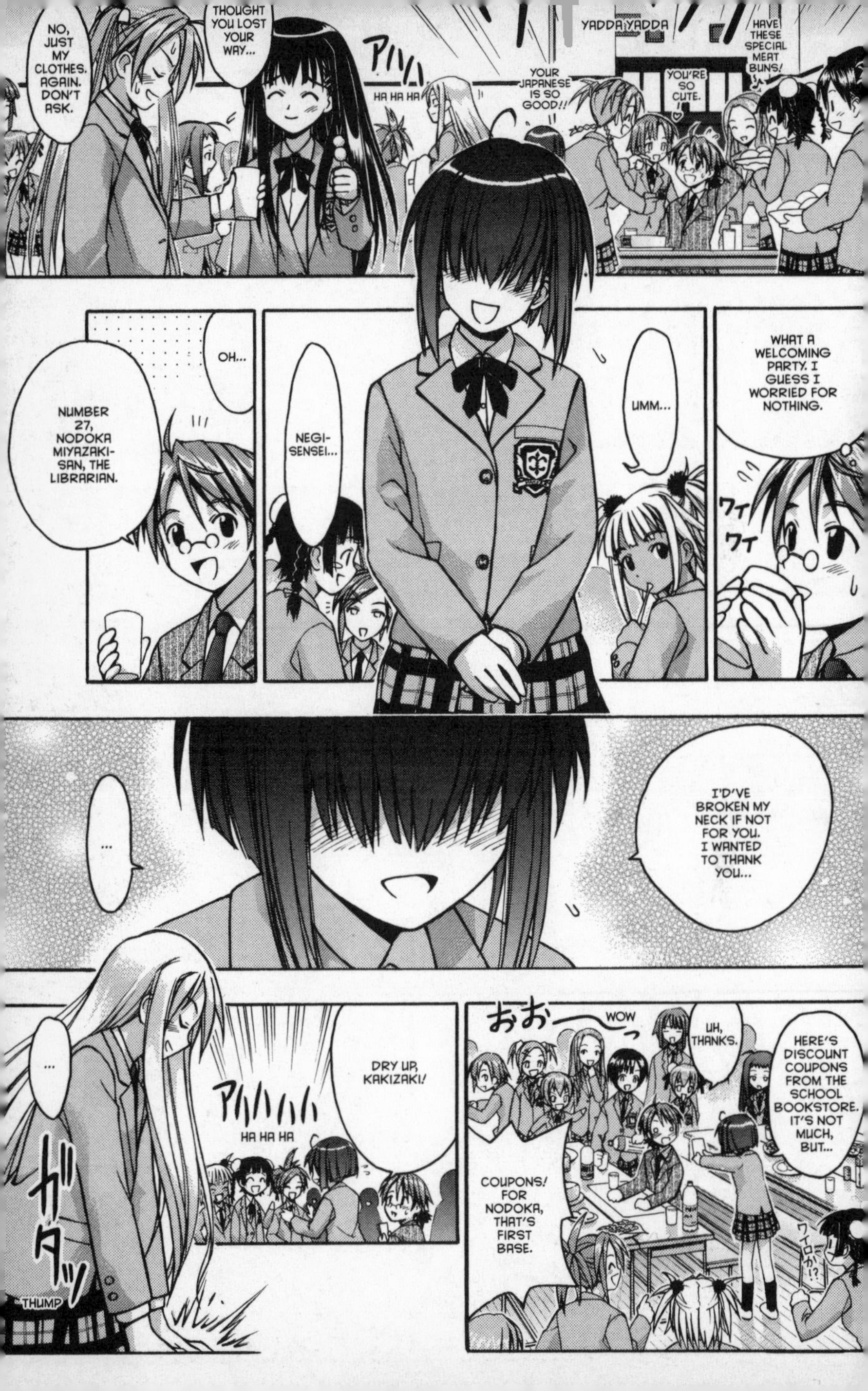
HAVE THESE SPECIAL MEAT BUNS!
YADDA YADDA
YOU'RE SO CUTE.
YOUR JAPANESE IS SO GOOD!!
アハハ
HA HA HA
THOUGHT YOU LOST YOUR WAY...
NO, JUST MY CLOTHES. AGAIN. DON'T ASK.
WHAT A WELCOMING PARTY. I GUESS I WORRIED FOR NOTHING.
ワイ ワイ
UMM...
NEGI-SENSEI...
OH...
NUMBER 27, NODOKA MIYAZAKI-SAN, THE LIBRARIAN.
I'D'VE BROKEN MY NECK IF NOT FOR YOU. I WANTED TO THANK YOU...
...
HERE'S DISCOUNT COUPONS FROM THE SCHOOL BOOKSTORE. IT'S NOT MUCH, BUT...
UH, THANKS.
おおー
WOW
COUPONS! FOR NODOKA, THAT'S FIRST BASE.
DRY UP, KAKIZAKI!
アハハハ
HA HA HA
...
ガタッ
THUMP

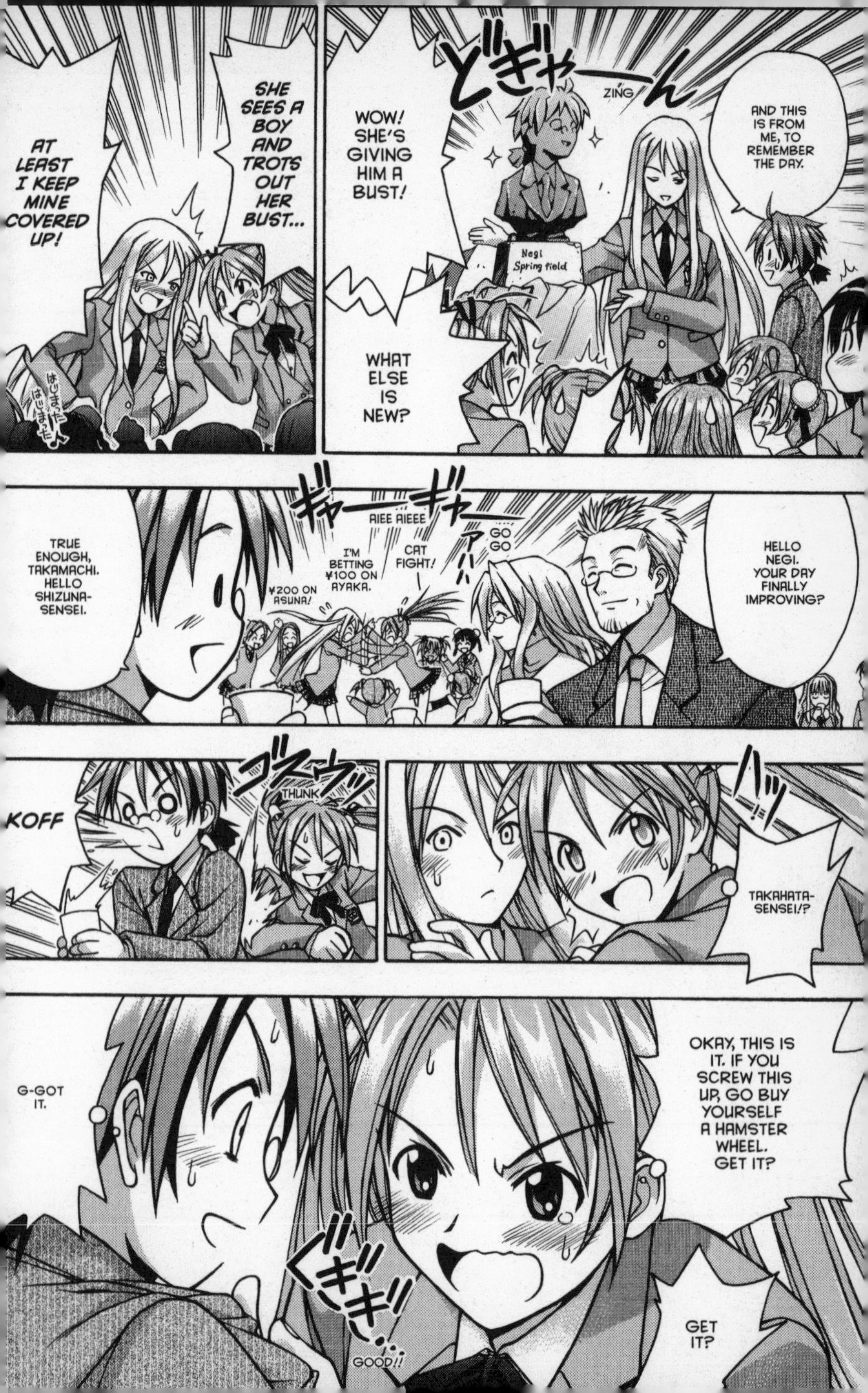
どぎゃーん
ZING
AND THIS IS FROM ME, TO REMEMBER THE DAY.
WOW! SHE'S GIVING HIM A BUST!
Negi Spring field
WHAT ELSE IS NEW?
SHE SEES A BOY AND TROTS OUT HER BUST...
AT LEAST I KEEP MINE COVERED UP!
はじまった はじまった
HELLO NEGI. YOUR DAY FINALLY IMPROVING?
ギャーギャー
AIEE AIEE
GO GO
アハハ
CAT FIGHT!
I'M BETTING ¥100 ON AYAKA.
¥200 ON ASUNA!
TRUE ENOUGH, TAKAMACHI. HELLO SHIZUNA-SENSEI.
TAKAHATA-SENSEI!?
THUNK
KOFF
OKAY, THIS IS IT. IF YOU SCREW THIS UP, GO BUY YOURSELF A HAMSTER WHEEL. GET IT?
GET IT?
GOOD!!
G-GOT IT.

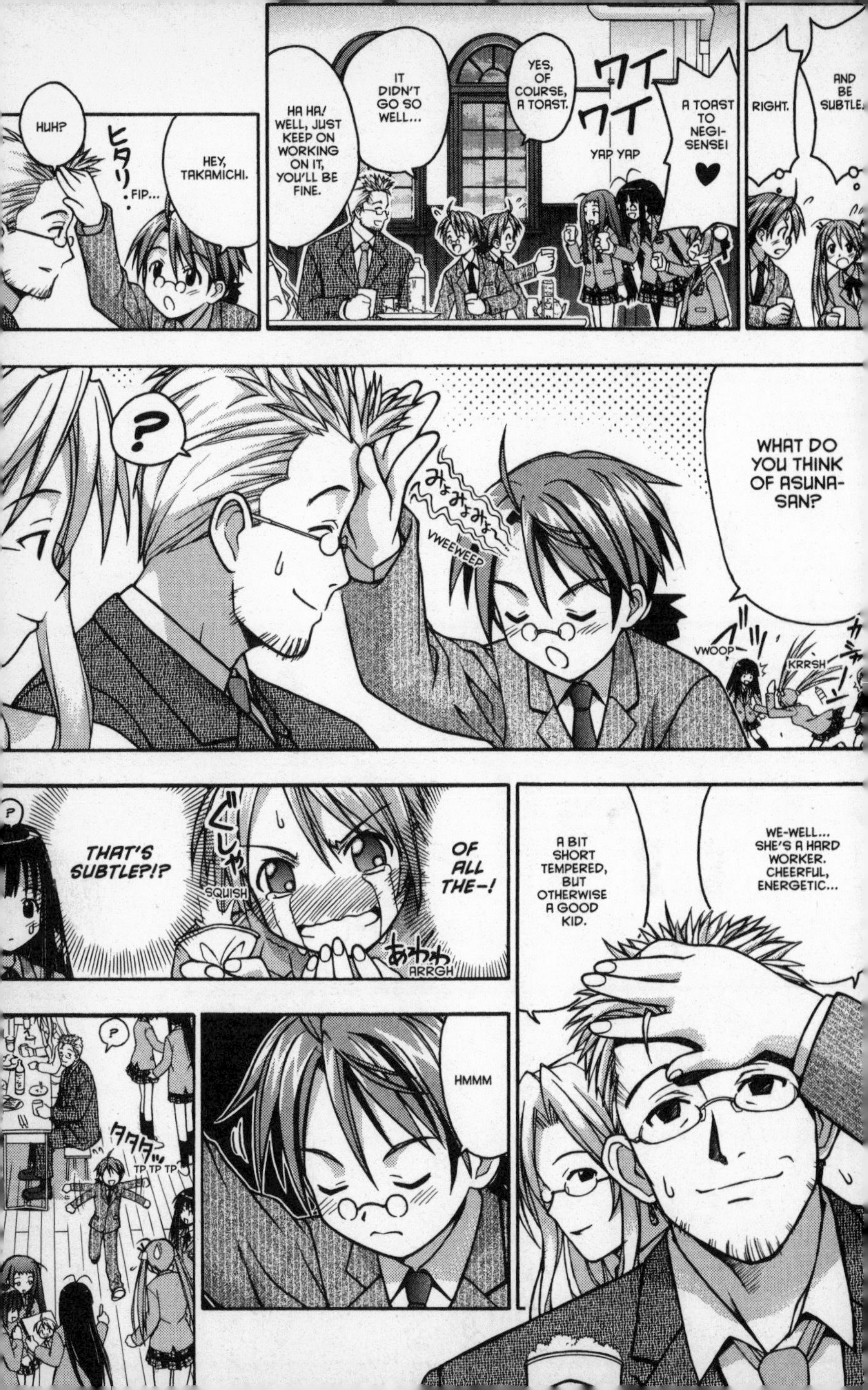
AND BE SUBTLE.
RIGHT.
A TOAST TO NEGI-SENSEI ♥
ワイワイ
YAP YAP
YES, OF COURSE, A TOAST.
IT DIDN'T GO SO WELL...
HA HA! WELL, JUST KEEP ON WORKING ON IT, YOU'LL BE FINE.
HEY, TAKAMICHI.
ヒタリ
FIP...
HUH?
WHAT DO YOU THINK OF ASUNA-SAN?
VWOOP
KRRSH
みょみょみょ~
VWEEWEEP
?
WE-WELL... SHE'S A HARD WORKER. CHEERFUL, ENERGETIC...
A BIT SHORT TEMPERED, BUT OTHERWISE A GOOD KID.
OF ALL THE-!
ぐしゃ
SQUISH
あわわ
ARRGH
THAT'S SUBTLE?!?
?
HMMM
タタタッ
TP TP TP
?

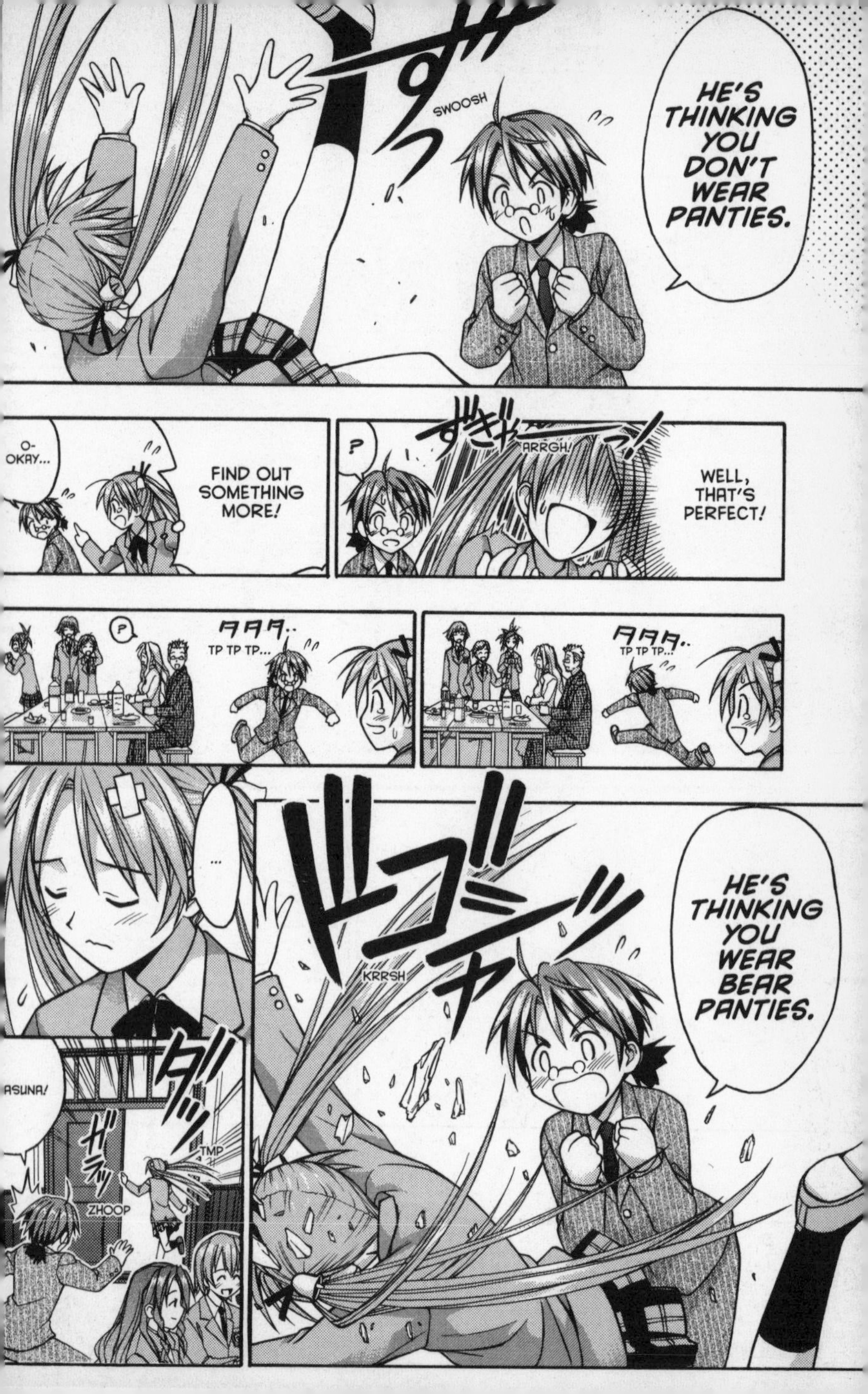
HE'S THINKING YOU DON'T WEAR PANTIES.
SWOOSH
WELL, THAT'S PERFECT!
ARRGH!
?
FIND OUT SOMETHING MORE!
O-OKAY...
TP TP TP...
?
TP TP TP...
HE'S THINKING YOU WEAR BEAR PANTIES.
KRRSH
...
ASUNA!
TMP
ZHOOP

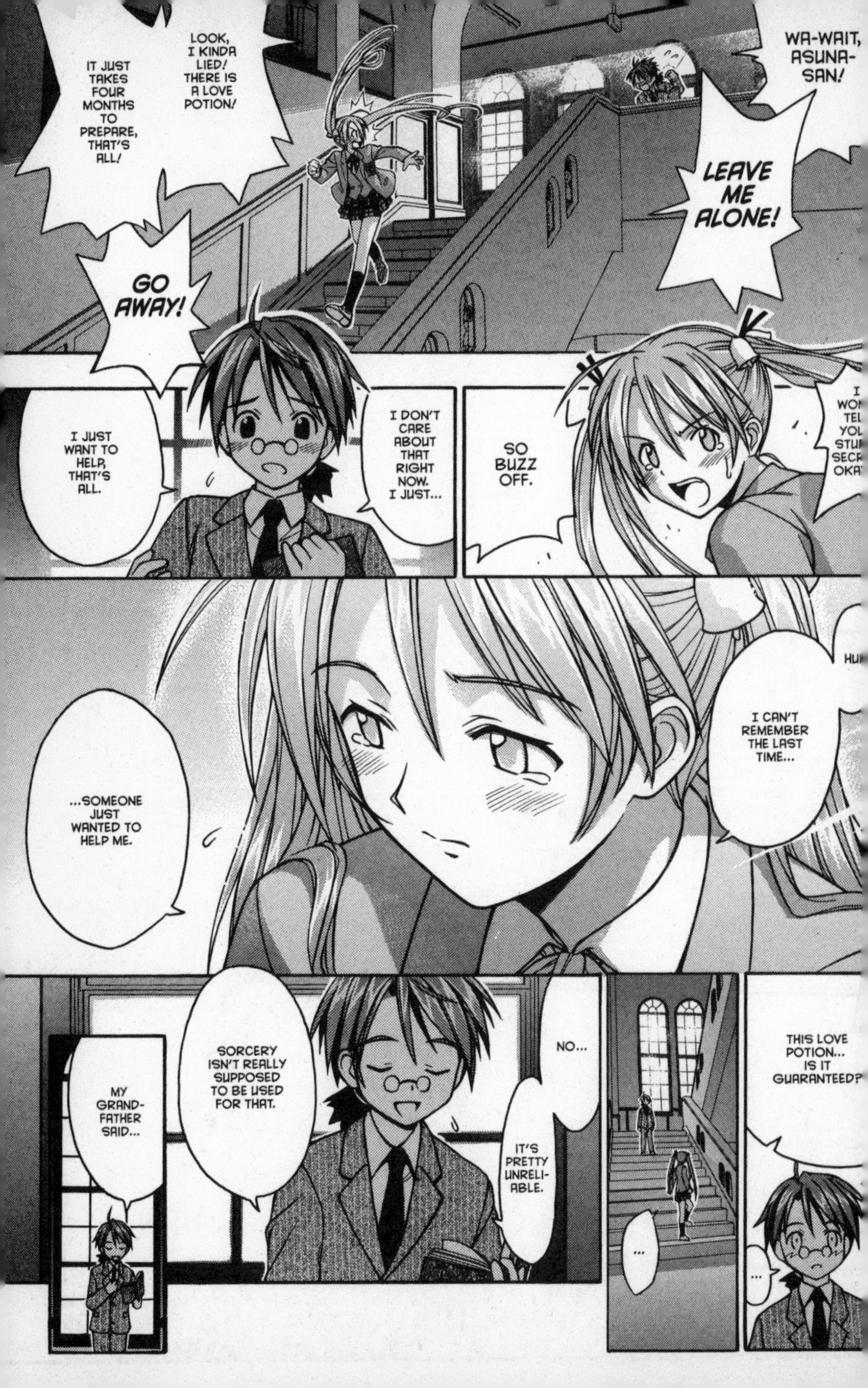
WA-WAIT, ASUNA-SAN!
LEAVE ME ALONE!
LOOK, I KINDA LIED! THERE IS A LOVE POTION!
IT JUST TAKES FOUR MONTHS TO PREPARE, THAT'S ALL!
GO AWAY!
SO BUZZ OFF.
I DON'T CARE ABOUT THAT RIGHT NOW. I JUST...
I JUST WANT TO HELP, THAT'S ALL.
I CAN'T REMEMBER THE LAST TIME...
...SOMEONE JUST WANTED TO HELP ME.
THIS LOVE POTION... IS IT GUARANTEED?
...
...
NO...
IT'S PRETTY UNRELI-ABLE.
SORCERY ISN'T REALLY SUPPOSED TO BE USED FOR THAT.
MY GRAND-FATHER SAID...

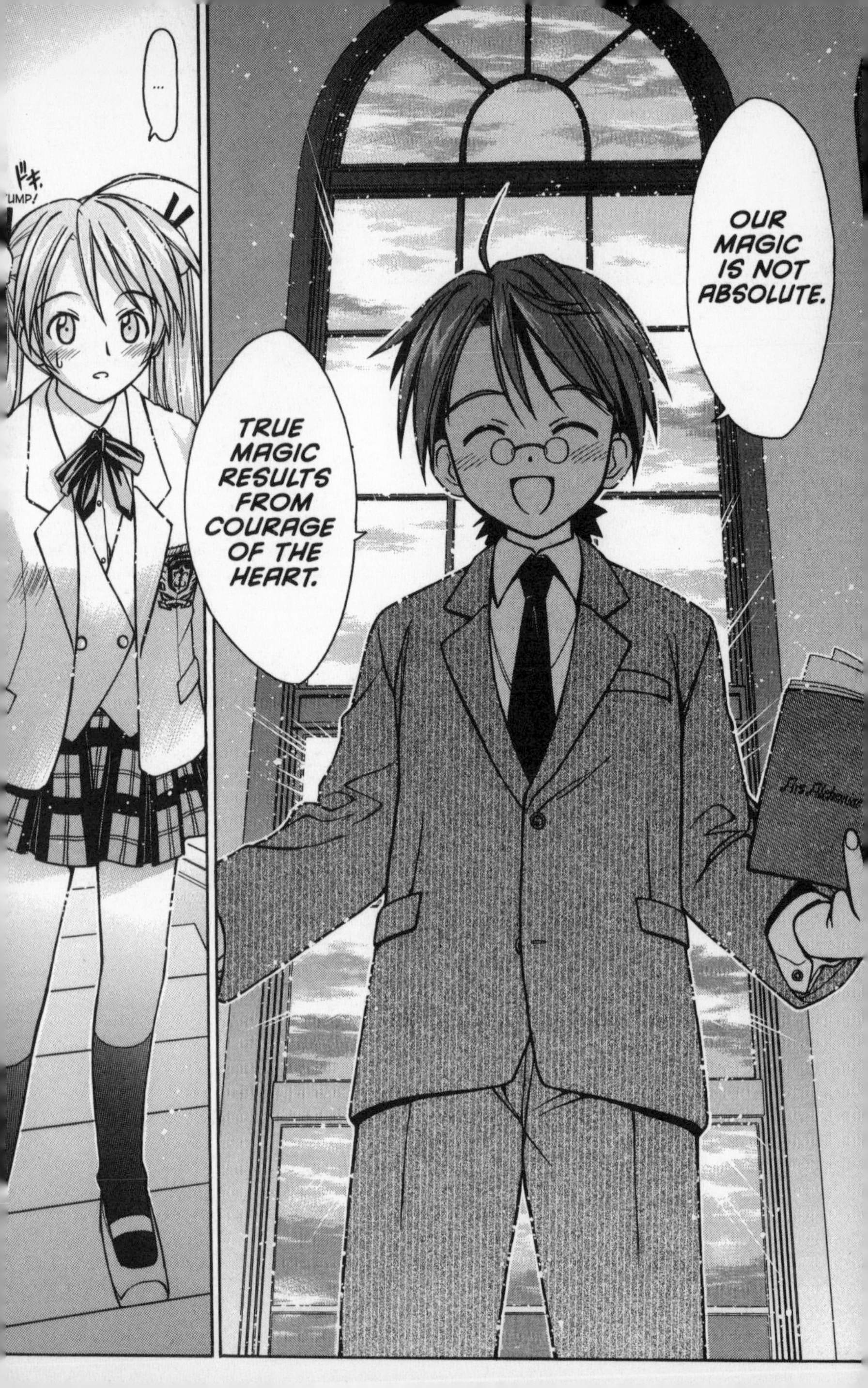
OUR MAGIC IS NOT ABSOLUTE.
TRUE MAGIC RESULTS FROM COURAGE OF THE HEART.
...

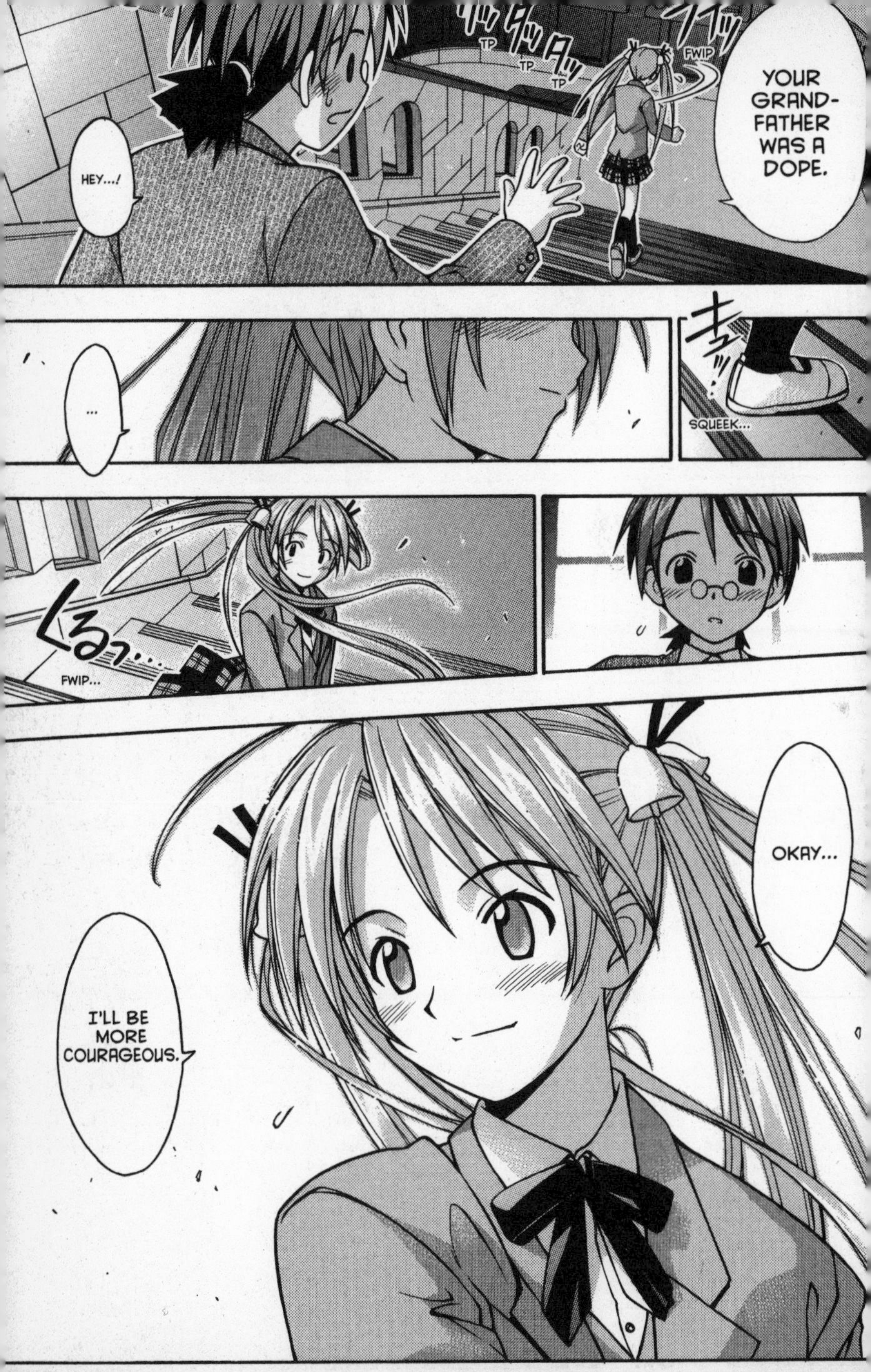
YOUR GRAND-FATHER WAS A DOPE.
FWIP
TP
TP
TP
HEY...!
SQUEEK...
...
FWIP...
OKAY...
I'LL BE MORE COURAGEOUS.

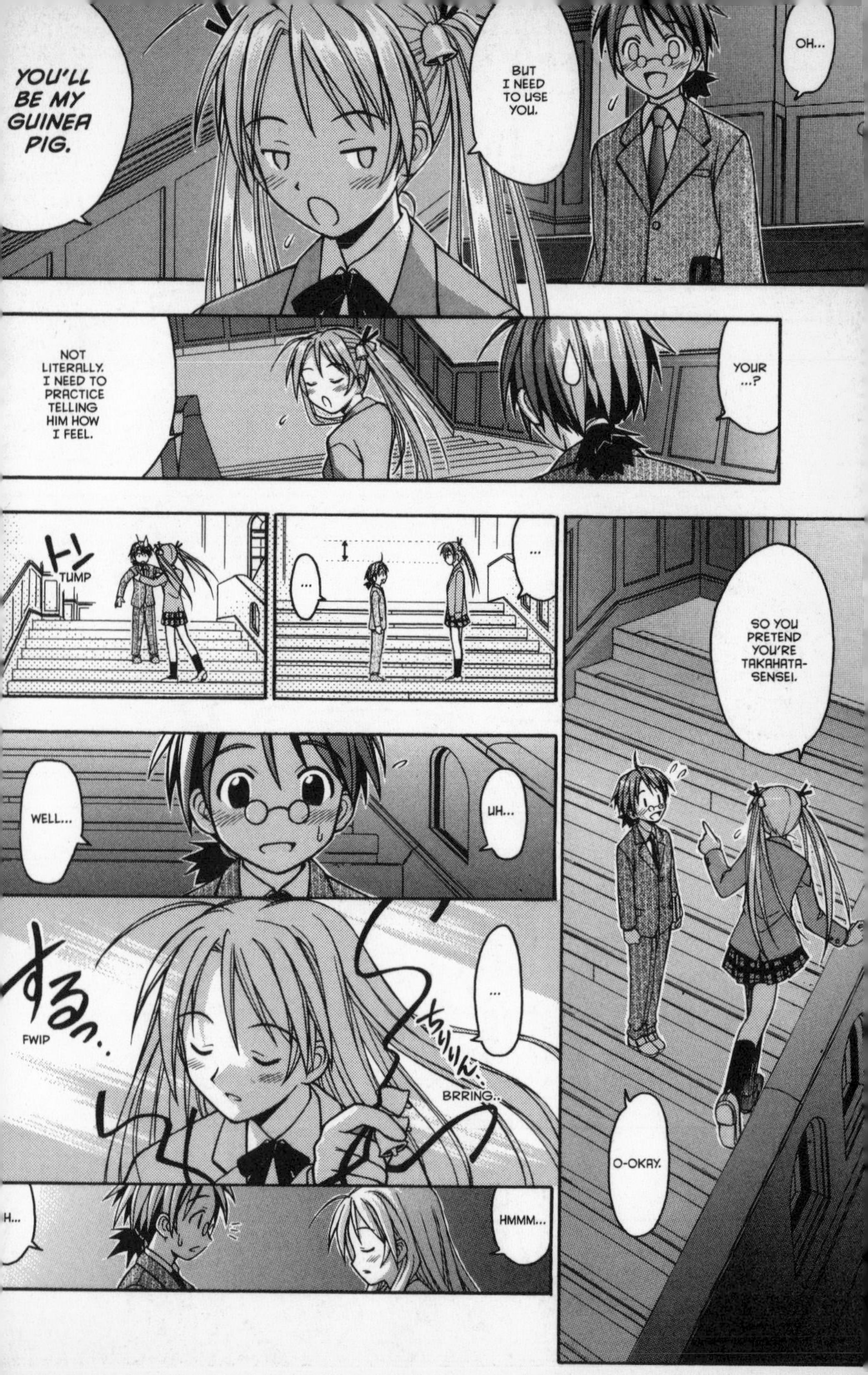
OH...
BUT I NEED TO USE YOU.
YOU'LL BE MY GUINEA PIG.
YOUR ...?
NOT LITERALLY. I NEED TO PRACTICE TELLING HIM HOW I FEEL.
SO YOU PRETEND YOU'RE TAKAHATA-SENSEI.
O-OKAY.
...
...
トン
TUMP
UH...
WELL...
...
ちりりん..
BRRING..
するっ..
FWIP
HMMM...
H...

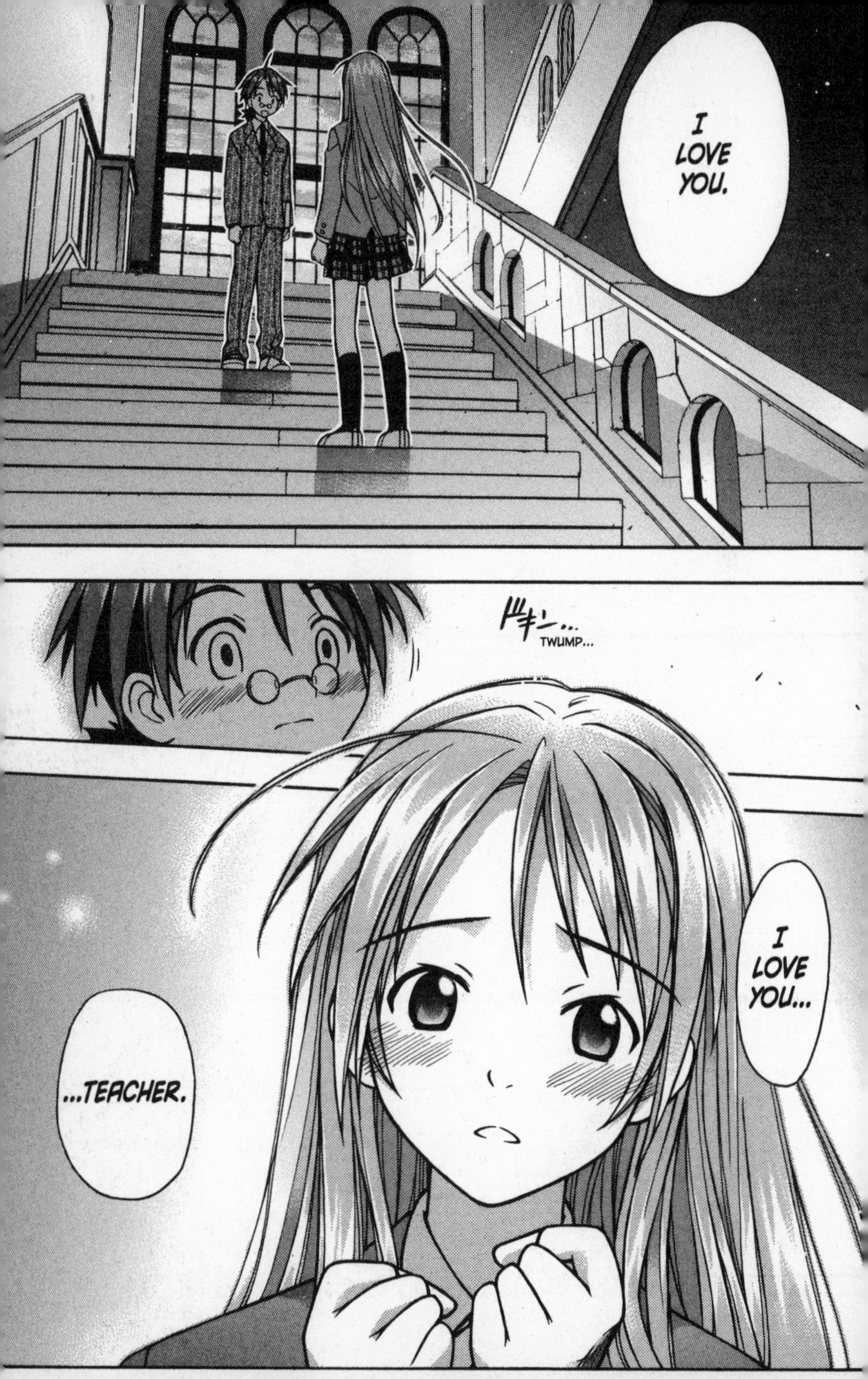
I LOVE YOU.
ドキン...
TWUMP...
I LOVE YOU...
...TEACHER.

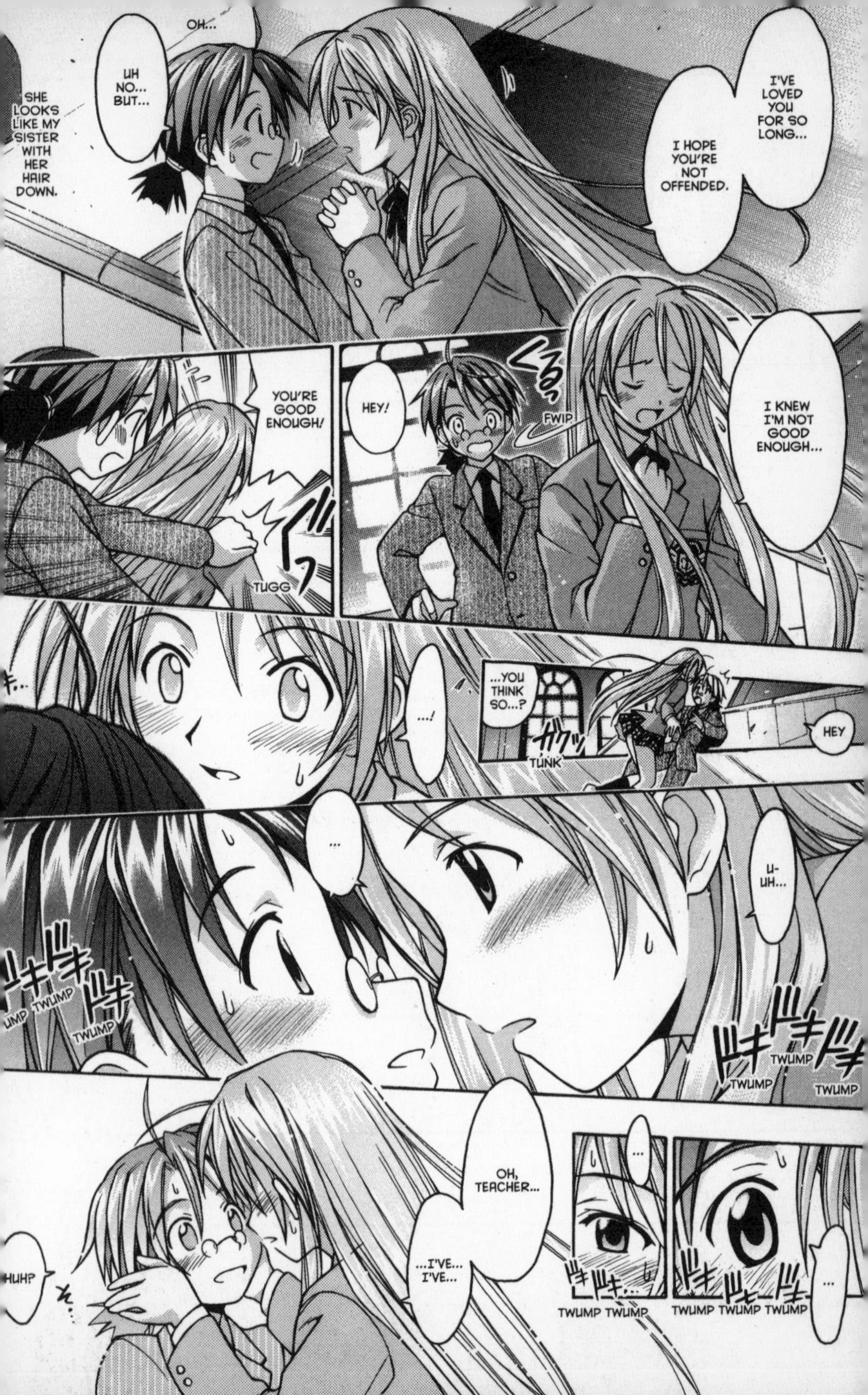
I'VE LOVED YOU FOR SO LONG...
I HOPE YOU'RE NOT OFFENDED.
OH...
UH NO... BUT...
SHE LOOKS LIKE MY SISTER WITH HER HAIR DOWN.
I KNEW I'M NOT GOOD ENOUGH...
FWIP
HEY!
YOU'RE GOOD ENOUGH!
TUGG
HEY
...YOU THINK SO...?
TUNK
...!
U-UH...
TWUMP
TWUMP
TWUMP
...
TWUMP
TWUMP
...
TWUMP TWUMP TWUMP
...
TWUMP TWUMP
OH, TEACHER...
...I'VE... I'VE...
HUH?

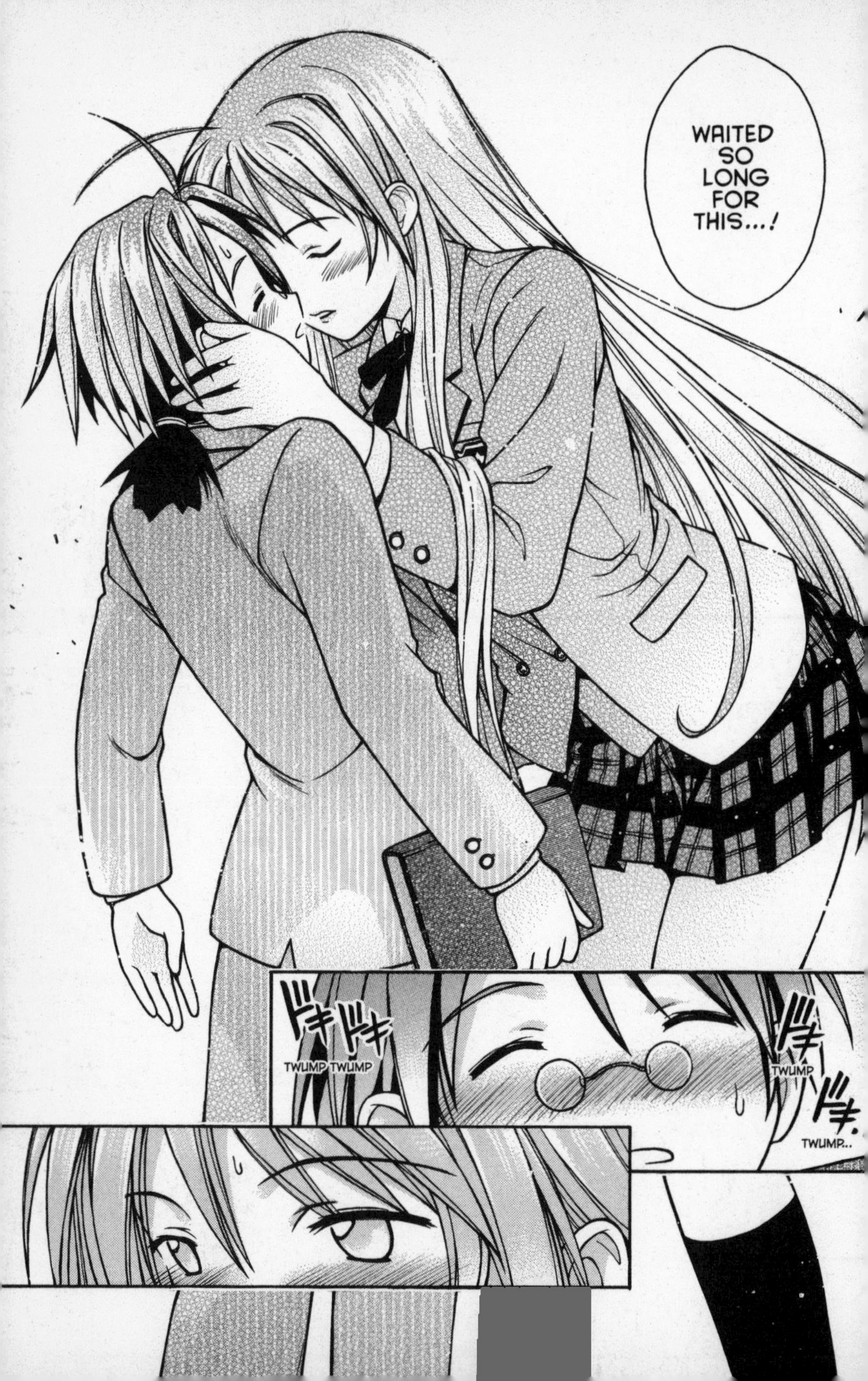
WAITED SO LONG FOR THIS...!
ドキ
TWUMP
ドキ.
TWUMP...
ドキドキ
TWUMP TWUMP

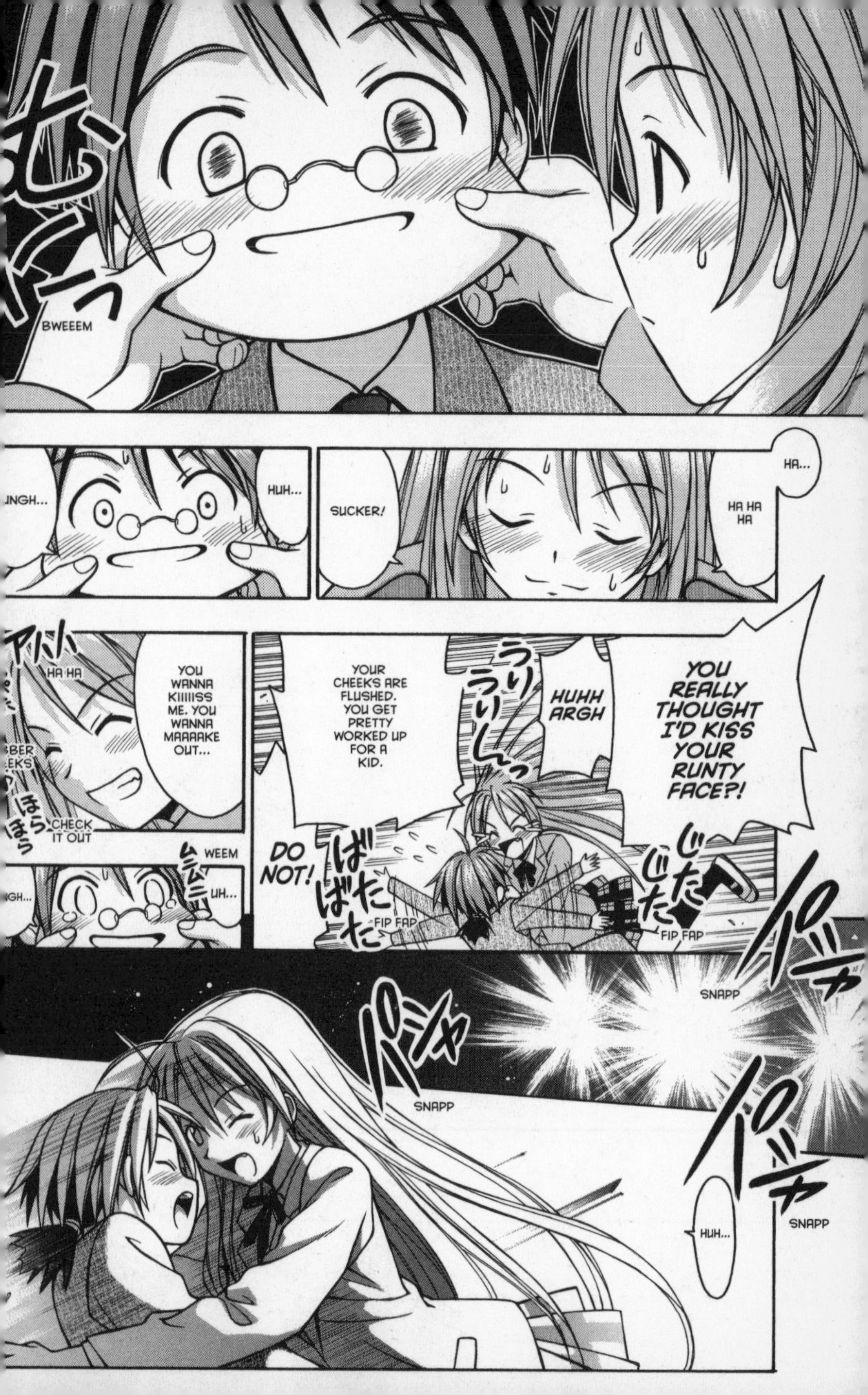
BWEEEM
HA...
HA HA HA
SUCKER!
HUH...
UNGH...
YOU REALLY THOUGHT I'D KISS YOUR RUNTY FACE?!
HUHH ARGH
YOUR CHEEKS ARE FLUSHED. YOU GET PRETTY WORKED UP FOR A KID.
DO NOT!
FIP FAP
FIP FAP
YOU WANNA KIIIIISS ME. YOU WANNA MAAAAAKE OUT...
HA HA
CHECK IT OUT
WEEM
UH...
NGH...
SNAPP
SNAPP
SNAPP
HUH...

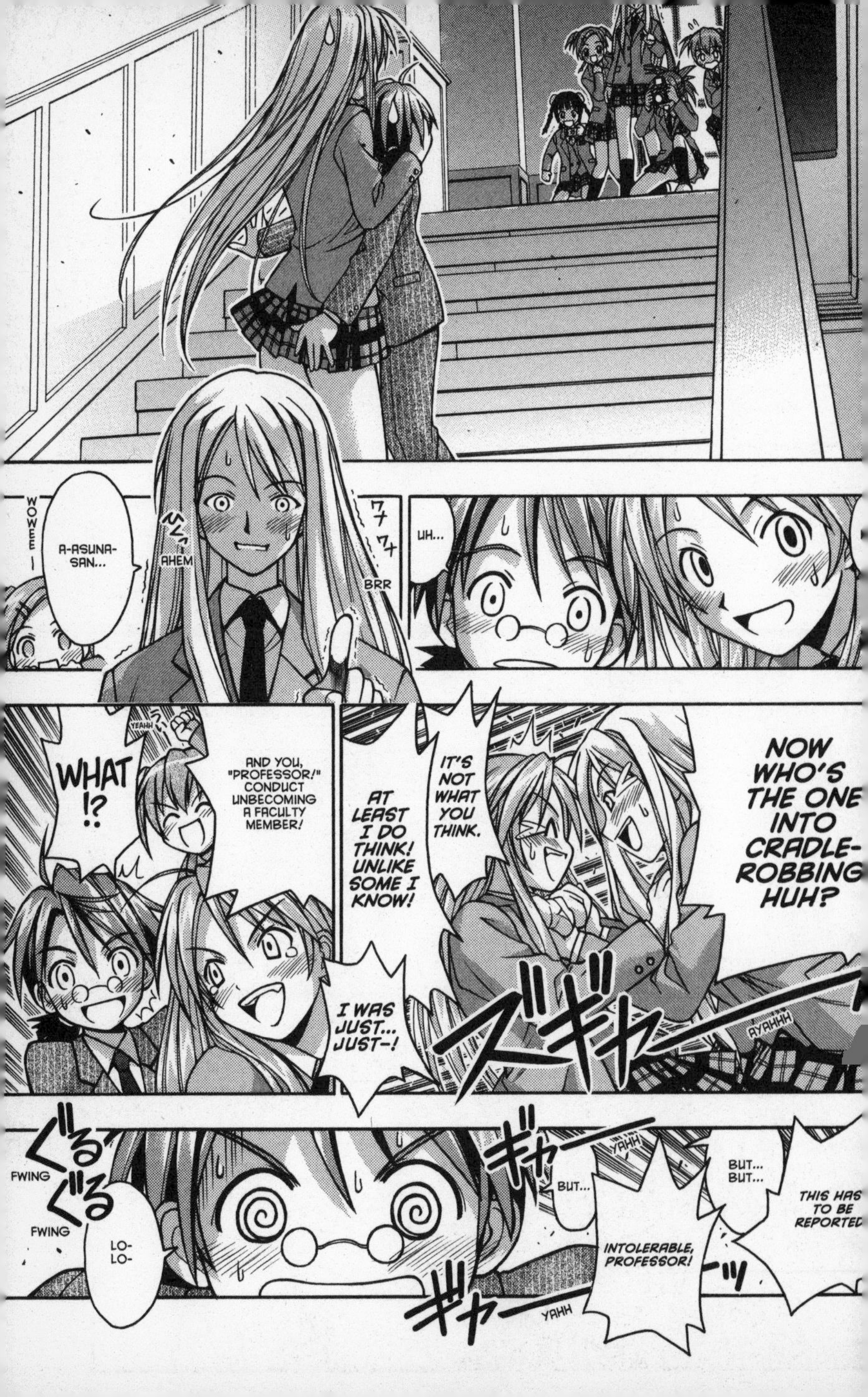

UH...
A-ASUNA-SAN...
AHEM
BRR
WOWEE
NOW WHO'S THE ONE INTO CRADLE-ROBBING HUH?
IT'S NOT WHAT YOU THINK.
AT LEAST I DO THINK! UNLIKE SOME I KNOW!
AYAHHH
I WAS JUST... JUST-!
AND YOU, "PROFESSOR!" CONDUCT UNBECOMING A FACULTY MEMBER!
YEAHH
WHAT!?
THIS HAS TO BE REPORTED
BUT... BUT...
YAHH
INTOLERABLE, PROFESSOR!
BUT...
YAHH
FWING
FWING
LO-LO-

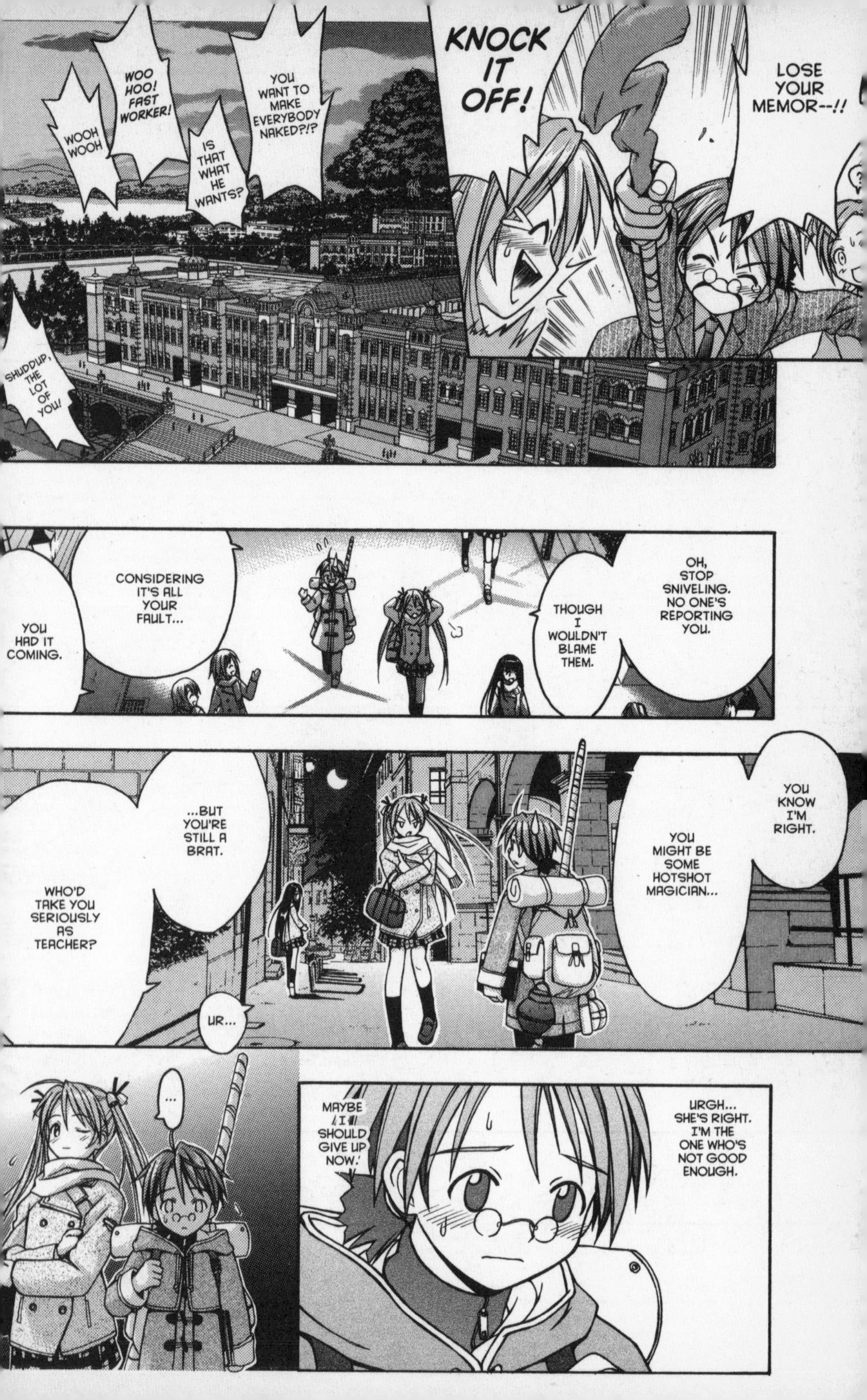
LOSE YOUR MEMOR--!!
KNOCK IT OFF!
YOU WANT TO MAKE EVERYBODY NAKED?!?
IS THAT WHAT HE WANTS?
WOO HOO! FAST WORKER!
WOOH WOOH
SHUDDUP, THE LOT OF YOU!
OH, STOP SNIVELING. NO ONE'S REPORTING YOU.
THOUGH I WOULDN'T BLAME THEM.
CONSIDERING IT'S ALL YOUR FAULT...
YOU HAD IT COMING.
YOU KNOW I'M RIGHT.
YOU MIGHT BE SOME HOTSHOT MAGICIAN...
...BUT YOU'RE STILL A BRAT.
WHO'D TAKE YOU SERIOUSLY AS TEACHER?
UR...
URGH... SHE'S RIGHT. I'M THE ONE WHO'S NOT GOOD ENOUGH.
MAYBE I SHOULD GIVE UP NOW.
...

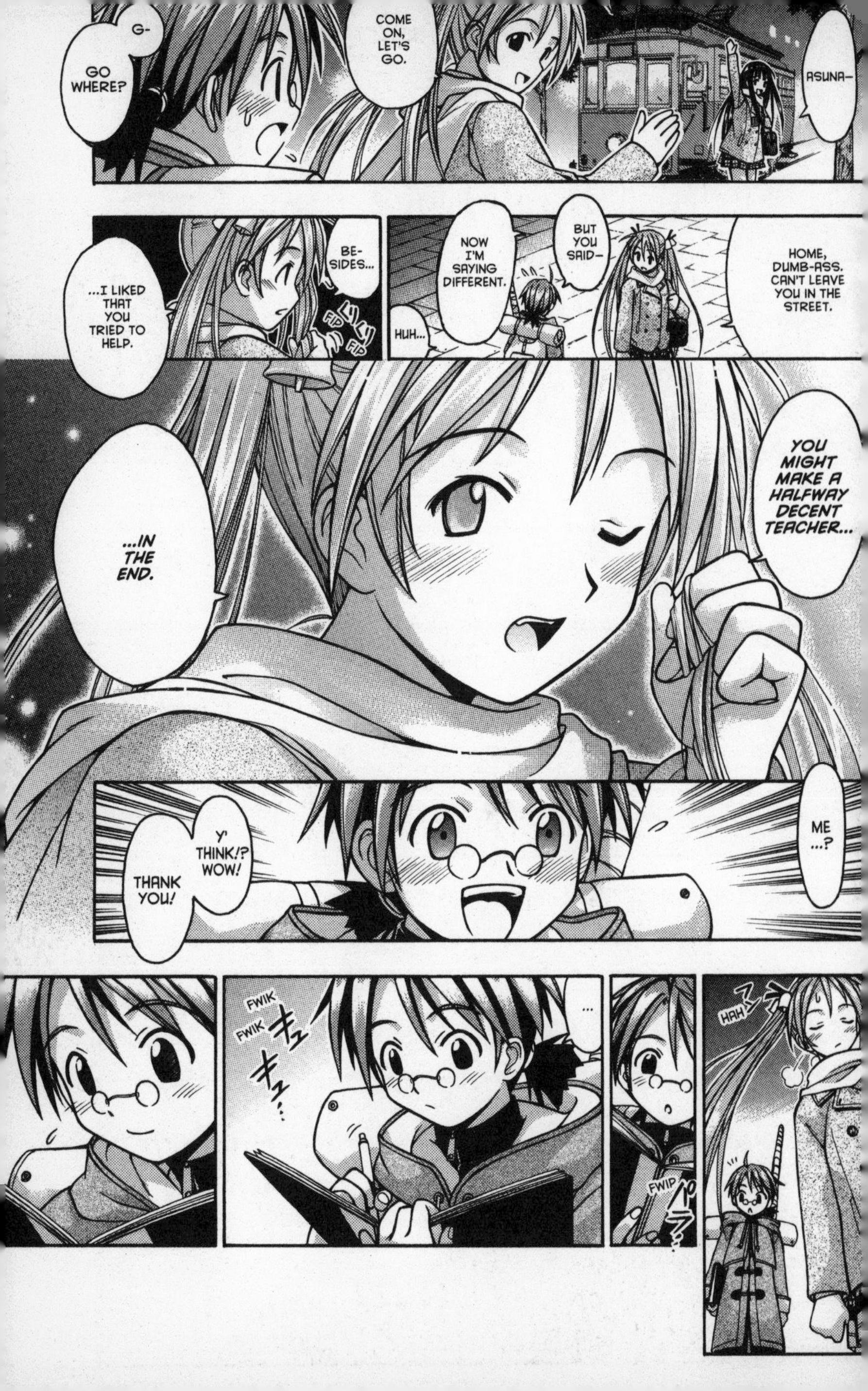
ASUNA—
COME ON, LET'S GO.
G-
GO WHERE?
HOME, DUMB-ASS. CAN'T LEAVE YOU IN THE STREET.
BUT YOU SAID—
NOW I'M SAYING DIFFERENT.
HUH...
BE-SIDES...
...I LIKED THAT YOU TRIED TO HELP.
FIP FIP FIP
YOU MIGHT MAKE A HALFWAY DECENT TEACHER...
...IN THE END.
ME ...?
Y' THINK!? WOW!
THANK YOU!
HAH
FWIP
...
FWIK
FWIK

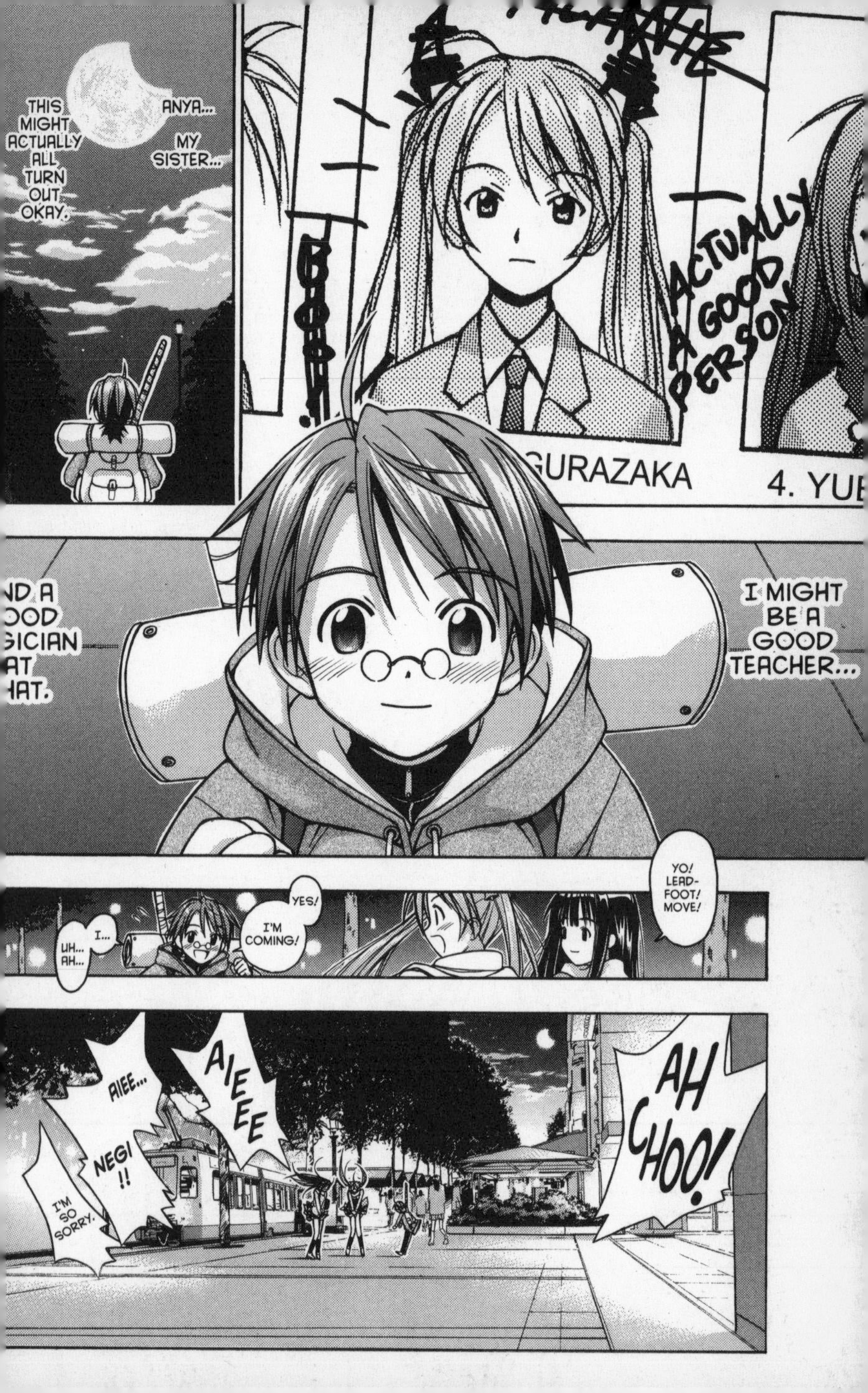
4. YU
GURAZAKA
ACTUALLY A GOOD PERSON
ANYA... MY SISTER...
THIS MIGHT ACTUALLY ALL TURN OUT OKAY.
I MIGHT BE A GOOD TEACHER...
ND A OOD GICIAN AT HAT.
YO! LEAD-FOOT! MOVE!
YES! I'M COMING!
I...
UH... AH...
AH CHOO!
AIEEE
AIEE...
NEGI !!
I'M SO SORRY.

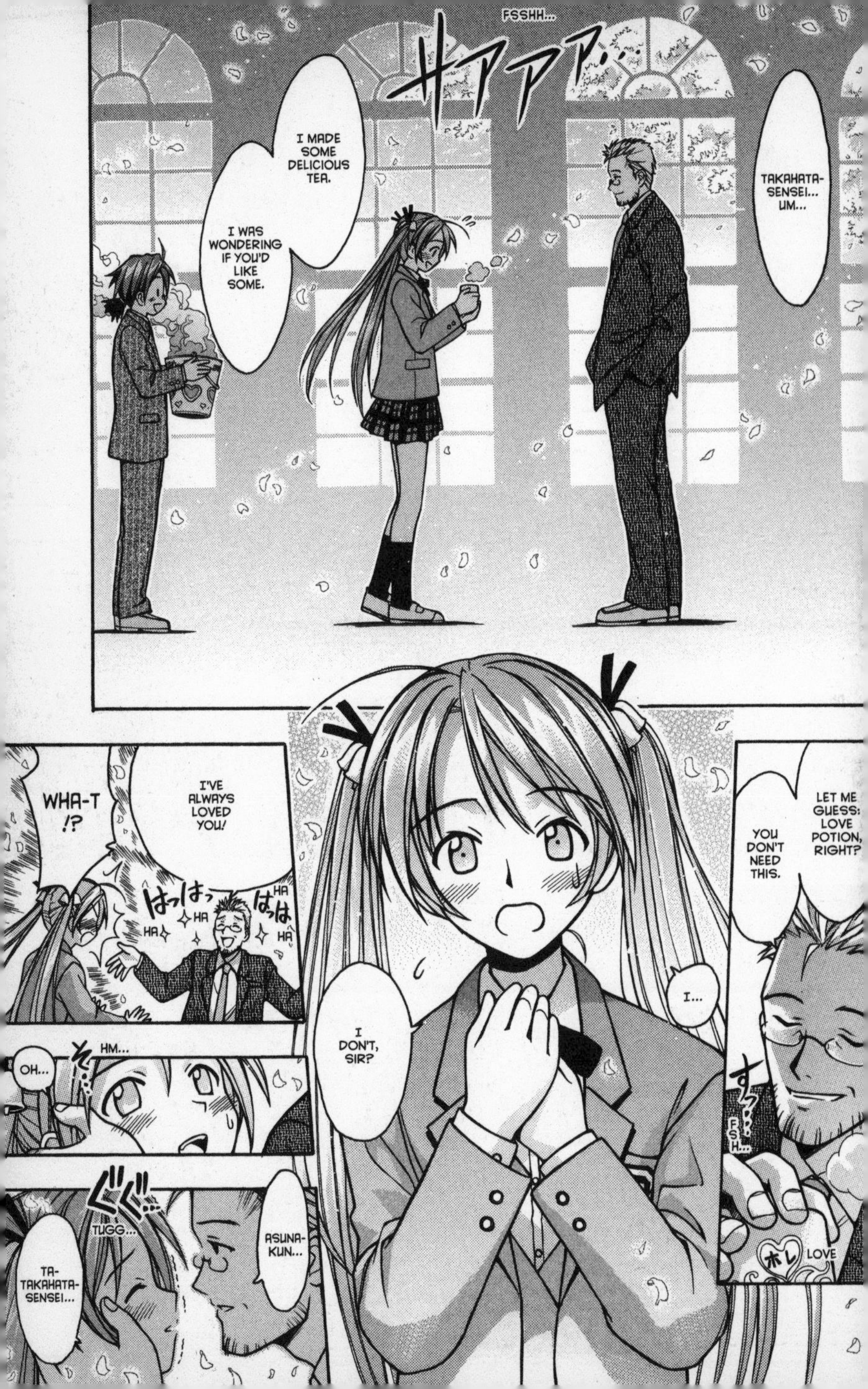
TAKAHATA-SENSEI... UM...
FSSHH...
I MADE SOME DELICIOUS TEA.
I WAS WONDERING IF YOU'D LIKE SOME.
LET ME GUESS: LOVE POTION, RIGHT?
YOU DON'T NEED THIS.
FSSH...
LOVE
I...
I DON'T, SIR?
I'VE ALWAYS LOVED YOU!
HA HA HA HA HA
WHA-T !?
HM...
OH...
ASUNA-KUN...
TUGG...
TA-TAKAHATA-SENSEI...

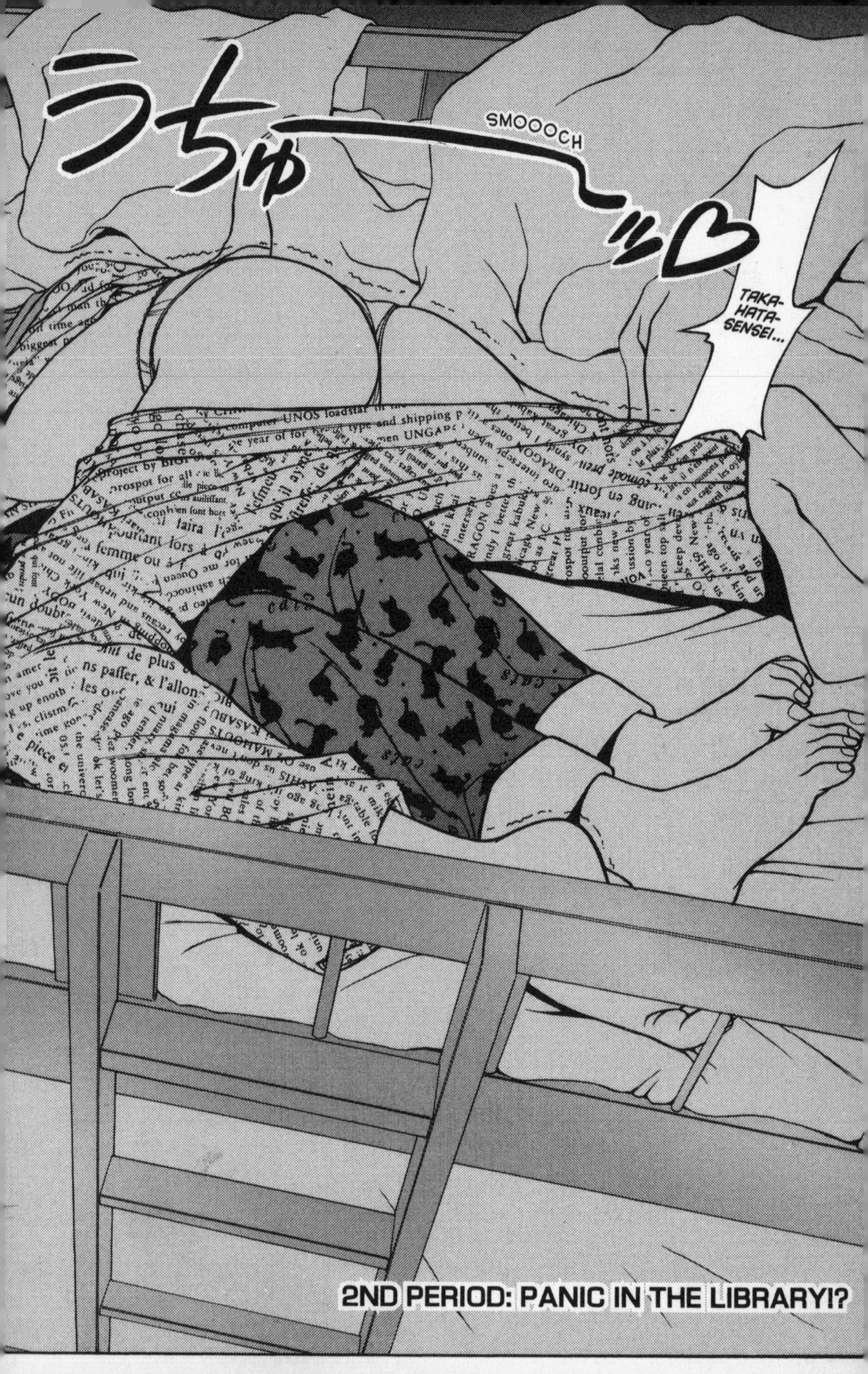
うちゅ
SMOOOCH
TAKA-HATA-SENSEI...
2ND PERIOD: PANIC IN THE LIBRARY!?

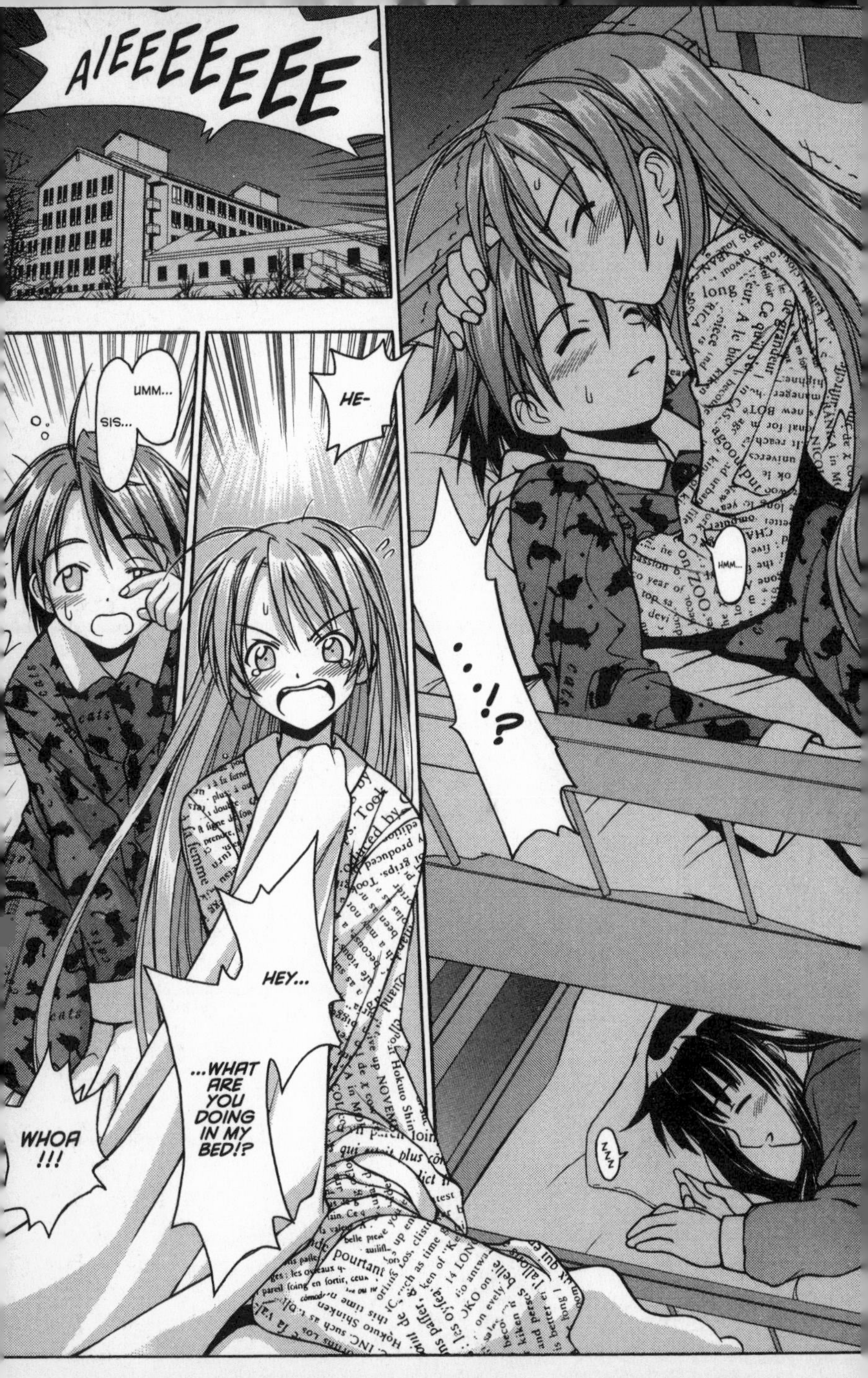
HMM...
...!?
NNN
AIEEEEEEE
HE-
HEY...
...WHAT ARE YOU DOING IN MY BED!?
UMM... SIS...
WHOA !!!

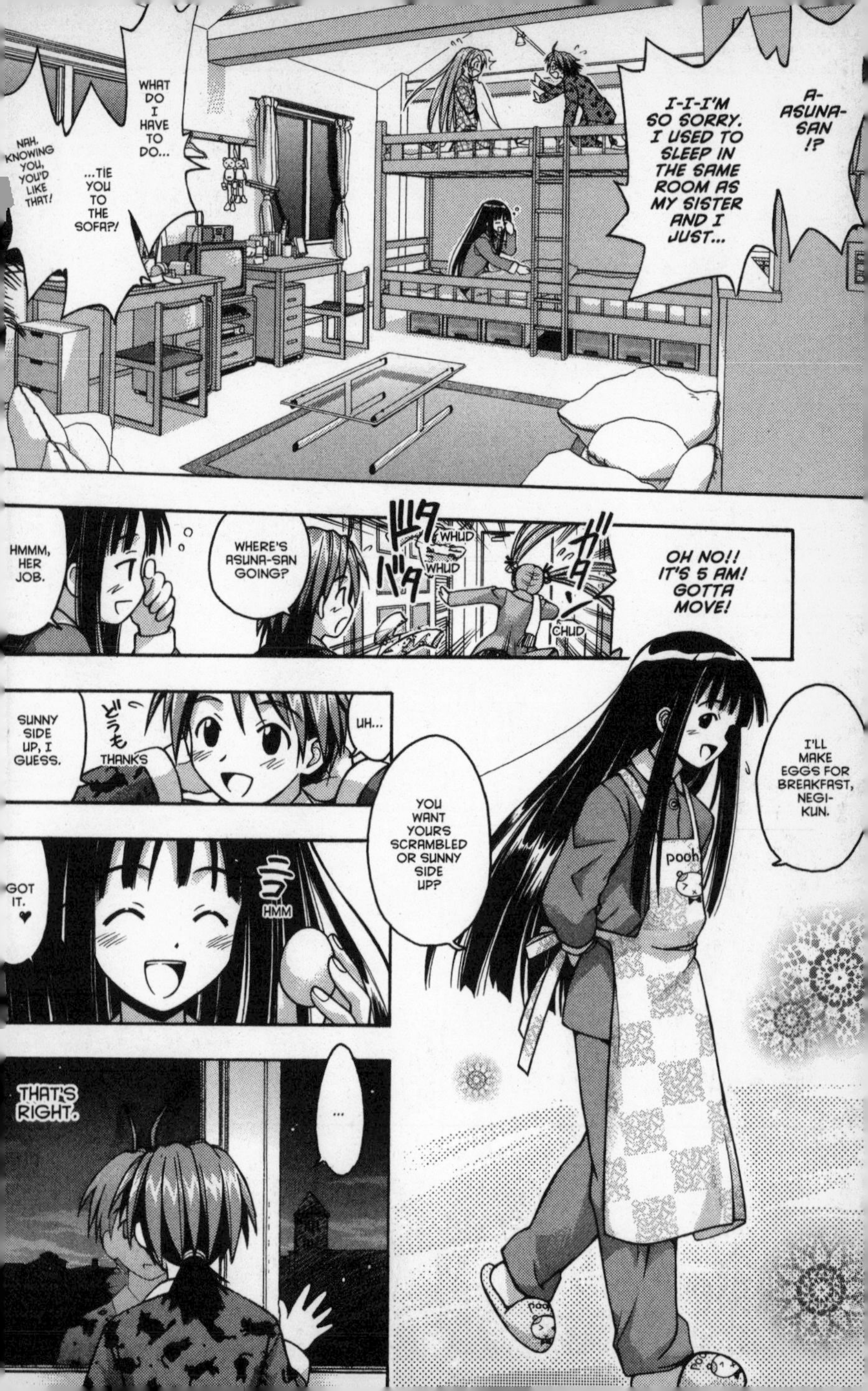
A-ASUNA-SAN!?
I-I-I'M SO SORRY. I USED TO SLEEP IN THE SAME ROOM AS MY SISTER AND I JUST...
WHAT DO I HAVE TO DO...
...TIE YOU TO THE SOFA?!
NAH. KNOWING YOU, YOU'D LIKE THAT!
OH NO!! IT'S 5 AM! GOTTA MOVE!
CHUD
ドタ WHUD
バタ WHUD
WHERE'S ASUNA-SAN GOING?
HMMM, HER JOB.
I'LL MAKE EGGS FOR BREAKFAST, NEGI-KUN.
YOU WANT YOURS SCRAMBLED OR SUNNY SIDE UP?
pooh
UH...
どうも THANKS
SUNNY SIDE UP, I GUESS.
HMM
GOT IT. ♥
...
THAT'S RIGHT.

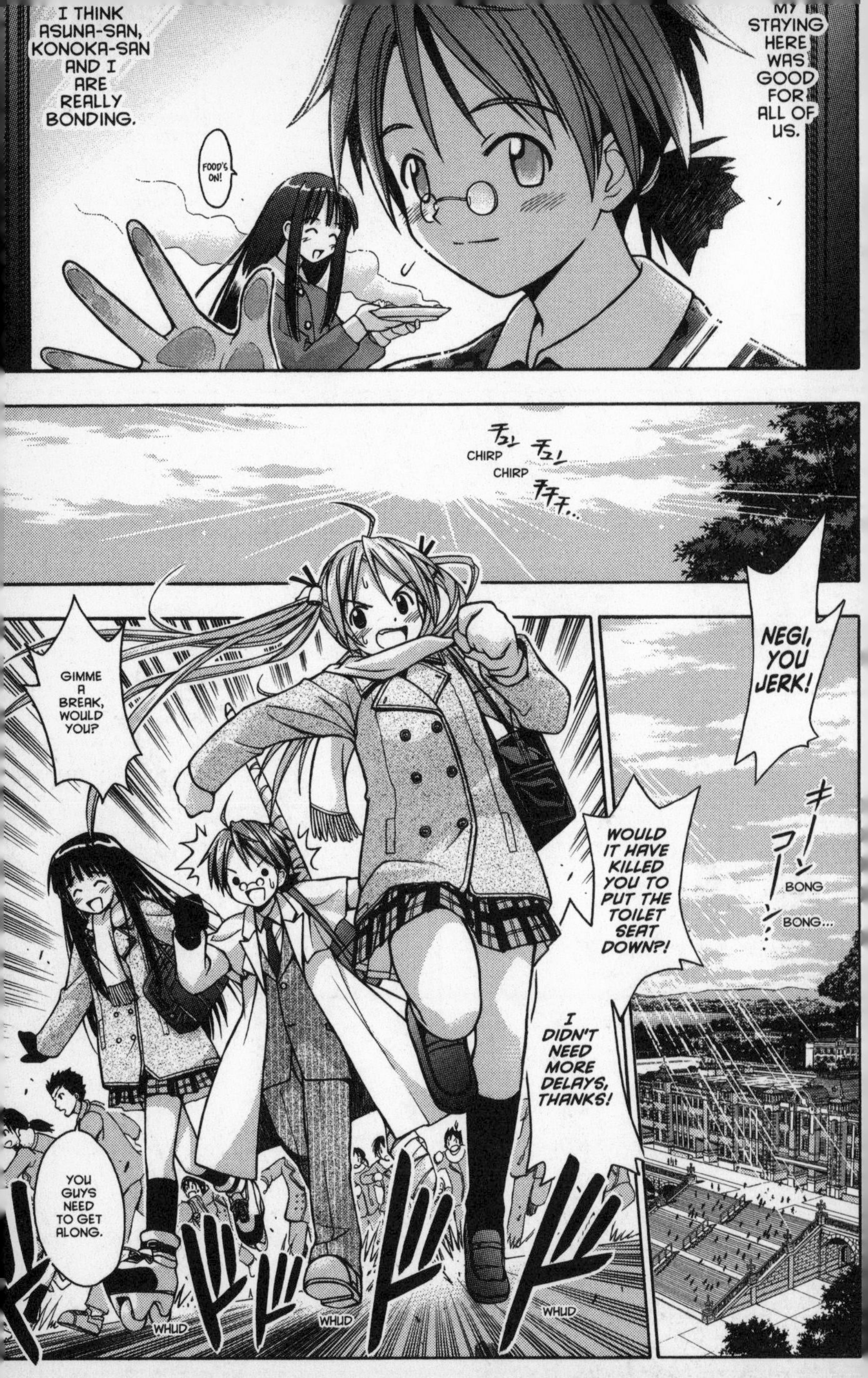
MY STAYING HERE WAS GOOD FOR ALL OF US.
I THINK ASUNA-SAN, KONOKA-SAN AND I ARE REALLY BONDING.
FOOD'S ON!
CHIRP
CHIRP
NEGI, YOU JERK!
WOULD IT HAVE KILLED YOU TO PUT THE TOILET SEAT DOWN?!
BONG
BONG...
I DIDN'T NEED MORE DELAYS, THANKS!
GIMME A BREAK, WOULD YOU?
YOU GUYS NEED TO GET ALONG.
WHUD
WHUD
WHUD

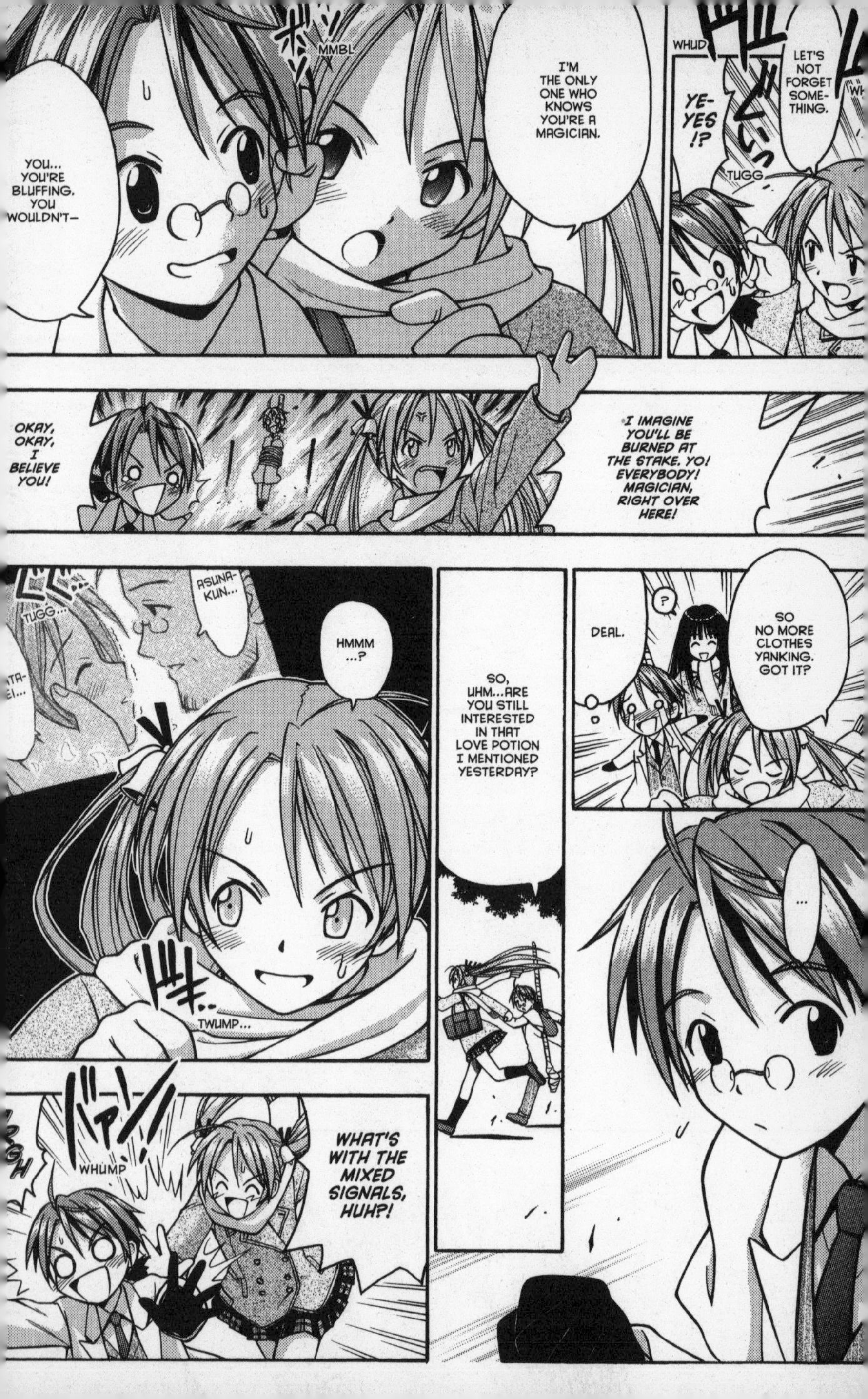
WHUD
LET'S NOT FORGET SOME-THING.
YE-YES!?
TUGG
MMBL
I'M THE ONLY ONE WHO KNOWS YOU'RE A MAGICIAN.
YOU... YOU'RE BLUFFING. YOU WOULDN'T—
I IMAGINE YOU'LL BE BURNED AT THE STAKE. YO! EVERYBODY! MAGICIAN, RIGHT OVER HERE!
OKAY, OKAY, I BELIEVE YOU!
SO NO MORE CLOTHES YANKING. GOT IT?
?
DEAL.
...
SO, UHM...ARE YOU STILL INTERESTED IN THAT LOVE POTION I MENTIONED YESTERDAY?
ASUNA-KUN...
TUGG...
HMMM...?
TWUMP...
WHUMP
WHAT'S WITH THE MIXED SIGNALS, HUH?!

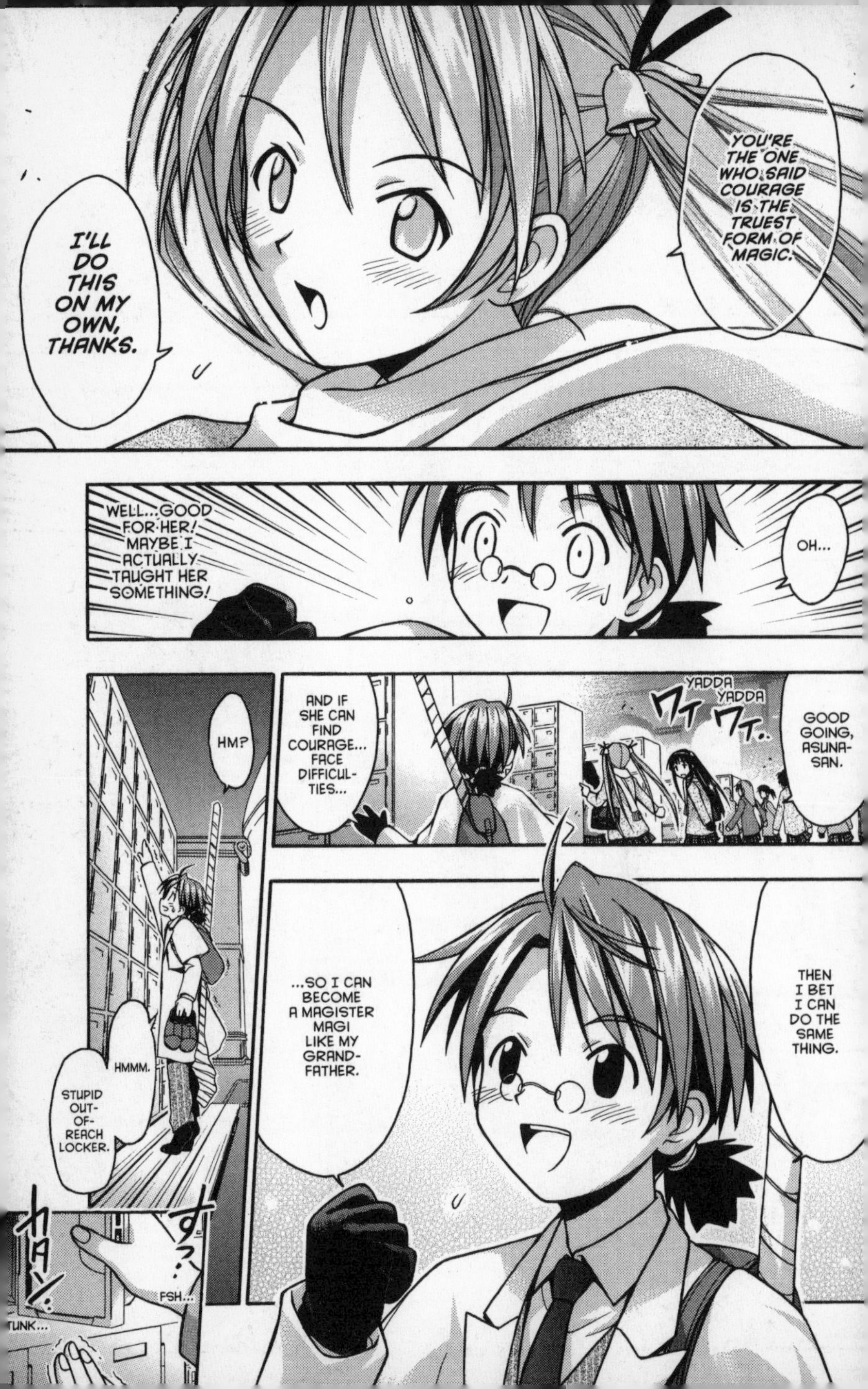
YOU'RE THE ONE WHO SAID COURAGE IS THE TRUEST FORM OF MAGIC.
I'LL DO THIS ON MY OWN, THANKS.
OH...
WELL...GOOD FOR HER! MAYBE I ACTUALLY TAUGHT HER SOMETHING!
GOOD GOING, ASUNA-SAN.
YADDA YADDA
AND IF SHE CAN FIND COURAGE... FACE DIFFICUL-TIES...
THEN I BET I CAN DO THE SAME THING.
...SO I CAN BECOME A MAGISTER MAGI LIKE MY GRAND-FATHER.
HM?
HMMM.
STUPID OUT-OF-REACH LOCKER.
FSH...
TUNK...

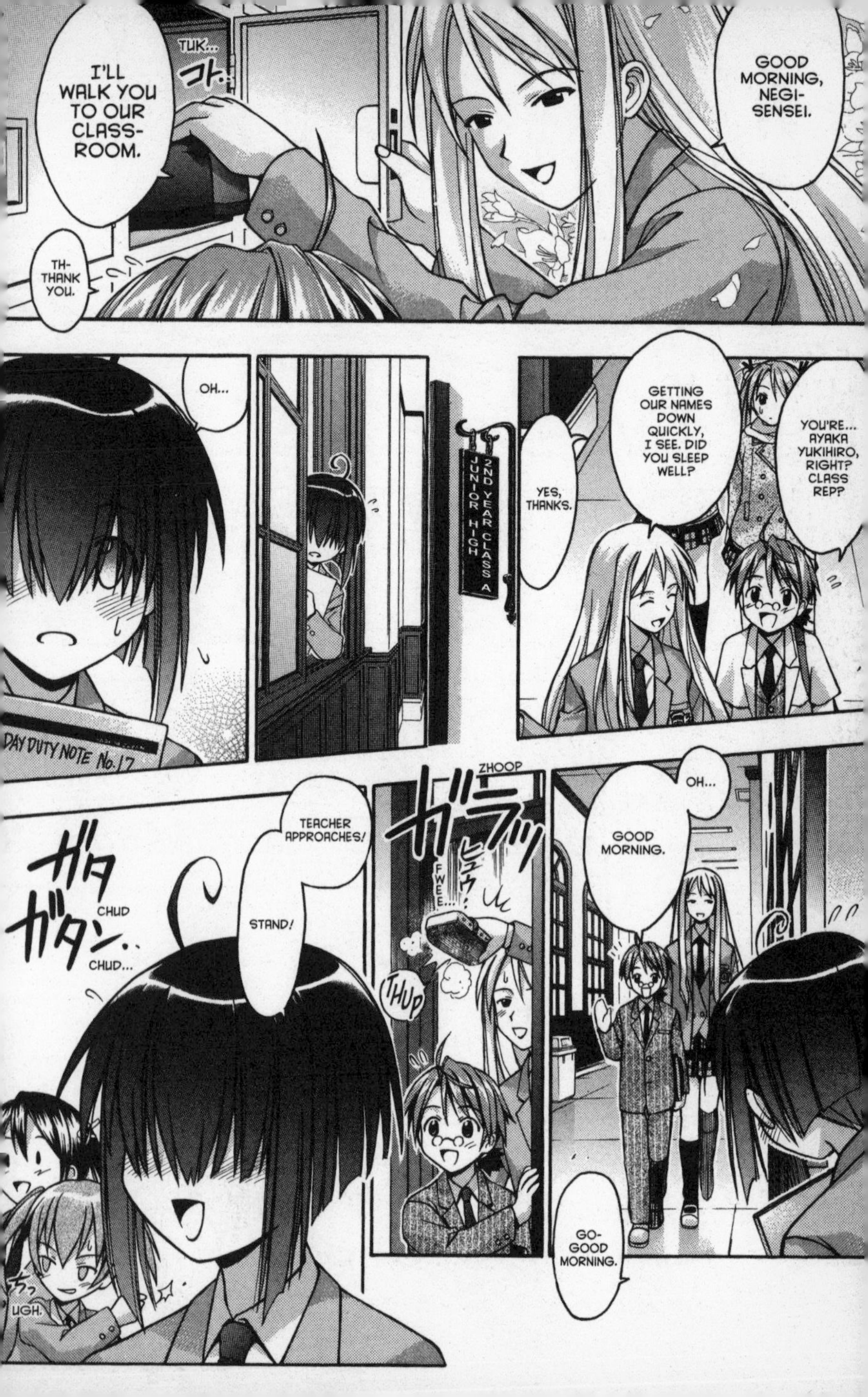
GOOD MORNING, NEGI-SENSEI.
TUK... コト..
I'LL WALK YOU TO OUR CLASS-ROOM.
TH-THANK YOU.
YOU'RE... AYAKA YUKIHIRO, RIGHT? CLASS REP?
GETTING OUR NAMES DOWN QUICKLY, I SEE. DID YOU SLEEP WELL?
YES, THANKS.
2ND YEAR CLASS A JUNIOR HIGH
OH...
DAY DUTY NOTE No.17
OH...
GOOD MORNING.
GO-GOOD MORNING.
ガラッ ZHOOP
ヒュウ! FWEE...
THUP
TEACHER APPROACHES!
STAND!
ガタ CHUD
ガタン.. CHUD...
ちっ
UGH.

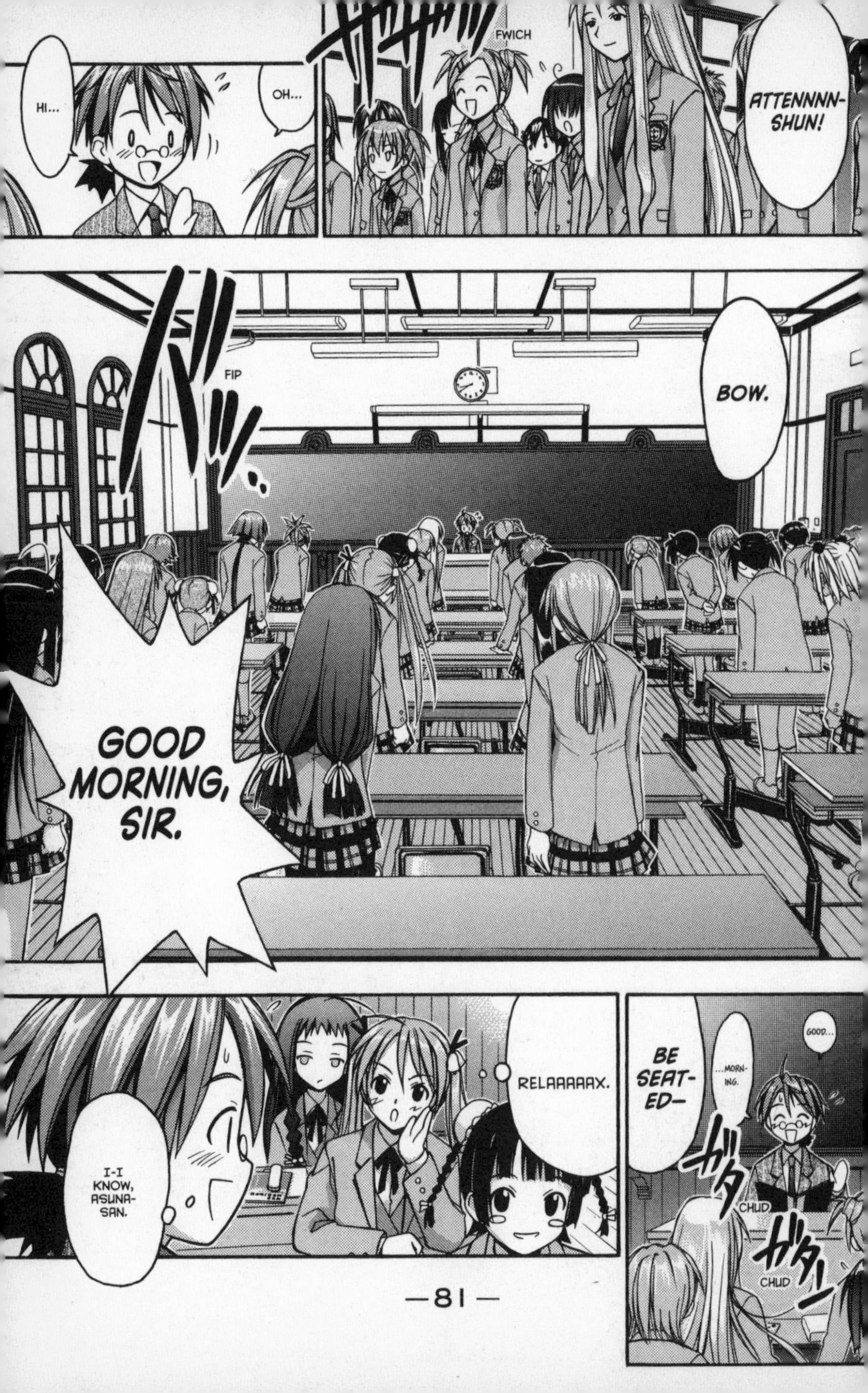
ATTENNNN-SHUN!
FWICH
OH...
HI...
BOW.
FIP
GOOD MORNING, SIR.
GOOD...
...MORN-ING.
BE SEAT-ED—
CHUD
CHUD
RELAAAAAX.
I-I KNOW, ASUNA-SAN.

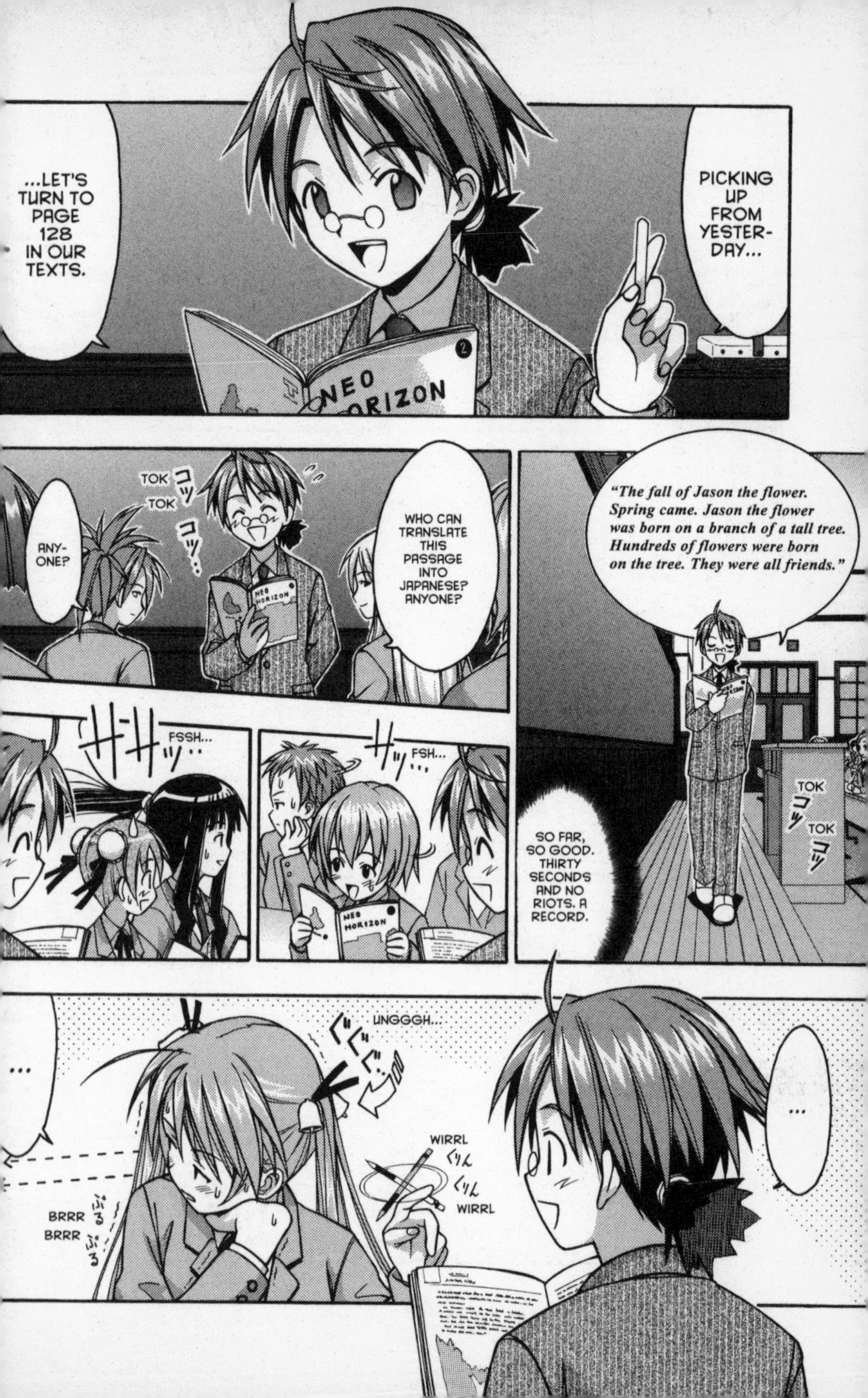
PICKING UP FROM YESTER-DAY...
...LET'S TURN TO PAGE 128 IN OUR TEXTS.
NEO HORIZON
"The fall of Jason the flower. Spring came. Jason the flower was born on a branch of a tall tree. Hundreds of flowers were born on the tree. They were all friends."
TOK TOK
SO FAR, SO GOOD. THIRTY SECONDS AND NO RIOTS. A RECORD.
WHO CAN TRANSLATE THIS PASSAGE INTO JAPANESE? ANYONE?
TOK TOK
ANY-ONE?
FSH...
FSSH...
...
UNGGGH...
WIRRL WIRRL
BRRR BRRR
...

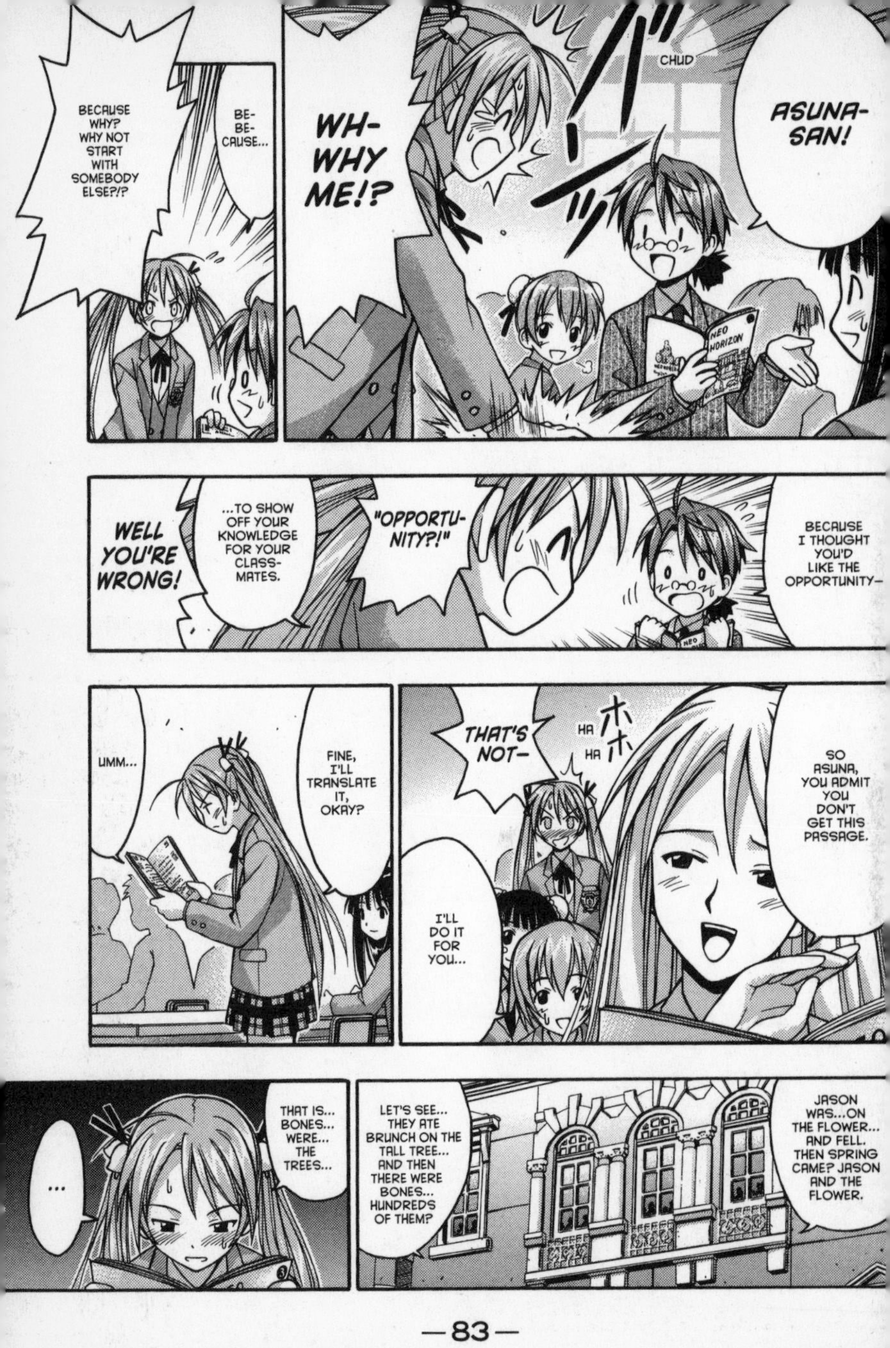
ASUNA-SAN!
CHUD
NEO HORIZON
WH-WHY ME!?
BE-BE-CAUSE...
BECAUSE WHY? WHY NOT START WITH SOMEBODY ELSE?!?
BECAUSE I THOUGHT YOU'D LIKE THE OPPORTUNITY—
"OPPORTU-NITY?!"
...TO SHOW OFF YOUR KNOWLEDGE FOR YOUR CLASS-MATES.
WELL YOU'RE WRONG!
SO ASUNA, YOU ADMIT YOU DON'T GET THIS PASSAGE.
HA HA
THAT'S NOT—
I'LL DO IT FOR YOU...
FINE, I'LL TRANSLATE IT, OKAY?
UMM...
JASON WAS...ON THE FLOWER... AND FELL. THEN SPRING CAME? JASON AND THE FLOWER.
LET'S SEE... THEY ATE BRUNCH ON THE TALL TREE... AND THEN THERE WERE BONES... HUNDREDS OF THEM?
THAT IS... BONES... WERE... THE TREES...
...

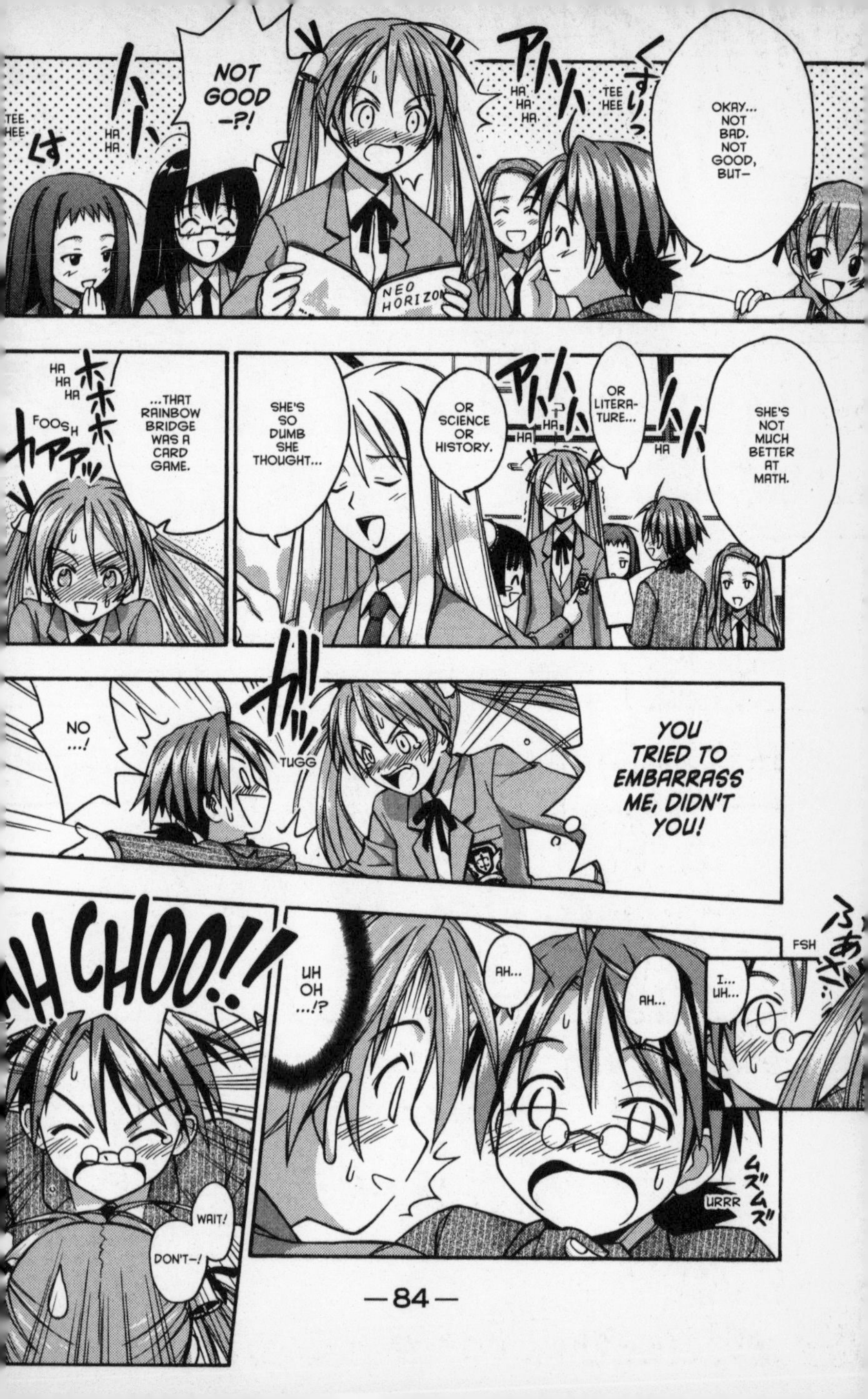

OKAY... NOT BAD. NOT GOOD, BUT—
TEE HEE
HA HA HA
NOT GOOD —?!
HA HA
TEE HEE
SHE'S NOT MUCH BETTER AT MATH.
HA
OR LITERATURE...
HA
HA
OR SCIENCE OR HISTORY.
SHE'S SO DUMB SHE THOUGHT...
...THAT RAINBOW BRIDGE WAS A CARD GAME.
HA HA HA
FOOSH
YOU TRIED TO EMBARRASS ME, DIDN'T YOU!
TUGG
NO ...!
FSH
I... UH...
AH...
AH...
UH OH ...!?
URRR
AH CHOO!!
WAIT!
DON'T—!

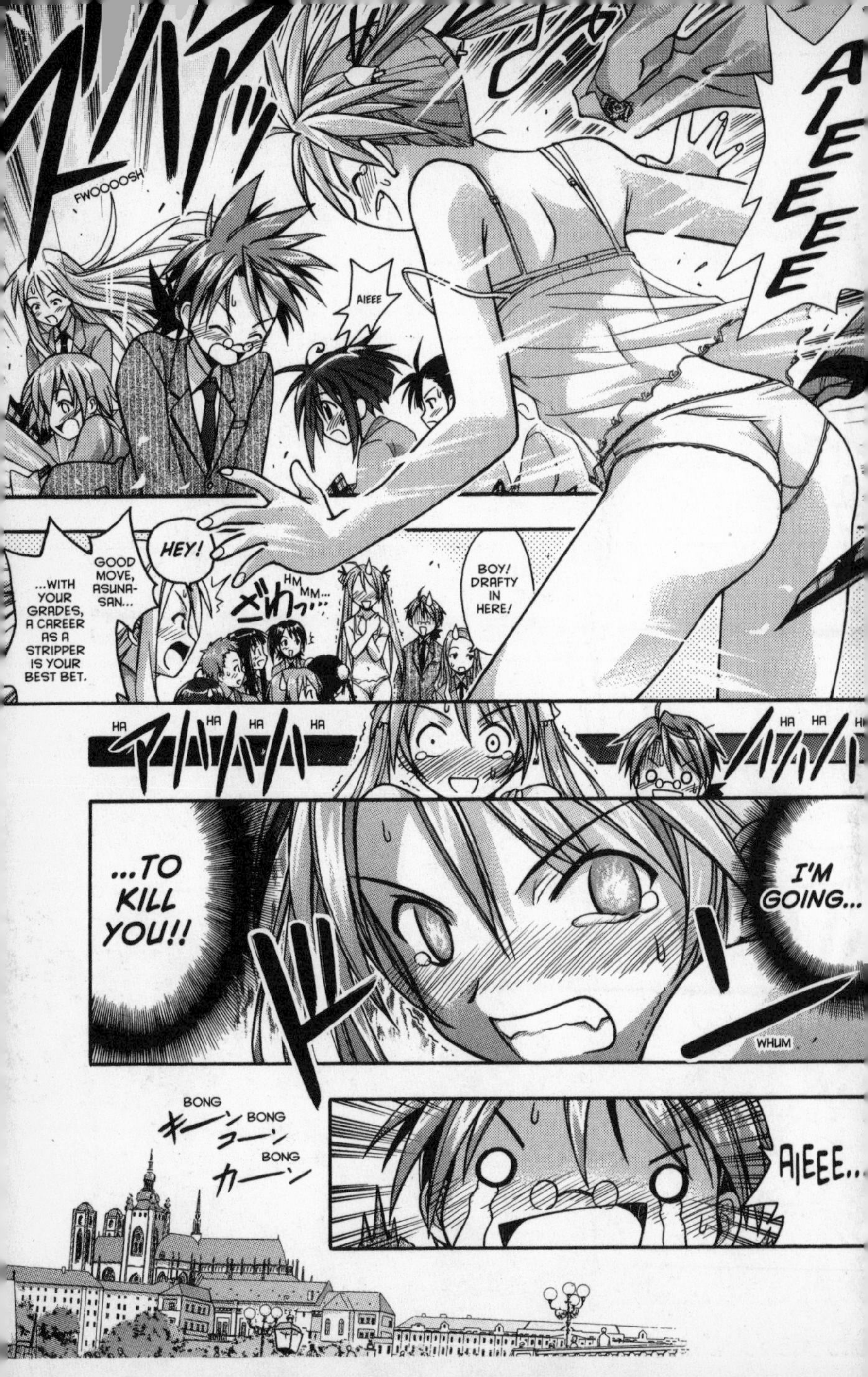
AIEEEE
AIEEE
FWOOOOSH
BOY! DRAFTY IN HERE!
HMMM...
ざわっ
HEY!
GOOD MOVE, ASUNA-SAN...
...WITH YOUR GRADES, A CAREER AS A STRIPPER IS YOUR BEST BET.
HA HA HA
HA HA HA HA
I'M GOING...
...TO KILL YOU!!
WHUM
AIEEE...
BONG BONG BONG

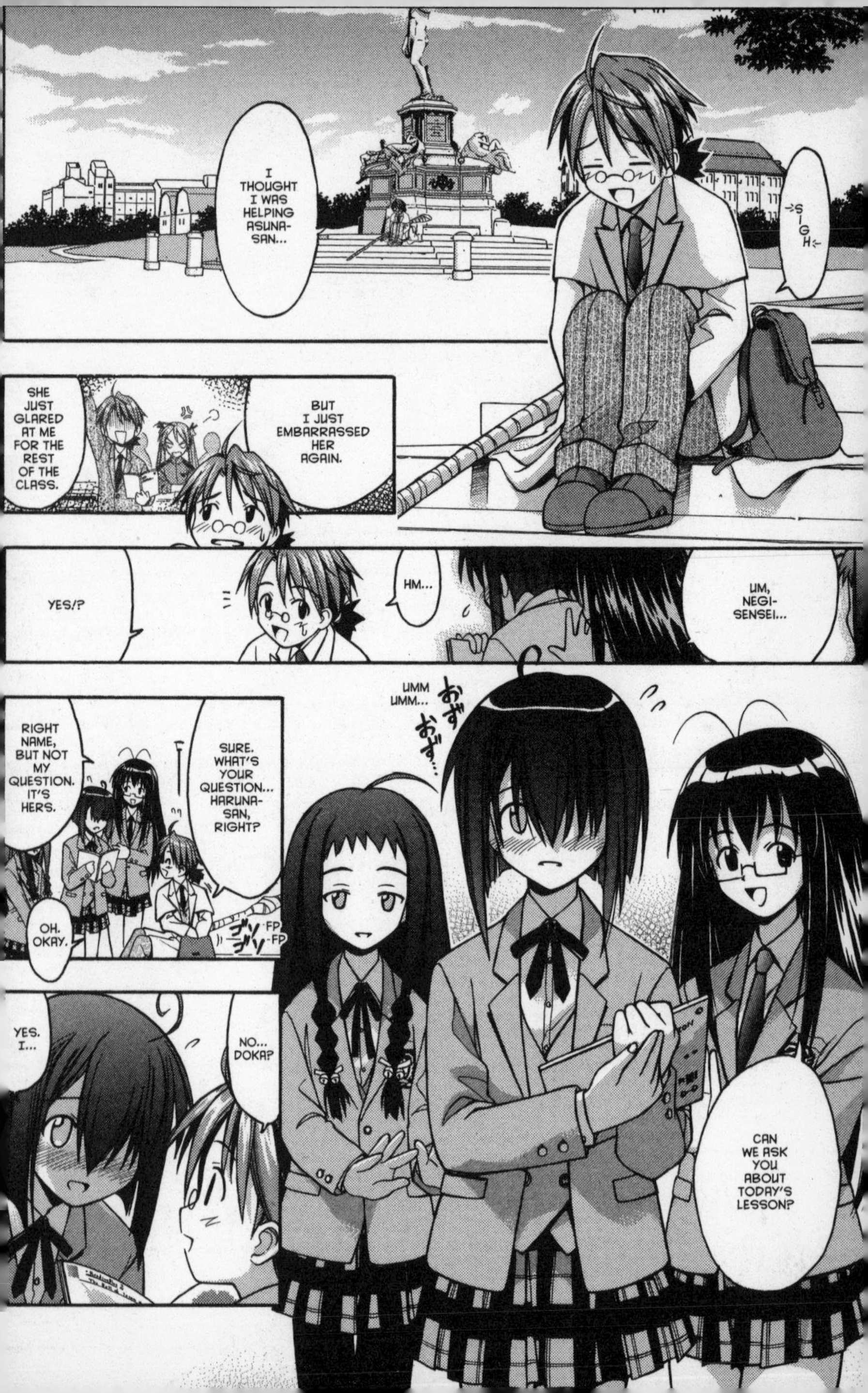
→SIGH←
I THOUGHT I WAS HELPING ASUNA-SAN...
BUT I JUST EMBARRASSED HER AGAIN.
SHE JUST GLARED AT ME FOR THE REST OF THE CLASS.
UM, NEGI-SENSEI...
HM...
YES!?
UMM UMM...
おず おず...
CAN WE ASK YOU ABOUT TODAY'S LESSON?
SURE. WHAT'S YOUR QUESTION... HARUNA-SAN, RIGHT?
RIGHT NAME, BUT NOT MY QUESTION. IT'S HERS.
OH. OKAY.
FP FP
NO... DOKA?
YES. I...

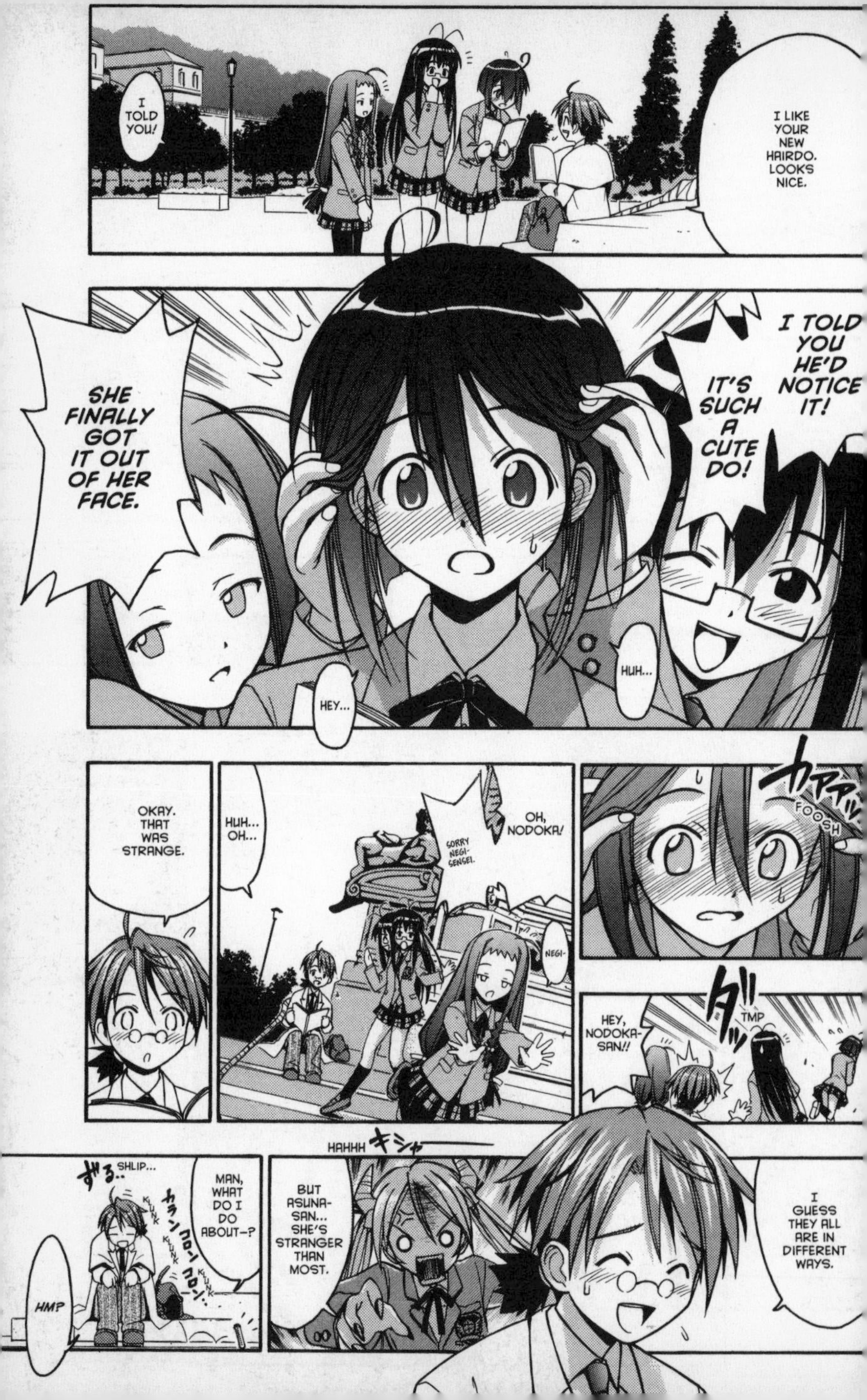
I LIKE YOUR NEW HAIRDO. LOOKS NICE.
I TOLD YOU!
I TOLD YOU HE'D NOTICE IT!
IT'S SUCH A CUTE DO!
SHE FINALLY GOT IT OUT OF HER FACE.
HUH...
HEY...
カァァ
FOOSH
タッ
TMP
HEY, NODOKA-SAN!!
OH, NODOKA!
SORRY NEGI-SENSEI.
NEGI-
HUH... OH...
OKAY. THAT WAS STRANGE.
I GUESS THEY ALL ARE IN DIFFERENT WAYS.
HAHHH キシャー
BUT ASUNA-SAN... SHE'S STRANGER THAN MOST.
MAN, WHAT DO I DO ABOUT—?
ずる..
SHLIP...
カランコロンコロン..
KLUNK KLUNK KLUNK
HM?

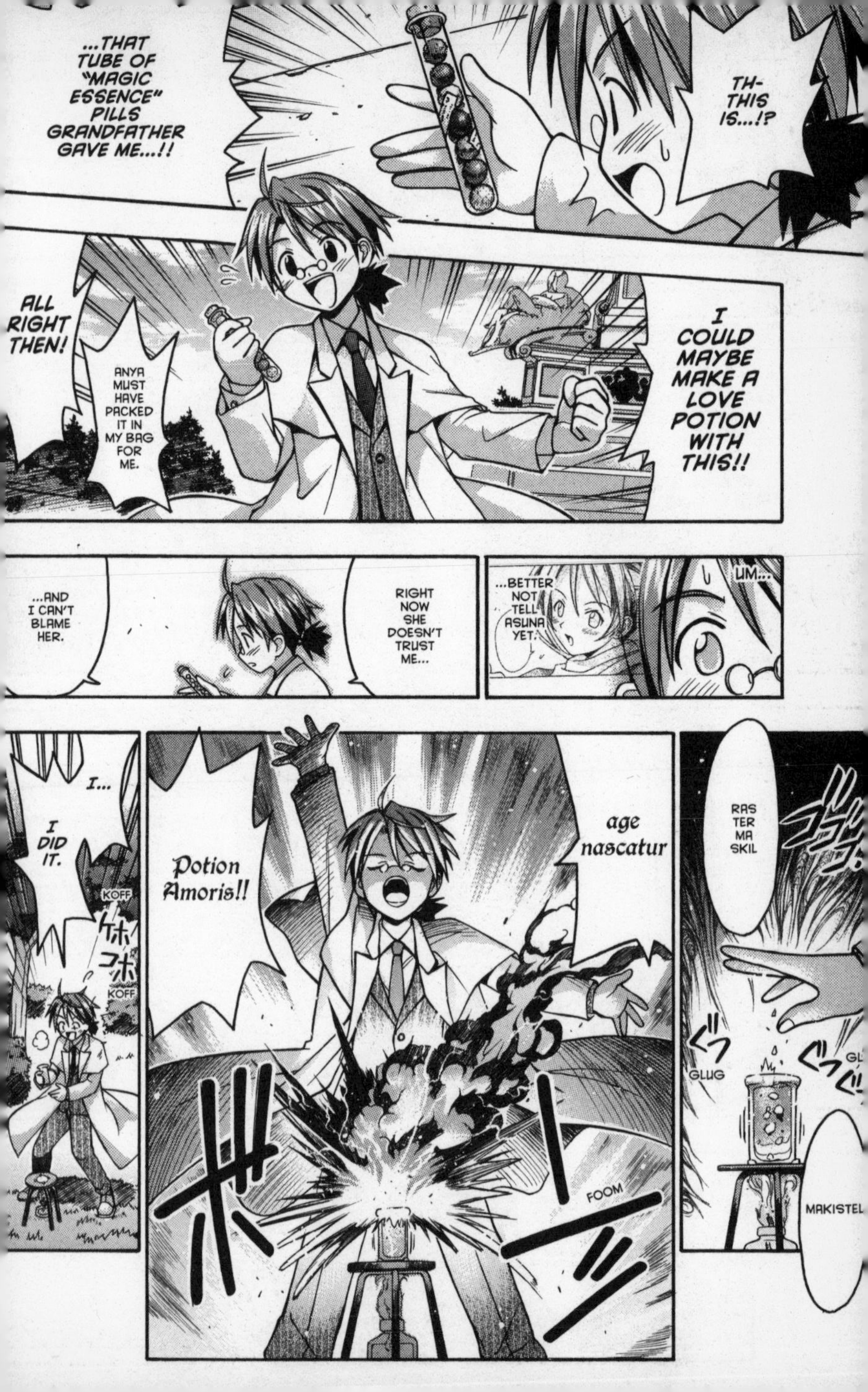
TH- THIS IS...!?
...THAT TUBE OF "MAGIC ESSENCE" PILLS GRANDFATHER GAVE ME...!!
I COULD MAYBE MAKE A LOVE POTION WITH THIS!!
ALL RIGHT THEN!
ANYA MUST HAVE PACKED IT IN MY BAG FOR ME.
UM...
...BETTER NOT TELL ASUNA YET.
RIGHT NOW SHE DOESN'T TRUST ME...
...AND I CAN'T BLAME HER.
RAS TER MA SKIL
GLUG
MAKISTEL
age nascatur
Potion Amoris!!
FOOM
I...
I DID IT.
KOFF
ケホ
コホ
KOFF

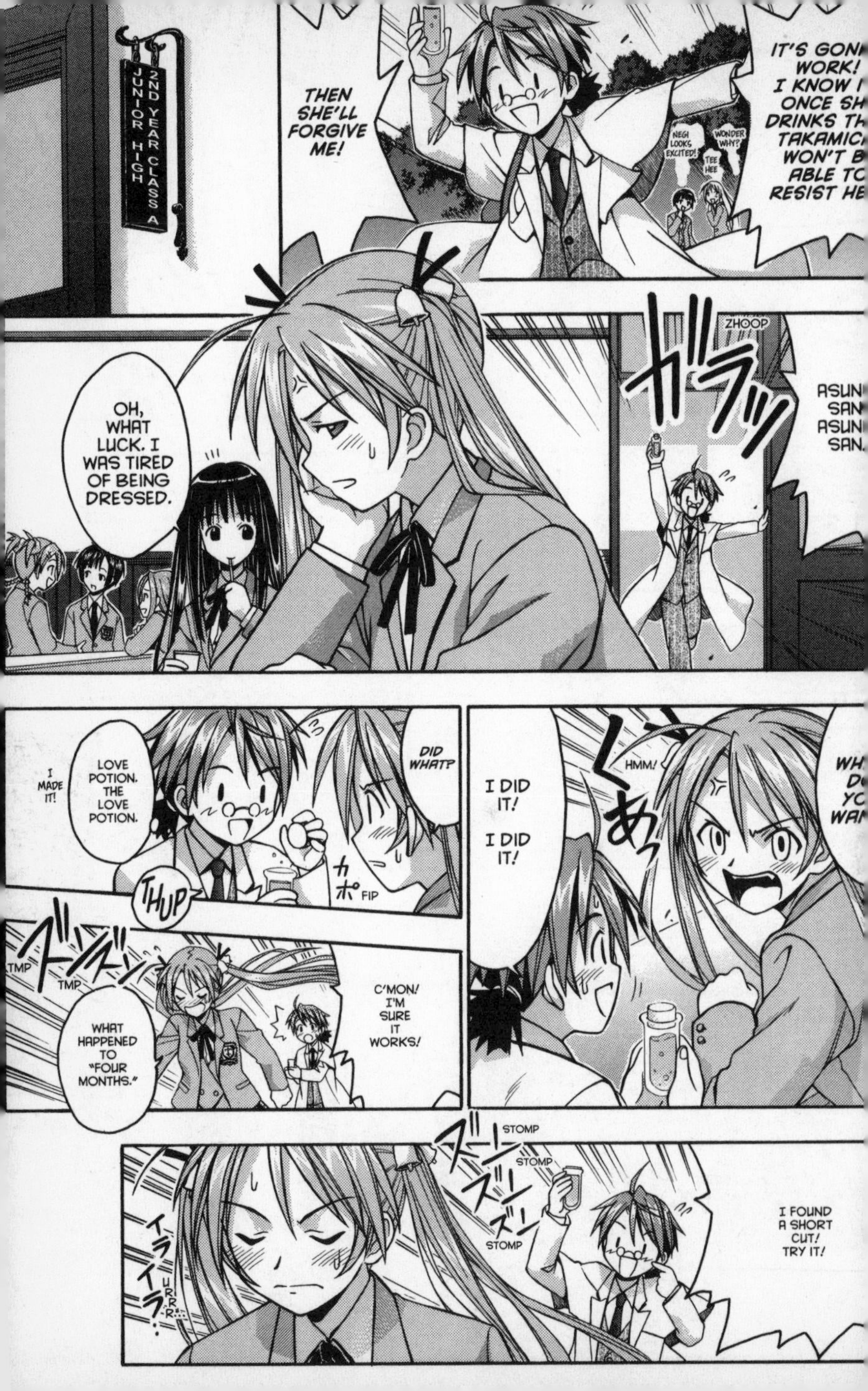
IT'S GONI WORK! I KNOW I ONCE SH DRINKS TH TAKAMICI WON'T B ABLE TO RESIST HE
WONDER WHY?
NEGI LOOKS EXCITED!
TEE HEE
THEN SHE'LL FORGIVE ME!
2ND YEAR CLASS A JUNIOR HIGH
ASUN SAN ASUN SAN.
ガラッ
ZHOOP
OH, WHAT LUCK. I WAS TIRED OF BEING DRESSED.
WH D YO WAN
くあっ
HMM!
I DID IT!
I DID IT!
DID WHAT?
カポ
FIP
LOVE POTION. THE LOVE POTION.
I MADE IT!
THUP
C'MON! I'M SURE IT WORKS!
WHAT HAPPENED TO "FOUR MONTHS."
ズンズン
TMP
TMP
I FOUND A SHORT CUT! TRY IT!
ズーズンズン
STOMP
STOMP
STOMP
イライラ
URRR

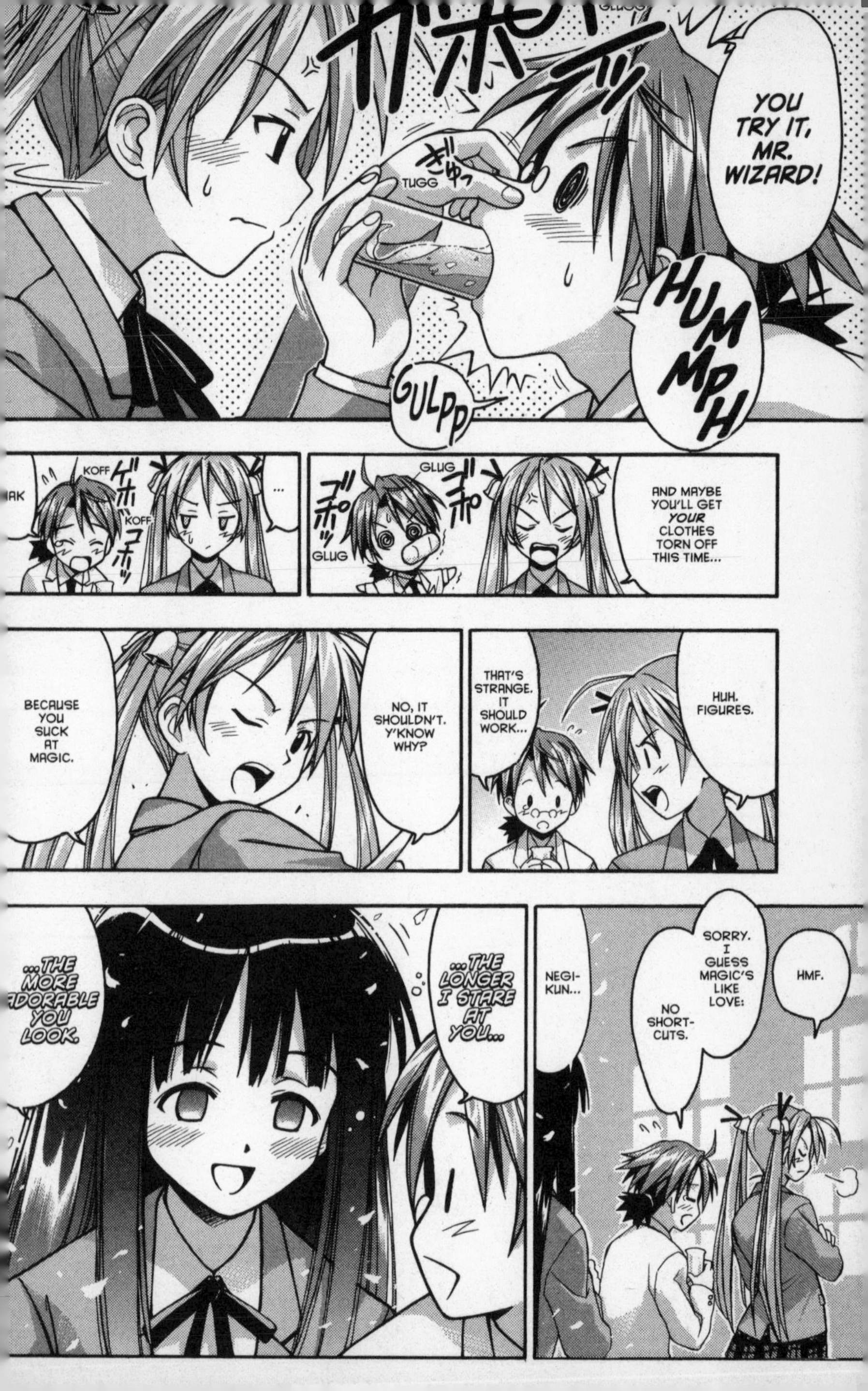
YOU TRY IT, MR. WIZARD!
ガボーッ
ぎゅっ
TUGG
HUMMPH
GULPP
AND MAYBE YOU'LL GET *YOUR* CLOTHES TORN OFF THIS TIME...
ゴポ
GLUG
ゴポッ
GLUG
...
KOFF
ゲホ
KOFF
ゴホッ
HUH. FIGURES.
THAT'S STRANGE. IT SHOULD WORK...
NO, IT SHOULDN'T. Y'KNOW WHY?
BECAUSE YOU SUCK AT MAGIC.
HMF.
SORRY. I GUESS MAGIC'S LIKE LOVE:
NO SHORT-CUTS.
NEGI-KUN...
...THE LONGER I STARE AT YOU...
...THE MORE ADORABLE YOU LOOK.

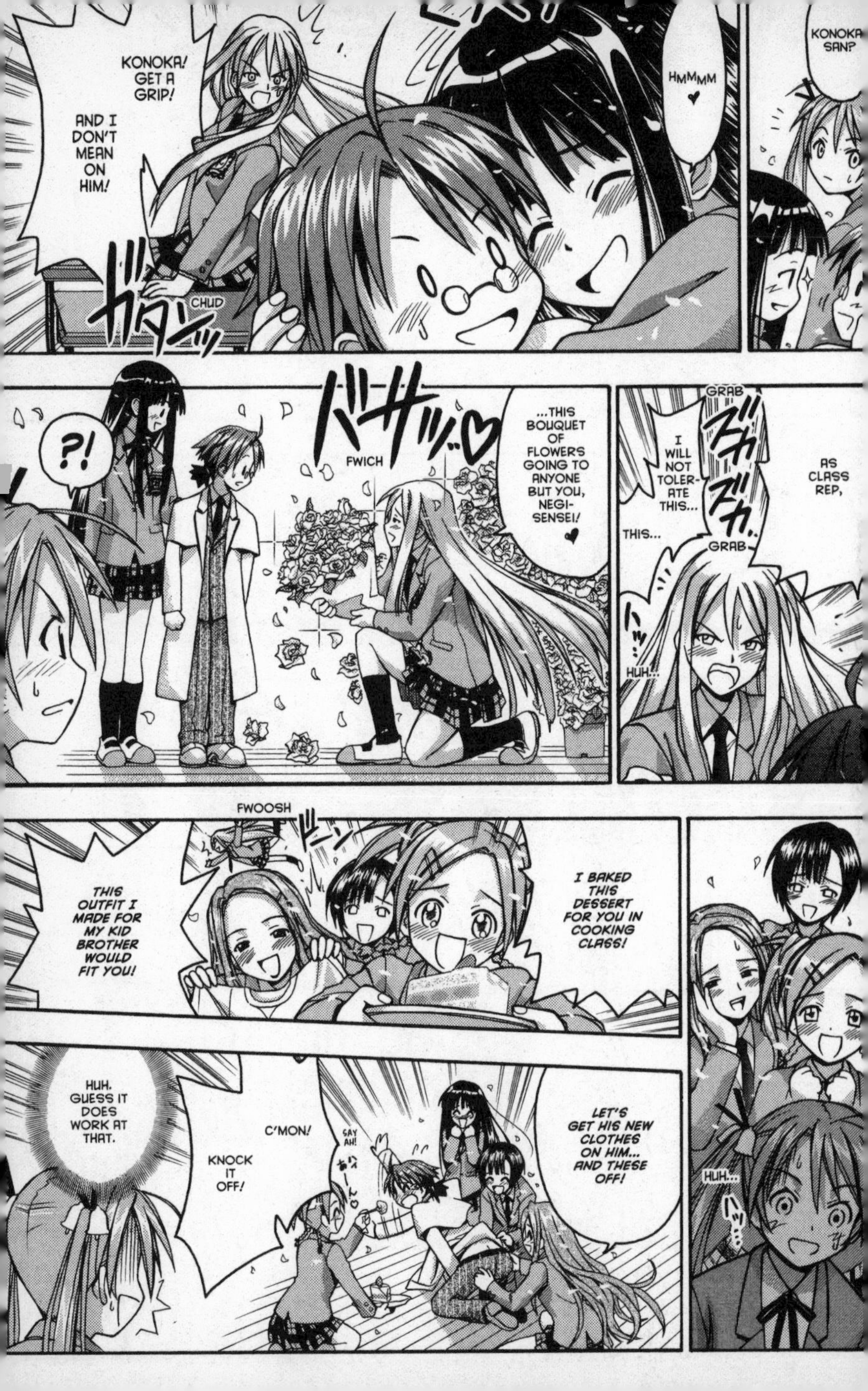
KONOKA-SAN?
HMMMM ♥
KONOKA! GET A GRIP!
AND I DON'T MEAN ON HIM!
CHUD
AS CLASS REP,
GRAB
I WILL NOT TOLERATE THIS...
THIS...
GRAB
HUH...
...THIS BOUQUET OF FLOWERS GOING TO ANYONE BUT YOU, NEGI-SENSEI! ♥
FWICH
?!
HUH...
I BAKED THIS DESSERT FOR YOU IN COOKING CLASS!
FWOOSH
THIS OUTFIT I MADE FOR MY KID BROTHER WOULD FIT YOU!
LET'S GET HIS NEW CLOTHES ON HIM... AND THESE OFF!
SAY AH!
C'MON!
KNOCK IT OFF!
HUH. GUESS IT DOES WORK AT THAT.

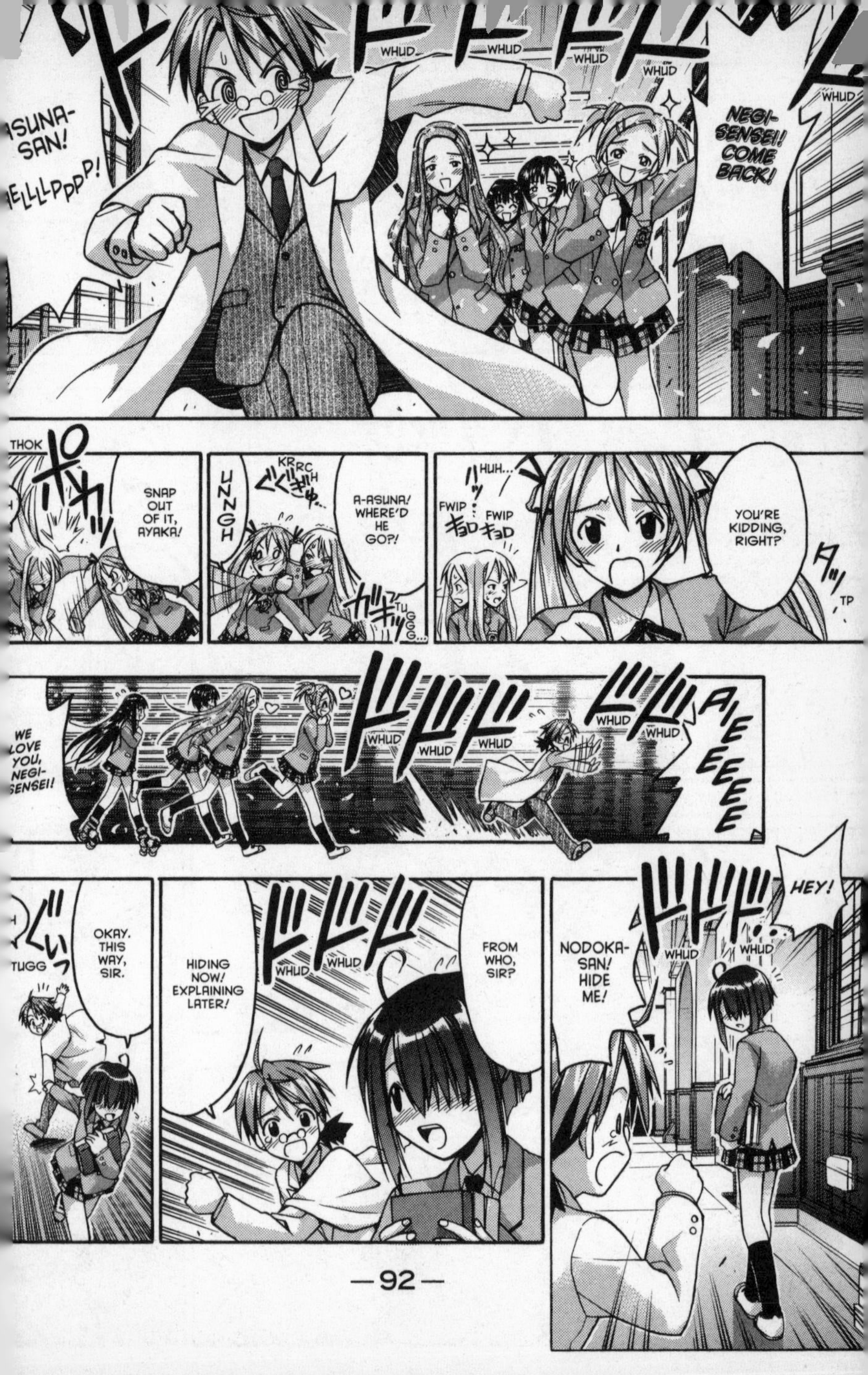
NEGI-SENSEI! COME BACK!
WHUD
WHUD
WHUD
WHUD
WHUD
ASUNA-SAN! HELLLLPPPP!
YOU'RE KIDDING, RIGHT?
TP
HUH...
FWIP
FWIP
A-ASUNA! WHERE'D HE GO?!
KRRCH
UNNGH
TUGGG...
SNAP OUT OF IT, AYAKA!
THOK
AIEEEEEE
WHUD
WHUD
WHUD
WHUD
WHUD
WE LOVE YOU, NEGI-SENSEI!
HEY!
WHUD
WHUD
NODOKA-SAN! HIDE ME!
FROM WHO, SIR?
WHUD
WHUD
HIDING NOW! EXPLAINING LATER!
OKAY. THIS WAY, SIR.
TUGG

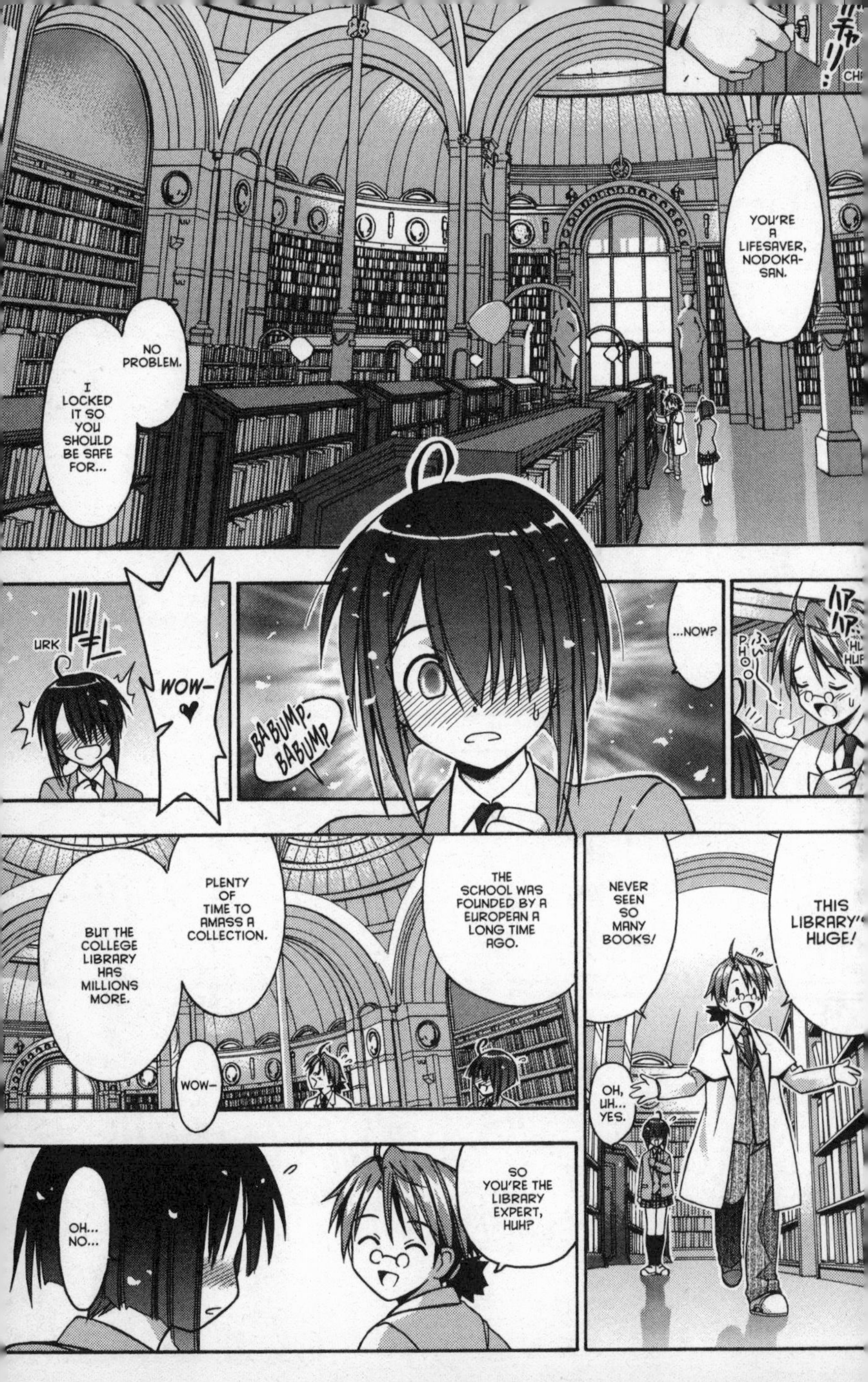

YOU'RE A LIFESAVER, NODOKA-SAN.
NO PROBLEM.
I LOCKED IT SO YOU SHOULD BE SAFE FOR...
...NOW?
BABUMP. BABUMP.
WOW-♥
URK
THIS LIBRARY'S HUGE!
NEVER SEEN SO MANY BOOKS!
OH, UH... YES.
THE SCHOOL WAS FOUNDED BY A EUROPEAN A LONG TIME AGO.
PLENTY OF TIME TO AMASS A COLLECTION.
BUT THE COLLEGE LIBRARY HAS MILLIONS MORE.
WOW-
SO YOU'RE THE LIBRARY EXPERT, HUH?
OH... NO...

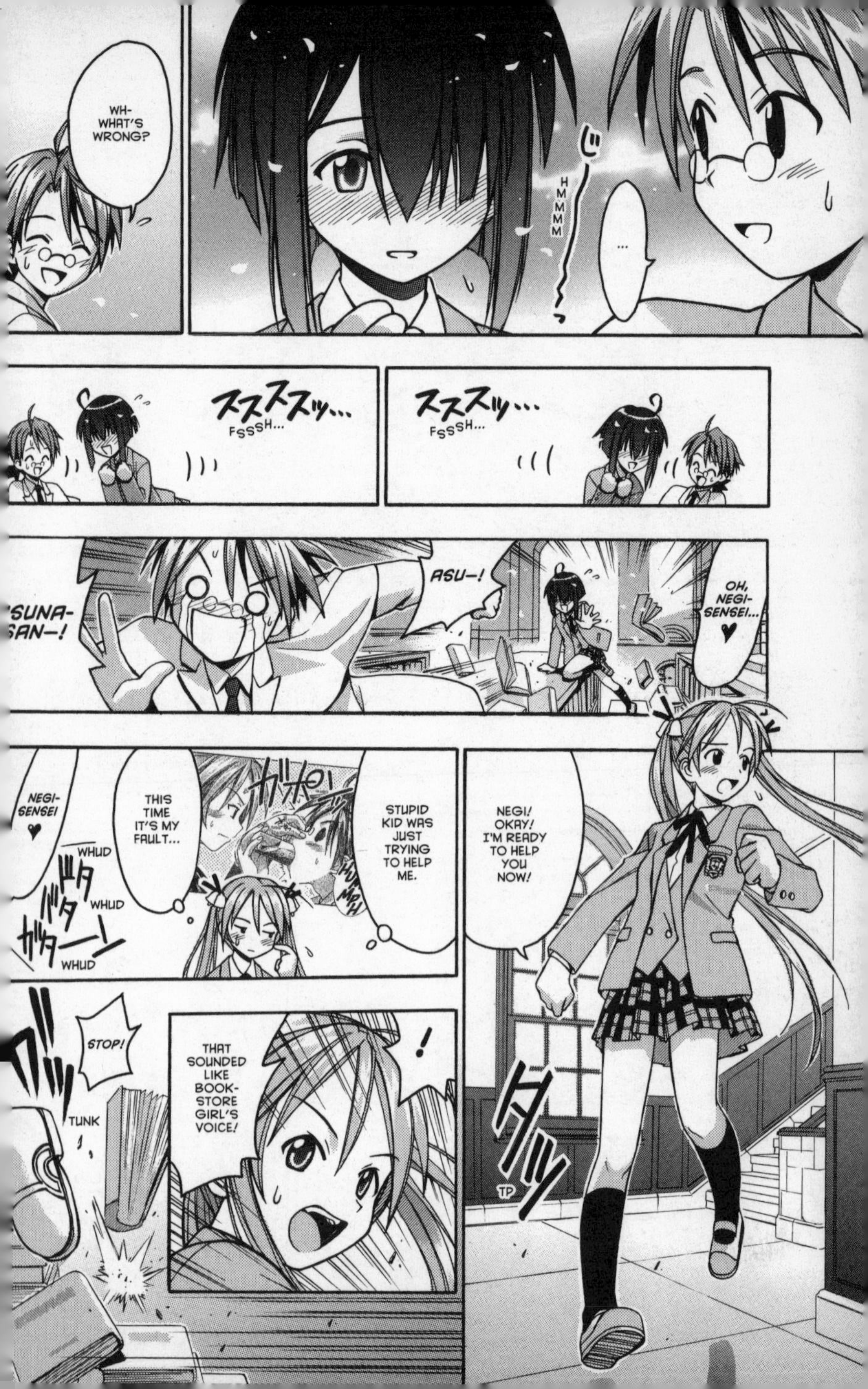
HMMMM
...
WH- WHAT'S WRONG?
スススッ…
FSSSH…
ススススッ…
FSSSH…
OH, NEGI-SENSEI... ♥
ASU–!
SUNA-SAN–!
NEGI! OKAY! I'M READY TO HELP YOU NOW!
TP
STUPID KID WAS JUST TRYING TO HELP ME.
THIS TIME IT'S MY FAULT...
NEGI-SENSEI ♥
WHUD
WHUD
WHUD
THAT SOUNDED LIKE BOOK-STORE GIRL'S VOICE!
!
STOP!
TUNK

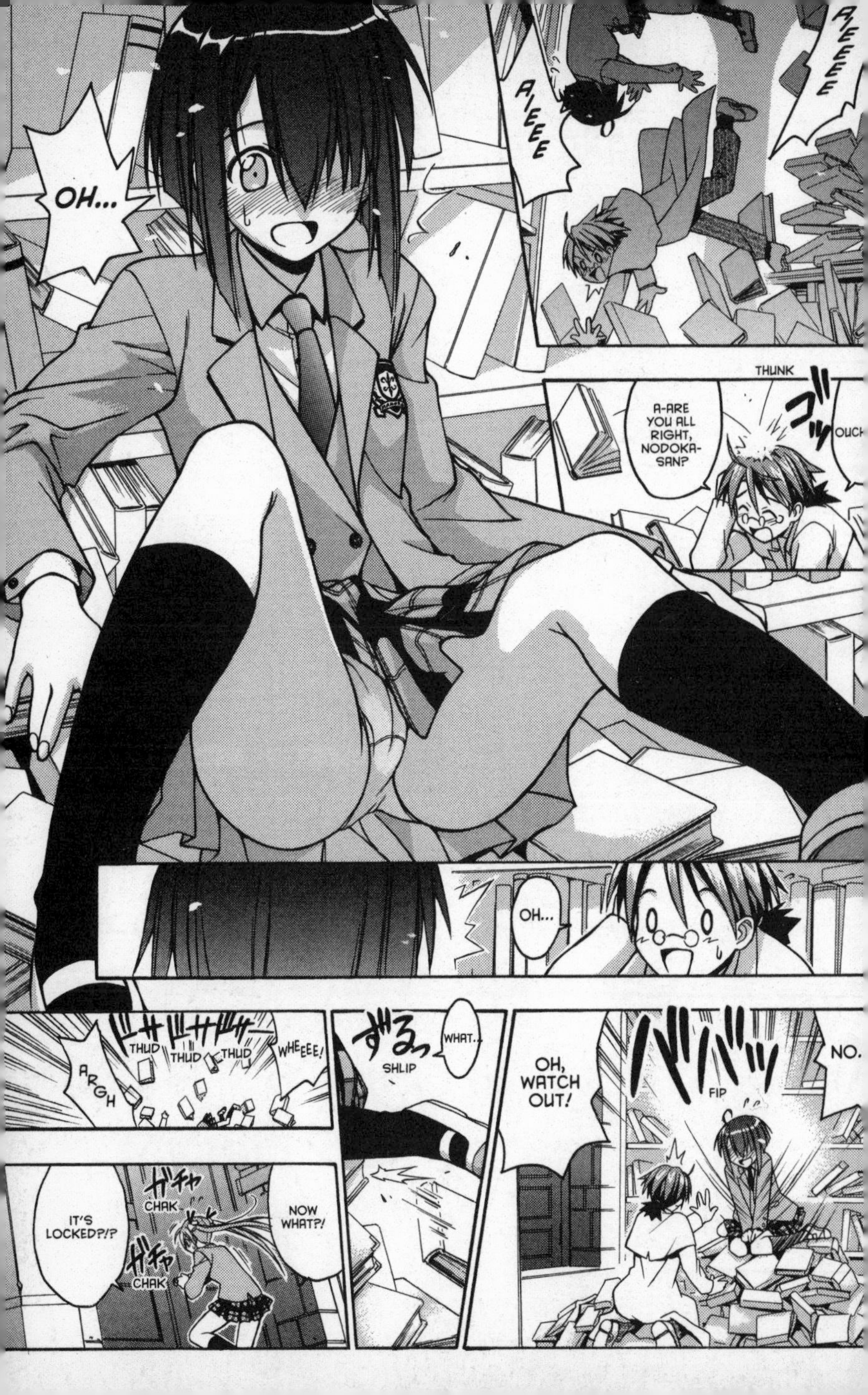
AIEEEE
AIEEE
OUCH
THUNK
A-ARE YOU ALL RIGHT, NODOKA-SAN?
OH...
OH...
NO.
FIP
OH, WATCH OUT!
WHAT...
SHLIP
WHEEEE!
THUD
THUD
THUD
ARGH
NOW WHAT?!
CHAK
CHAK
IT'S LOCKED?!?

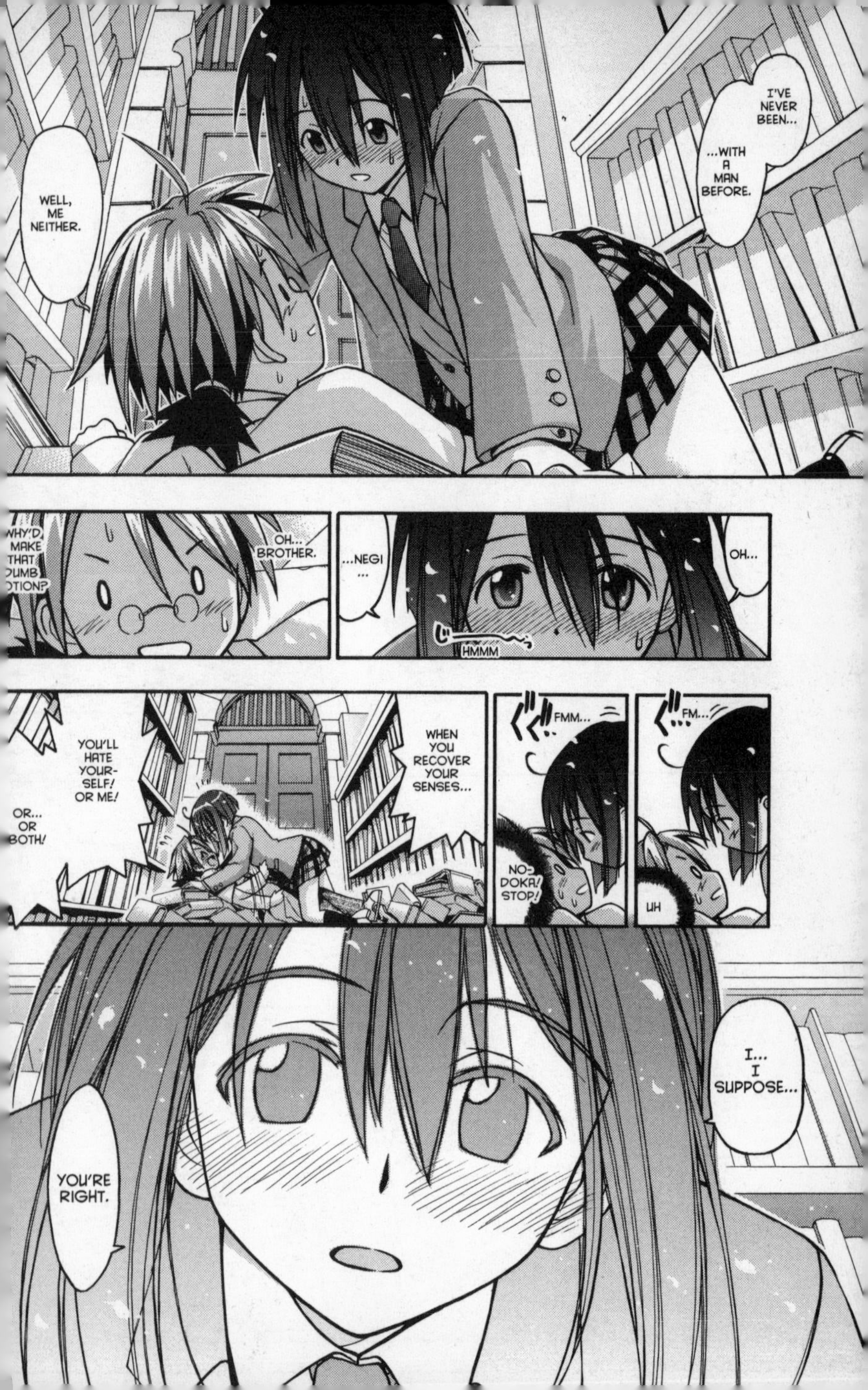
I'VE NEVER BEEN...
...WITH A MAN BEFORE.
WELL, ME NEITHER.
OH...
...NEGI ...
HMMM
OH... BROTHER.
WHY'D MAKE THAT UMB OTION?
FM...
UH
FMM...
NO-DOKA! STOP!
WHEN YOU RECOVER YOUR SENSES...
YOU'LL HATE YOURSELF! OR ME!
OR... OR BOTH!
I... I SUPPOSE...
YOU'RE RIGHT.

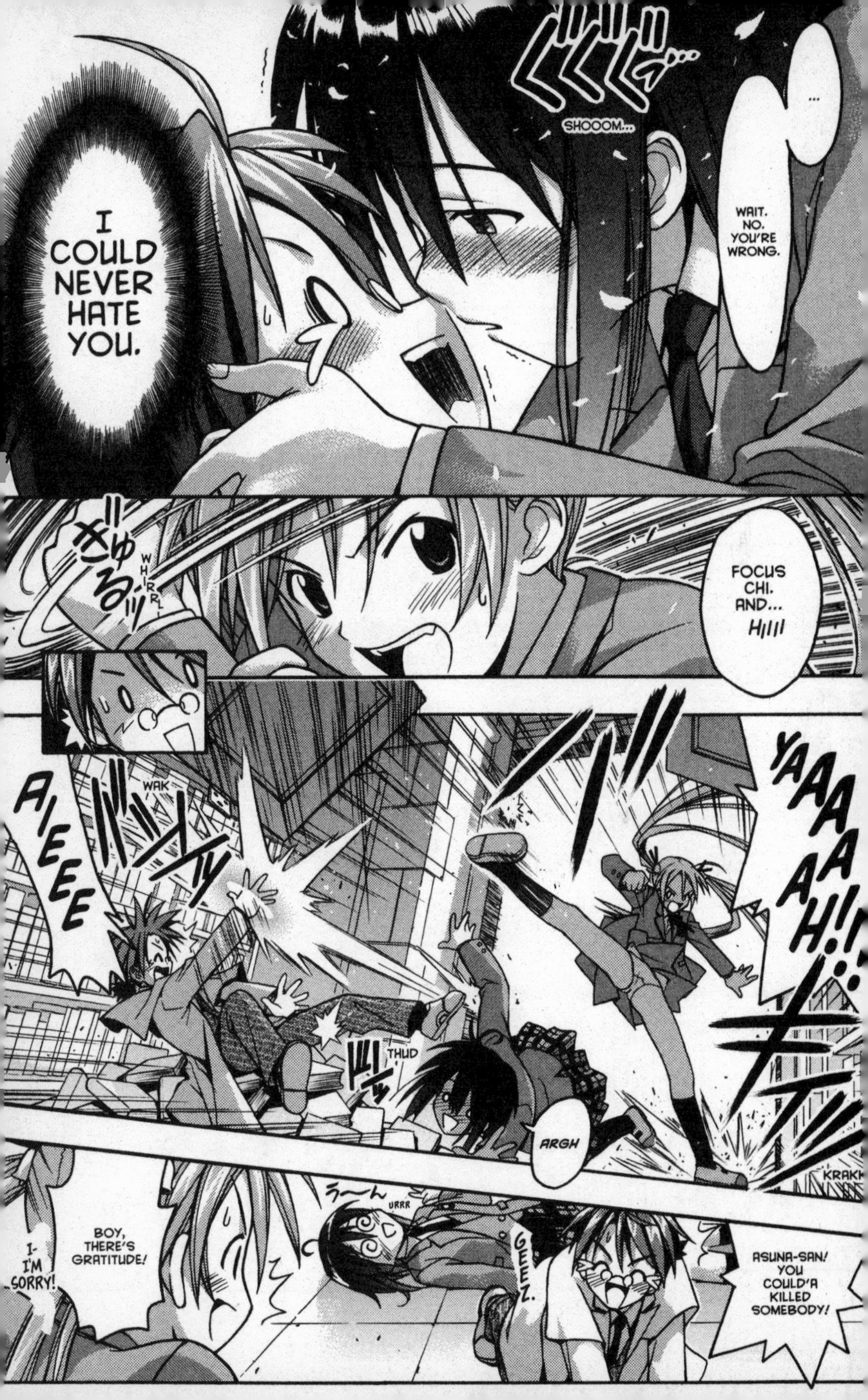
...
SHOOOM...
WAIT. NO. YOU'RE WRONG.
I COULD NEVER HATE YOU.
FOCUS CHI. AND... H!!!!
WHIRRL
YAAAAAH!!!
AIEEE
WAK
THUD
ARGH
KRAKK
ASUNA-SAN! YOU COULD'A KILLED SOMEBODY!
GEEZ.
URRR
BOY, THERE'S GRATITUDE!
I- I'M SORRY!

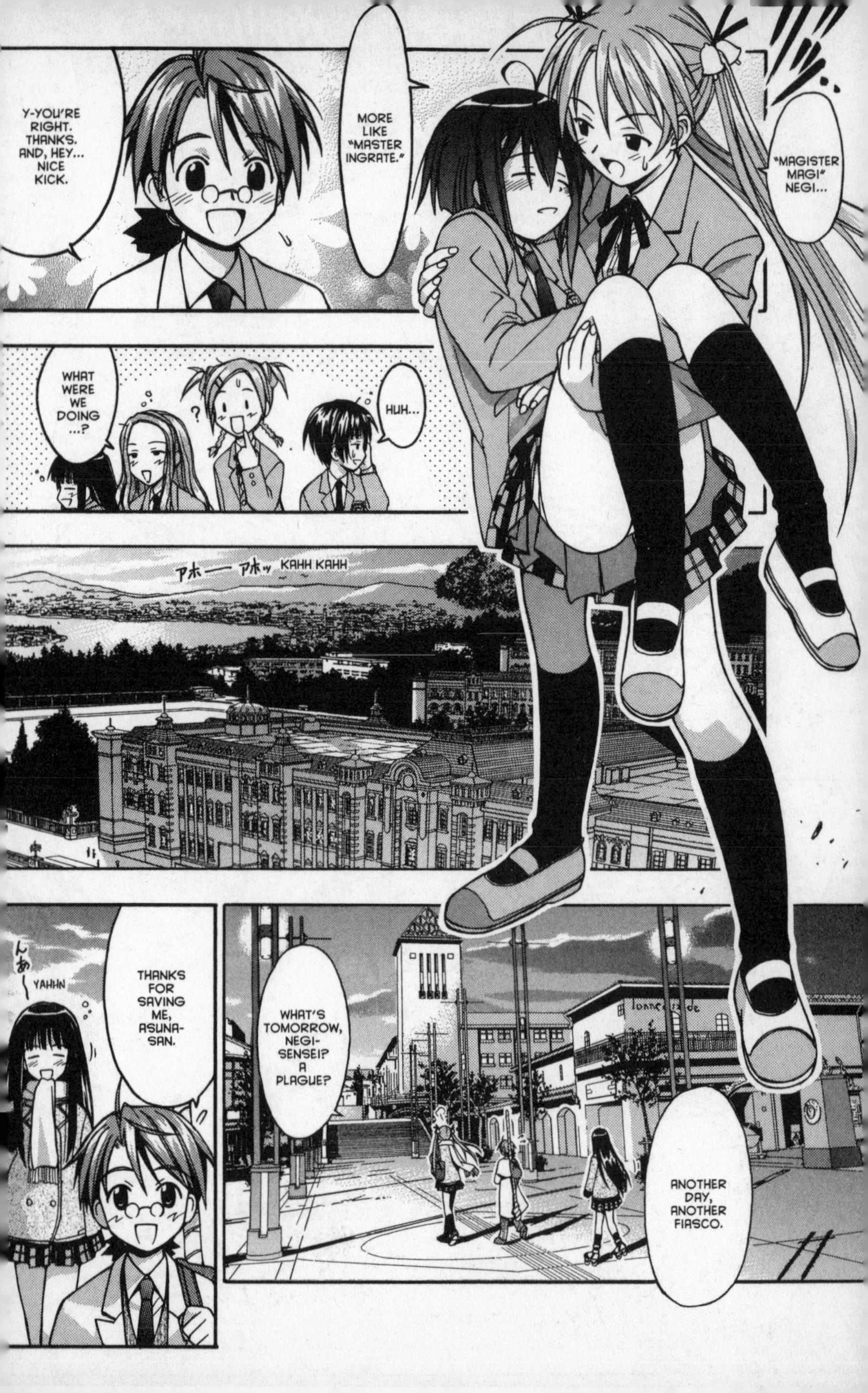
"MAGISTER MAGI" NEGI...
MORE LIKE "MASTER INGRATE."
Y-YOU'RE RIGHT. THANKS. AND, HEY... NICE KICK.
HUH...
WHAT WERE WE DOING ...?
アホー アホッ KAHH KAHH
ANOTHER DAY, ANOTHER FIASCO.
WHAT'S TOMORROW, NEGI-SENSEI!? A PLAGUE?
THANKS FOR SAVING ME, ASUNA-SAN.
んあ～ YAHHN

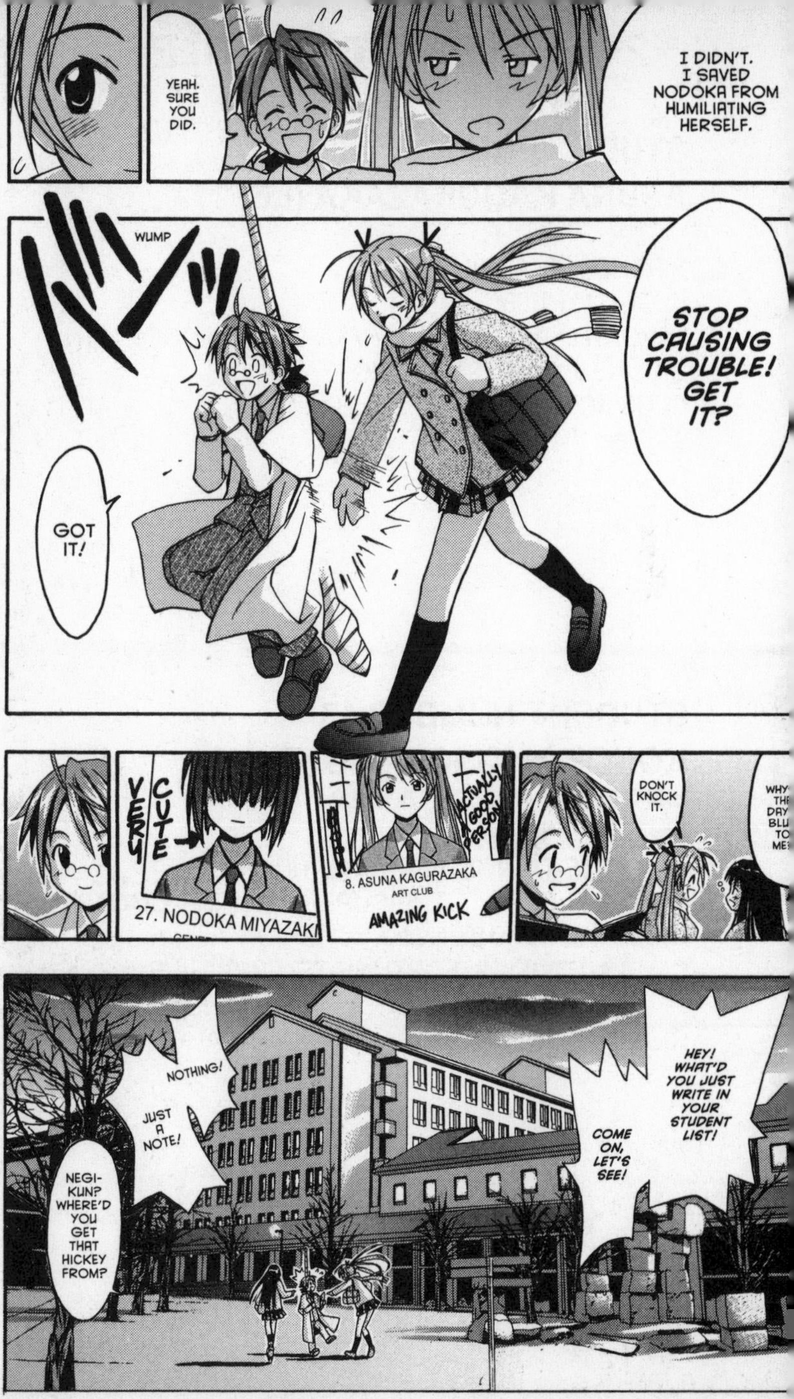
I DIDN'T. I SAVED NODOKA FROM HUMILIATING HERSELF.
YEAH. SURE YOU DID.
STOP CAUSING TROUBLE! GET IT?
WUMP
GOT IT!
DON'T KNOCK IT.
8. ASUNA KAGURAZAKA
ART CLUB
ACTUALLY A GOOD PERSON
AMAZING KICK
VERY CUTE
27. NODOKA MIYAZAKI
HEY! WHAT'D YOU JUST WRITE IN YOUR STUDENT LIST!
COME ON, LET'S SEE!
NOTHING!
JUST A NOTE!
NEGI-KUN? WHERE'D YOU GET THAT HICKEY FROM?

STUDENT NUMBER 8
ASUNA KAGURAZAKA (LEFT)

BIRTHDATE: APRIL 21, 1988
BLOODTYPE: B
FAVORITE THINGS: TAKAHATA-SENSEI, COOL MEN
DISLIKES: KIDS, STUDYING
CLUB ACTIVITIES: ART CLUB

STUDENT NUMBER 13
KONOKA KONOE (RIGHT)
BIRTHDATE: MARCH 18, 1989
BLOODTYPE: AB
FAVORITE THINGS: FORTUNE-TELLING,
                   THE SUPERNATURAL, COOKING
DISLIKES: ALMOST NONE
CLUB ACTIVITIES: FORTUNE-TELLING CLUB,
                   LIBRARY EXPLORATION CLUB
REMARKS: SCHOOL DEAN'S GRANDDAUGHTER

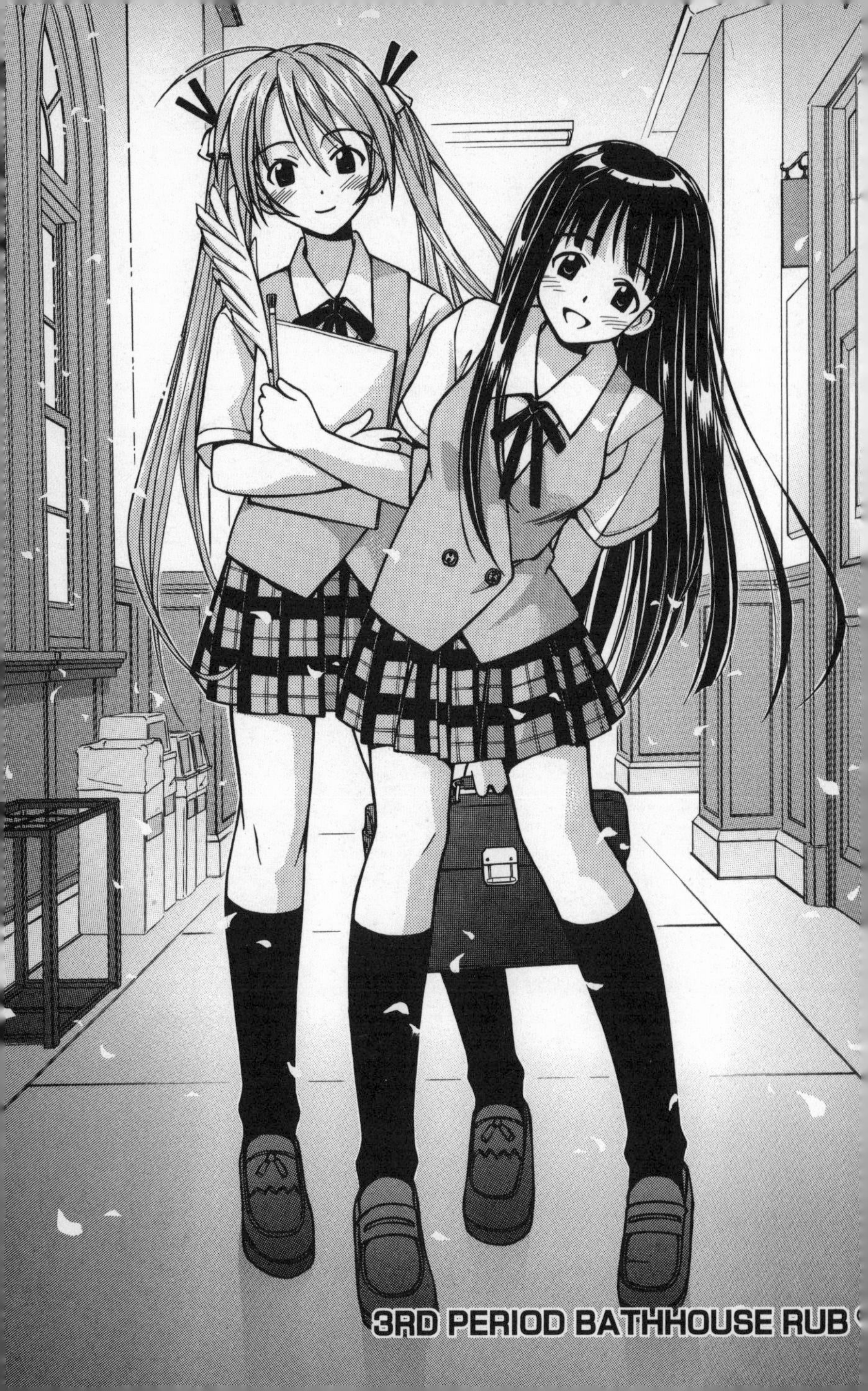

3RD PERIOD BATHHOUSE RUB

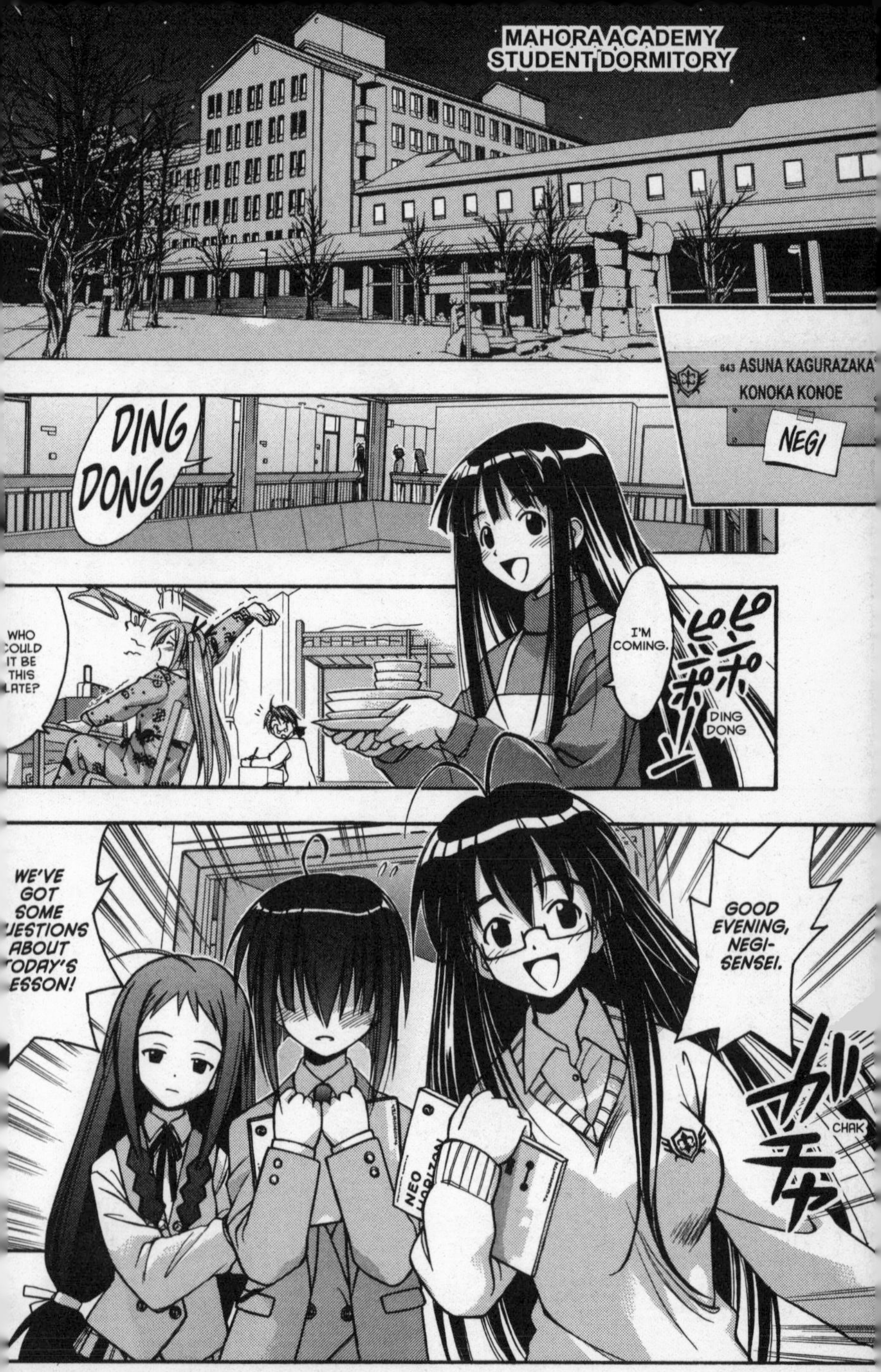
MAHORA ACADEMY
STUDENT DORMITORY
643 ASUNA KAGURAZAKA
KONOKA KONOE
NEGI
DING DONG
I'M COMING.
ピンポーン
DING DONG
WHO COULD IT BE THIS LATE?
GOOD EVENING, NEGI-SENSEI.
ガチャ
CHAK
WE'VE GOT SOME UESTIONS ABOUT ODAY'S ESSON!
NEO HORIZON

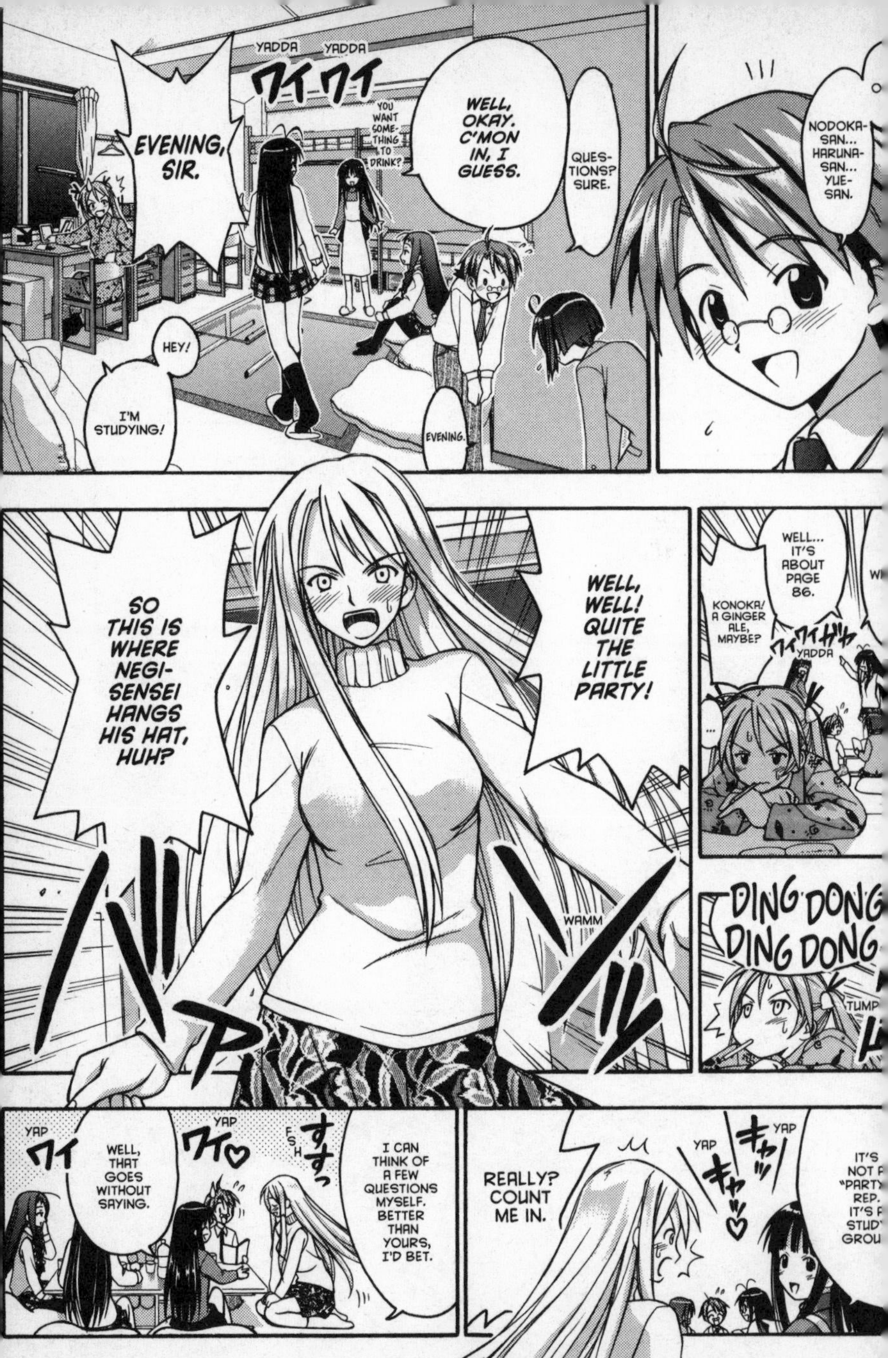

NODOKA-SAN... HARUNA-SAN... YUE-SAN.
QUES-TIONS? SURE.
WELL, OKAY. C'MON IN, I GUESS.
YOU WANT SOME-THING TO DRINK?
YADDA YADDA
ワイワイ
EVENING, SIR.
HEY!
I'M STUDYING!
EVENING.
WELL... IT'S ABOUT PAGE 86.
KONOKA! A GINGER ALE, MAYBE?
ワイワイガヤ
YADDA
...
DING DONG DING DONG
TUMP
WELL, WELL! QUITE THE LITTLE PARTY!
SO THIS IS WHERE NEGI-SENSEI HANGS HIS HAT, HUH?
WAMM
REALLY? COUNT ME IN.
YAP
キャッ
YAP
キャッ
I CAN THINK OF A FEW QUESTIONS MYSELF. BETTER THAN YOURS, I'D BET.
FSH
すすっ
YAP
ワイ♡
WELL, THAT GOES WITHOUT SAYING.
YAP
ワイ

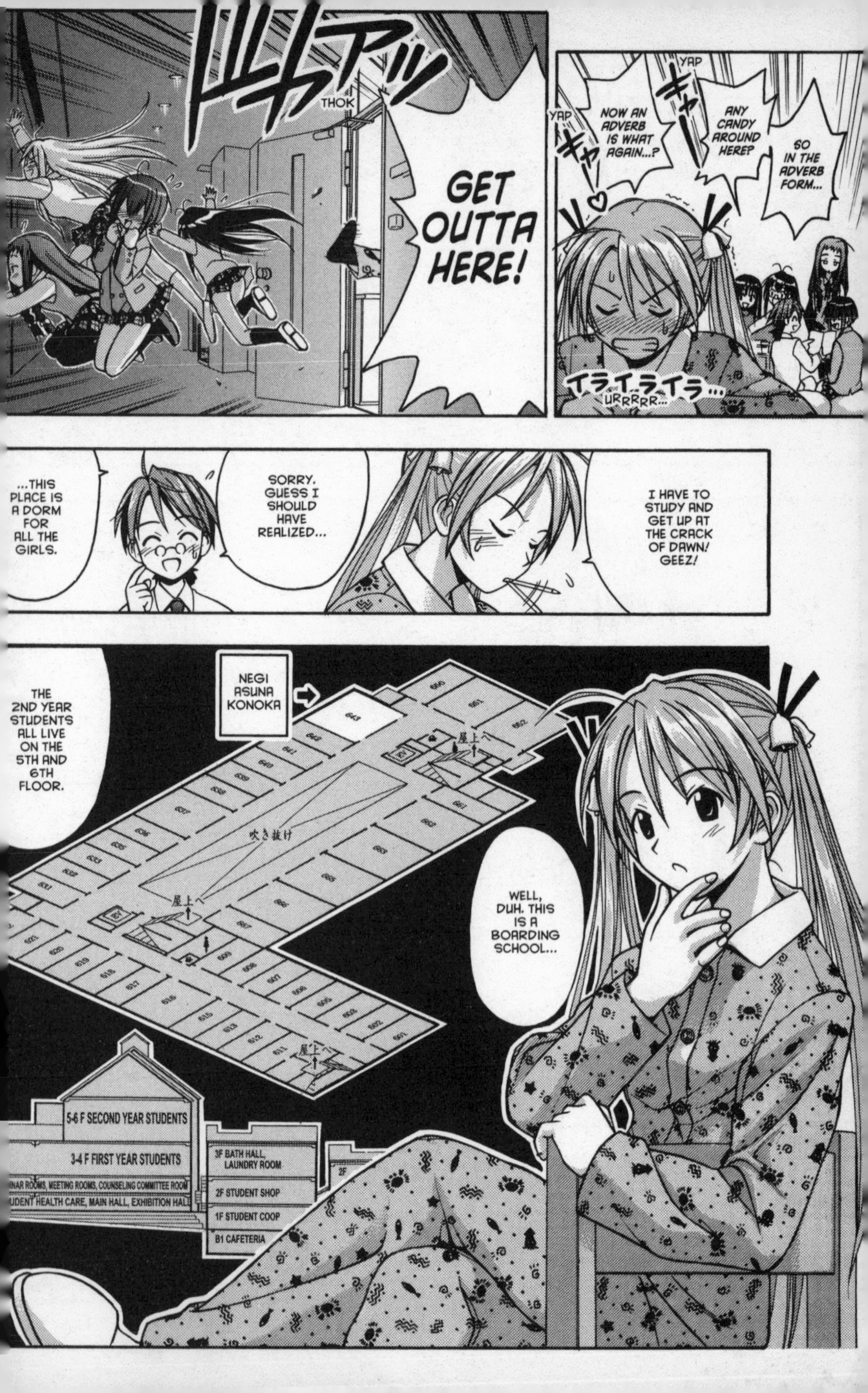
SO IN THE ADVERB FORM...
ANY CANDY AROUND HERE?
YAP
キャー
NOW AN ADVERB IS WHAT AGAIN...?
YAP
キャー
イライライラ...
URRRRR...
THOK
GET OUTTA HERE!
I HAVE TO STUDY AND GET UP AT THE CRACK OF DAWN! GEEZ!
SORRY. GUESS I SHOULD HAVE REALIZED...
...THIS PLACE IS A DORM FOR ALL THE GIRLS.
WELL, DUH. THIS IS A BOARDING SCHOOL...
THE 2ND YEAR STUDENTS ALL LIVE ON THE 5TH AND 6TH FLOOR.
NEGI
ASUNA
KONOKA
屋上へ
吹き抜け
屋上へ
屋上へ
5-6 F SECOND YEAR STUDENTS
3-4 F FIRST YEAR STUDENTS
INAR ROOMS, MEETING ROOMS, COUNSELING COMMITTEE ROOM
UDENT HEALTH CARE, MAIN HALL, EXHIBITION HALL
3F BATH HALL, LAUNDRY ROOM
2F STUDENT SHOP
1F STUDENT COOP
B1 CAFETERIA

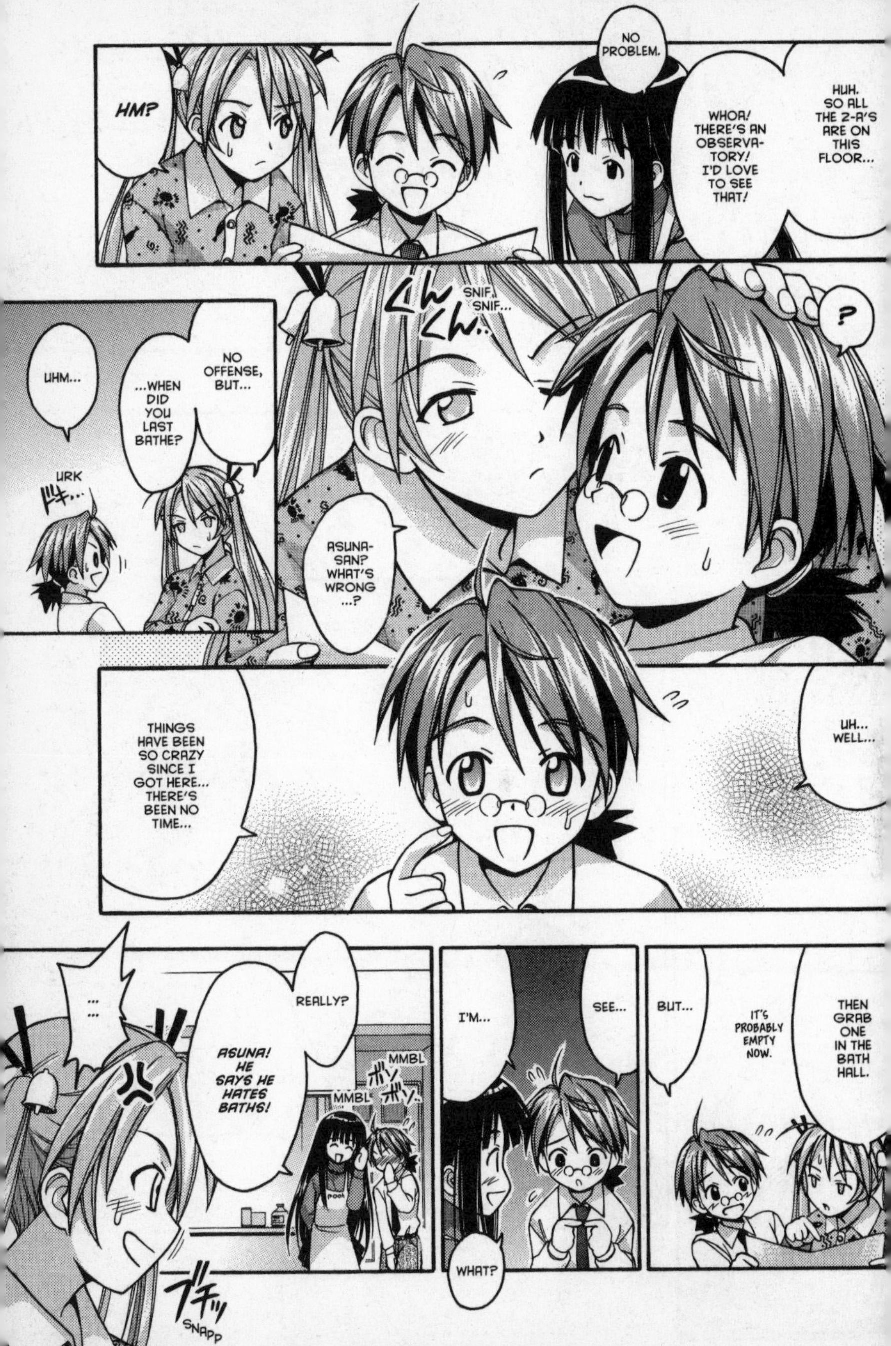
HUH. SO ALL THE 2-A'S ARE ON THIS FLOOR...
WHOA! THERE'S AN OBSERVATORY! I'D LOVE TO SEE THAT!
NO PROBLEM.
HM?
?
くんくん
SNIF, SNIF...
ASUNA-SAN? WHAT'S WRONG ...?
NO OFFENSE, BUT...
...WHEN DID YOU LAST BATHE?
UHM...
ドキ...
URK
UH... WELL...
THINGS HAVE BEEN SO CRAZY SINCE I GOT HERE... THERE'S BEEN NO TIME...
THEN GRAB ONE IN THE BATH HALL.
IT'S PROBABLY EMPTY NOW.
BUT...
SEE...
I'M...
WHAT?
REALLY?
ASUNA! HE SAYS HE HATES BATHS!
ボソ ボソ
MMBL
MMBL
... ...
ブチッ
SNAPP

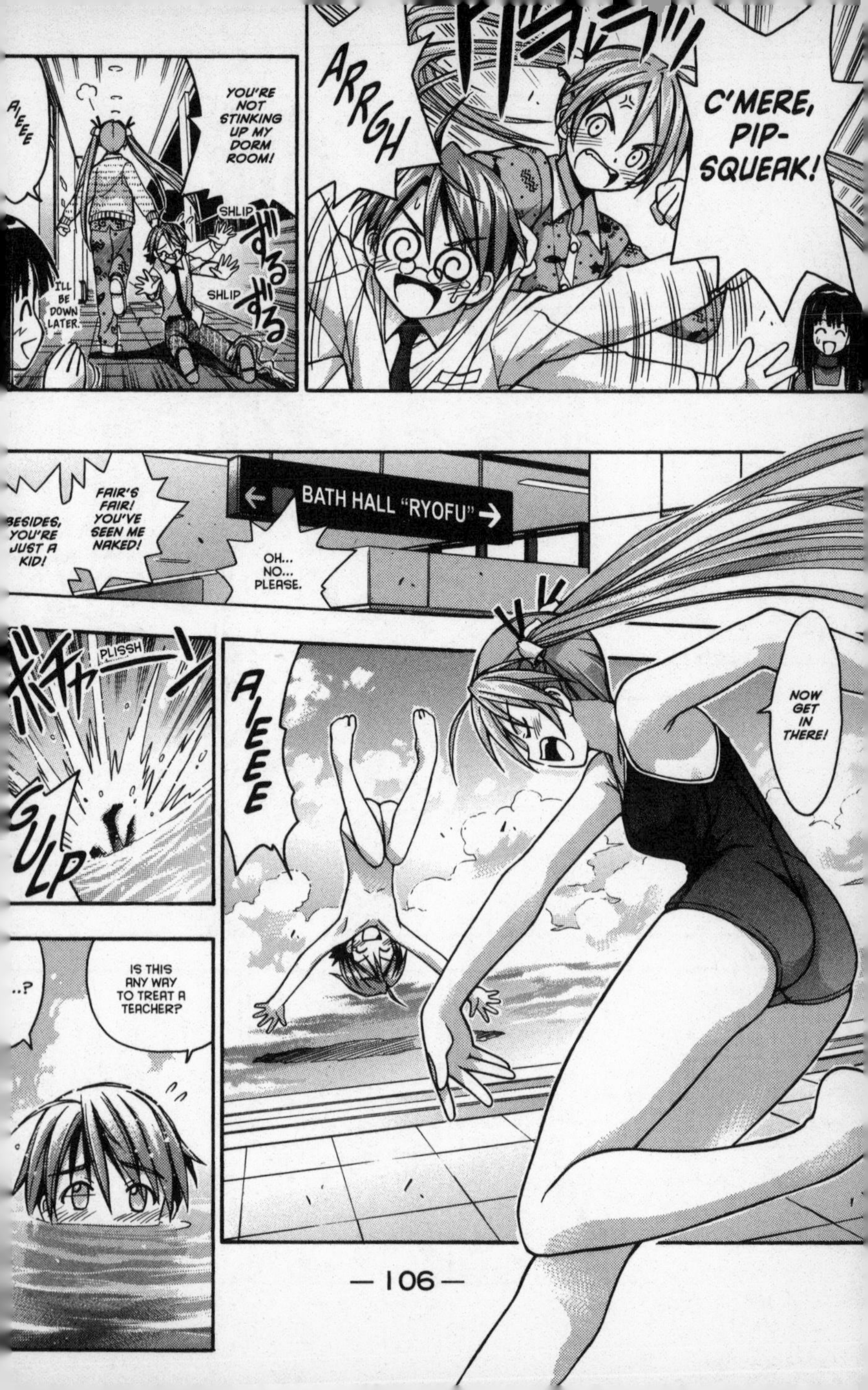
ARRGH
C'MERE, PIP-SQUEAK!
YOU'RE NOT STINKING UP MY DORM ROOM!
SHLIP
SHLIP
AIEEE
I'LL BE DOWN LATER.
BATH HALL "RYOFU"
OH... NO... PLEASE.
FAIR'S FAIR! YOU'VE SEEN ME NAKED!
BESIDES, YOU'RE JUST A KID!
NOW GET IN THERE!
AIEEE
PLISSH
GULP
IS THIS ANY WAY TO TREAT A TEACHER?
..?

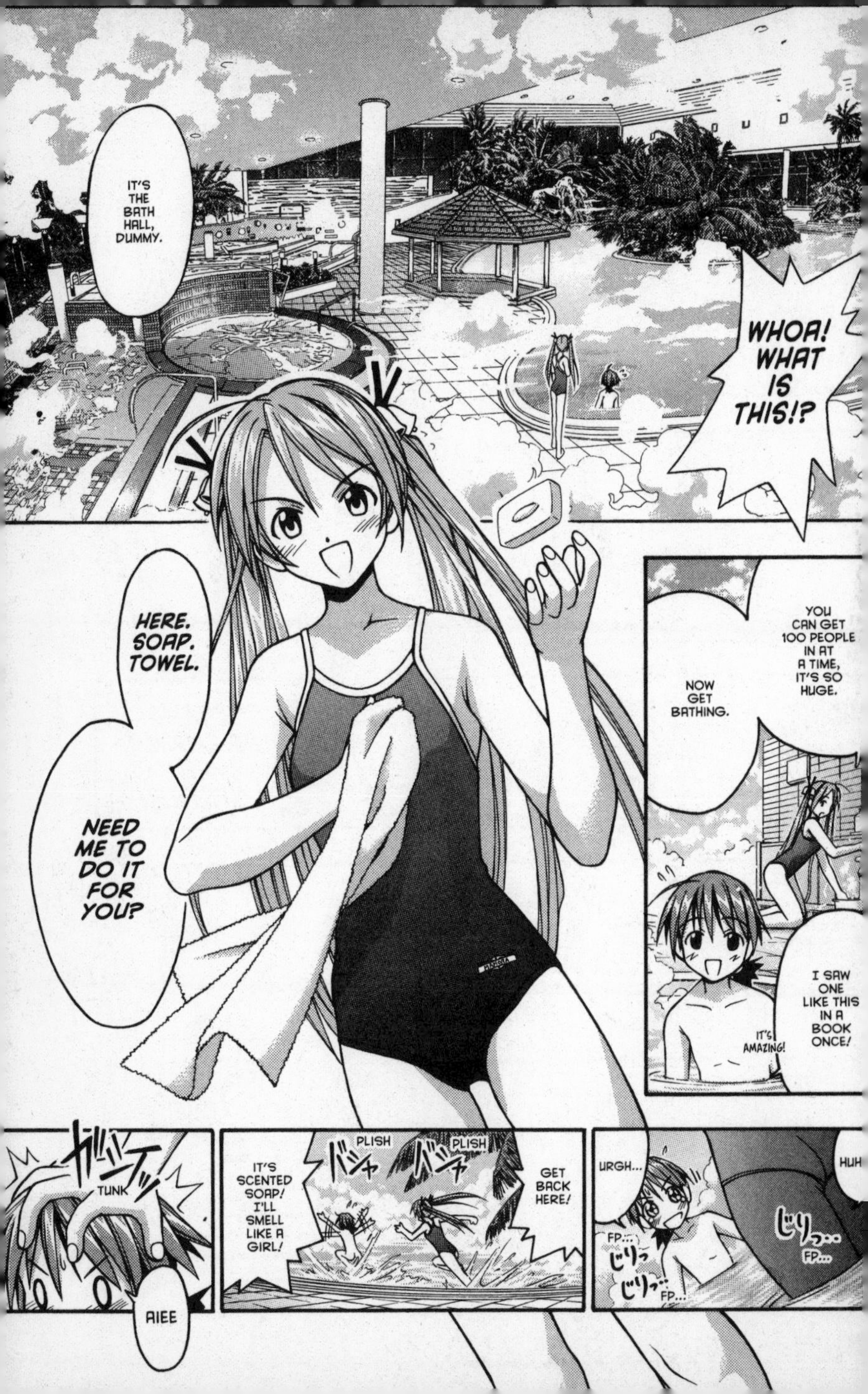
WHOA! WHAT IS THIS!?
IT'S THE BATH HALL, DUMMY.
YOU CAN GET 100 PEOPLE IN AT A TIME, IT'S SO HUGE.
NOW GET BATHING.
I SAW ONE LIKE THIS IN A BOOK ONCE!
IT'S AMAZING!
HERE. SOAP. TOWEL.
NEED ME TO DO IT FOR YOU?
HUH
じりっ‥
FP...
URGH...
FP...
じりっ
じりっ‥
FP...
PLISH
バシャ
PLISH
バシャ
GET BACK HERE!
IT'S SCENTED SOAP! I'LL SMELL LIKE A GIRL!
TUNK
AIEE

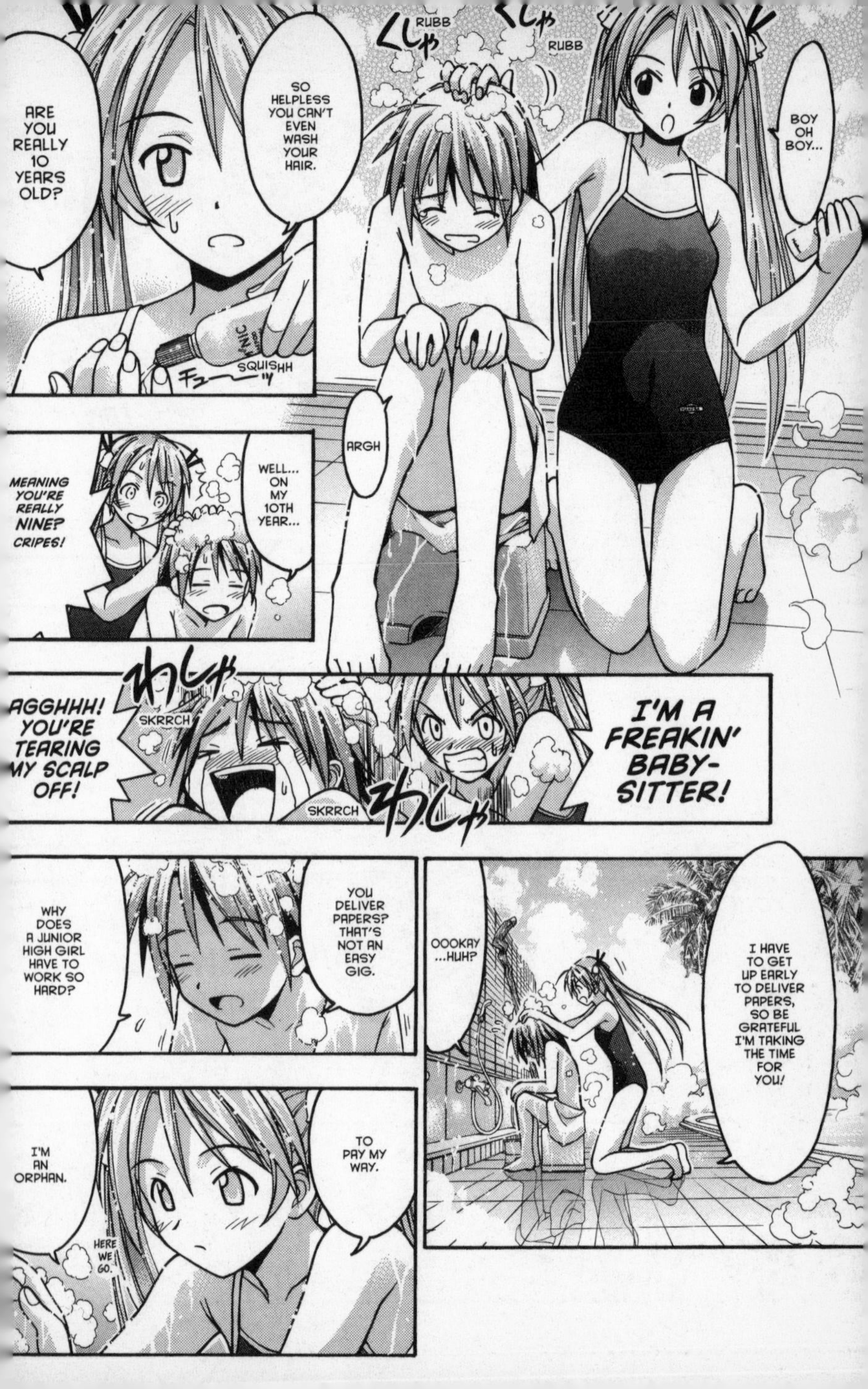
くしゃ RUBB
くしゃ RUBB
BOY OH BOY...
ARGH
SO HELPLESS YOU CAN'T EVEN WASH YOUR HAIR.
ARE YOU REALLY 10 YEARS OLD?
SQUISHH
WELL... ON MY 10TH YEAR...
MEANING YOU'RE REALLY NINE? CRIPES!
I'M A FREAKIN' BABY-SITTER!
SKRRCH
SKRRCH
AGGHHH! YOU'RE TEARING MY SCALP OFF!
I HAVE TO GET UP EARLY TO DELIVER PAPERS, SO BE GRATEFUL I'M TAKING THE TIME FOR YOU!
OOOKAY ...HUH?
YOU DELIVER PAPERS? THAT'S NOT AN EASY GIG.
WHY DOES A JUNIOR HIGH GIRL HAVE TO WORK SO HARD?
TO PAY MY WAY.
I'M AN ORPHAN.
HERE WE GO.

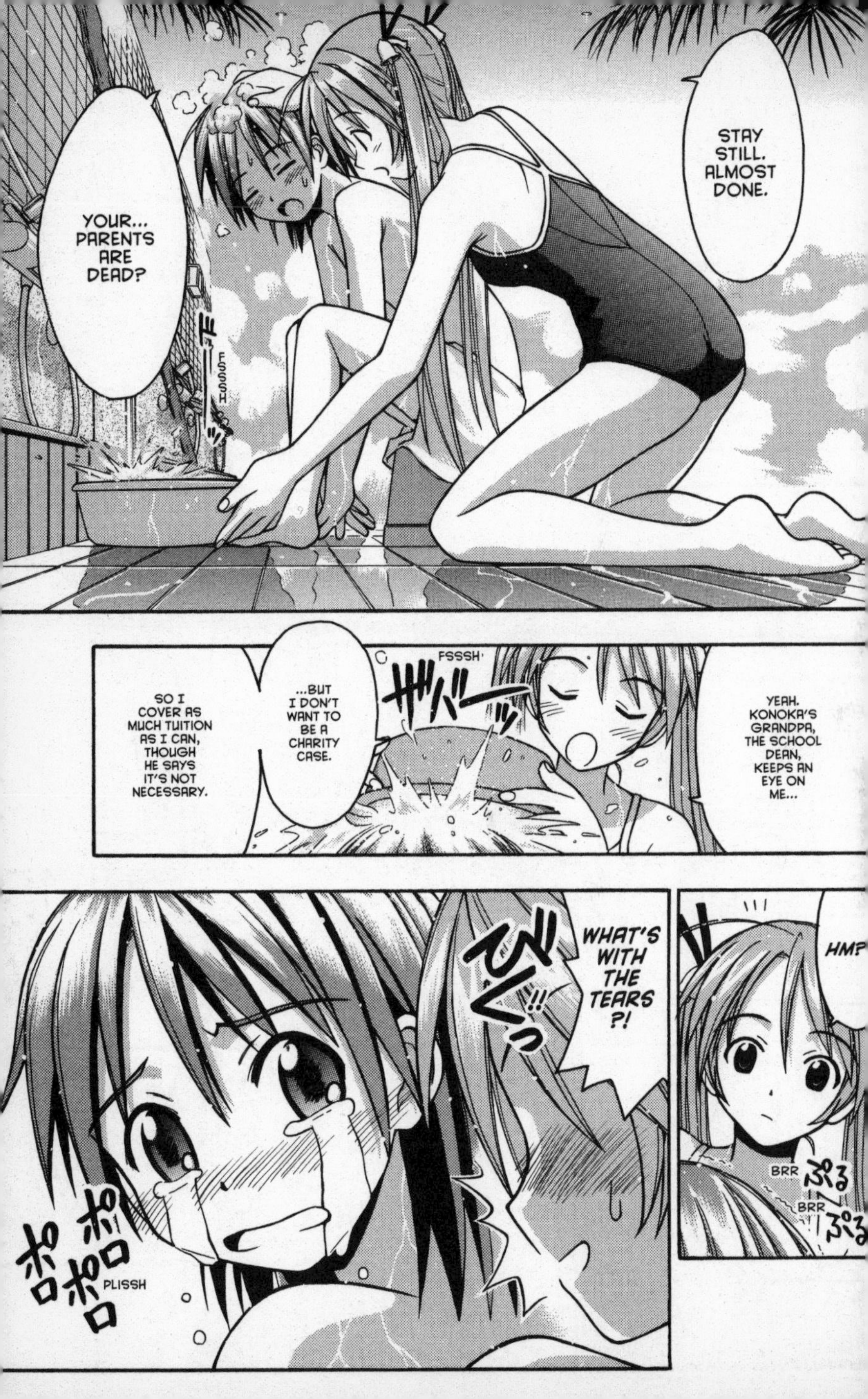
STAY STILL. ALMOST DONE.
YOUR... PARENTS ARE DEAD?
FSSSH
YEAH. KONOKA'S GRANDPA, THE SCHOOL DEAN, KEEPS AN EYE ON ME...
FSSSH
ザバーッ
...BUT I DON'T WANT TO BE A CHARITY CASE.
SO I COVER AS MUCH TUITION AS I CAN, THOUGH HE SAYS IT'S NOT NECESSARY.
HM?
ぷる BRR
ぷる BRR
WHAT'S WITH THE TEARS?!
びくっ!!
ポロポロ
PLISSH
ポロポロ

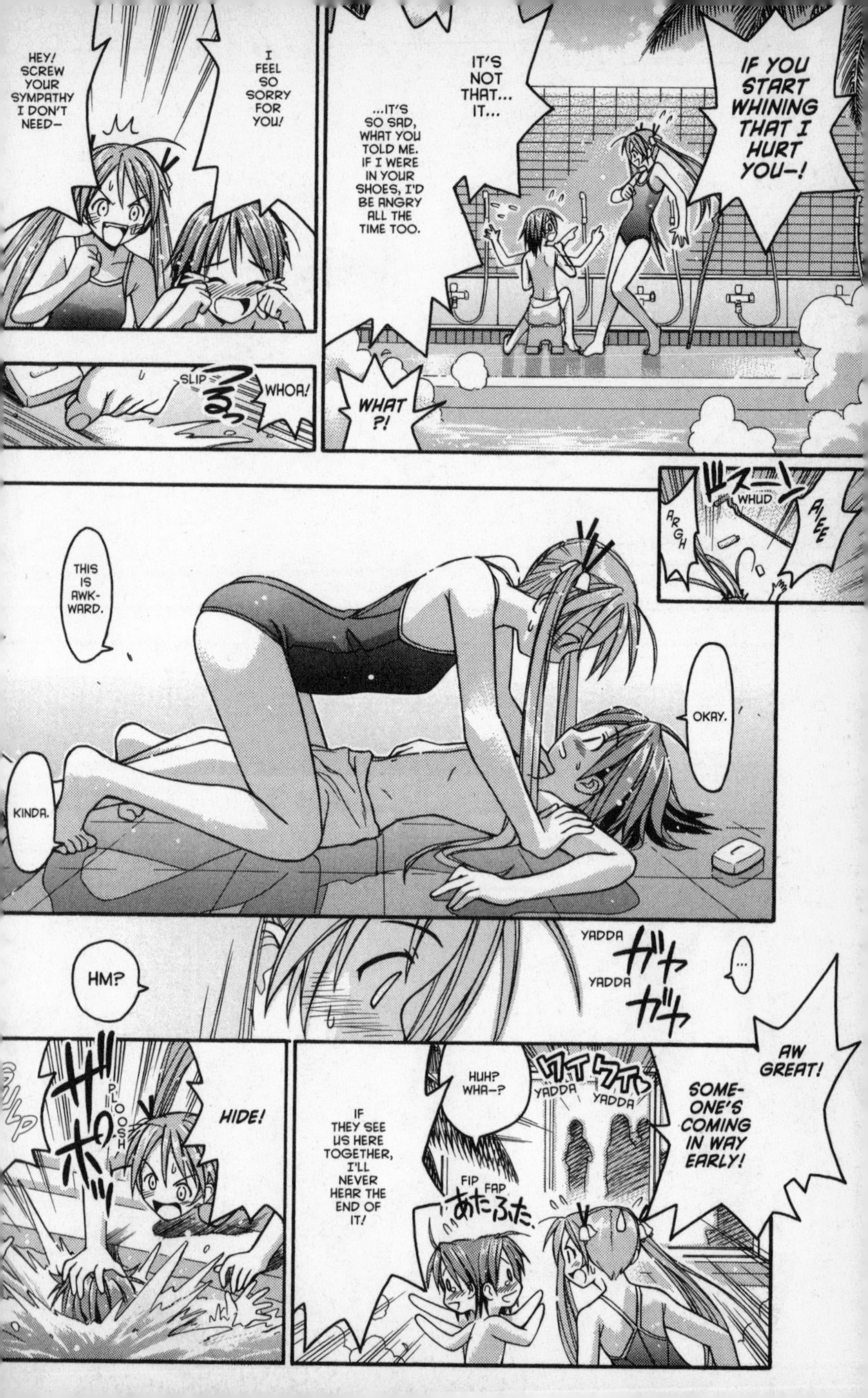
IF YOU START WHINING THAT I HURT YOU–!
IT'S NOT THAT... IT...
...IT'S SO SAD, WHAT YOU TOLD ME. IF I WERE IN YOUR SHOES, I'D BE ANGRY ALL THE TIME TOO.
WHAT ?!
I FEEL SO SORRY FOR YOU!
HEY! SCREW YOUR SYMPATHY I DON'T NEED–
SLIP
WHOA!
WHUD
AIEE
ARGH
OKAY.
THIS IS AWK-WARD.
KINDA.
YADDA
YADDA
...
HM?
AW GREAT!
SOME-ONE'S COMING IN WAY EARLY!
YADDA
YADDA
HUH? WHA–?
IF THEY SEE US HERE TOGETHER, I'LL NEVER HEAR THE END OF IT!
FIP
FAP
あたふた
HIDE!
PLOOSH

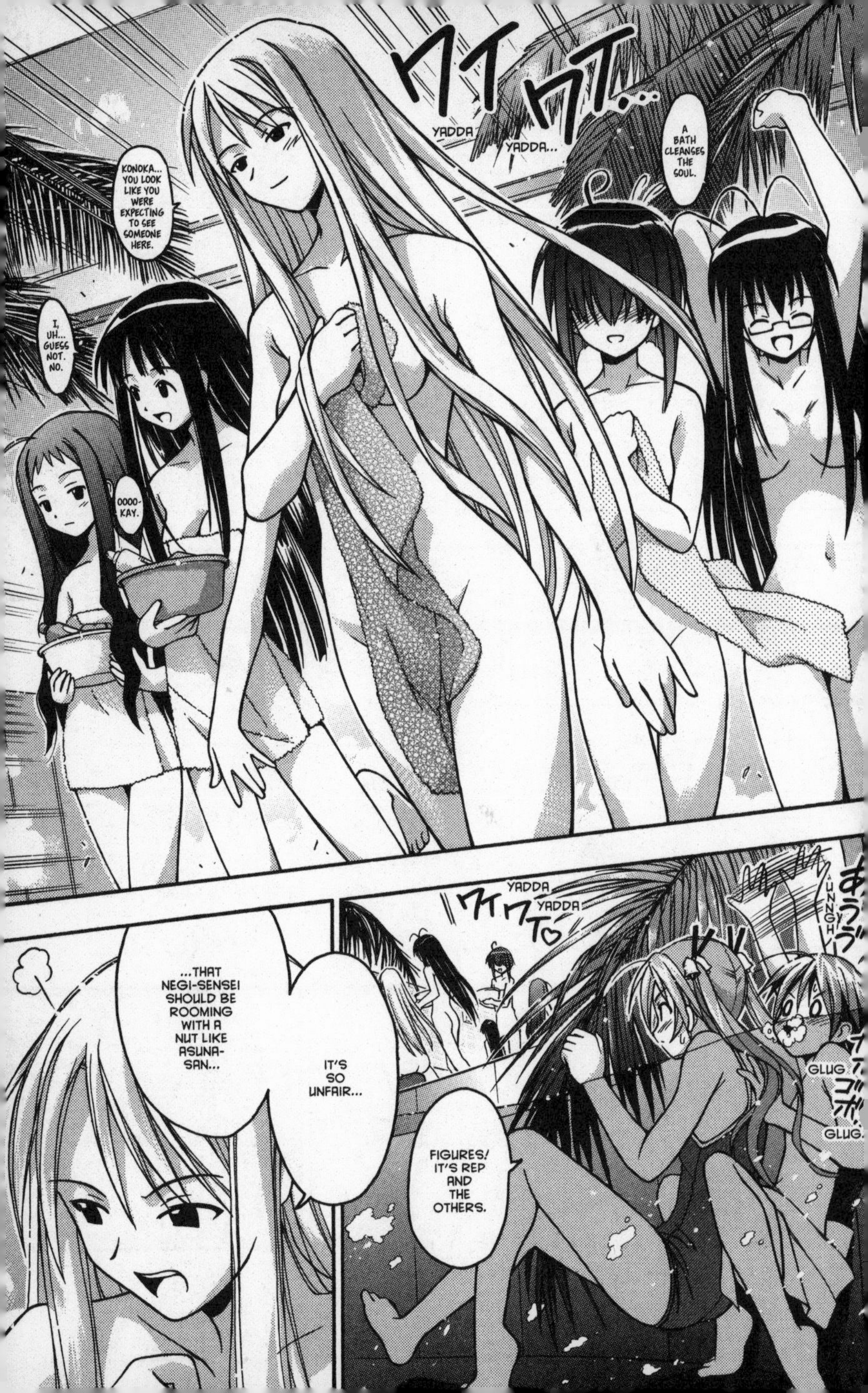
ワイワイ...
YADDA YADDA...
A BATH CLEANSES THE SOUL.
KONOKA... YOU LOOK LIKE YOU WERE EXPECTING TO SEE SOMEONE HERE.
I, UH... GUESS NOT. NO.
OOOO-KAY.
UNNGH!
ワイワイ♡
YADDA YADDA
GLUG, GLUG.
FIGURES! IT'S REP AND THE OTHERS.
...THAT NEGI-SENSEI SHOULD BE ROOMING WITH A NUT LIKE ASUNA-SAN...
IT'S SO UNFAIR...

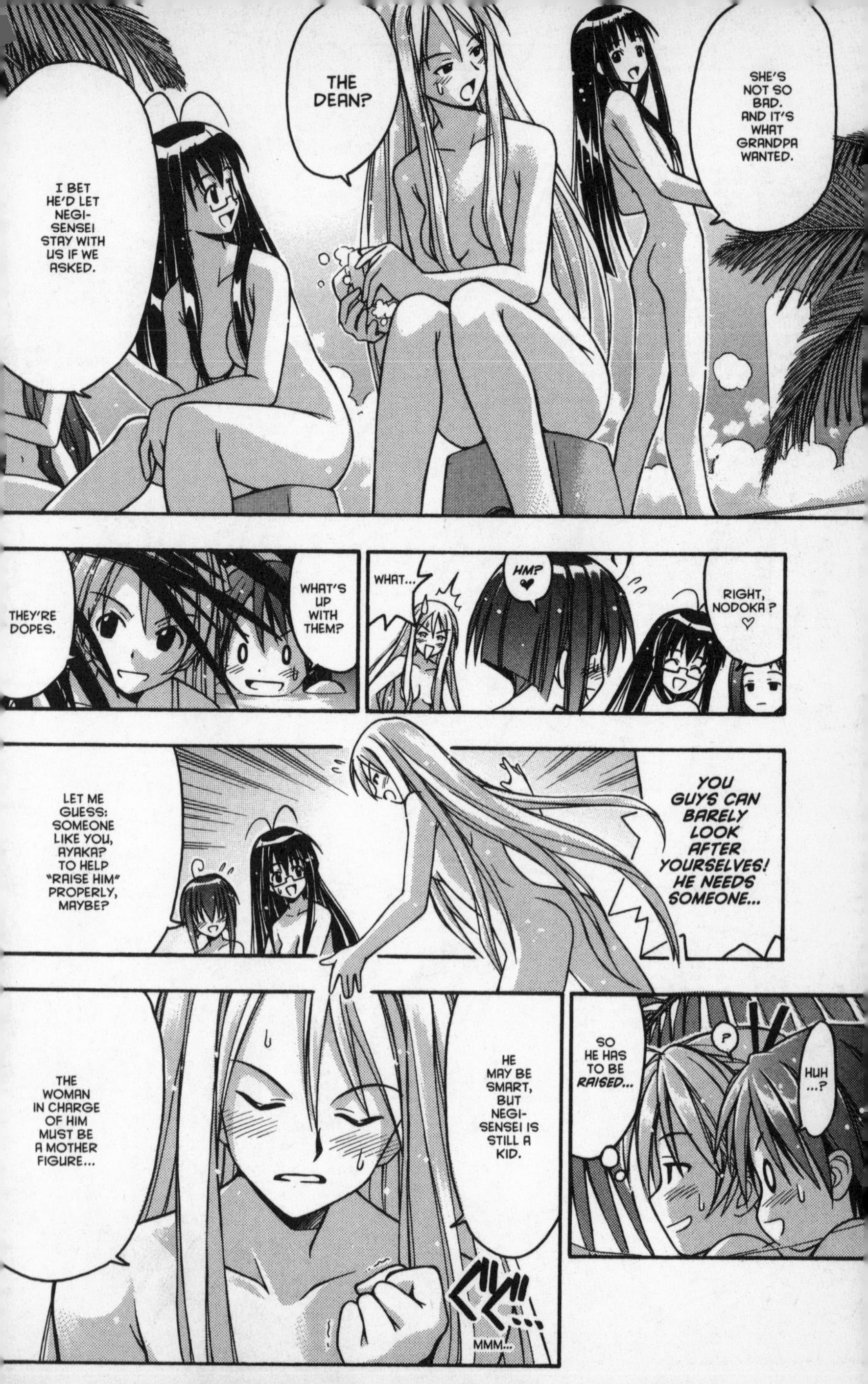
SHE'S NOT SO BAD. AND IT'S WHAT GRANDPA WANTED.
THE DEAN?
I BET HE'D LET NEGI-SENSEI STAY WITH US IF WE ASKED.
RIGHT, NODOKA? ♡
HM? ♥
WHAT...
WHAT'S UP WITH THEM?
THEY'RE DOPES.
YOU GUYS CAN BARELY LOOK AFTER YOURSELVES! HE NEEDS SOMEONE...
LET ME GUESS: SOMEONE LIKE YOU, AYAKA? TO HELP "RAISE HIM" PROPERLY, MAYBE?
HUH ...?
?
SO HE HAS TO BE *RAISED...*
HE MAY BE SMART, BUT NEGI-SENSEI IS STILL A KID.
THE WOMAN IN CHARGE OF HIM MUST BE A MOTHER FIGURE...
MMM...

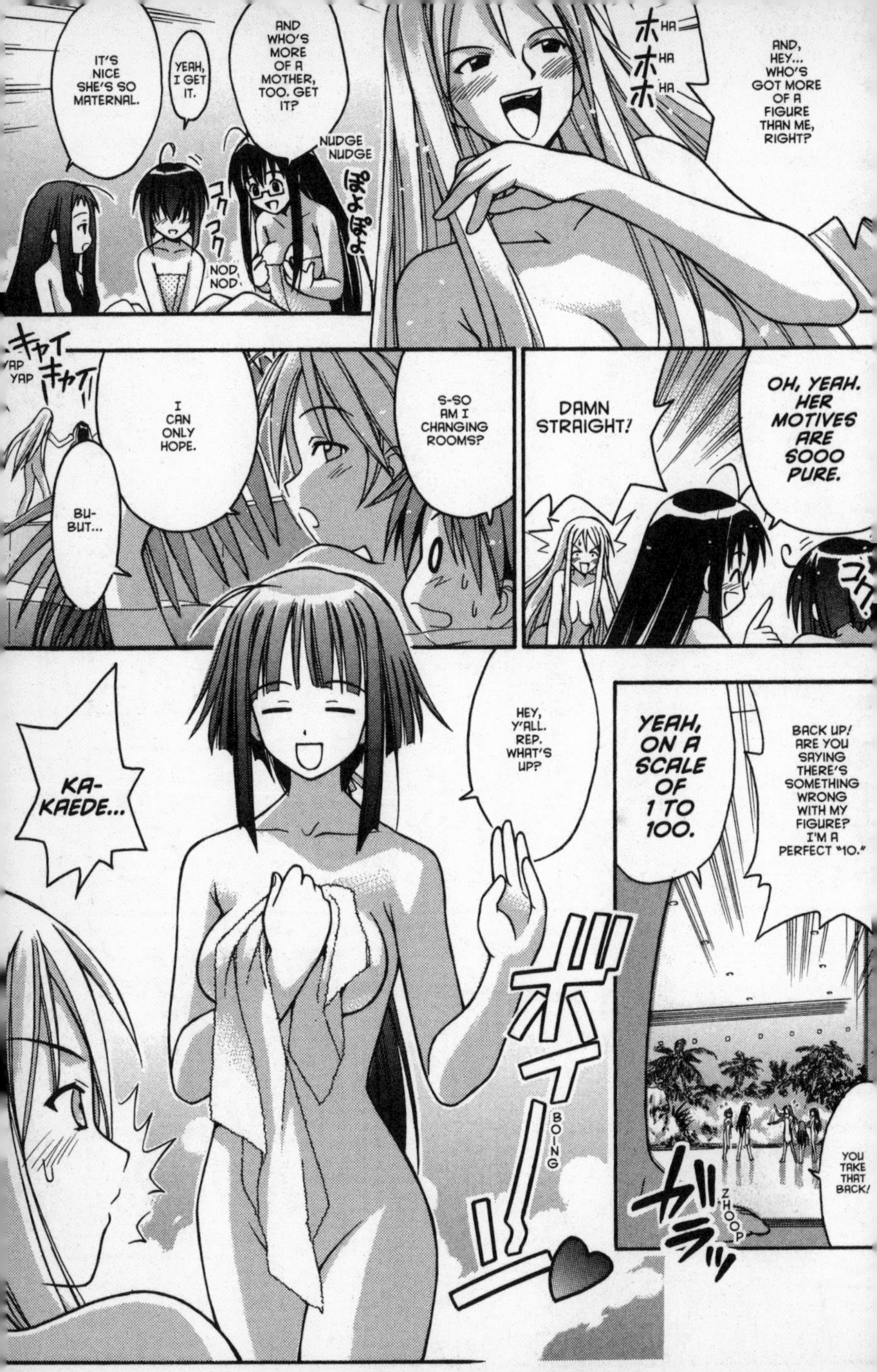
HA HA HA
AND, HEY... WHO'S GOT MORE OF A FIGURE THAN ME, RIGHT?
AND WHO'S MORE OF A MOTHER, TOO. GET IT?
NUDGE NUDGE
YEAH, I GET IT.
IT'S NICE SHE'S SO MATERNAL.
NOD NOD
OH, YEAH. HER MOTIVES ARE SOOO PURE.
DAMN STRAIGHT!
S-SO AM I CHANGING ROOMS?
I CAN ONLY HOPE.
YAP YAP
BU-BUT...
BACK UP! ARE YOU SAYING THERE'S SOMETHING WRONG WITH MY FIGURE? I'M A PERFECT "10."
YEAH, ON A SCALE OF 1 TO 100.
YOU TAKE THAT BACK!
ZHOOP
HEY, Y'ALL. REP. WHAT'S UP?
BOING
KA-KAEDE...

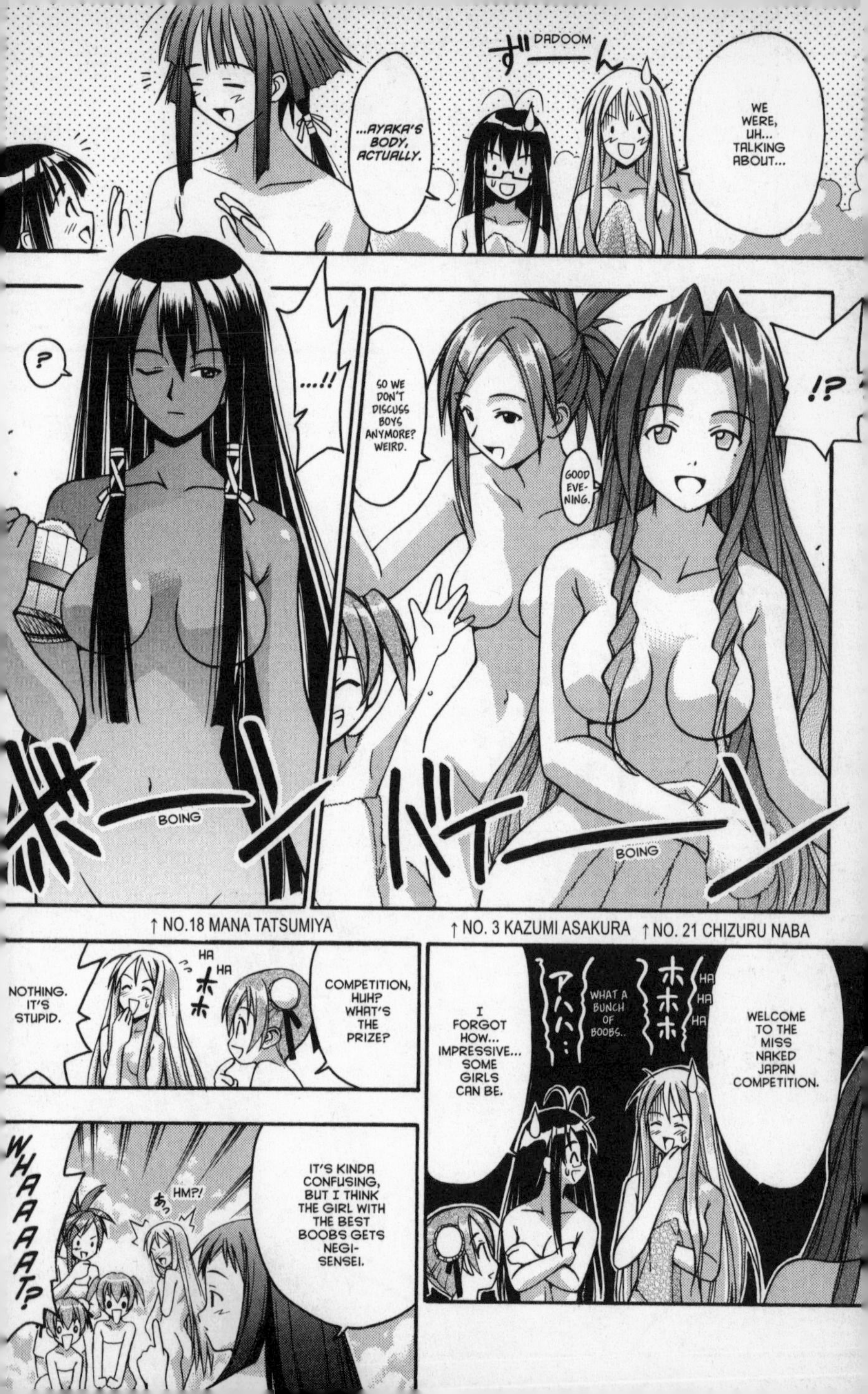
WE WERE, UH... TALKING ABOUT...
ずーん
DADOOM
...AYAKA'S BODY, ACTUALLY.
!?
GOOD EVE-NING.
SO WE DON'T DISCUSS BOYS ANYMORE? WEIRD.
BOING
...!!
?
BOING
↑ NO.18 MANA TATSUMIYA
↑ NO. 3 KAZUMI ASAKURA
↑ NO. 21 CHIZURU NABA
WELCOME TO THE MISS NAKED JAPAN COMPETITION.
ホホホ
HA HA HA
WHAT A BUNCH OF BOOBS..
I FORGOT HOW... IMPRESSIVE... SOME GIRLS CAN BE.
COMPETITION, HUH? WHAT'S THE PRIZE?
HA HA
NOTHING. IT'S STUPID.
IT'S KINDA CONFUSING, BUT I THINK THE GIRL WITH THE BEST BOOBS GETS NEGI-SENSEI.
HM?!
WHAAAAAT?

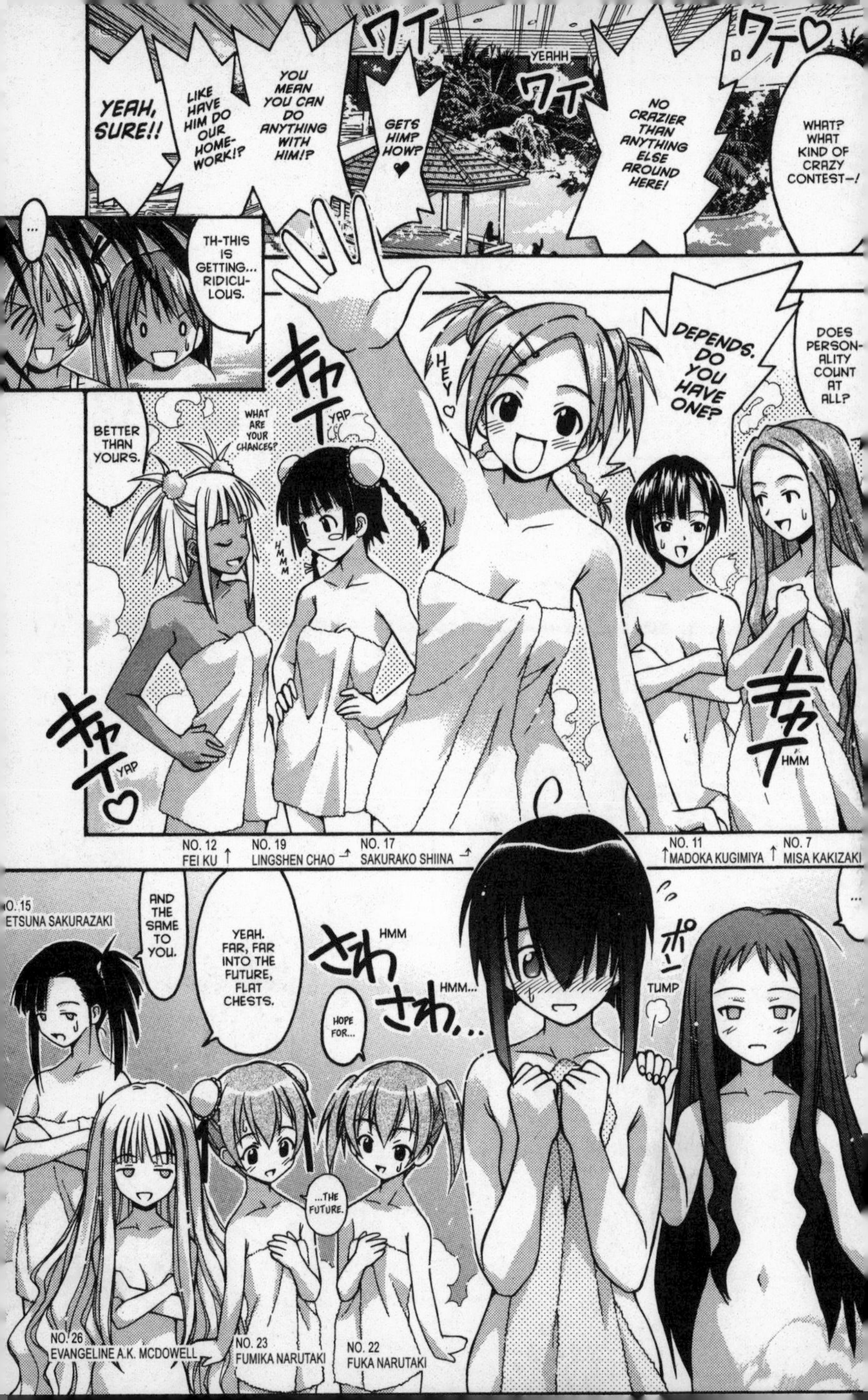
ワイ ワイ♡
WHAT? WHAT KIND OF CRAZY CONTEST—!
NO CRAZIER THAN ANYTHING ELSE AROUND HERE!
ワイ
YEAHH
GETS HIM? HOW? ♥
YOU MEAN YOU CAN DO ANYTHING WITH HIM!?
LIKE HAVE HIM DO OUR HOMEWORK!?
YEAH, SURE!!
DOES PERSONALITY COUNT AT ALL?
DEPENDS. DO YOU HAVE ONE?
HEY ♡
キャー YAP
WHAT ARE YOUR CHANCES?
BETTER THAN YOURS.
HMMM
キャー HMM
キャー YAP ♡
NO. 7 MISA KAKIZAKI
NO. 11 MADOKA KUGIMIYA
NO. 17 SAKURAKO SHIINA
NO. 19 LINGSHEN CHAO
NO. 12 FEI KU
...
TH-THIS IS GETTING... RIDICULOUS.
...
ポー TUMP
HMM...
さわさわ... HMM
YEAH. FAR, FAR INTO THE FUTURE, FLAT CHESTS.
AND THE SAME TO YOU.
HOPE FOR...
...THE FUTURE.
O. 15
ETSUNA SAKURAZAKI
NO. 22 FUKA NARUTAKI
NO. 23 FUMIKA NARUTAKI
NO. 26 EVANGELINE A.K. MCDOWELL

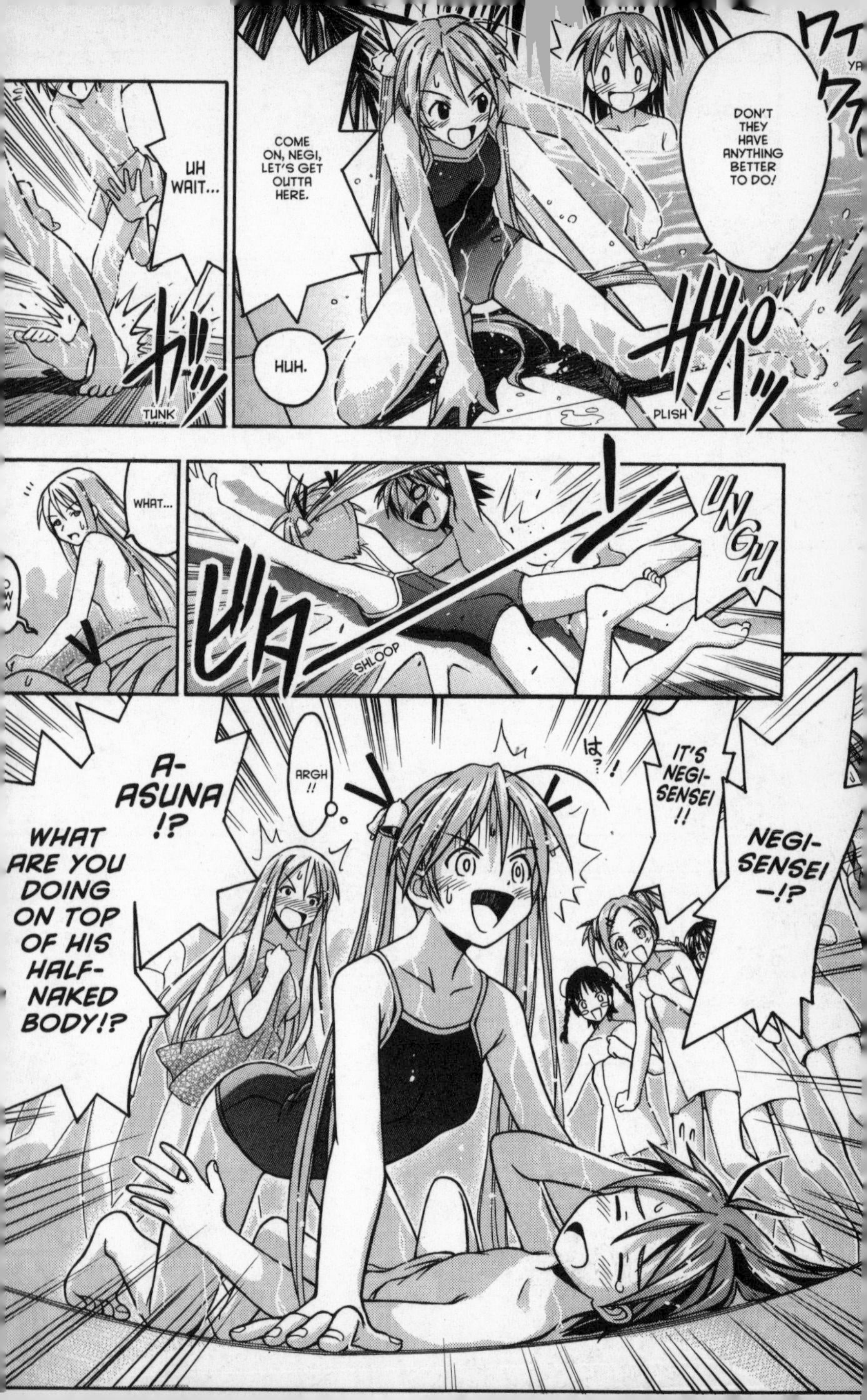
DON'T THEY HAVE ANYTHING BETTER TO DO!
PLISH
COME ON, NEGI, LET'S GET OUTTA HERE.
HUH.
UH WAIT...
TUNK
UNGH
SHLOOP
WHAT...
NEGI-SENSEI—!?
IT'S NEGI-SENSEI!!
ARGH!!
A-ASUNA!?
WHAT ARE YOU DOING ON TOP OF HIS HALF-NAKED BODY!?

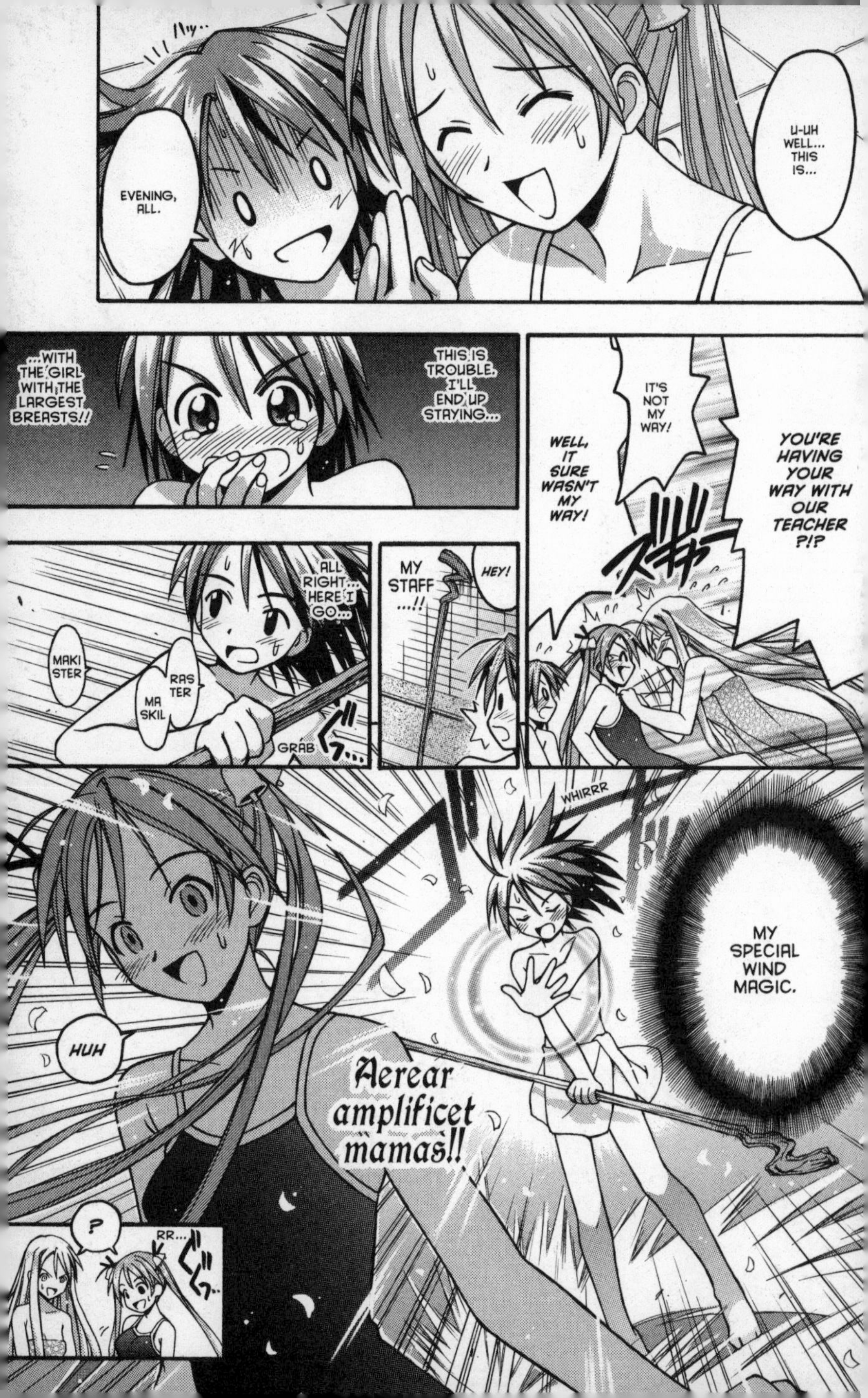
U-UH WELL... THIS IS...
EVENING, ALL.
YOU'RE HAVING YOUR WAY WITH OUR TEACHER?!?
IT'S NOT MY WAY!
WELL, IT SURE WASN'T MY WAY!
THIS IS TROUBLE. I'LL END UP STAYING...
...WITH THE GIRL WITH THE LARGEST BREASTS!!
HEY!
MY STAFF...!!
ALL RIGHT... HERE I GO...
RAS TER
MA SKIL
MAKI STER
GRAB
MY SPECIAL WIND MAGIC.
WHIRRR
Aerear amplificet mamas!!
HUH
RR...
?

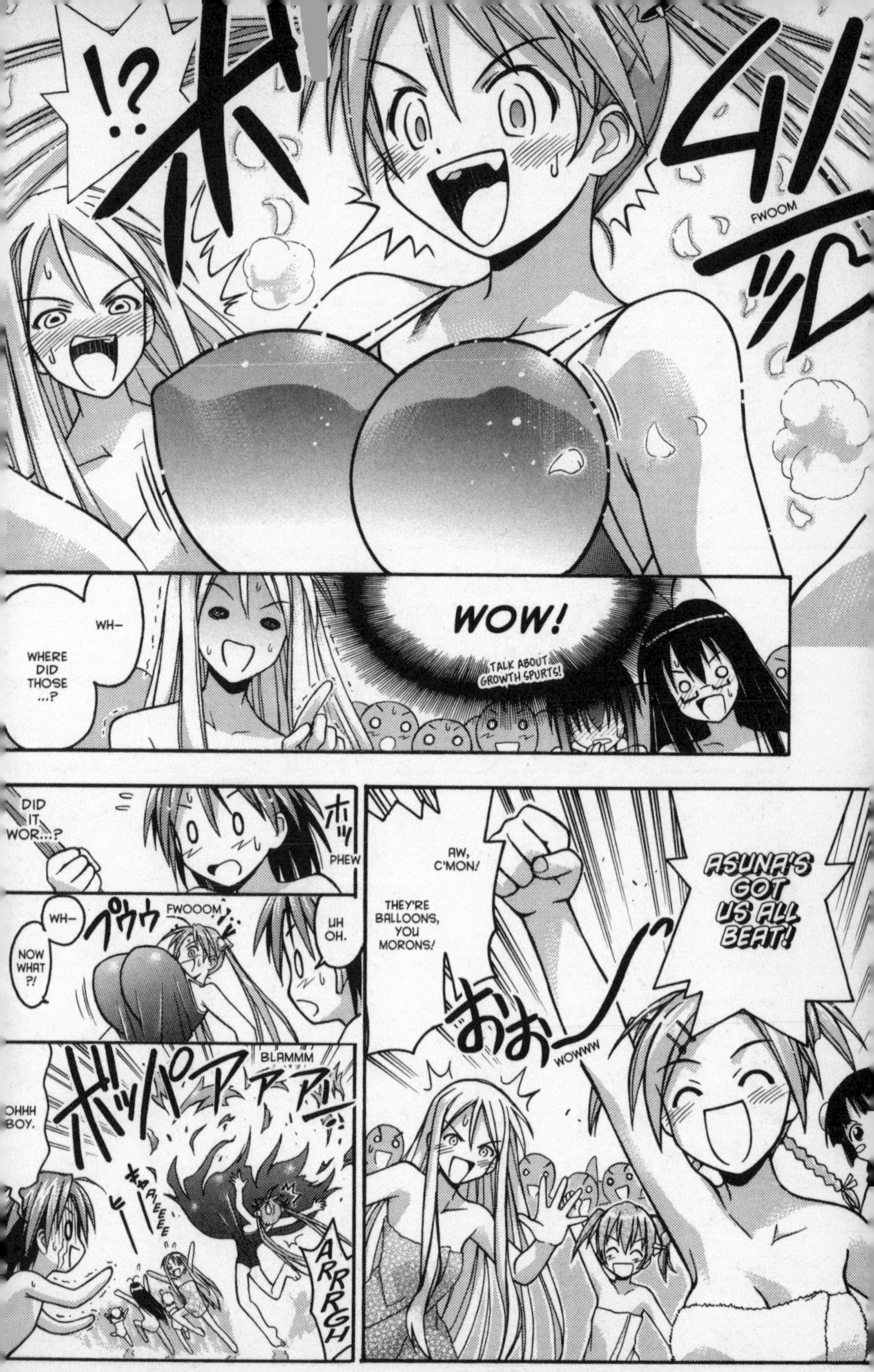
FWOOM
!?
WOW!
TALK ABOUT GROWTH SPURTS!
WH–
WHERE DID THOSE ...?
ASUNA'S GOT US ALL BEAT!
AW, C'MON!
THEY'RE BALLOONS, YOU MORONS!
おぉ〜
WOWWW
ホッ
PHEW
DID IT WOR...?
UH OH.
プウウ
FWOOOM
WH–
NOW WHAT?!
BLAMMM
ARRRGH
AIEEE
OHHH BOY.

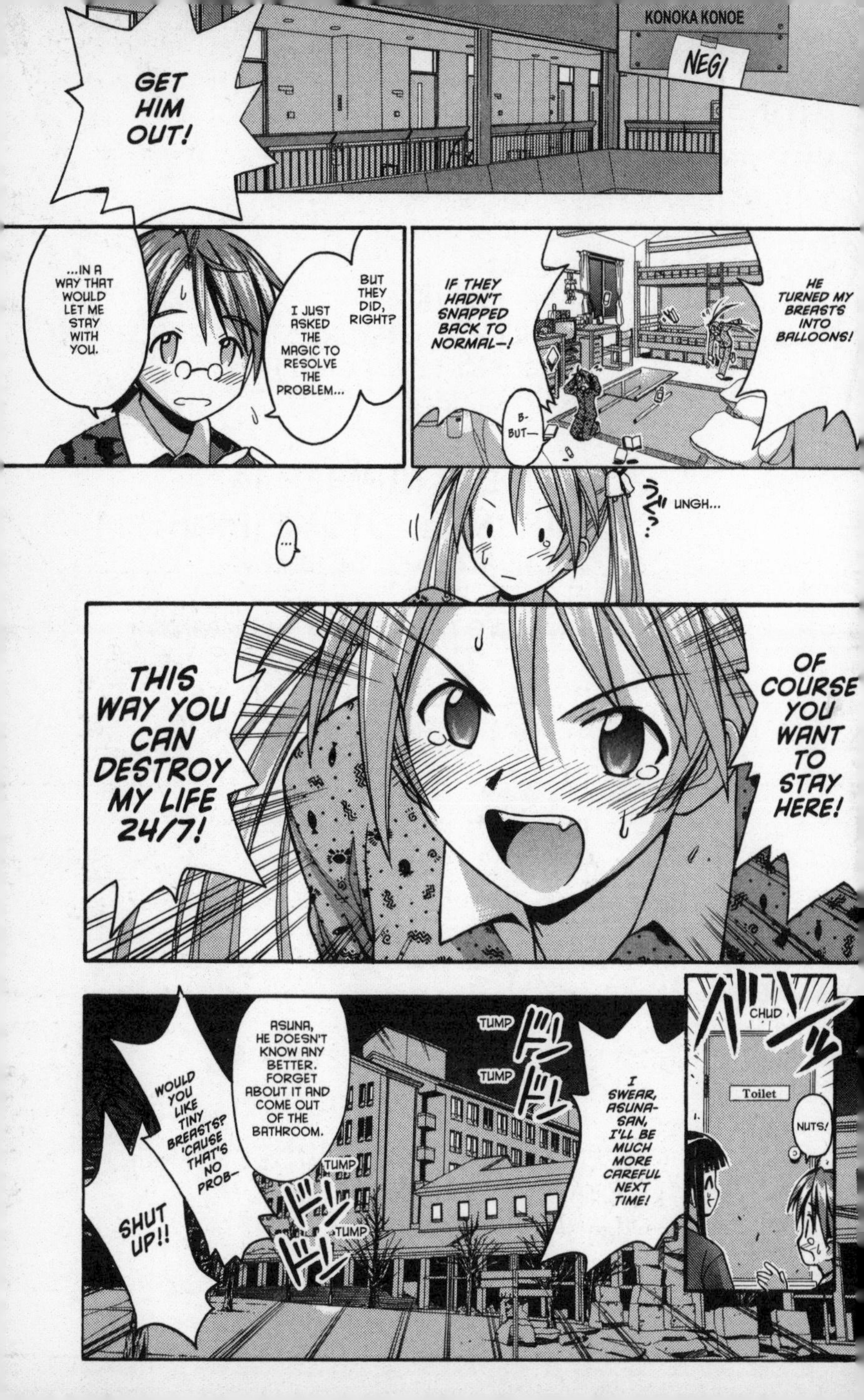
KONOKA KONOE
NEGI
GET HIM OUT!
HE TURNED MY BREASTS INTO BALLOONS!
IF THEY HADN'T SNAPPED BACK TO NORMAL—!
B-BUT—
BUT THEY DID, RIGHT?
I JUST ASKED THE MAGIC TO RESOLVE THE PROBLEM...
...IN A WAY THAT WOULD LET ME STAY WITH YOU.
UNGH...
...
OF COURSE YOU WANT TO STAY HERE!
THIS WAY YOU CAN DESTROY MY LIFE 24/7!
CHUD
Toilet
NUTS!
TUMP
TUMP
I SWEAR, ASUNA-SAN, I'LL BE MUCH MORE CAREFUL NEXT TIME!
ASUNA, HE DOESN'T KNOW ANY BETTER. FORGET ABOUT IT AND COME OUT OF THE BATHROOM.
TUMP
TUMP
WOULD YOU LIKE TINY BREASTS? 'CAUSE THAT'S NO PROB-
SHUT UP!!

2-A STUDENT PROFILE

STUDENT NUMBER 4
YUE AYASE (LEFT)
BIRTHDATE: NOVEMBER 16, 1988
BLOODTYPE: AB
FAVORITE THINGS: READING
DISLIKES: STUDYING FOR SCHOOL
CLUB ACTIVITIES: CHILDREN'S LITERATURE STUDY GROUP,
PHILOSOPHY STUDY GROUP,
LIBRARY CLUB

STUDENT NUMBER 14
HARUNA SAOTOME (RIGHT)
BIRTHDATE: AUGUST 18, 1988
BLOODTYPE: B
FAVORITE THINGS: TEA CEREMONY;
LOTS OF TROUBLE
DISLIKES: REPTILES, DEADLINES
CLUB ACTIVITIES: MANGA CLUB,
LIBRARY EXPLORATION
GROUP
REMARKS: PSEUDONYM "PAL"

STUDENT NUMBER 27
NODOKA MIYAZAKI (MIDDLE)
BIRTHDATE: MAY 10, 1988
BLOODTYPE: O
FAVORITE THINGS: TO BE SURROUNDED BY BOOKS,
ORGANIZING BOOKS
DISLIKES: GUYS
CLUB ACTIVITIES: GENERAL LIBRARY COMMITTEE MEMBER,
LIBRARY REPRESENTATIVE,
LIBRARY CLUB

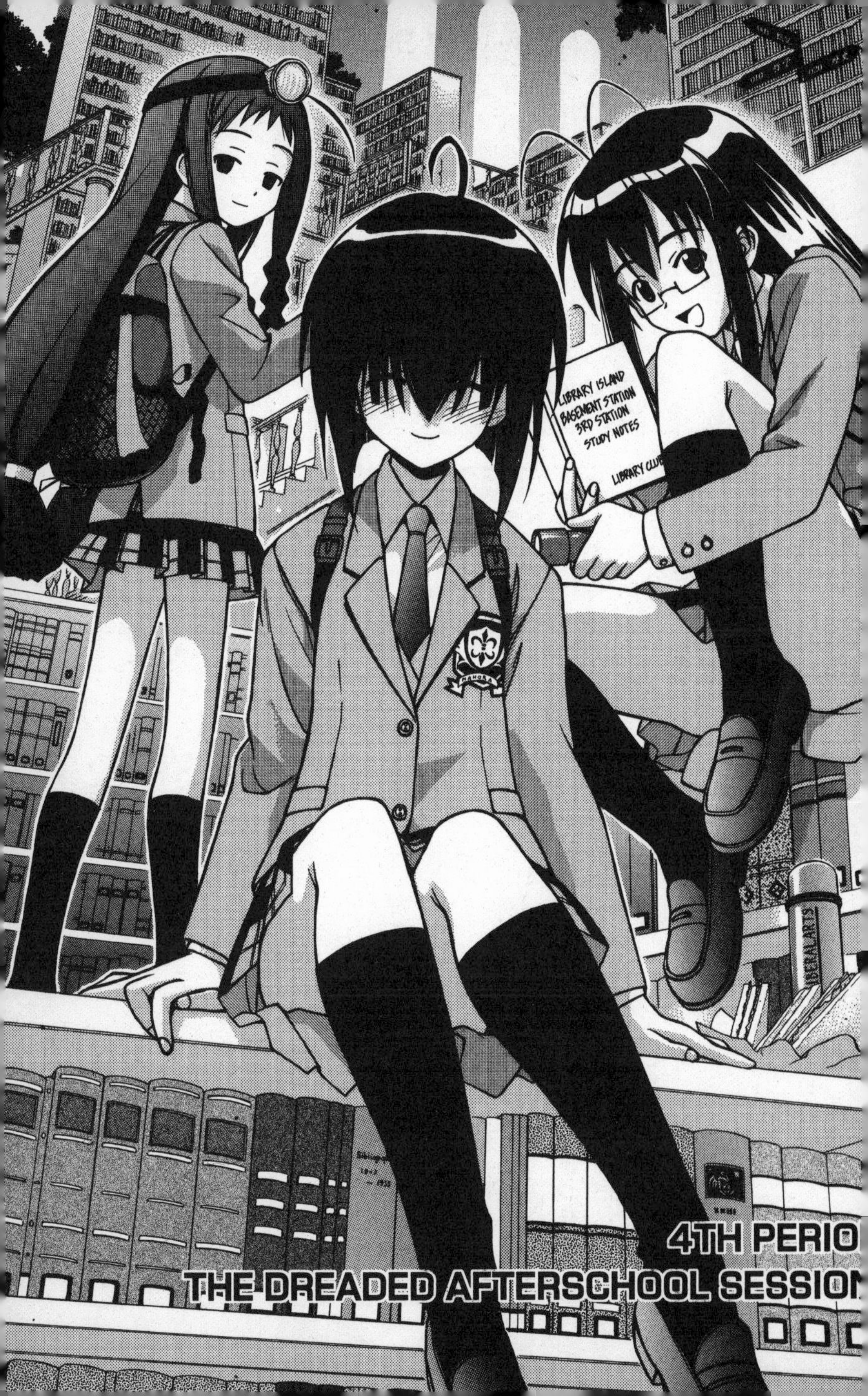
LIBRARY ISLAND
BASEMENT STATION
3RD STATION
STUDY NOTES
LIBRARY CLUB
LIBERAL ARTS
4TH PERIO
THE DREADED AFTERSCHOOL SESSION

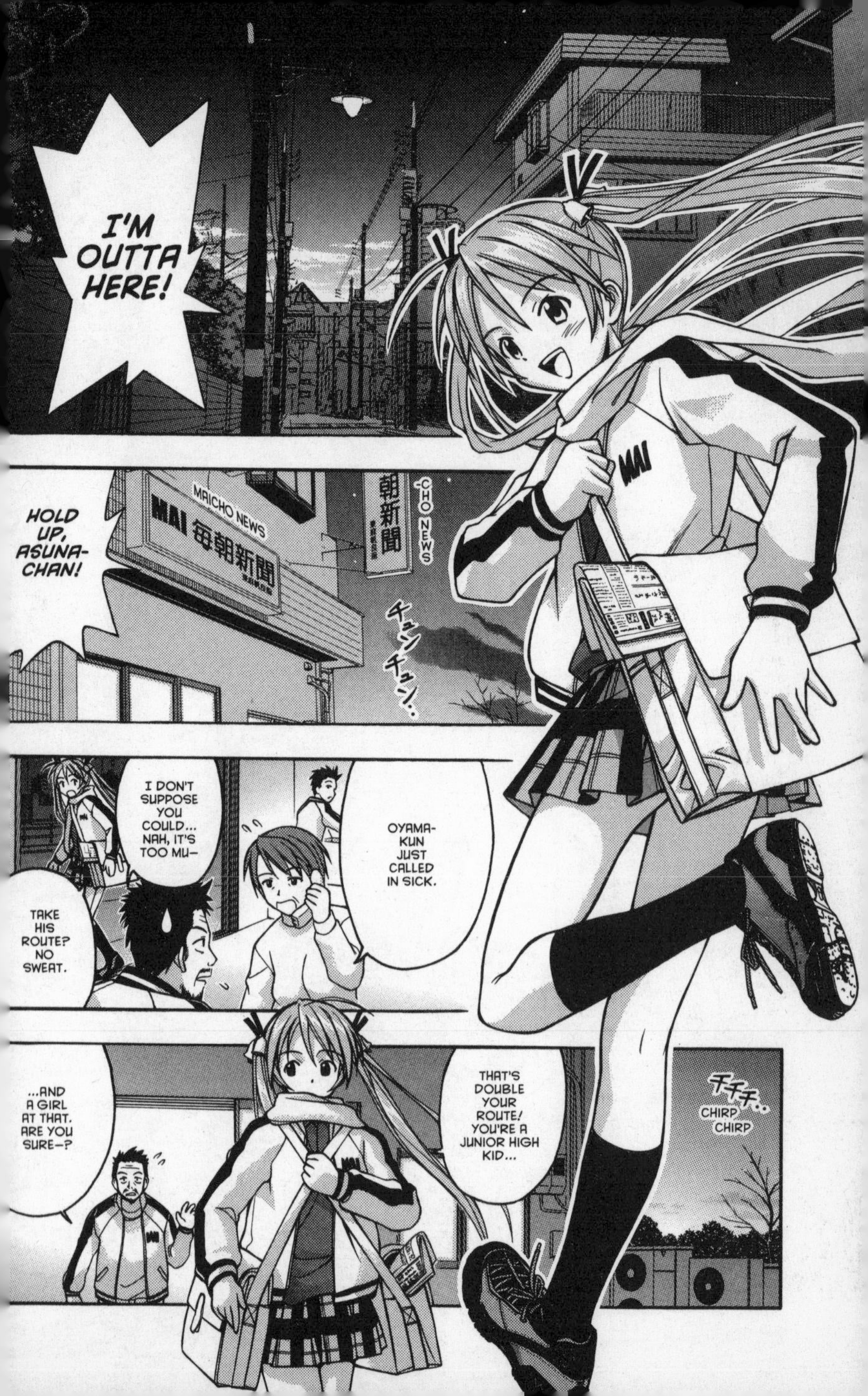
I'M OUTTA HERE!
チュンチュン..
-CHO NEWS
朝新聞
MAICHO NEWS
MAI 毎朝新聞
HOLD UP, ASUNA-CHAN!
OYAMA-KUN JUST CALLED IN SICK.
I DON'T SUPPOSE YOU COULD... NAH, IT'S TOO MU–
TAKE HIS ROUTE? NO SWEAT.
MAI
チチチ..
CHIRP CHIRP
THAT'S DOUBLE YOUR ROUTE! YOU'RE A JUNIOR HIGH KID...
...AND A GIRL AT THAT. ARE YOU SURE–?
MAI

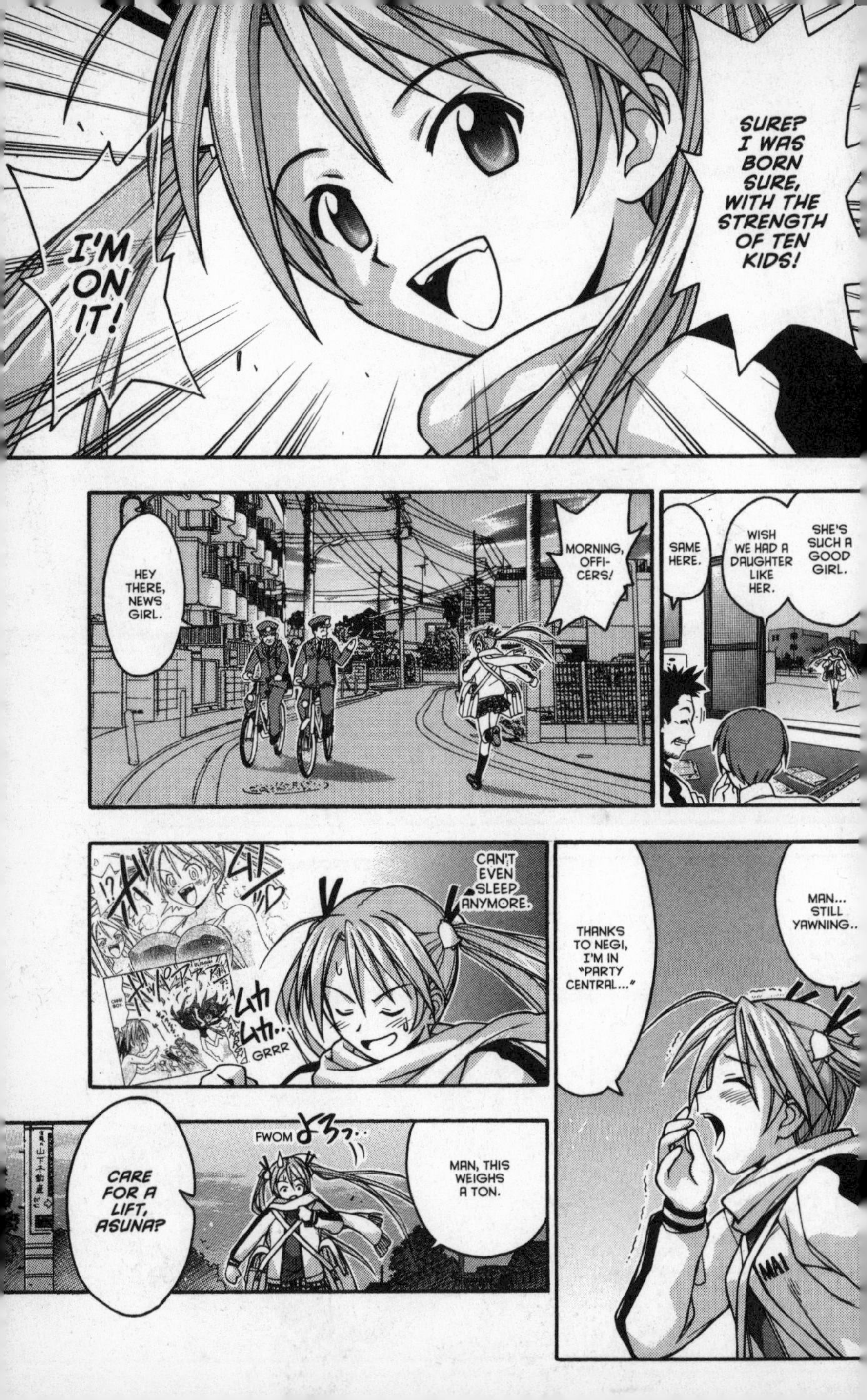
SURE? I WAS BORN SURE, WITH THE STRENGTH OF TEN KIDS!
I'M ON IT!
SHE'S SUCH A GOOD GIRL.
WISH WE HAD A DAUGHTER LIKE HER.
SAME HERE.
MORNING, OFFICERS!
HEY THERE, NEWS GIRL.
MAN... STILL YAWNING...
THANKS TO NEGI, I'M IN "PARTY CENTRAL..."
MAI
CAN'T EVEN SLEEP ANYMORE.
GRRR
MAN, THIS WEIGHS A TON.
FWOM
CARE FOR A LIFT, ASUNA?

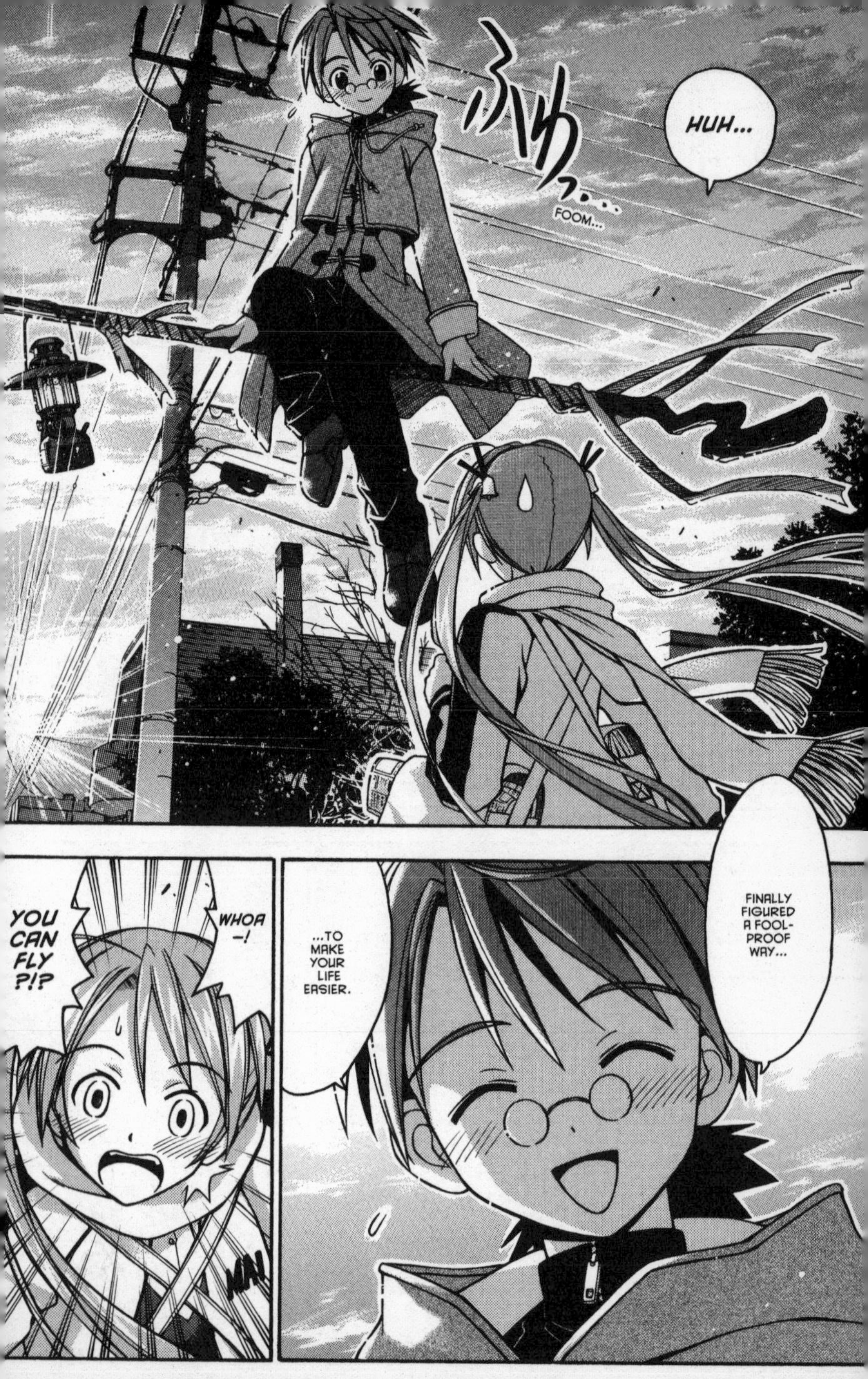
ふわっ…
FOOM...
HUH...
FINALLY FIGURED A FOOL-PROOF WAY...
...TO MAKE YOUR LIFE EASIER.
WHOA—!
YOU CAN FLY?!?

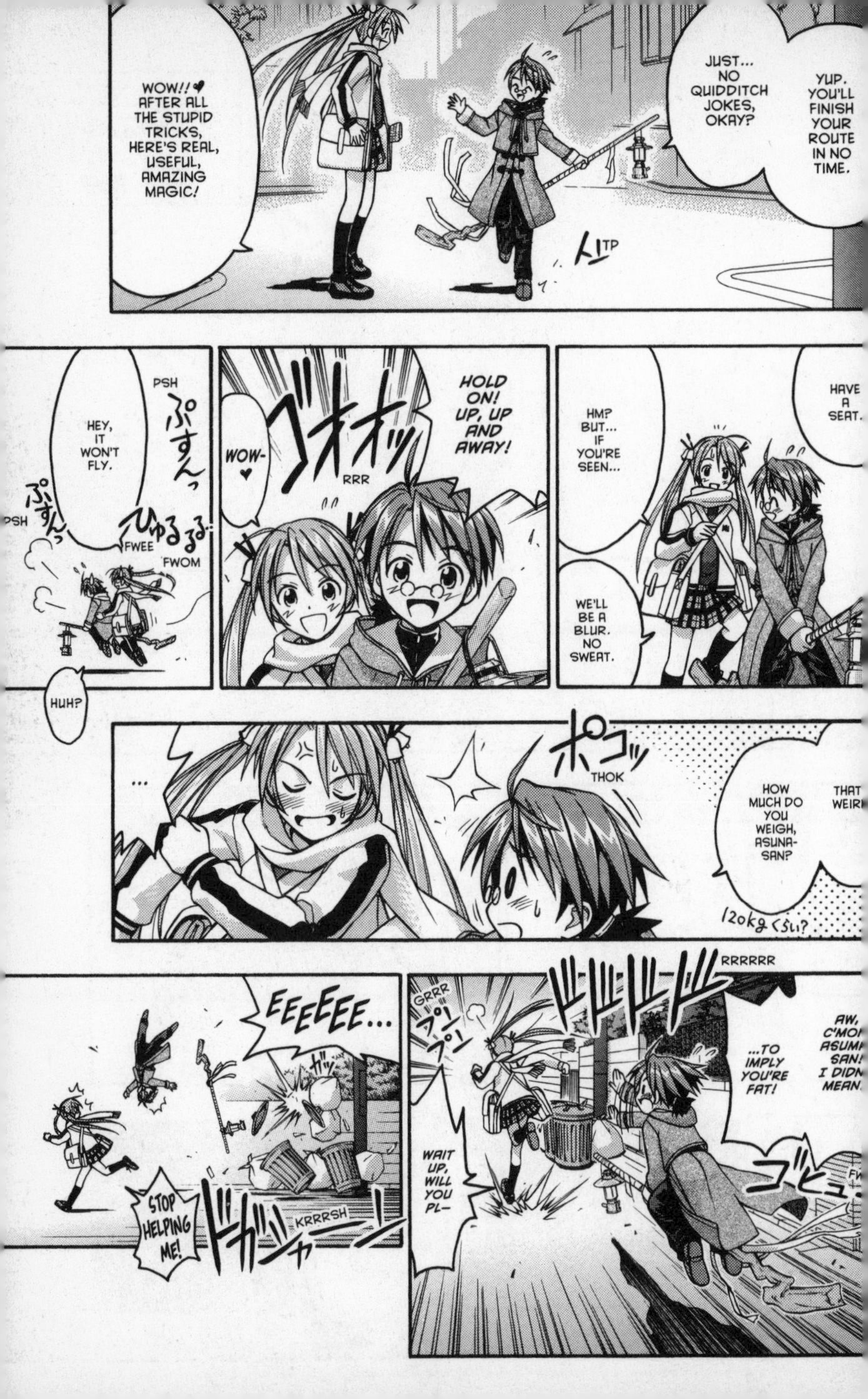

YUP. YOU'LL FINISH YOUR ROUTE IN NO TIME.
JUST... NO QUIDDITCH JOKES, OKAY?
TP
WOW!!♥ AFTER ALL THE STUPID TRICKS, HERE'S REAL, USEFUL, AMAZING MAGIC!
HAVE A SEAT.
HM? BUT... IF YOU'RE SEEN...
WE'LL BE A BLUR. NO SWEAT.
HOLD ON! UP, UP AND AWAY!
ゴオオッ
RRR
WOW-♥
PSH
ぷすんっ
HEY, IT WON'T FLY.
ひゅるるる
FWEE
FWOM
ぷすんっ
PSH
HUH?
THAT WEIR
HOW MUCH DO YOU WEIGH, ASUNA-SAN?
120kgくらい?
ポコッ
THOK
...
AW, C'MO ASUNA SAN! I DIDN MEAN
...TO IMPLY YOU'RE FAT!
ドドドド
RRRRRR
GRRR
プンプン
ゴヒュ
WAIT UP, WILL YOU PL—
EEEEEE...
ガッ
STOP HELPING ME!
ドガシャ
KRRRSH

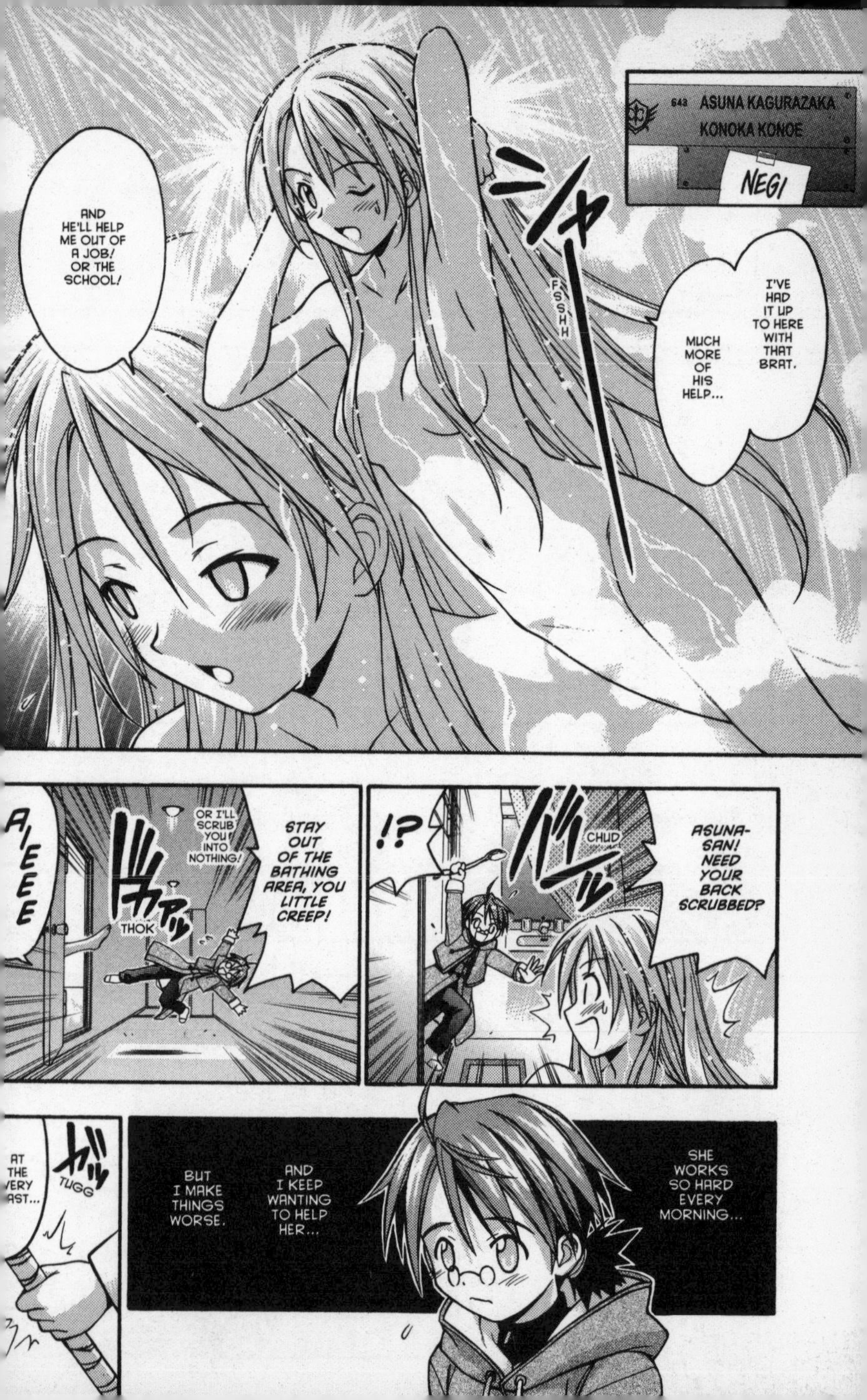
643 ASUNA KAGURAZAKA
KONOKA KONOE
NEGI
I'VE HAD IT UP TO HERE WITH THAT BRAT.
MUCH MORE OF HIS HELP...
FSSHH
AND HE'LL HELP ME OUT OF A JOB! OR THE SCHOOL!
ASUNA-SAN! NEED YOUR BACK SCRUBBED?
CHUD
!?
STAY OUT OF THE BATHING AREA, YOU LITTLE CREEP!
OR I'LL SCRUB YOU INTO NOTHING!
THOK
AIEEE
SHE WORKS SO HARD EVERY MORNING...
AND I KEEP WANTING TO HELP HER...
BUT I MAKE THINGS WORSE.
TUGG
AT THE ERY AST...

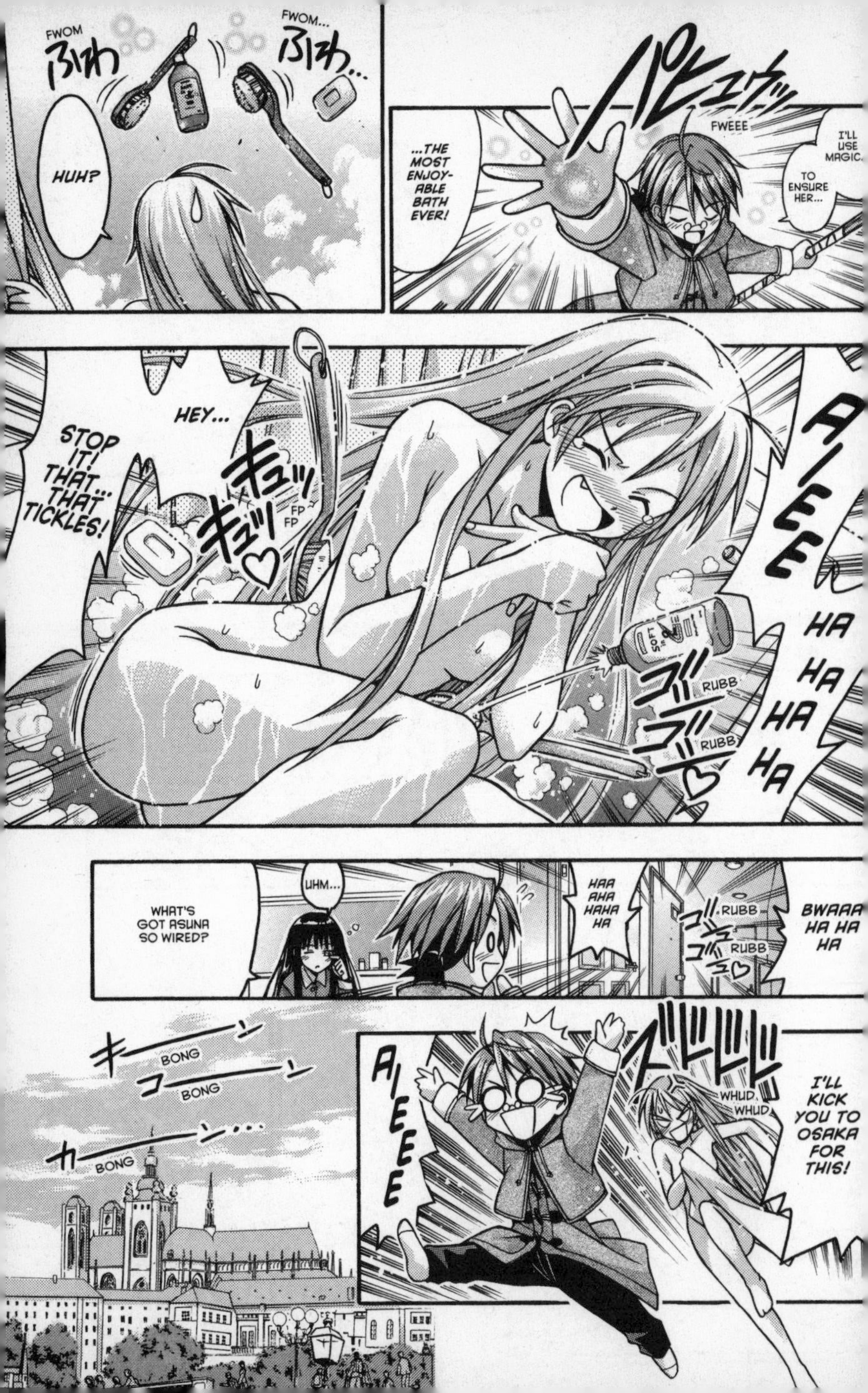
FWEEE
I'LL USE MAGIC...
TO ENSURE HER...
...THE MOST ENJOY-ABLE BATH EVER!
FWOM... ふわ...
FWOM ふわ
HUH?
AIEEE
HA HA HA HA HA
RUBB
RUBB
HEY...
STOP IT! THAT... THAT TICKLES!
FP FP
BWAAA HA HA HA
RUBB
RUBB
HAA AHA HAHA HA
UHM...
WHAT'S GOT ASUNA SO WIRED?
I'LL KICK YOU TO OSAKA FOR THIS!
WHUD, WHUD
AIEEE
BONG
BONG
BONG

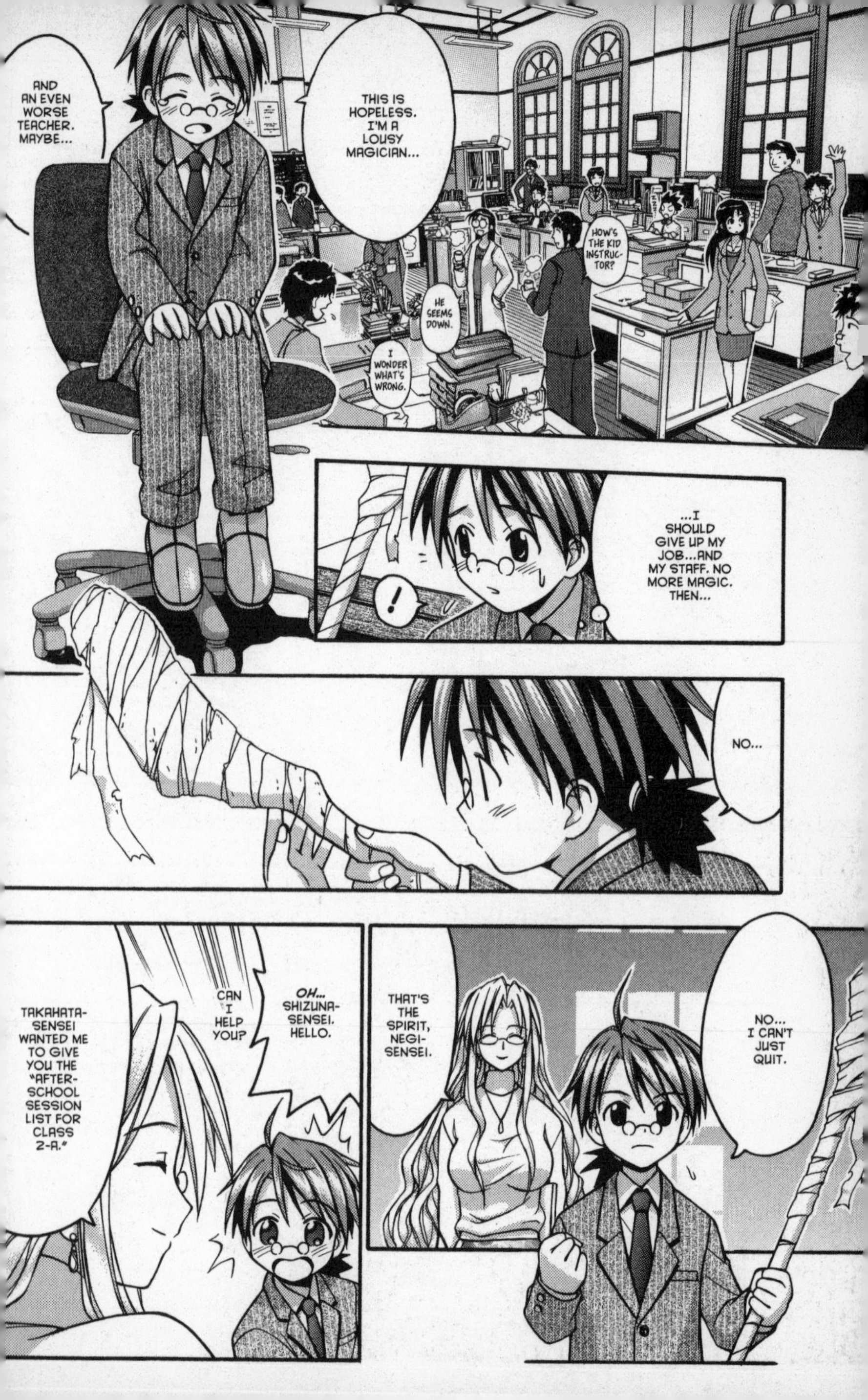
HOW'S THE KID INSTRUCTOR?
HE SEEMS DOWN.
I WONDER WHAT'S WRONG.
THIS IS HOPELESS. I'M A LOUSY MAGICIAN...
AND AN EVEN WORSE TEACHER. MAYBE...
...I SHOULD GIVE UP MY JOB...AND MY STAFF. NO MORE MAGIC. THEN...
!
NO...
NO... I CAN'T JUST QUIT.
THAT'S THE SPIRIT, NEGI-SENSEI.
OH... SHIZUNA-SENSEI. HELLO.
CAN I HELP YOU?
TAKAHATA-SENSEI WANTED ME TO GIVE YOU THE "AFTER-SCHOOL SESSION LIST FOR CLASS 2-A."

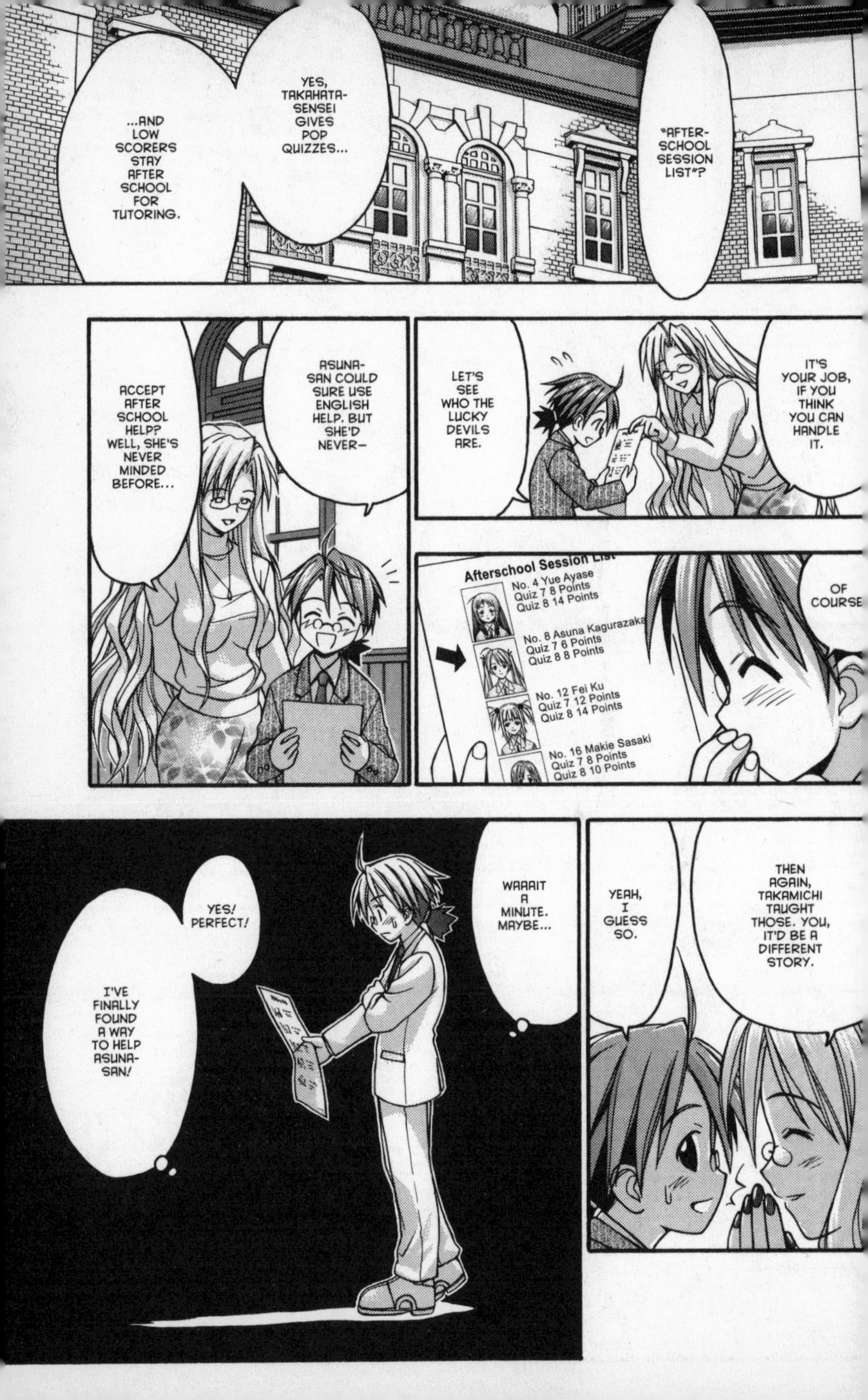
"AFTER-SCHOOL SESSION LIST"?
YES, TAKAHATA-SENSEI GIVES POP QUIZZES...
...AND LOW SCORERS STAY AFTER SCHOOL FOR TUTORING.
IT'S YOUR JOB, IF YOU THINK YOU CAN HANDLE IT.
LET'S SEE WHO THE LUCKY DEVILS ARE.
OF COURSE
Afterschool Session List
No. 4 Yue Ayase Quiz 7 8 Points Quiz 8 14 Points
No. 8 Asuna Kagurazaka Quiz 7 6 Points Quiz 8 8 Points
No. 12 Fei Ku Quiz 7 12 Points Quiz 8 14 Points
No. 16 Makie Sasaki Quiz 7 8 Points Quiz 8 10 Points
ASUNA-SAN COULD SURE USE ENGLISH HELP. BUT SHE'D NEVER—
ACCEPT AFTER SCHOOL HELP? WELL, SHE'S NEVER MINDED BEFORE...
THEN AGAIN, TAKAMICHI TAUGHT THOSE. YOU, IT'D BE A DIFFERENT STORY.
YEAH, I GUESS SO.
WAAAIT A MINUTE. MAYBE...
YES! PERFECT!
I'VE FINALLY FOUND A WAY TO HELP ASUNA-SAN!

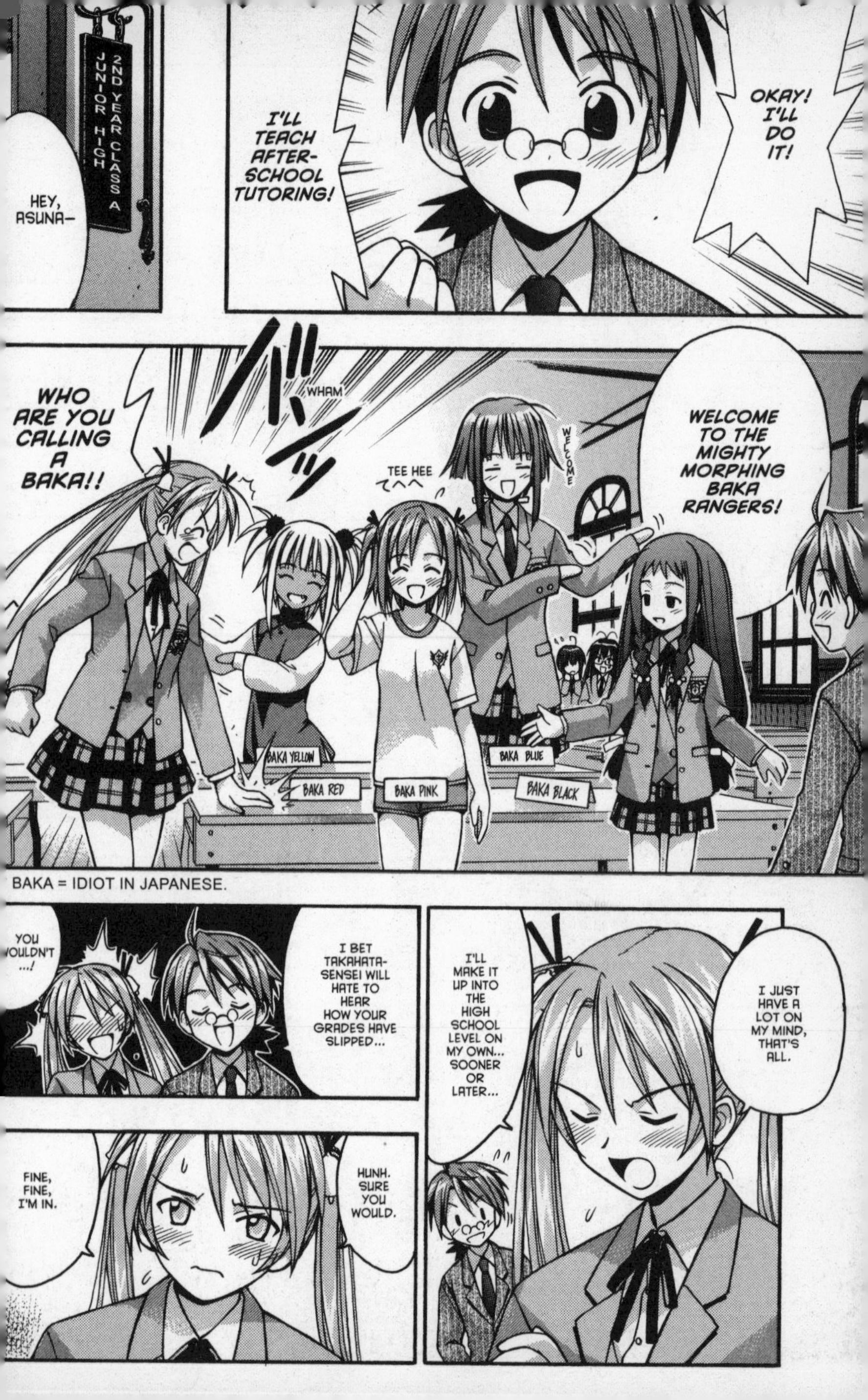
OKAY! I'LL DO IT!
I'LL TEACH AFTER-SCHOOL TUTORING!
2ND YEAR CLASS A JUNIOR HIGH
HEY, ASUNA—
WELCOME TO THE MIGHTY MORPHING BAKA RANGERS!
WELCOME
TEE HEE てへへ
WHAM
WHO ARE YOU CALLING A BAKA!!
BAKA BLUE
BAKA BLACK
BAKA PINK
BAKA YELLOW
BAKA RED
I JUST HAVE A LOT ON MY MIND, THAT'S ALL.
I'LL MAKE IT UP INTO THE HIGH SCHOOL LEVEL ON MY OWN... SOONER OR LATER...
I BET TAKAHATA-SENSEI WILL HATE TO HEAR HOW YOUR GRADES HAVE SLIPPED...
YOU WOULDN'T ...!
HUNH. SURE YOU WOULD.
FINE, FINE, I'M IN.

BAKA = IDIOT IN JAPANESE.

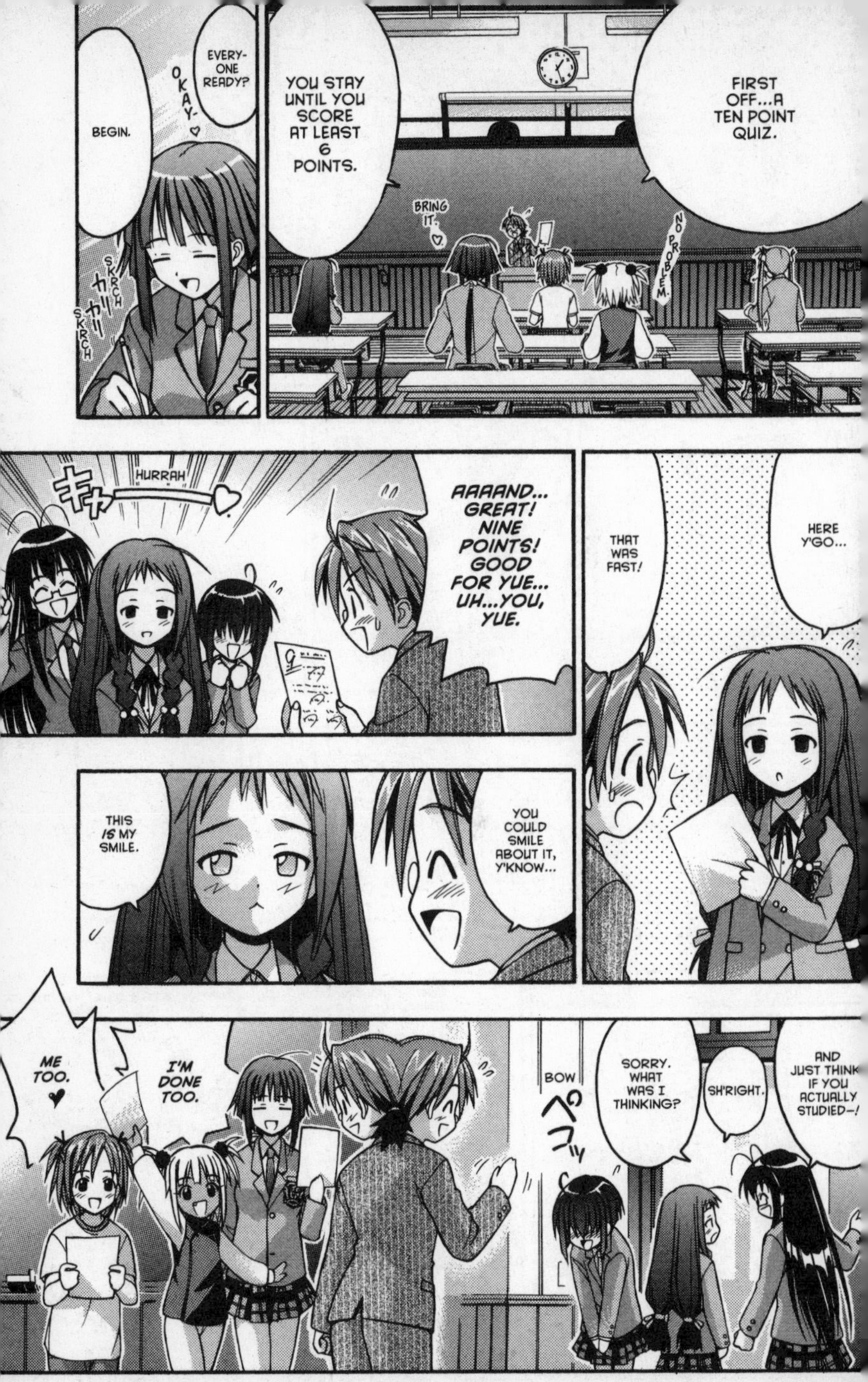
FIRST OFF...A TEN POINT QUIZ.
NO PROBLEM.
YOU STAY UNTIL YOU SCORE AT LEAST 6 POINTS.
BRING IT. ♥
EVERY-ONE READY?
OKAY-♥
BEGIN.
SKRCH
SKRCH
HERE Y'GO...
THAT WAS FAST!
AAAAND... GREAT! NINE POINTS! GOOD FOR YUE... UH...YOU, YUE.
HURRAH
YOU COULD SMILE ABOUT IT, Y'KNOW...
THIS *IS* MY SMILE.
AND JUST THINK IF YOU ACTUALLY STUDIED—!
SH'RIGHT.
SORRY. WHAT WAS I THINKING?
BOW
I'M DONE TOO.
ME TOO. ♥

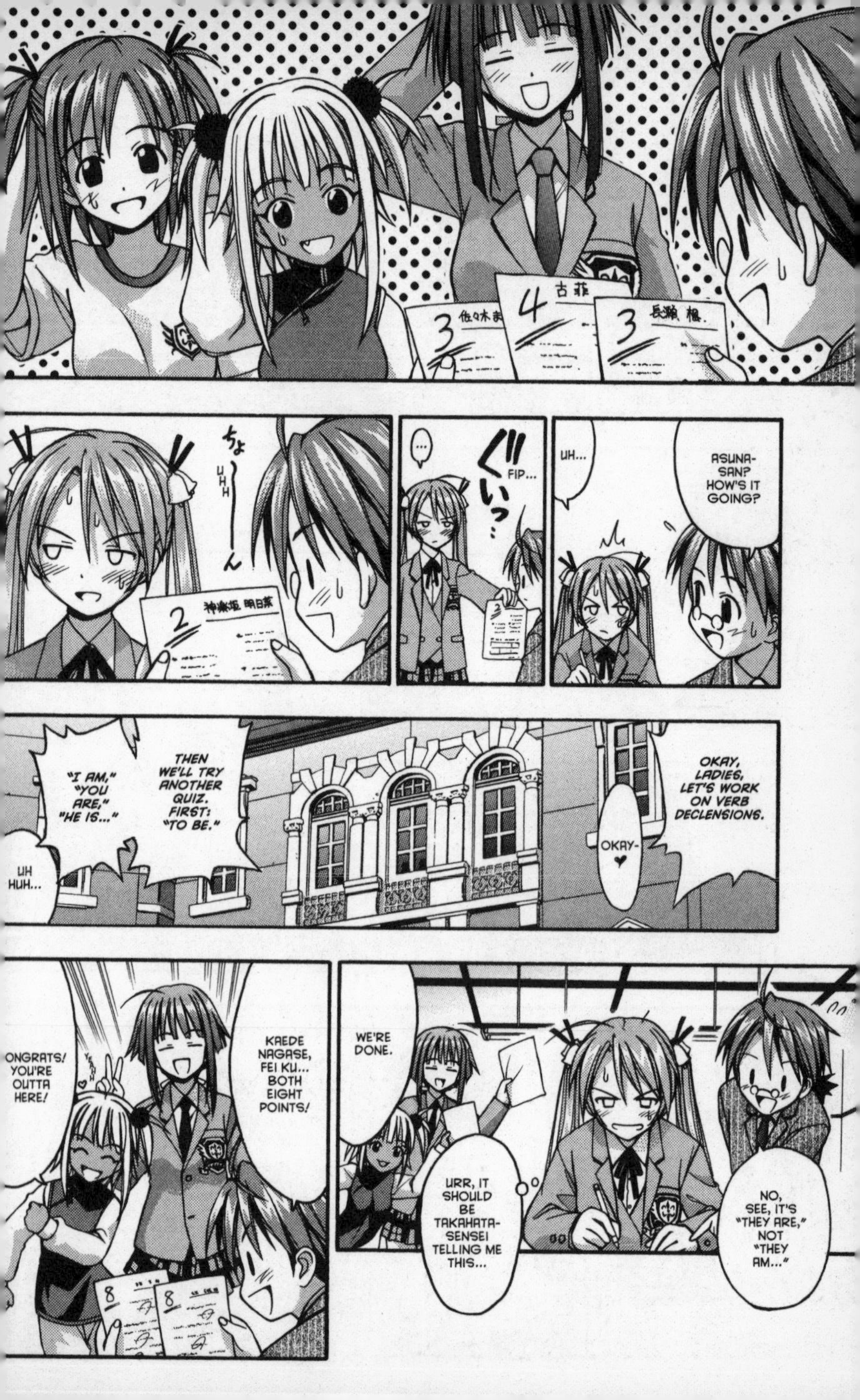

3 長瀬 楓.
4 古菲
3 佐々木ま
ASUNA-SAN? HOW'S IT GOING?
UH...
...
ぐいっ
FIP...
ちょ～ん
UHH
2 神楽坂 明日菜
OKAY, LADIES, LET'S WORK ON VERB DECLENSIONS.
OKAY-♥
THEN WE'LL TRY ANOTHER QUIZ. FIRST: "TO BE."
"I AM," "YOU ARE," "HE IS..."
UH HUH...
NO, SEE, IT'S "THEY ARE," NOT "THEY AM..."
URR, IT SHOULD BE TAKAHATA-SENSEI TELLING ME THIS...
WE'RE DONE.
KAEDE NAGASE, FEI KU... BOTH EIGHT POINTS!
ONGRATS! YOU'RE OUTTA HERE!

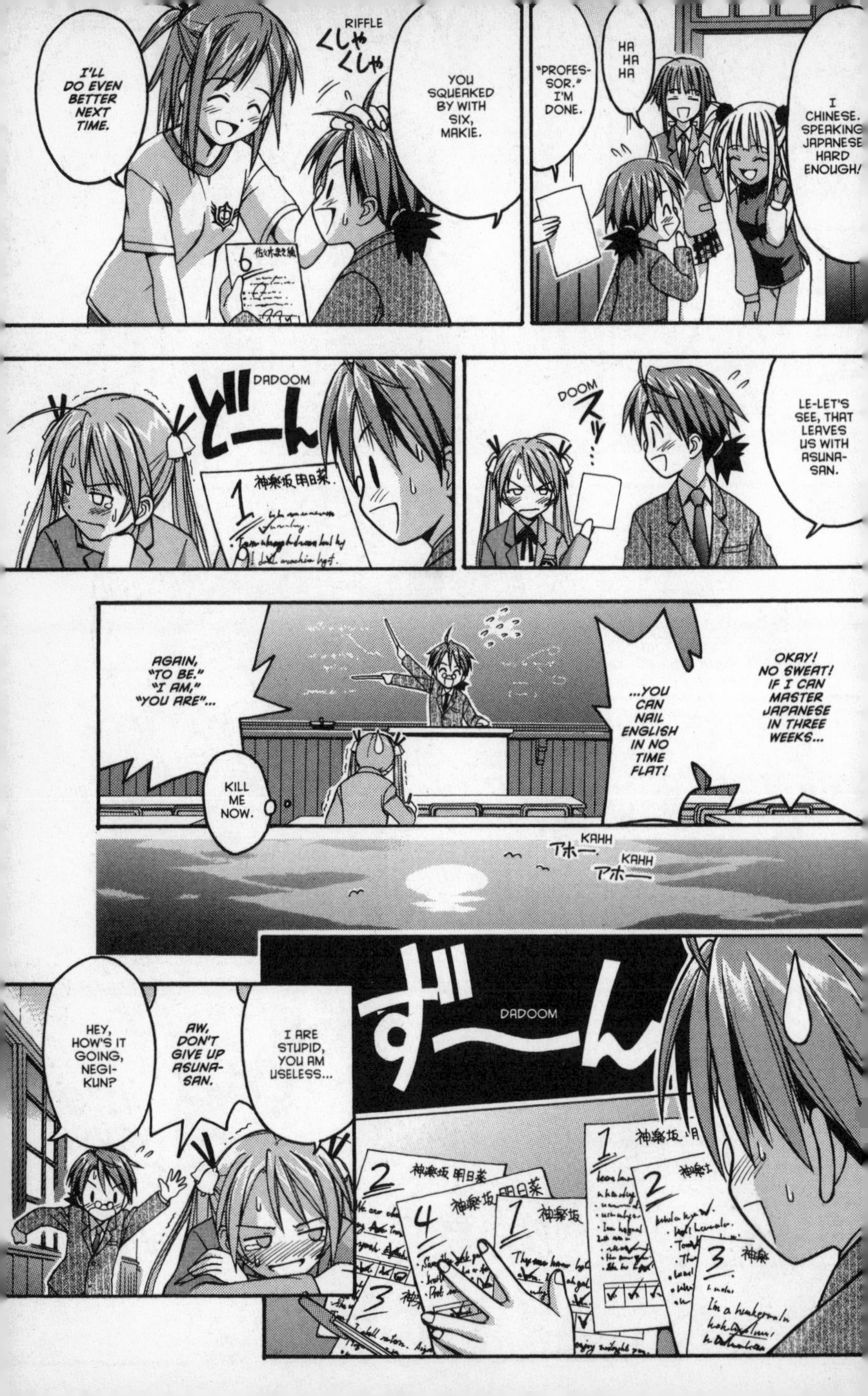
I CHINESE. SPEAKING JAPANESE HARD ENOUGH!
HA HA HA
"PROFES-SOR." I'M DONE.
YOU SQUEAKED BY WITH SIX, MAKIE.
RIFFLE
くしゃくしゃ
I'LL DO EVEN BETTER NEXT TIME.
LE-LET'S SEE, THAT LEAVES US WITH ASUNA-SAN.
DOOM
スッ…
DADOOM
どーん
神楽坂明日菜
OKAY! NO SWEAT! IF I CAN MASTER JAPANESE IN THREE WEEKS...
...YOU CAN NAIL ENGLISH IN NO TIME FLAT!
AGAIN, "TO BE." "I AM," "YOU ARE"...
KILL ME NOW.
KAHH
アホー
KAHH
アホー
ずーん
DADOOM
I ARE STUPID, YOU AM USELESS...
AW, DON'T GIVE UP ASUNA-SAN.
HEY, HOW'S IT GOING, NEGI-KUN?

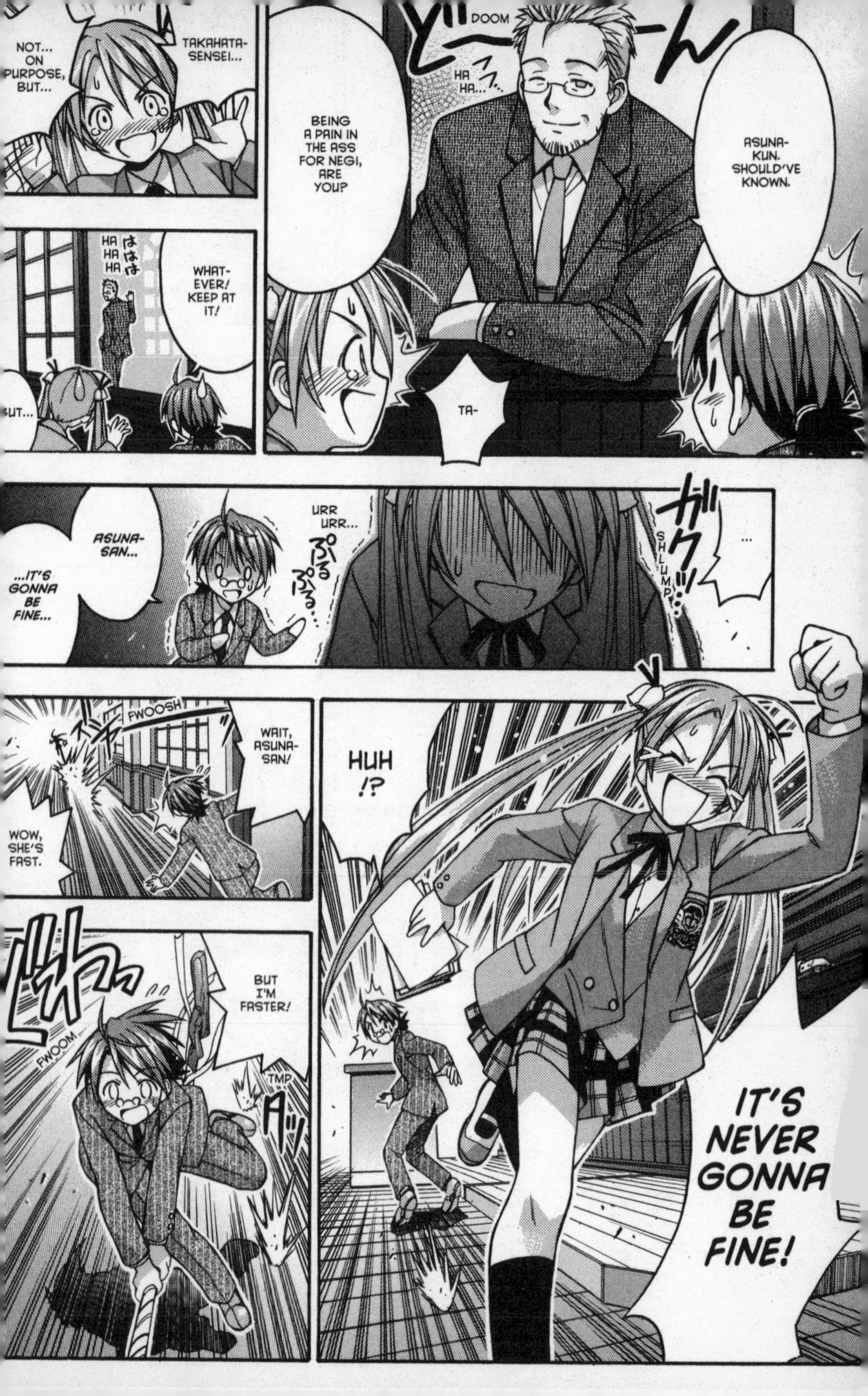

ASUNA-KUN. SHOULD'VE KNOWN.
DOOM
HA HA...
BEING A PAIN IN THE ASS FOR NEGI, ARE YOU?
TA-
TAKAHATA-SENSEI...
NOT... ON PURPOSE, BUT...
HA HA HA
ははは
WHAT-EVER! KEEP AT IT!
UT...
...
SHLUMP
URR URR...
ぷるぷる...
ASUNA-SAN...
...IT'S GONNA BE FINE...
HUH !?
IT'S NEVER GONNA BE FINE!
FWOOSH
WAIT, ASUNA-SAN!
WOW, SHE'S FAST.
BUT I'M FASTER!
FWOOM
TMP

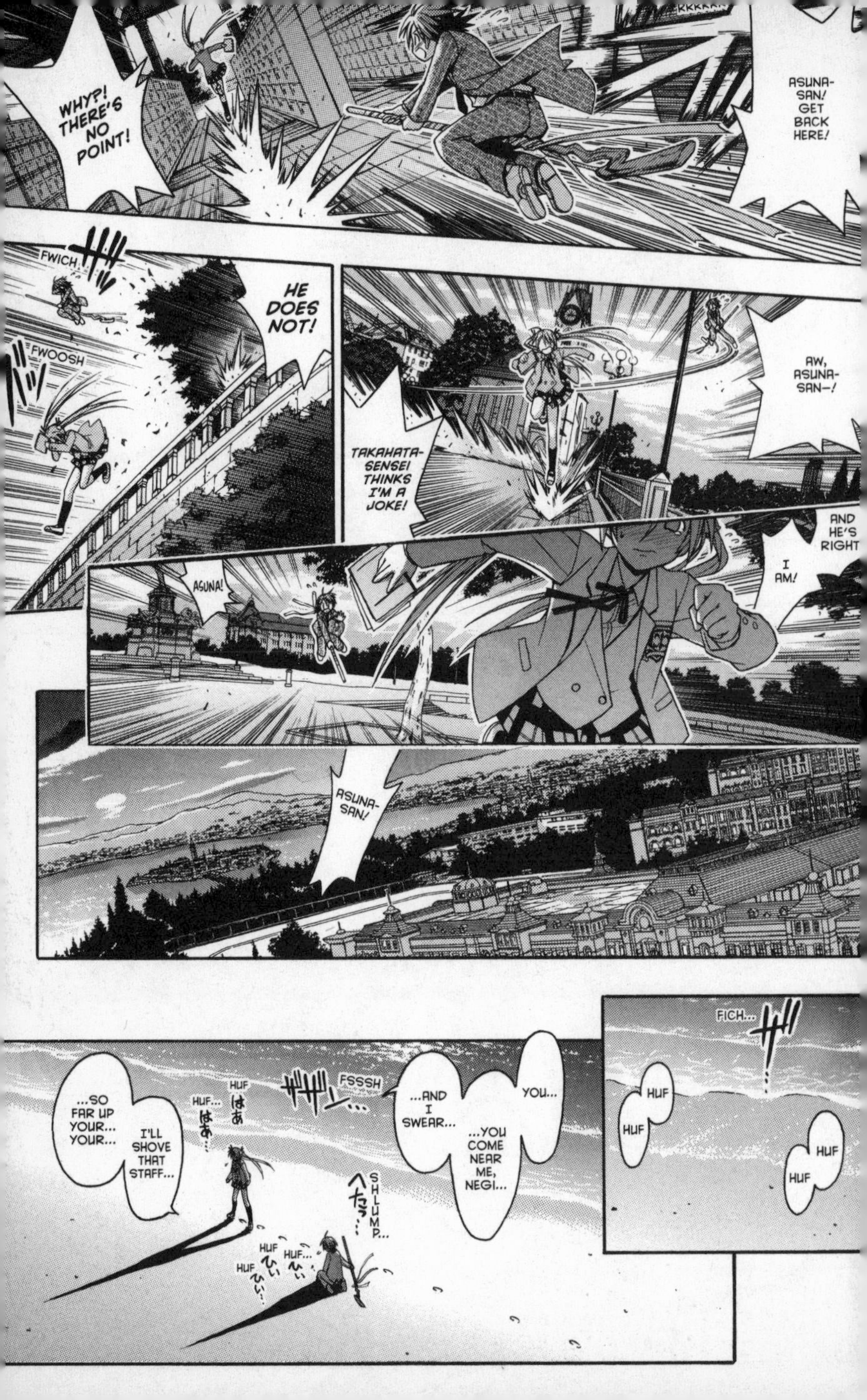
ASUNA-SAN! GET BACK HERE!
WHY?! THERE'S NO POINT!
AW, ASUNA-SAN—!
TAKAHATA-SENSEI THINKS I'M A JOKE!
FWICH
HE DOES NOT!
FWOOSH
AND HE'S RIGHT
I AM!
ASUNA!
ASUNA-SAN!
FICH...
HUF
HUF
HUF
HUF
YOU...
...YOU COME NEAR ME, NEGI...
...AND I SWEAR...
FSSSH
I'LL SHOVE THAT STAFF...
...SO FAR UP YOUR... YOUR...
HUF...
HUF
SHLUMP...
HUF...
HUF
HUF

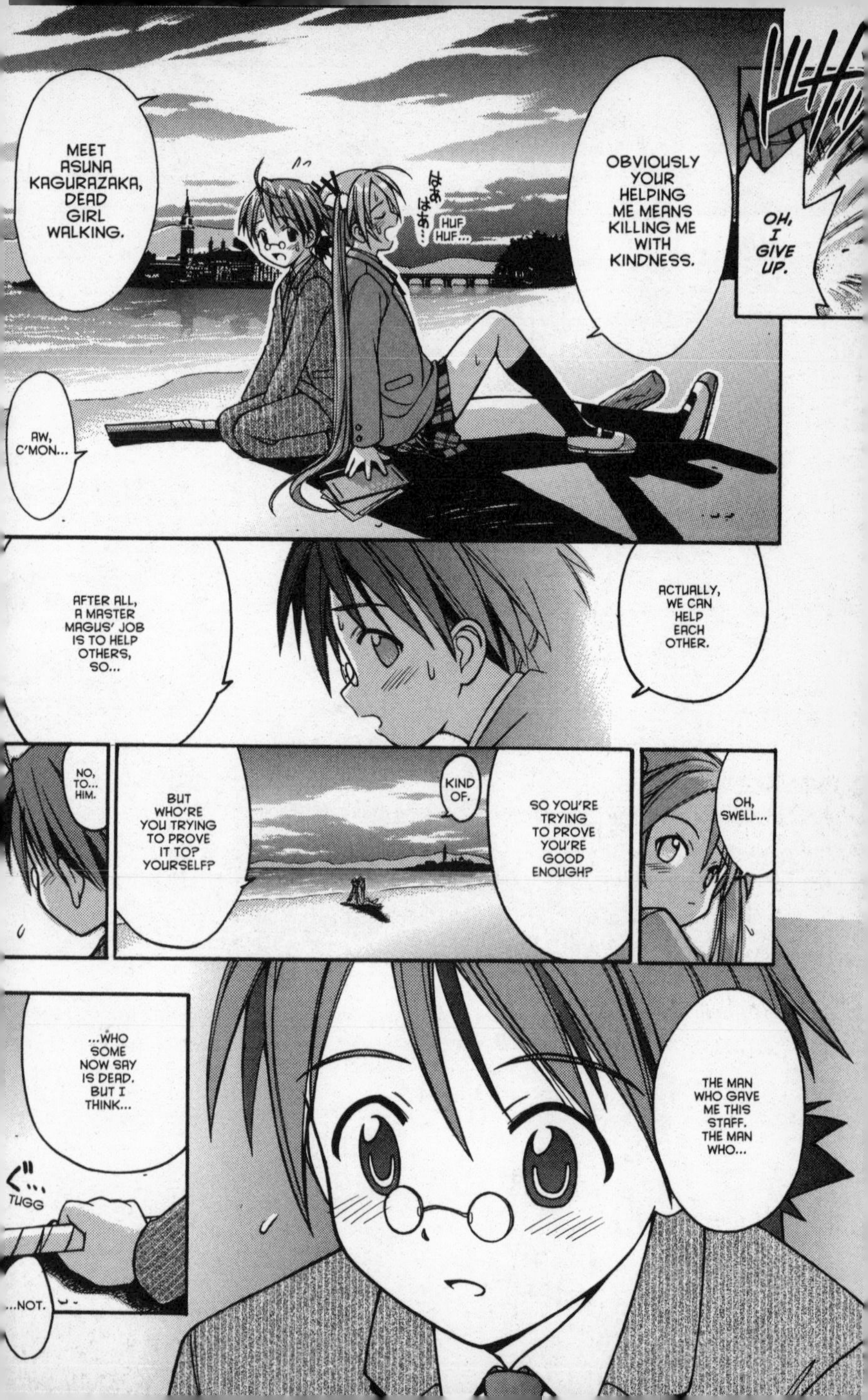
OH, I GIVE UP.
OBVIOUSLY YOUR HELPING ME MEANS KILLING ME WITH KINDNESS.
はあ はあ… HUF HUF...
MEET ASUNA KAGURAZAKA, DEAD GIRL WALKING.
AW, C'MON...
ACTUALLY, WE CAN HELP EACH OTHER.
AFTER ALL, A MASTER MAGUS' JOB IS TO HELP OTHERS, SO...
OH, SWELL...
SO YOU'RE TRYING TO PROVE YOU'RE GOOD ENOUGH?
KIND OF.
BUT WHO'RE YOU TRYING TO PROVE IT TO? YOURSELF?
NO, TO... HIM.
THE MAN WHO GAVE ME THIS STAFF. THE MAN WHO...
...WHO SOME NOW SAY IS DEAD. BUT I THINK...
ぐ… TUGG
...NOT.

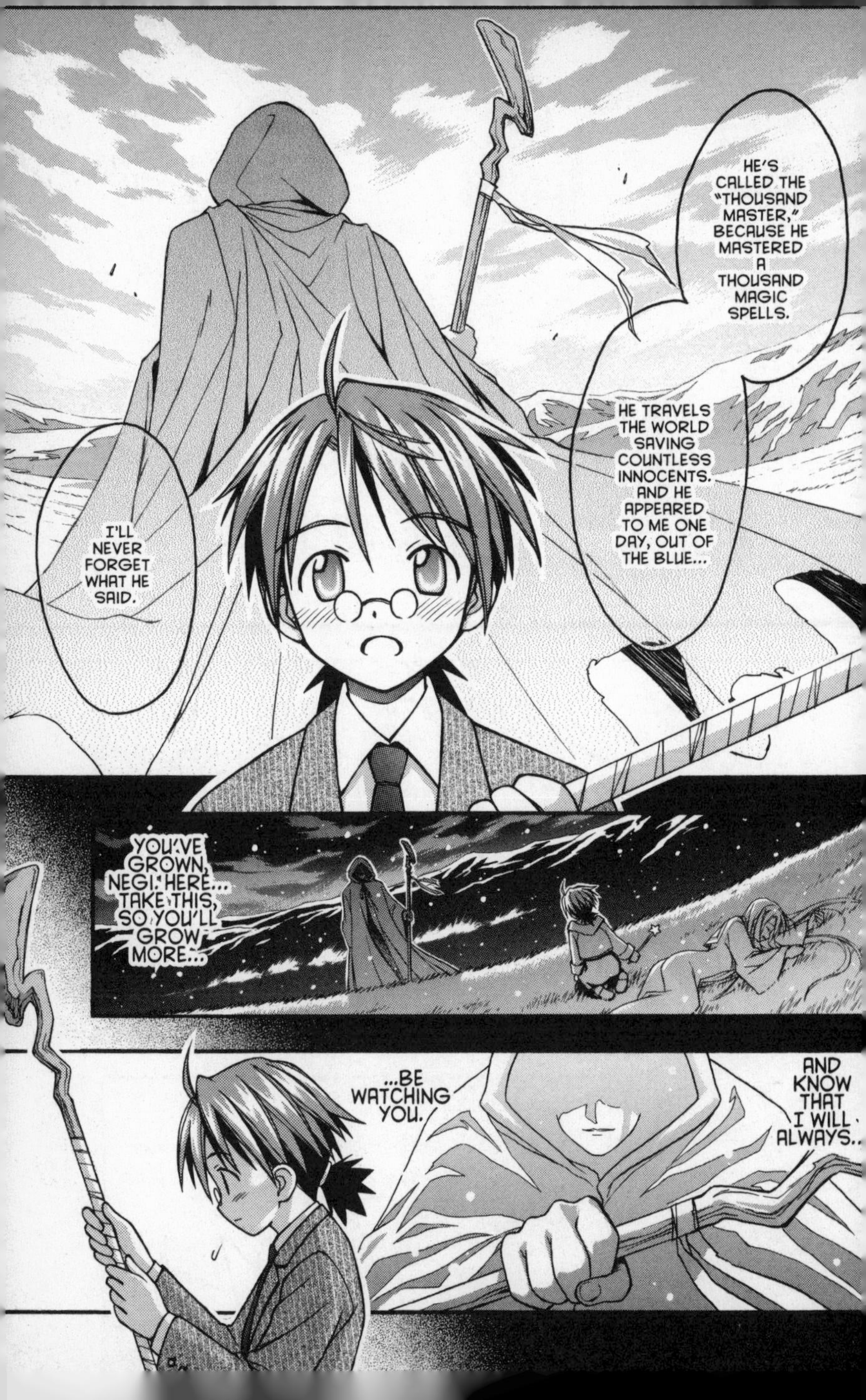
HE'S CALLED THE "THOUSAND MASTER," BECAUSE HE MASTERED A THOUSAND MAGIC SPELLS.
HE TRAVELS THE WORLD SAVING COUNTLESS INNOCENTS. AND HE APPEARED TO ME ONE DAY, OUT OF THE BLUE...
I'LL NEVER FORGET WHAT HE SAID.
YOU'VE GROWN, NEGI. HERE... TAKE THIS, SO YOU'LL GROW MORE...
AND KNOW THAT I WILL ALWAYS...
...BE WATCHING YOU.

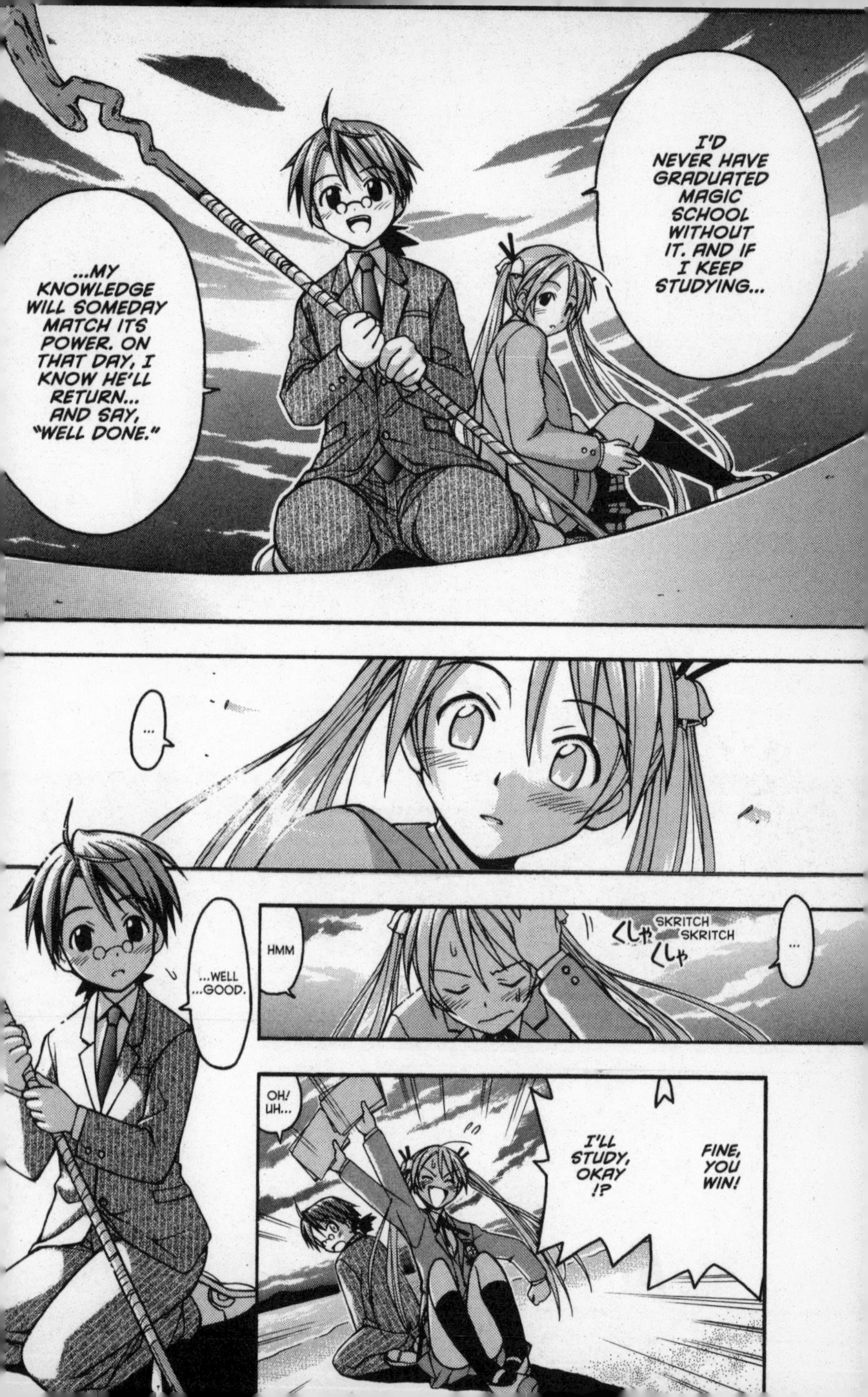
I'D NEVER HAVE GRADUATED MAGIC SCHOOL WITHOUT IT. AND IF I KEEP STUDYING...
...MY KNOWLEDGE WILL SOMEDAY MATCH ITS POWER. ON THAT DAY, I KNOW HE'LL RETURN... AND SAY, "WELL DONE."
...
...
くしゃ SKRITCH
くしゃ SKRITCH
HMM
FINE, YOU WIN!
I'LL STUDY, OKAY !?
OH! UH...
...WELL ...GOOD.

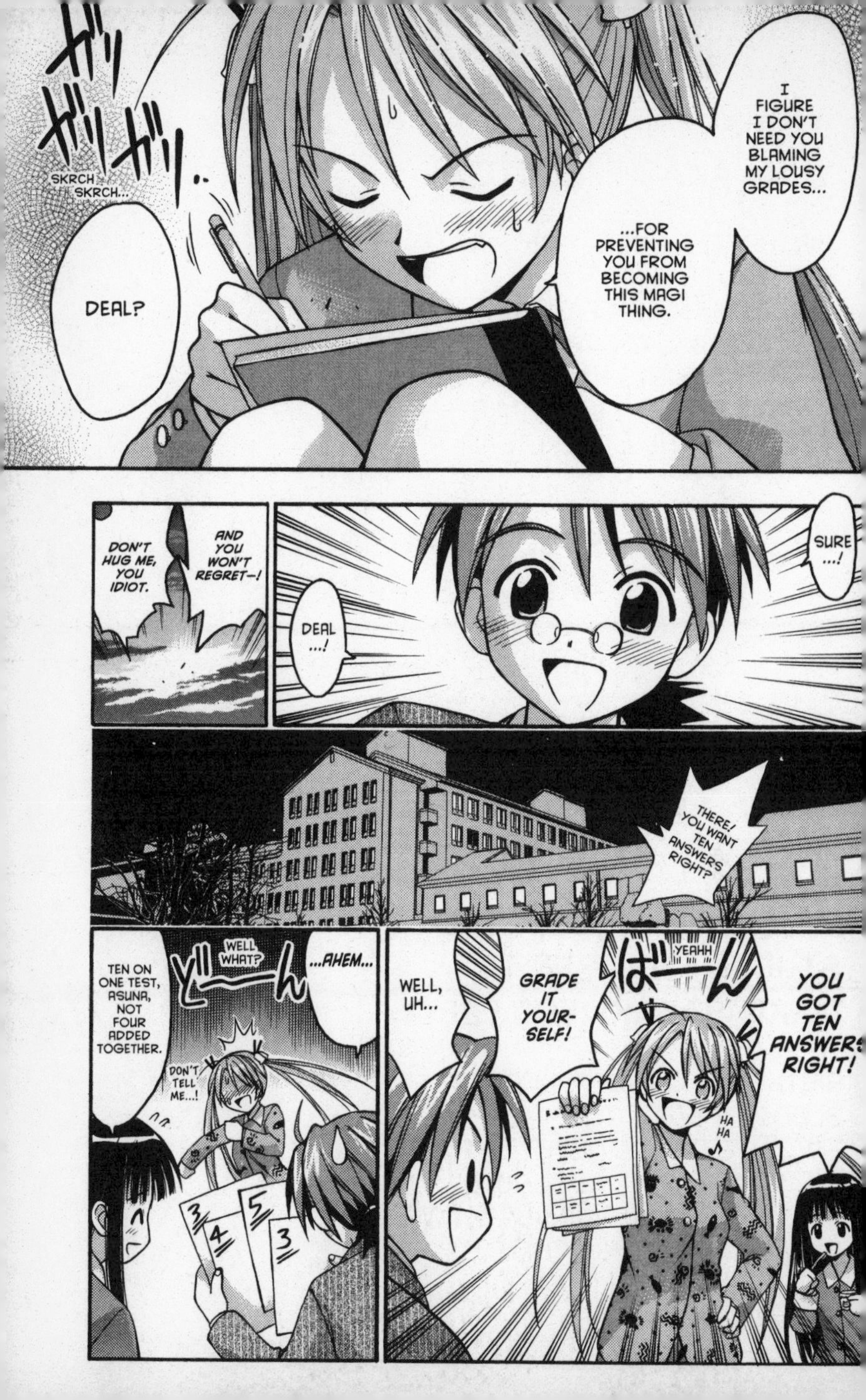

I FIGURE I DON'T NEED YOU BLAMING MY LOUSY GRADES...
...FOR PREVENTING YOU FROM BECOMING THIS MAGI THING.
SKRCH SKRCH...
DEAL?
SURE ...!
DEAL ...!
AND YOU WON'T REGRET—!
DON'T HUG ME, YOU IDIOT.
THERE! YOU WANT TEN ANSWERS RIGHT?
YOU GOT TEN ANSWERS RIGHT!
YEAHH
GRADE IT YOURSELF!
WELL, UH...
HA HA ♪
...AHEM...
WELL WHAT?
TEN ON ONE TEST, ASUNA, NOT FOUR ADDED TOGETHER.
DON'T TELL ME...!

2-A STUDENT PROFILE

STUDENT NUMBER 2
YUNA AKASHI (BOTTOM)

BIRTHDATE: JUNE 1, 1988
BLOODTYPE: A
FAVORITE THINGS: FATHER
DISLIKES: BAD CLOTHES,
            SHIRTS HANGING OUT,
            SLOPPY LIFESTYLE
CLUB ACTIVITIES: BASKETBALL

STUDENT NUMBER 5
AKO IZUMI (RIGHT)

BIRTHDATE: NOVEMBER 21, 1988
BLOODTYPE: A
FAVORITE THINGS: CUTE BANDAIDS,
            DOING LAUNDRY
DISLIKES: BLOOD, FIGHTS
CLUB ACTIVITIES: NURSE'S OFFICE,
            BOYS' SOCCER
              TEAM MANAGER

STUDENT NUMBER 16
MAKIE SASAKI (TOP LEFT)

BIRTHDATE: MARCH 7, 1989
BLOODTYPE: O
FAVORITE THINGS: DEVOTED TO RHYTHMIC GYMNASTICS,
            NEGI, CUTE THINGS
DISLIKES: SLIMY THINGS LIKE NATTO
CLUB ACTIVITIES: RHYTHMIC GYMNASTICS

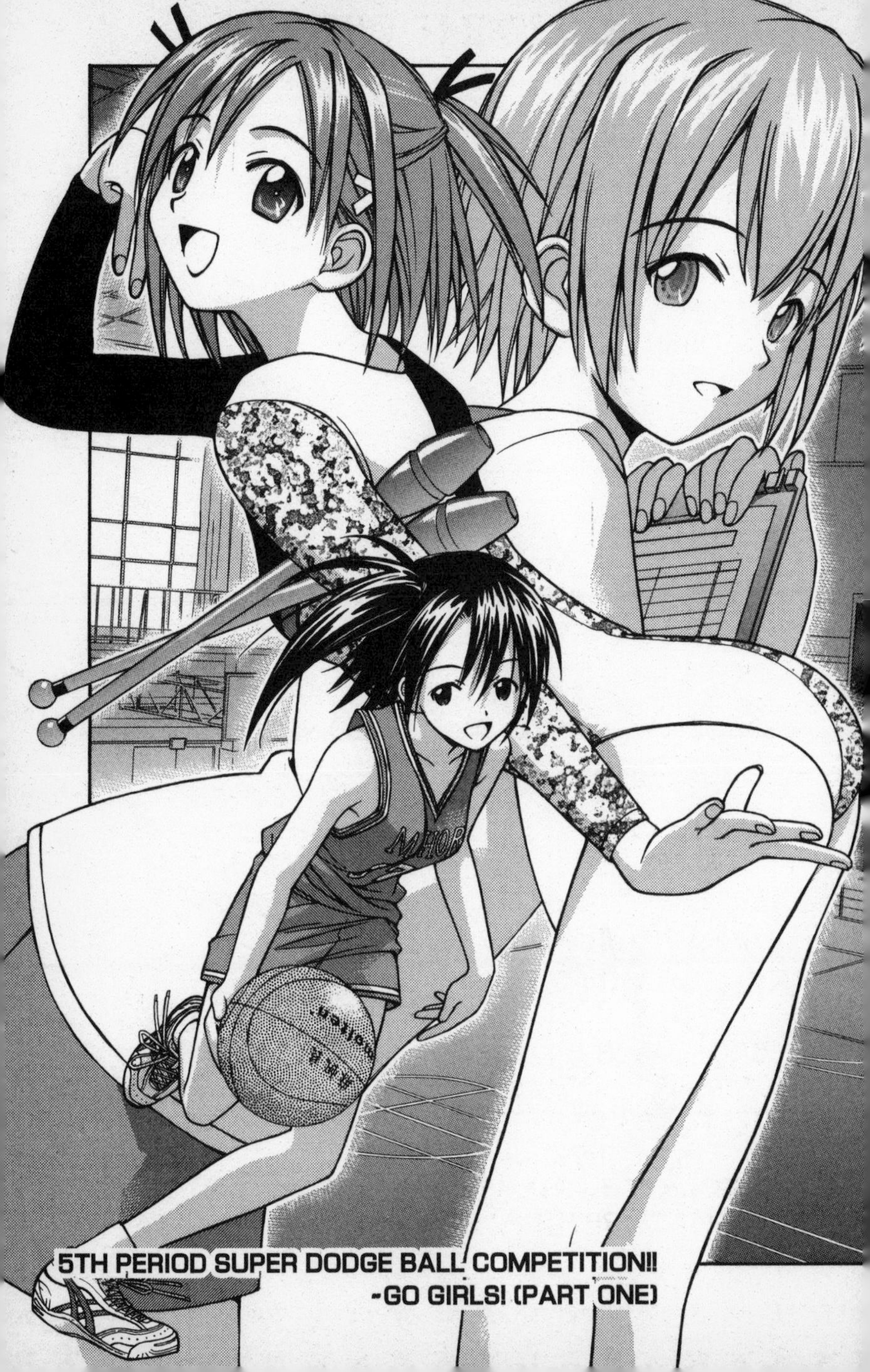

5TH PERIOD SUPER DODGE BALL COMPETITION!! -GO GIRLS! (PART ONE)

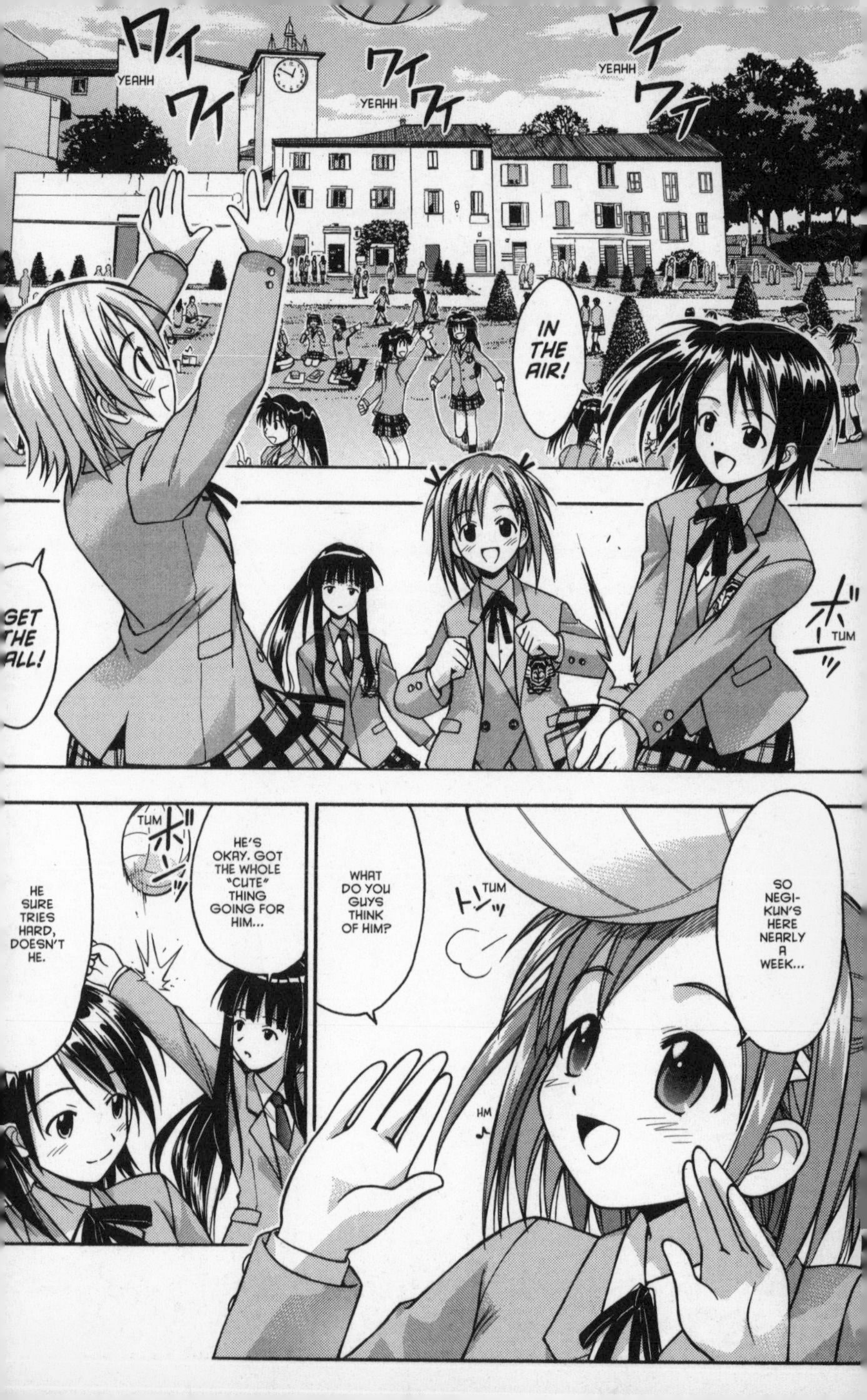

ワイワイ
YEAHH
ワイワイ
YEAHH
ワイワイ
YEAHH
IN THE AIR!
ボッ
TUM
GET THE ALL!
SO NEGI-KUN'S HERE NEARLY A WEEK...
トンッ
TUM
HM
WHAT DO YOU GUYS THINK OF HIM?
ボン
TUM
HE'S OKAY. GOT THE WHOLE "CUTE" THING GOING FOR HIM...
HE SURE TRIES HARD, DOESN'T HE.

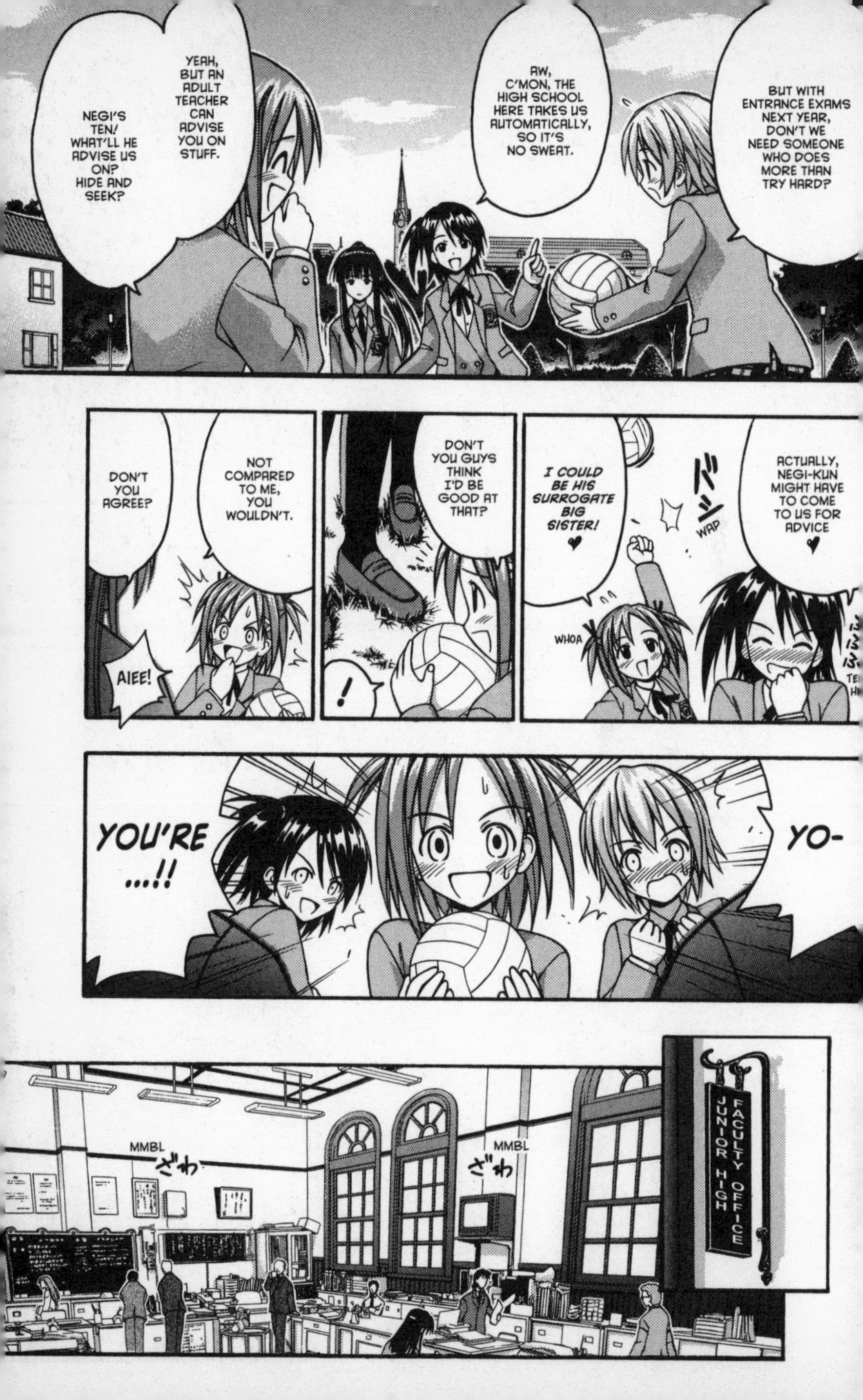
BUT WITH ENTRANCE EXAMS NEXT YEAR, DON'T WE NEED SOMEONE WHO DOES MORE THAN TRY HARD?
AW, C'MON, THE HIGH SCHOOL HERE TAKES US AUTOMATICALLY, SO IT'S NO SWEAT.
YEAH, BUT AN ADULT TEACHER CAN ADVISE YOU ON STUFF.
NEGI'S TEN! WHAT'LL HE ADVISE US ON? HIDE AND SEEK?
ACTUALLY, NEGI-KUN MIGHT HAVE TO COME TO US FOR ADVICE ♥
バッ
WAP
I COULD BE HIS SURROGATE BIG SISTER! ♥
WHOA
DON'T YOU GUYS THINK I'D BE GOOD AT THAT?
!
NOT COMPARED TO ME, YOU WOULDN'T.
DON'T YOU AGREE?
AIEE!
YO-
YOU'RE ...!!
JUNIOR HIGH FACULTY OFFICE
ざわ
MMBL
ざわ
MMBL

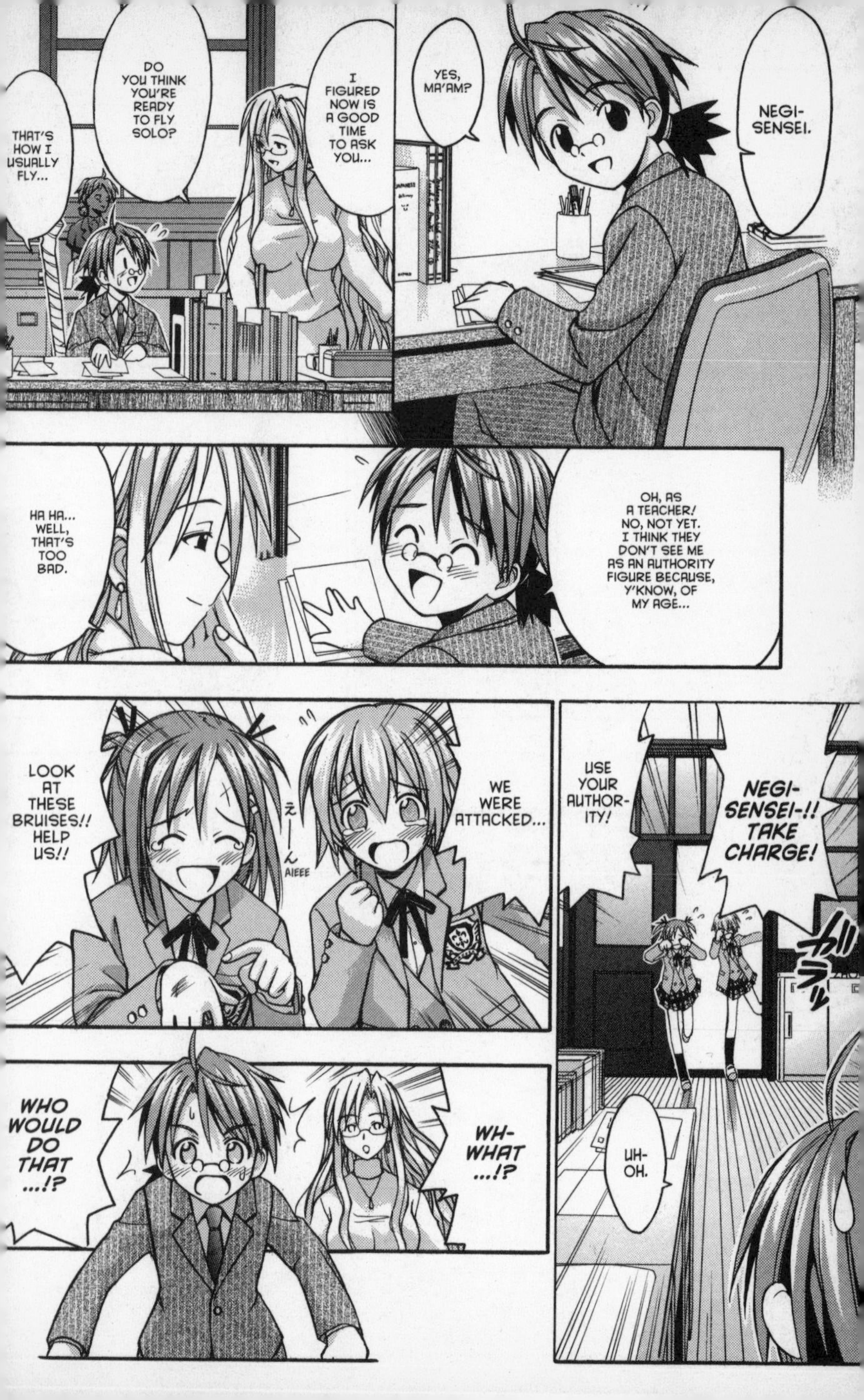
NEGI-SENSEI.
YES, MA'AM?
I FIGURED NOW IS A GOOD TIME TO ASK YOU...
DO YOU THINK YOU'RE READY TO FLY SOLO?
THAT'S HOW I USUALLY FLY...
OH, AS A TEACHER! NO, NOT YET. I THINK THEY DON'T SEE ME AS AN AUTHORITY FIGURE BECAUSE, Y'KNOW, OF MY AGE...
HA HA... WELL, THAT'S TOO BAD.
ガラッ
NEGI-SENSEI-!! TAKE CHARGE!
USE YOUR AUTHORITY!
UH-OH.
WE WERE ATTACKED...
えーん
AIEEE
LOOK AT THESE BRUISES!! HELP US!!
WH-WHAT ...!?
WHO WOULD DO THAT ...!?

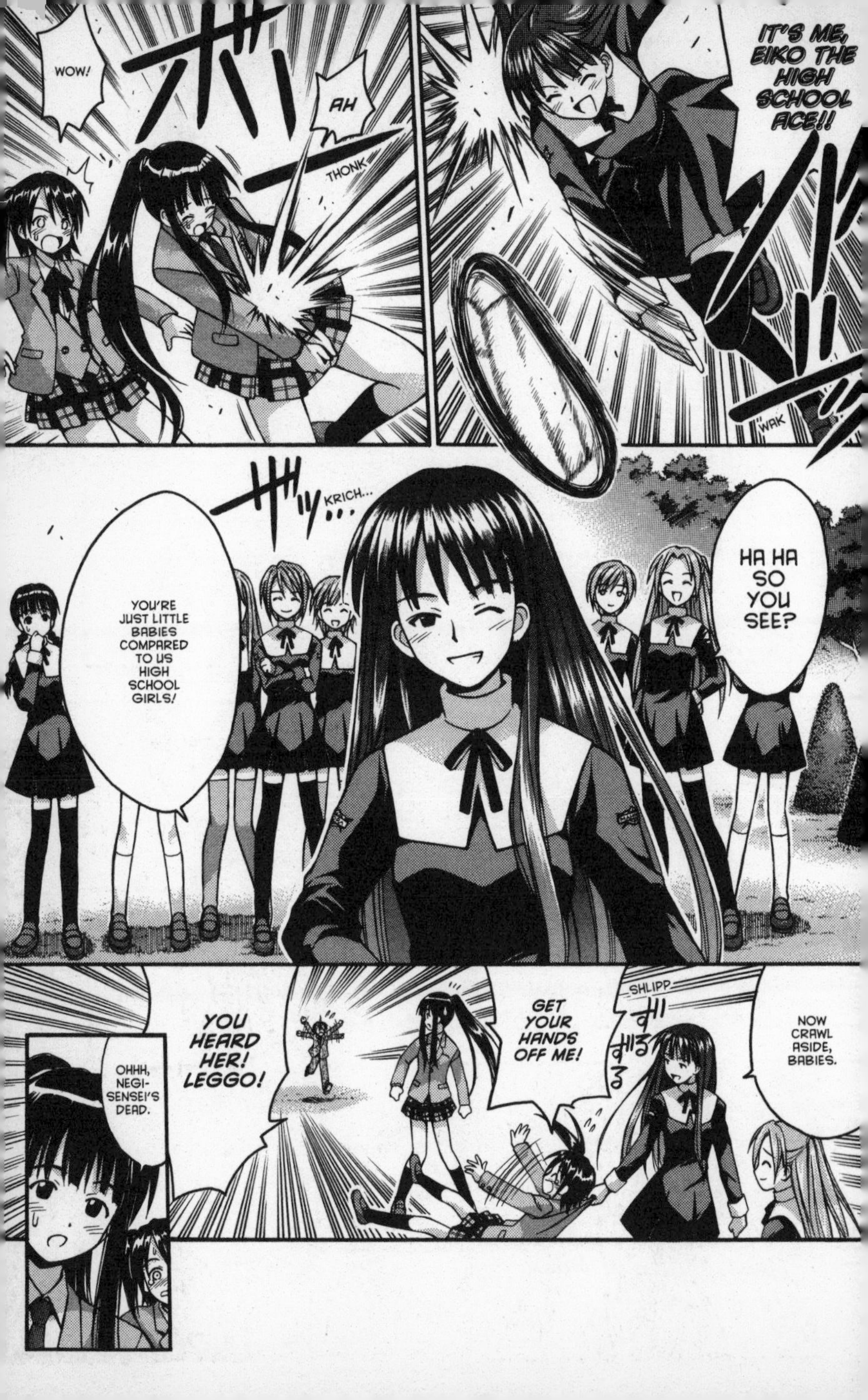
IT'S ME, EIKO THE HIGH SCHOOL ACE!!
WAK
AH
WOW!
THONK
HA HA SO YOU SEE?
KRICH...
YOU'RE JUST LITTLE BABIES COMPARED TO US HIGH SCHOOL GIRLS!
NOW CRAWL ASIDE, BABIES.
SHLIPP
GET YOUR HANDS OFF ME!
YOU HEARD HER! LEGGO!
OHHH, NEGI-SENSEI'S DEAD.

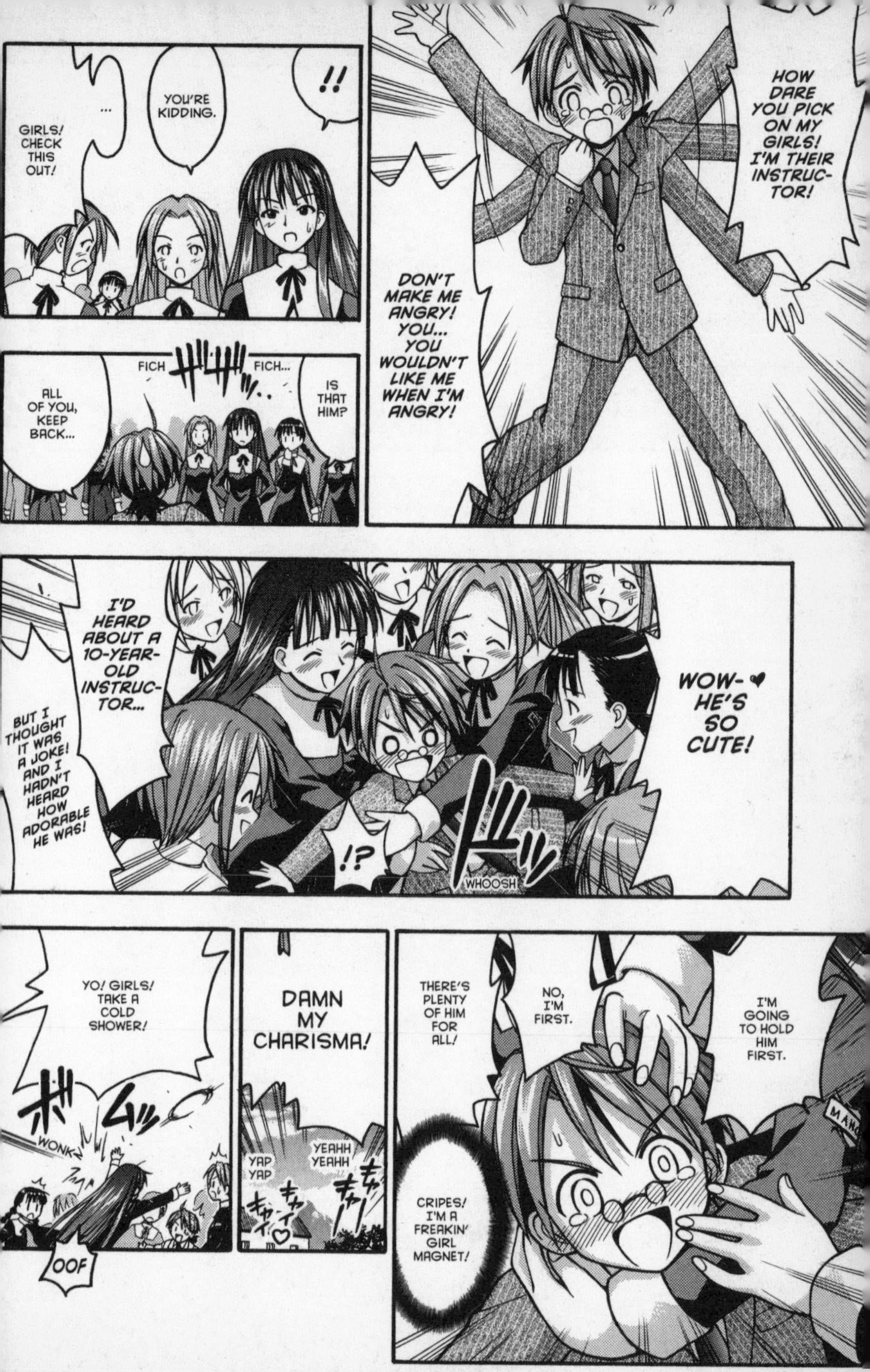
HOW DARE YOU PICK ON MY GIRLS! I'M THEIR INSTRUCTOR!
DON'T MAKE ME ANGRY! YOU... YOU WOULDN'T LIKE ME WHEN I'M ANGRY!
!!
YOU'RE KIDDING.
...
GIRLS! CHECK THIS OUT!
IS THAT HIM?
FICH...
FICH
ALL OF YOU, KEEP BACK...
WOW-♥ HE'S SO CUTE!
I'D HEARD ABOUT A 10-YEAR-OLD INSTRUCTOR...
BUT I THOUGHT IT WAS A JOKE! AND I HADN'T HEARD HOW ADORABLE HE WAS!
WHOOSH
!?
I'M GOING TO HOLD HIM FIRST.
NO, I'M FIRST.
THERE'S PLENTY OF HIM FOR ALL!
CRIPES! I'M A FREAKIN' GIRL MAGNET!
DAMN MY CHARISMA!
YEAHH YEAHH
YAP YAP
YO! GIRLS! TAKE A COLD SHOWER!
WONK
OOF

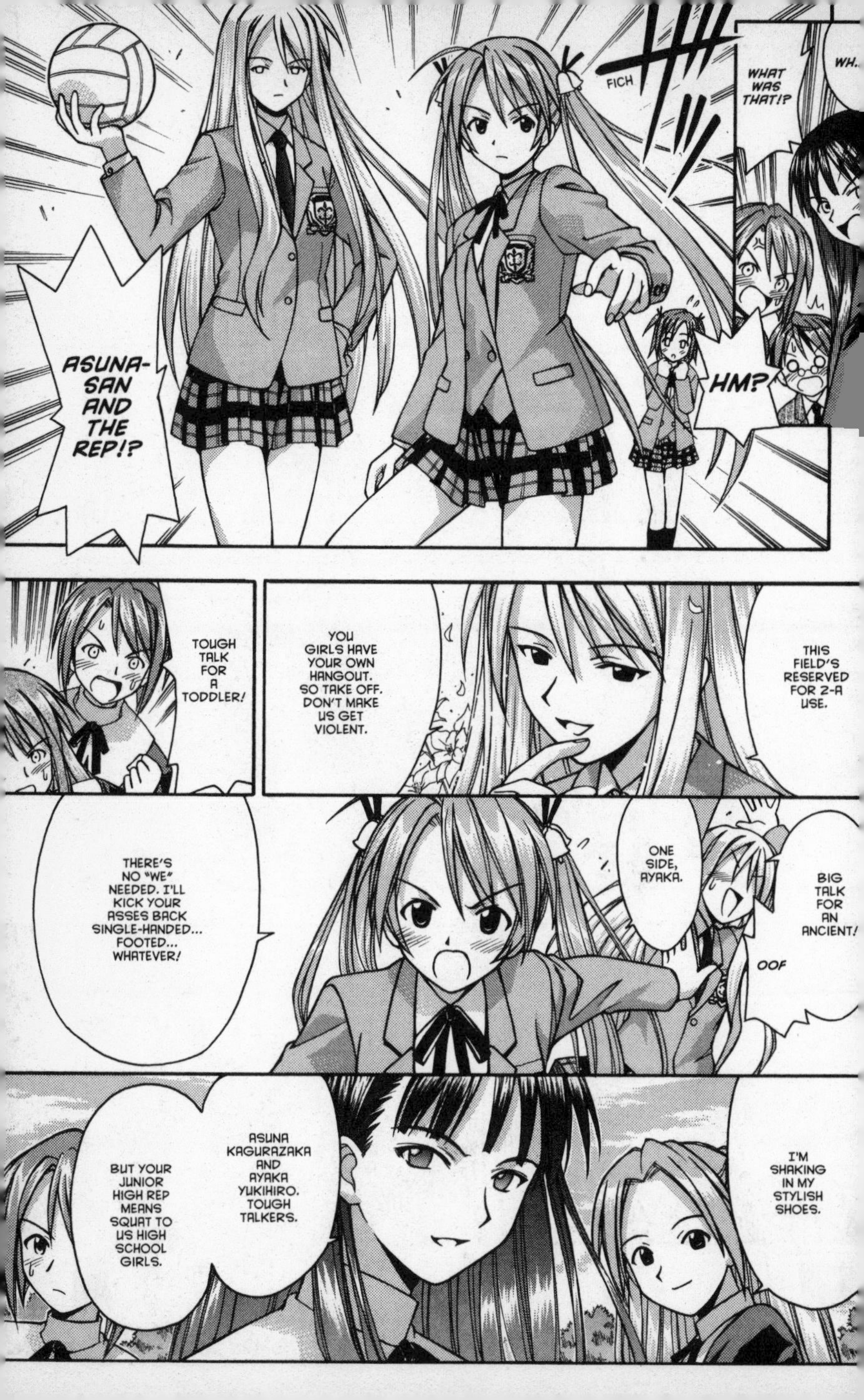
WH...
WHAT WAS THAT!?
FICH
HM?
ASUNA-SAN AND THE REP!?
THIS FIELD'S RESERVED FOR 2-A USE.
YOU GIRLS HAVE YOUR OWN HANGOUT. SO TAKE OFF. DON'T MAKE US GET VIOLENT.
TOUGH TALK FOR A TODDLER!
BIG TALK FOR AN ANCIENT!
OOF
ONE SIDE, AYAKA.
THERE'S NO "WE" NEEDED. I'LL KICK YOUR ASSES BACK SINGLE-HANDED... FOOTED... WHATEVER!
I'M SHAKING IN MY STYLISH SHOES.
ASUNA KAGURAZAKA AND AYAKA YUKIHIRO. TOUGH TALKERS.
BUT YOUR JUNIOR HIGH REP MEANS SQUAT TO US HIGH SCHOOL GIRLS.

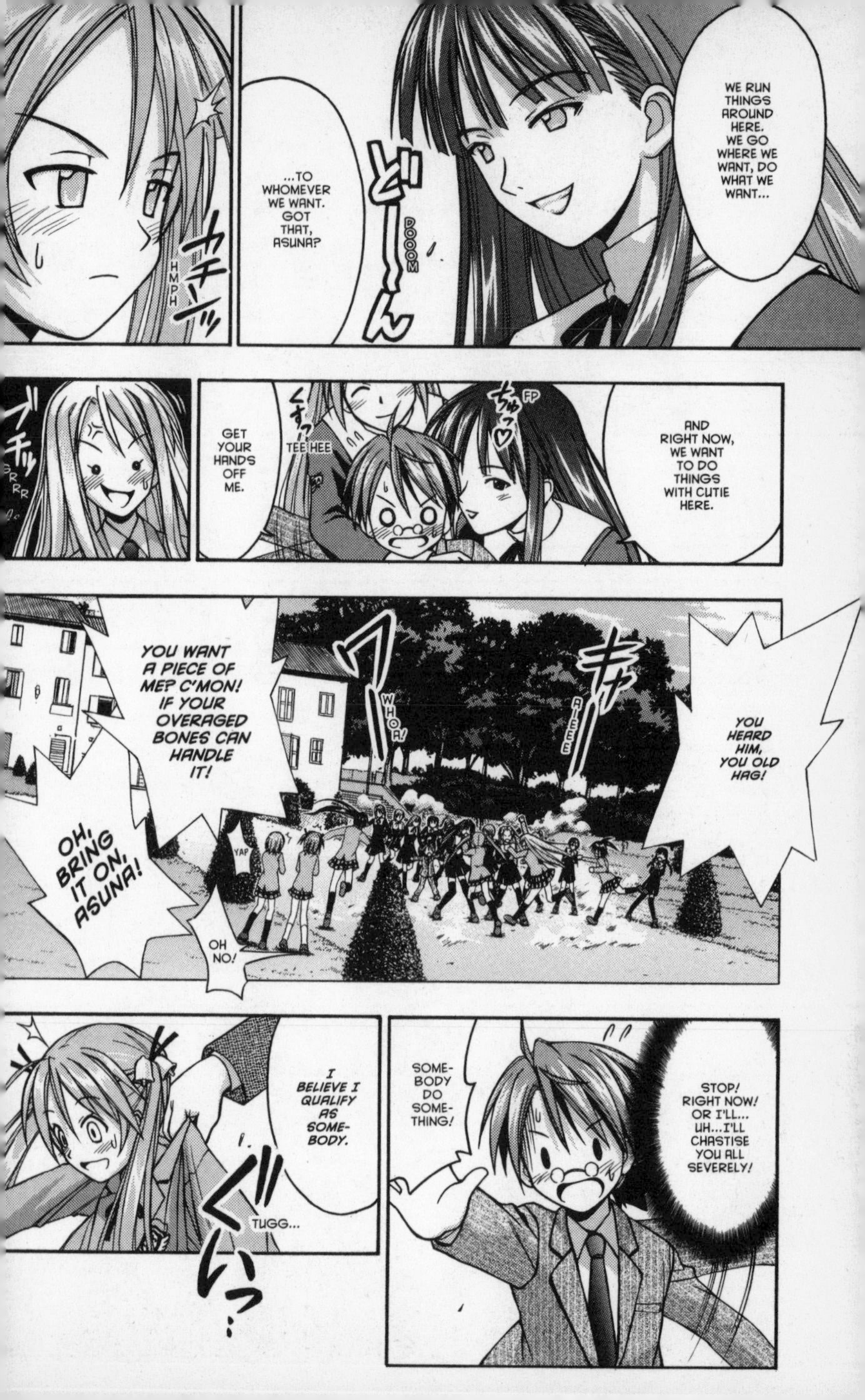
WE RUN THINGS AROUND HERE. WE GO WHERE WE WANT, DO WHAT WE WANT...
どーーん
DOOOM
...TO WHOMEVER WE WANT. GOT THAT, ASUNA?
カチーンッ
HMPH
AND RIGHT NOW, WE WANT TO DO THINGS WITH CUTIE HERE.
ちゅっ♡
FP
くすっ
TEE HEE
GET YOUR HANDS OFF ME.
ブチッ
GRRR
YOU HEARD HIM, YOU OLD HAG!
キャ
RIEEE
ワー
WHOA!
YOU WANT A PIECE OF ME? C'MON! IF YOUR OVERAGED BONES CAN HANDLE IT!
YAP
OH, BRING IT ON, ASUNA!
OH NO!
STOP! RIGHT NOW! OR I'LL... UH...I'LL CHASTISE YOU ALL SEVERELY!
SOME-BODY DO SOME-THING!
I BELIEVE I QUALIFY AS SOME-BODY.
ぐい
TUGG...
ぐいっ

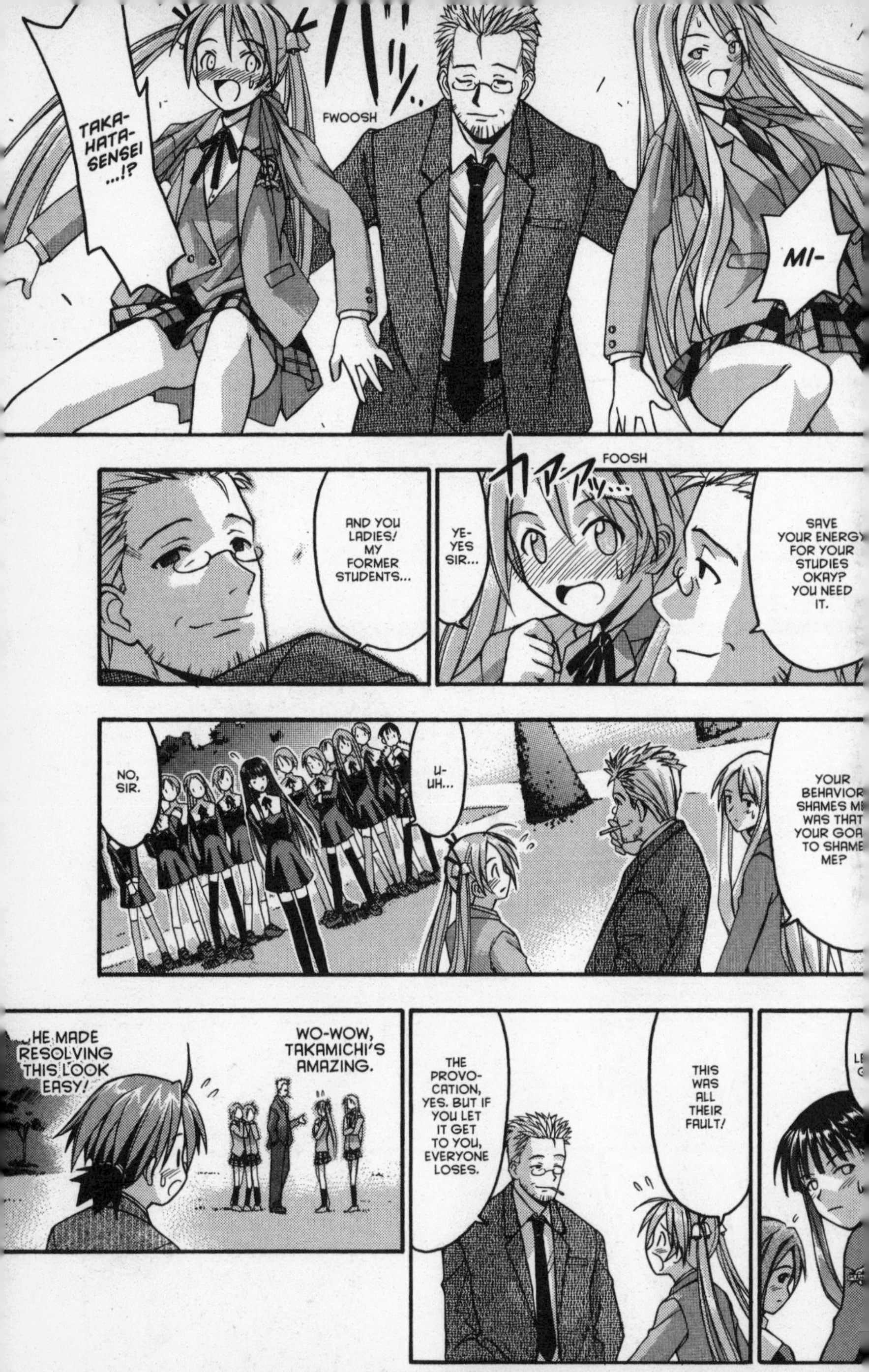
MI-
FWOOSH
TAKA-HATA-SENSEI ...!?
FOOSH
SAVE YOUR ENERGY FOR YOUR STUDIES OKAY? YOU NEED IT.
YE-YES SIR...
AND YOU LADIES! MY FORMER STUDENTS...
YOUR BEHAVIOR SHAMES ME WAS THAT YOUR GOA TO SHAME ME?
U-UH...
NO, SIR.
THIS WAS ALL THEIR FAULT!
THE PROVOCATION, YES. BUT IF YOU LET IT GET TO YOU, EVERYONE LOSES.
WO-WOW, TAKAMICHI'S AMAZING.
HE MADE RESOLVING THIS LOOK EASY!

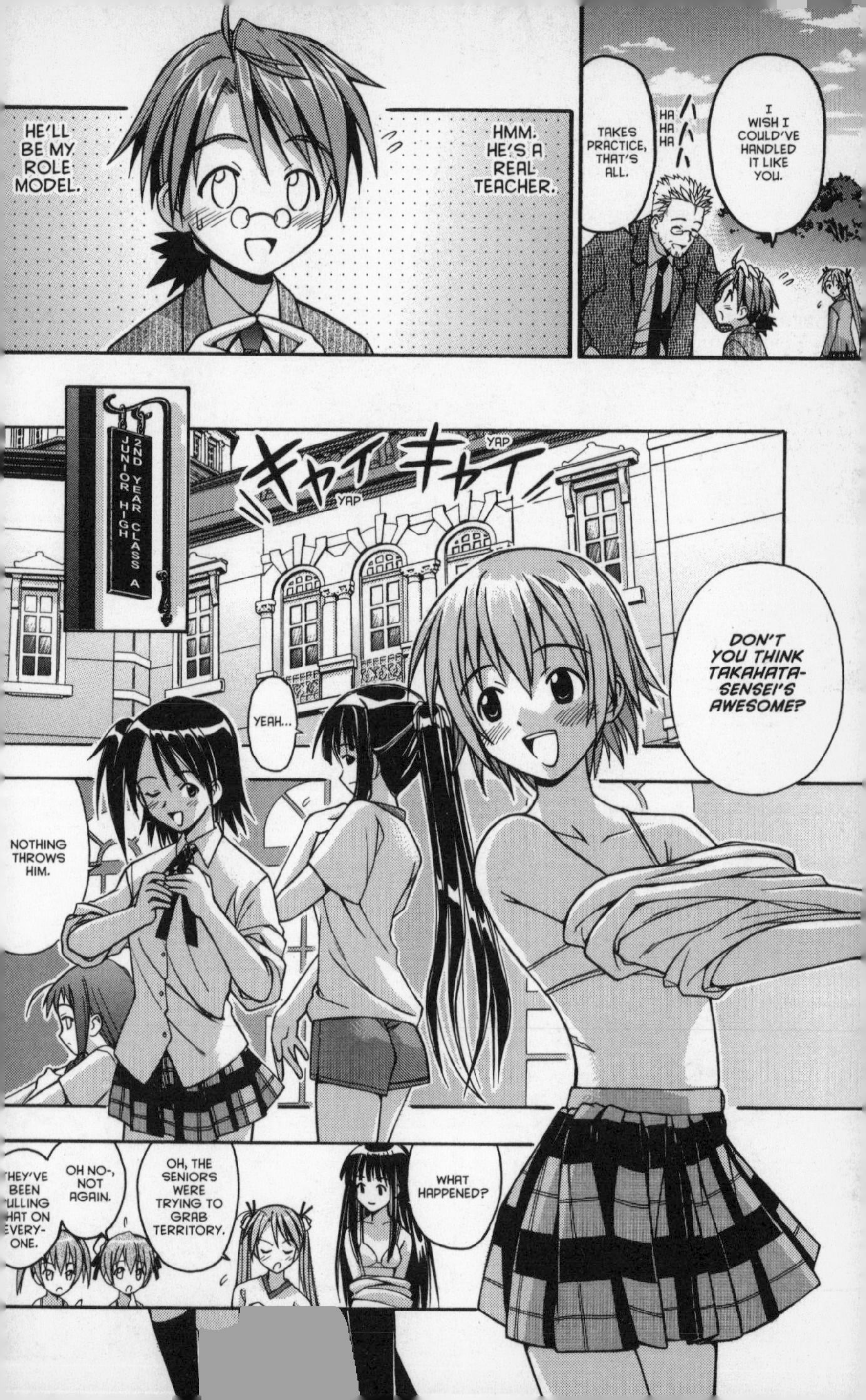
I WISH I COULD'VE HANDLED IT LIKE YOU.
HA HA HA
ハハハ
TAKES PRACTICE, THAT'S ALL.
HMM. HE'S A REAL TEACHER.
HE'LL BE MY ROLE MODEL.
2ND YEAR CLASS A JUNIOR HIGH
キャイ キャイ
YAP YAP
DON'T YOU THINK TAKAHATA-SENSEI'S AWESOME?
YEAH...
NOTHING THROWS HIM.
WHAT HAPPENED?
OH, THE SENIORS WERE TRYING TO GRAB TERRITORY.
OH NO-, NOT AGAIN.
THEY'VE BEEN ULLING HAT ON EVERY-ONE.

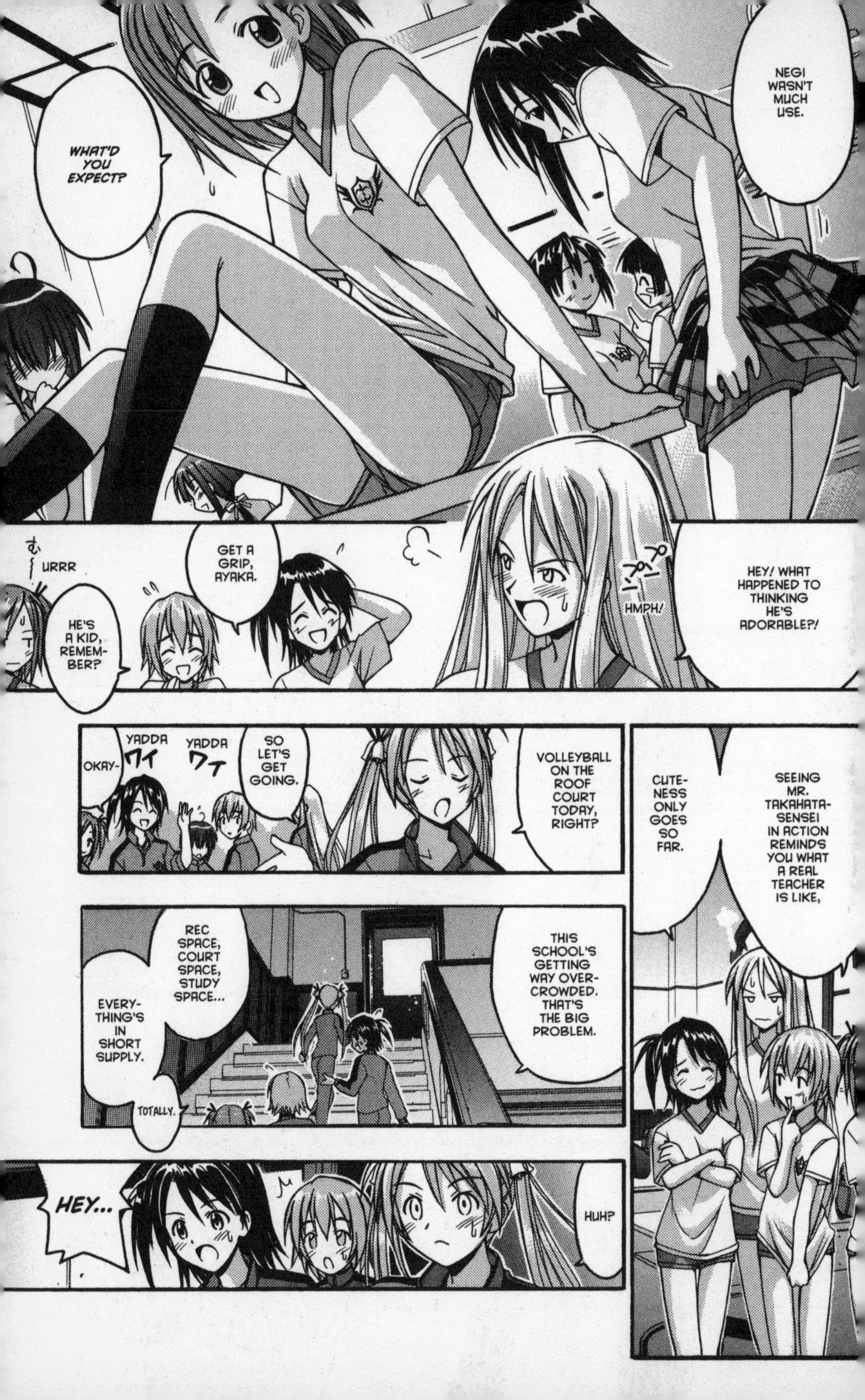
NEGI WASN'T MUCH USE.
WHAT'D YOU EXPECT?
HEY! WHAT HAPPENED TO THINKING HE'S ADORABLE?!
HMPH!
GET A GRIP, AYAKA.
HE'S A KID, REMEMBER?
URRR
SEEING MR. TAKAHATA-SENSEI IN ACTION REMINDS YOU WHAT A REAL TEACHER IS LIKE,
CUTENESS ONLY GOES SO FAR.
VOLLEYBALL ON THE ROOF COURT TODAY, RIGHT?
SO LET'S GET GOING.
YADDA ワイ
YADDA ワイ
OKAY-
THIS SCHOOL'S GETTING WAY OVER-CROWDED. THAT'S THE BIG PROBLEM.
REC SPACE, COURT SPACE, STUDY SPACE...
EVERY-THING'S IN SHORT SUPPLY.
TOTALLY.
HUH?
HEY...

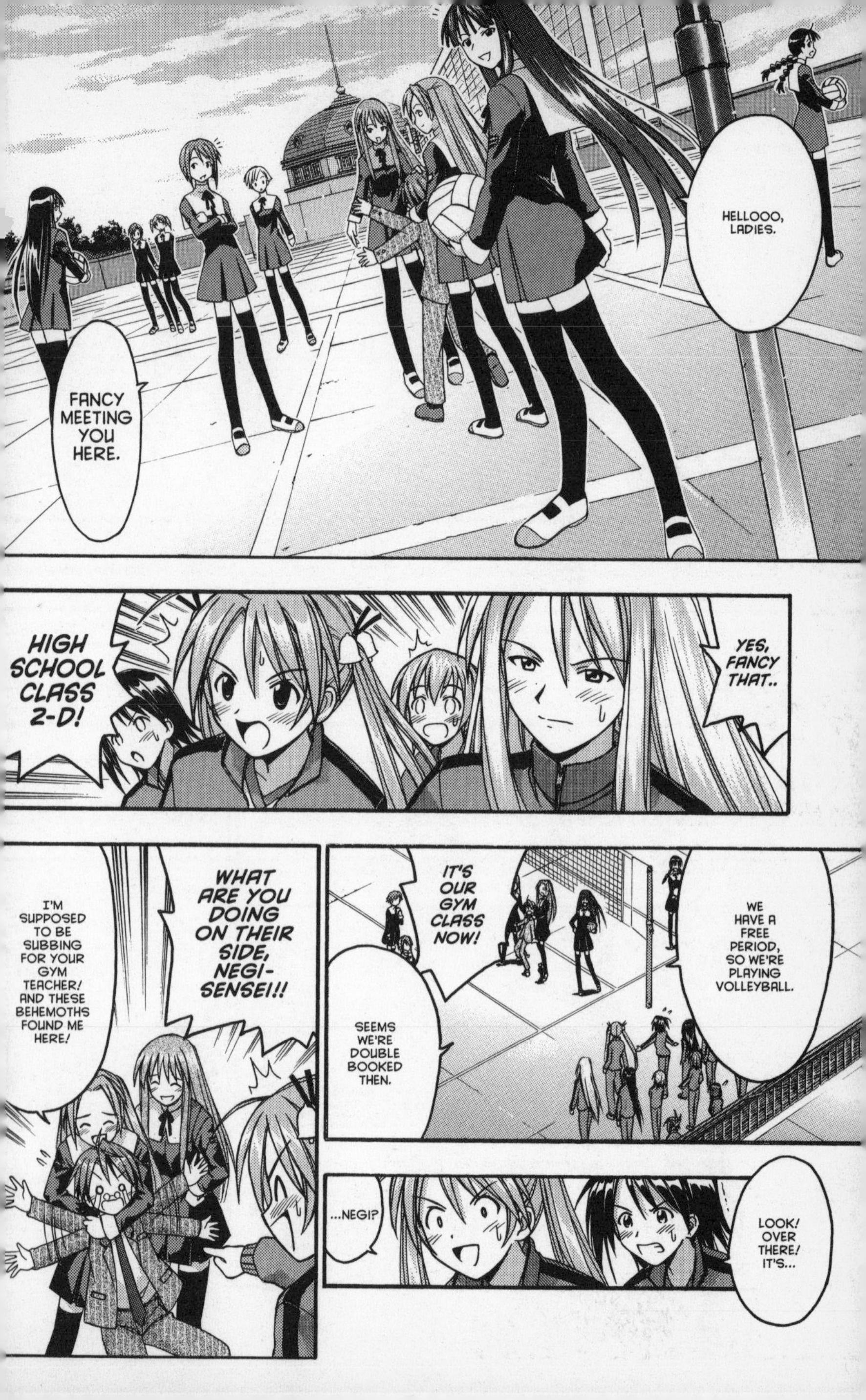
HELLOOO, LADIES.
FANCY MEETING YOU HERE.
YES, FANCY THAT..
HIGH SCHOOL CLASS 2-D!
WE HAVE A FREE PERIOD, SO WE'RE PLAYING VOLLEYBALL.
IT'S OUR GYM CLASS NOW!
SEEMS WE'RE DOUBLE BOOKED THEN.
LOOK! OVER THERE! IT'S...
...NEGI?
WHAT ARE YOU DOING ON THEIR SIDE, NEGI-SENSEI!!
I'M SUPPOSED TO BE SUBBING FOR YOUR GYM TEACHER! AND THESE BEHEMOTHS FOUND ME HERE!

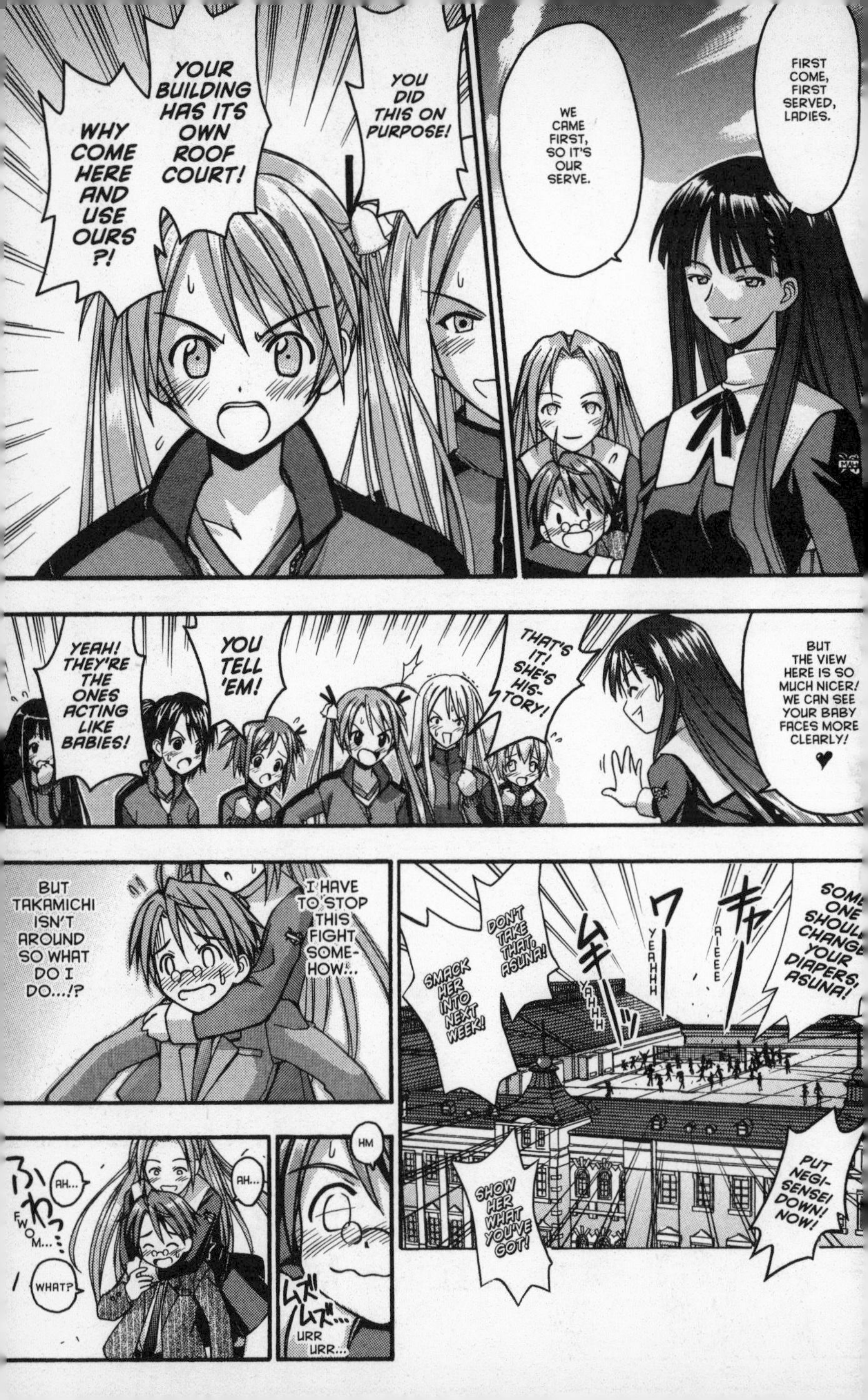
FIRST COME, FIRST SERVED, LADIES.
WE CAME FIRST, SO IT'S OUR SERVE.
YOU DID THIS ON PURPOSE!
YOUR BUILDING HAS ITS OWN ROOF COURT!
WHY COME HERE AND USE OURS?!
BUT THE VIEW HERE IS SO MUCH NICER! WE CAN SEE YOUR BABY FACES MORE CLEARLY! ♥
THAT'S IT! SHE'S HISTORY!
YOU TELL 'EM!
YEAH! THEY'RE THE ONES ACTING LIKE BABIES!
SOMEONE SHOULD CHANGE YOUR DIAPERS, ASUNA!
AIEEE
YEAHHH
YAHHH
DON'T TAKE THAT, ASUNA!
SMACK HER INTO NEXT WEEK!
PUT NEGI-SENSEI DOWN! NOW!
SHOW HER WHAT YOU'VE GOT!
I HAVE TO STOP THIS FIGHT SOMEHOW...
BUT TAKAMICHI ISN'T AROUND SO WHAT DO I DO...!?
HM
URR URR...
AH...
AH...
FWOM...
WHAT?

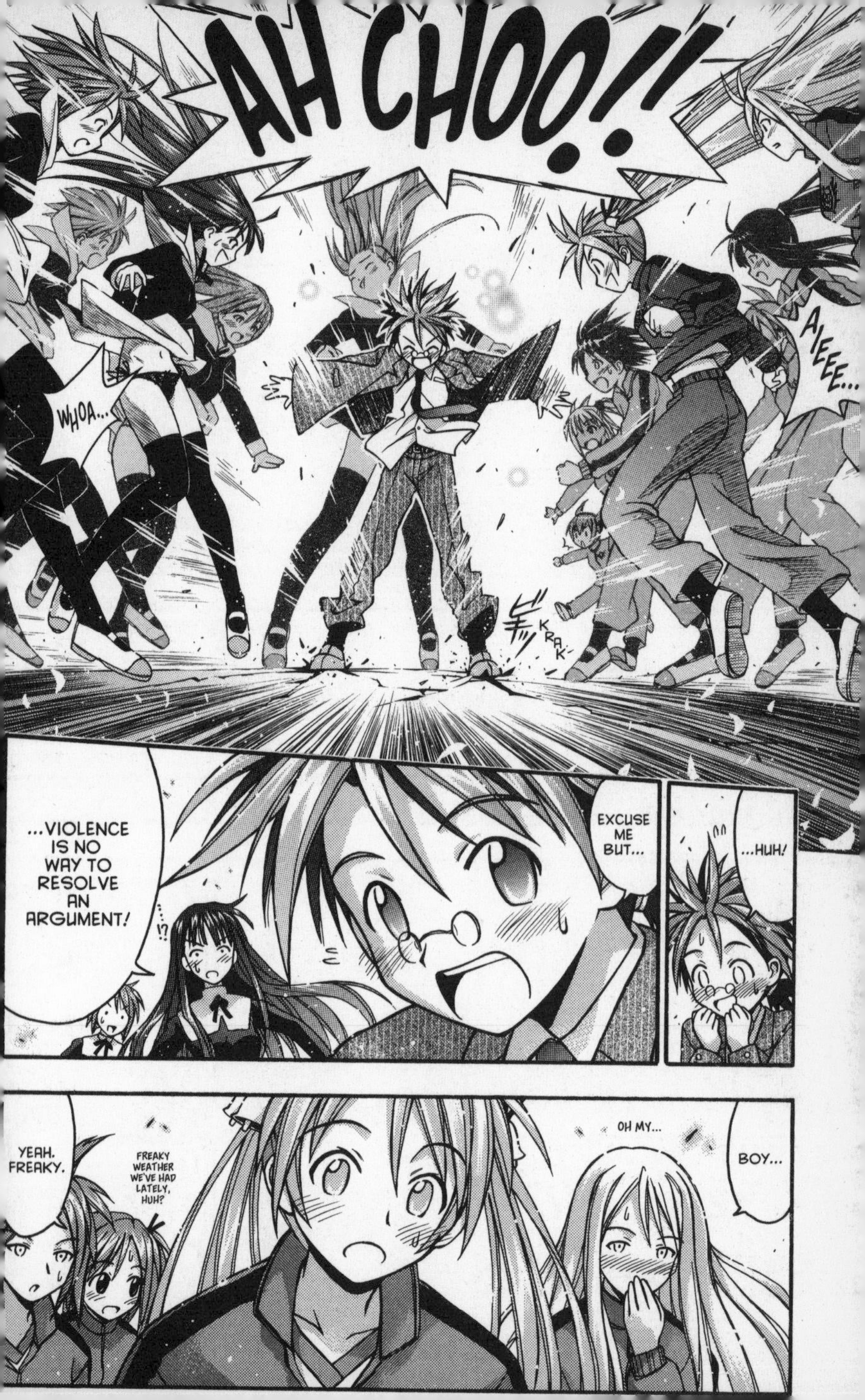
AH CHOO!!
AIEEE...
KRAK
WHOA...
...HUH!
EXCUSE ME BUT...
...VIOLENCE IS NO WAY TO RESOLVE AN ARGUMENT!
...!?
BOY...
OH MY...
FREAKY WEATHER WE'VE HAD LATELY, HUH?
YEAH. FREAKY.

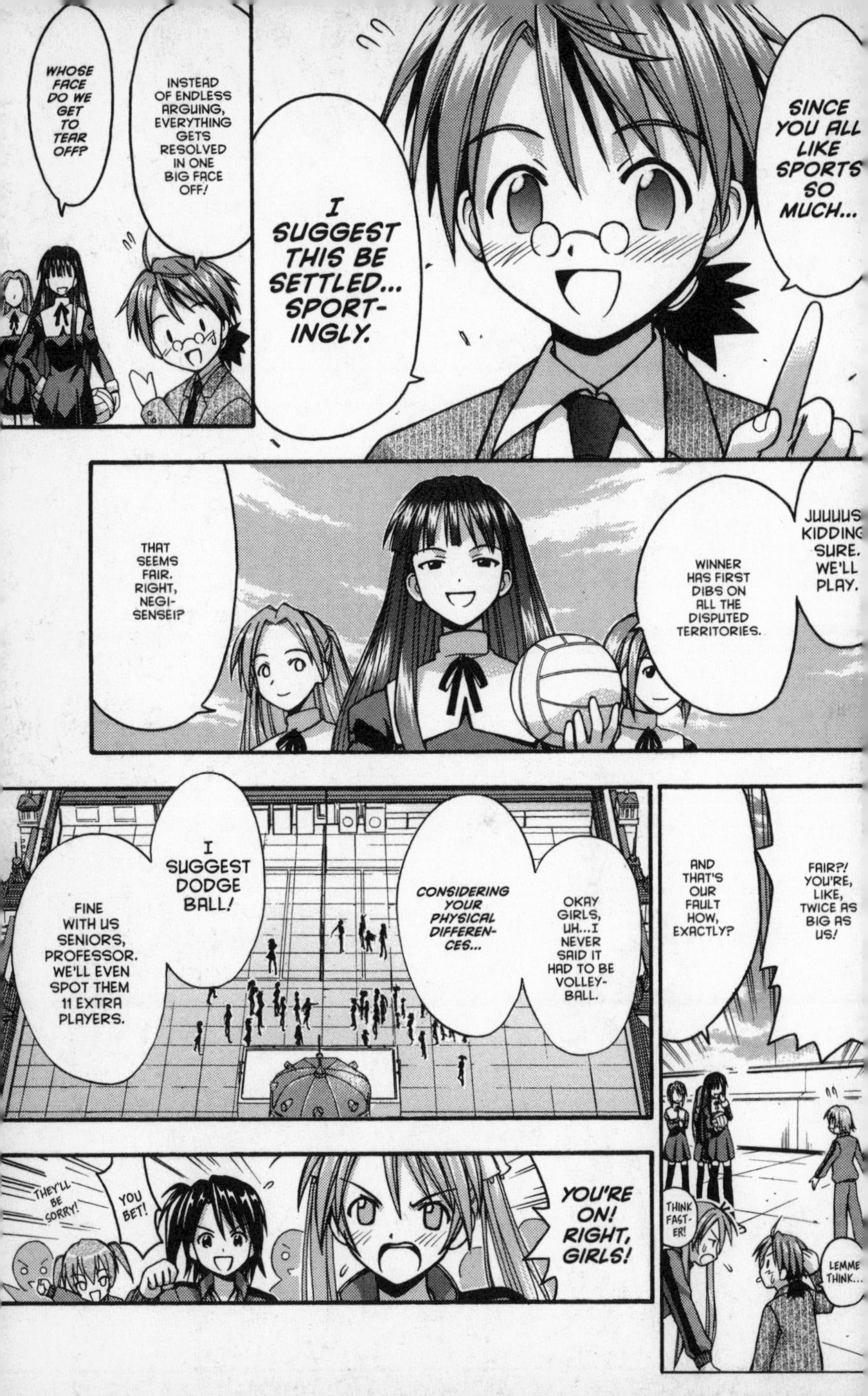
SINCE YOU ALL LIKE SPORTS SO MUCH...
I SUGGEST THIS BE SETTLED... SPORT-INGLY.
INSTEAD OF ENDLESS ARGUING, EVERYTHING GETS RESOLVED IN ONE BIG FACE OFF!
WHOSE FACE DO WE GET TO TEAR OFF?
JUUUUS KIDDING SURE. WE'LL PLAY.
WINNER HAS FIRST DIBS ON ALL THE DISPUTED TERRITORIES.
THAT SEEMS FAIR. RIGHT, NEGI-SENSEI?
FAIR?! YOU'RE, LIKE, TWICE AS BIG AS US!
AND THAT'S OUR FAULT HOW, EXACTLY?
THINK FAST-ER!
LEMME THINK...
OKAY GIRLS, UH...I NEVER SAID IT HAD TO BE VOLLEY-BALL.
CONSIDERING YOUR PHYSICAL DIFFEREN-CES...
I SUGGEST DODGE BALL!
FINE WITH US SENIORS, PROFESSOR. WE'LL EVEN SPOT THEM 11 EXTRA PLAYERS.
YOU'RE ON! RIGHT, GIRLS!
YOU BET!
THEY'LL BE SORRY!

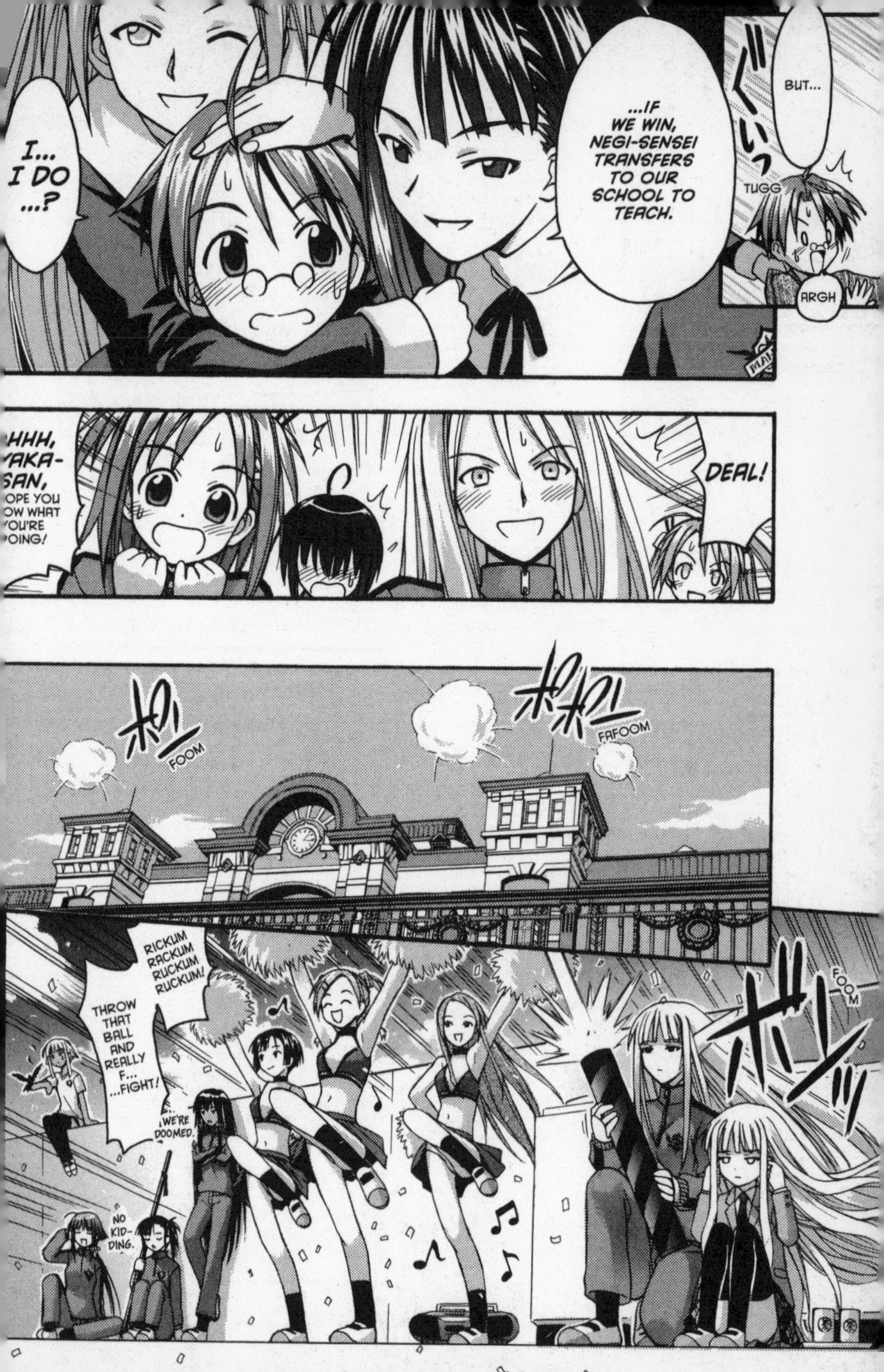

BUT...
ぐいっ
TUGG
ARGH
...IF WE WIN, NEGI-SENSEI TRANSFERS TO OUR SCHOOL TO TEACH.
I... I DO ...?
DEAL!
HHH, YAKA-SAN, OPE YOU OW WHAT YOU'RE OING!
ポポン
FAFOOM
ポン
FOOM
ザンッ
FOOM
RICKUM RACKUM RUCKUM RUCKUM!
THROW THAT BALL AND REALLY F... ...FIGHT!
...WE'RE DOOMED.
NO KID-DING.

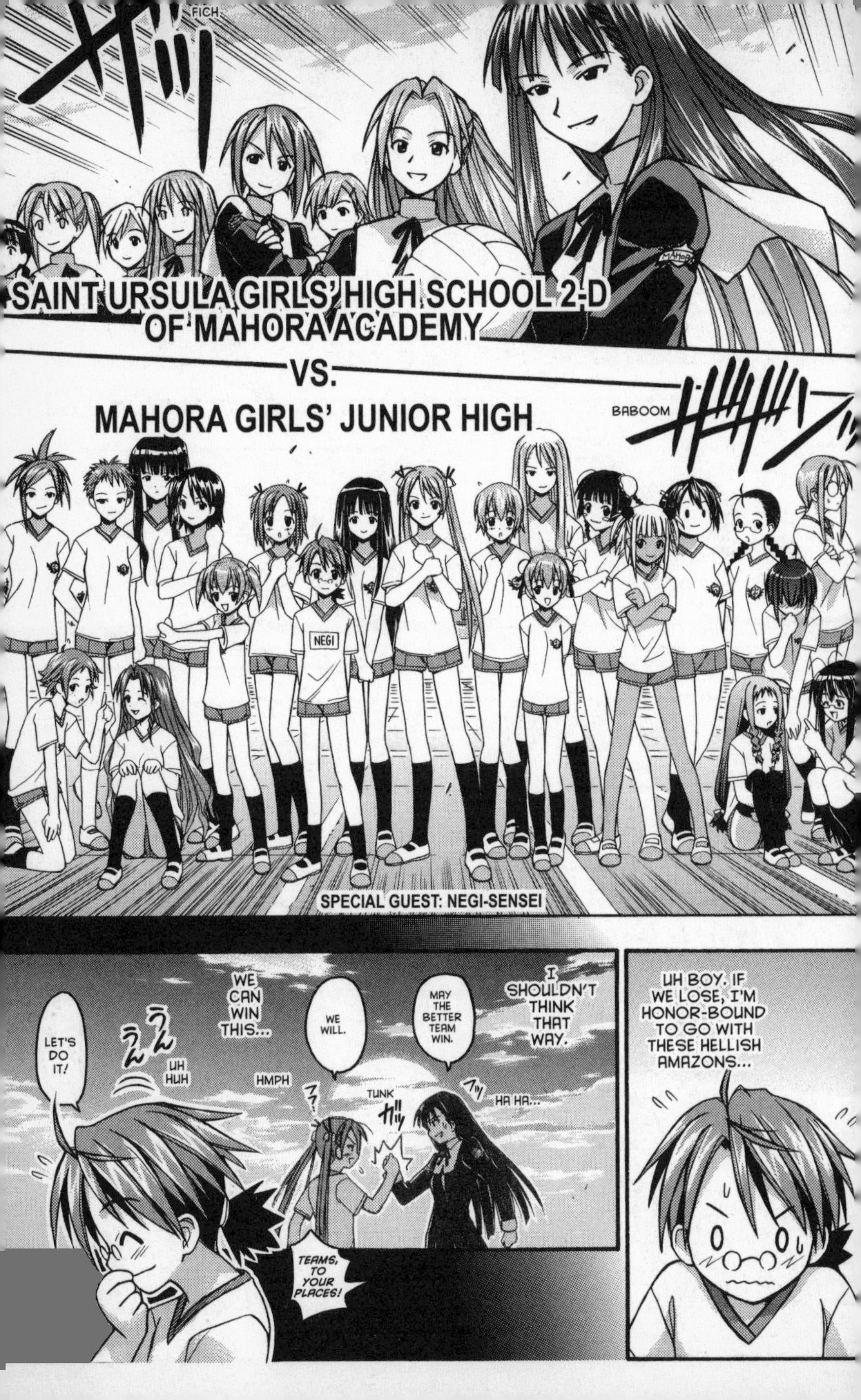
FICH
SAINT URSULA GIRLS' HIGH SCHOOL 2-D
OF MAHORA ACADEMY
VS.
MAHORA GIRLS' JUNIOR HIGH
BABOOM
NEGI
SPECIAL GUEST: NEGI-SENSEI
UH BOY. IF WE LOSE, I'M HONOR-BOUND TO GO WITH THESE HELLISH AMAZONS...
I SHOULDN'T THINK THAT WAY.
HA HA...
MAY THE BETTER TEAM WIN.
TUNK
WE WILL.
HMPH
WE CAN WIN THIS...
UH HUH
LET'S DO IT!
TEAMS, TO YOUR PLACES!

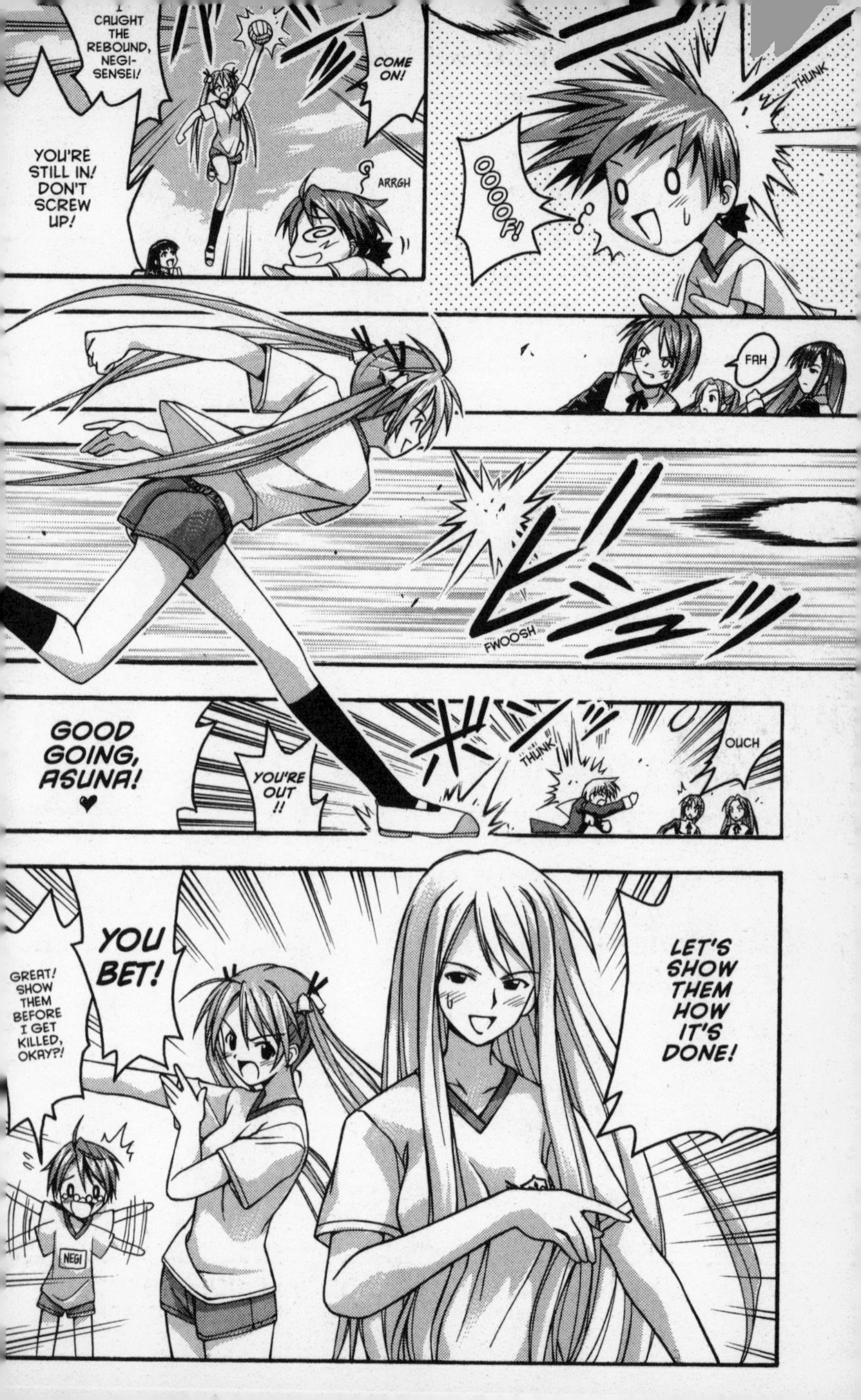
THUNK
OOOOF!
I CAUGHT THE REBOUND, NEGI-SENSEI!
COME ON!
ARRGH
YOU'RE STILL IN! DON'T SCREW UP!
FAH
FWOOSH
OUCH
THUNK
YOU'RE OUT!!
GOOD GOING, ASUNA! ♥
LET'S SHOW THEM HOW IT'S DONE!
YOU BET!
GREAT! SHOW THEM BEFORE I GET KILLED, OKAY?!
NEGI

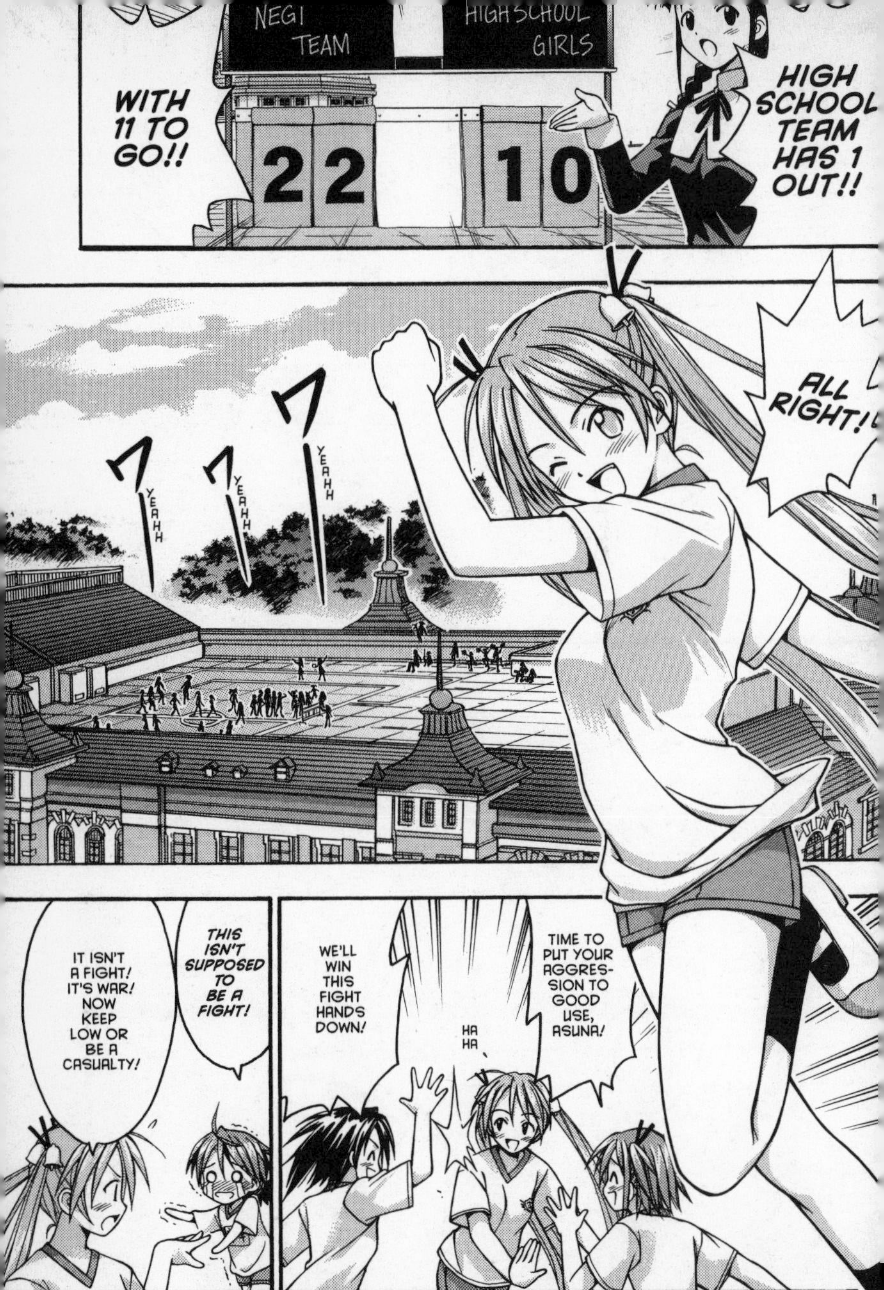
NEGI TEAM
HIGH SCHOOL GIRLS
22
10
HIGH SCHOOL TEAM HAS 1 OUT!!
WITH 11 TO GO!!
ALL RIGHT!!
YEAHH
YEAHH
YEAHH
TIME TO PUT YOUR AGGRESSION TO GOOD USE, ASUNA!
WE'LL WIN THIS FIGHT HANDS DOWN!
HA HA
THIS ISN'T SUPPOSED TO BE A FIGHT!
IT ISN'T A FIGHT! IT'S WAR! NOW KEEP LOW OR BE A CASUALTY!

6TH PERIOD SUPER DODGE BALL COMPETITION!!
~GO GIRLS! (PART TWO)

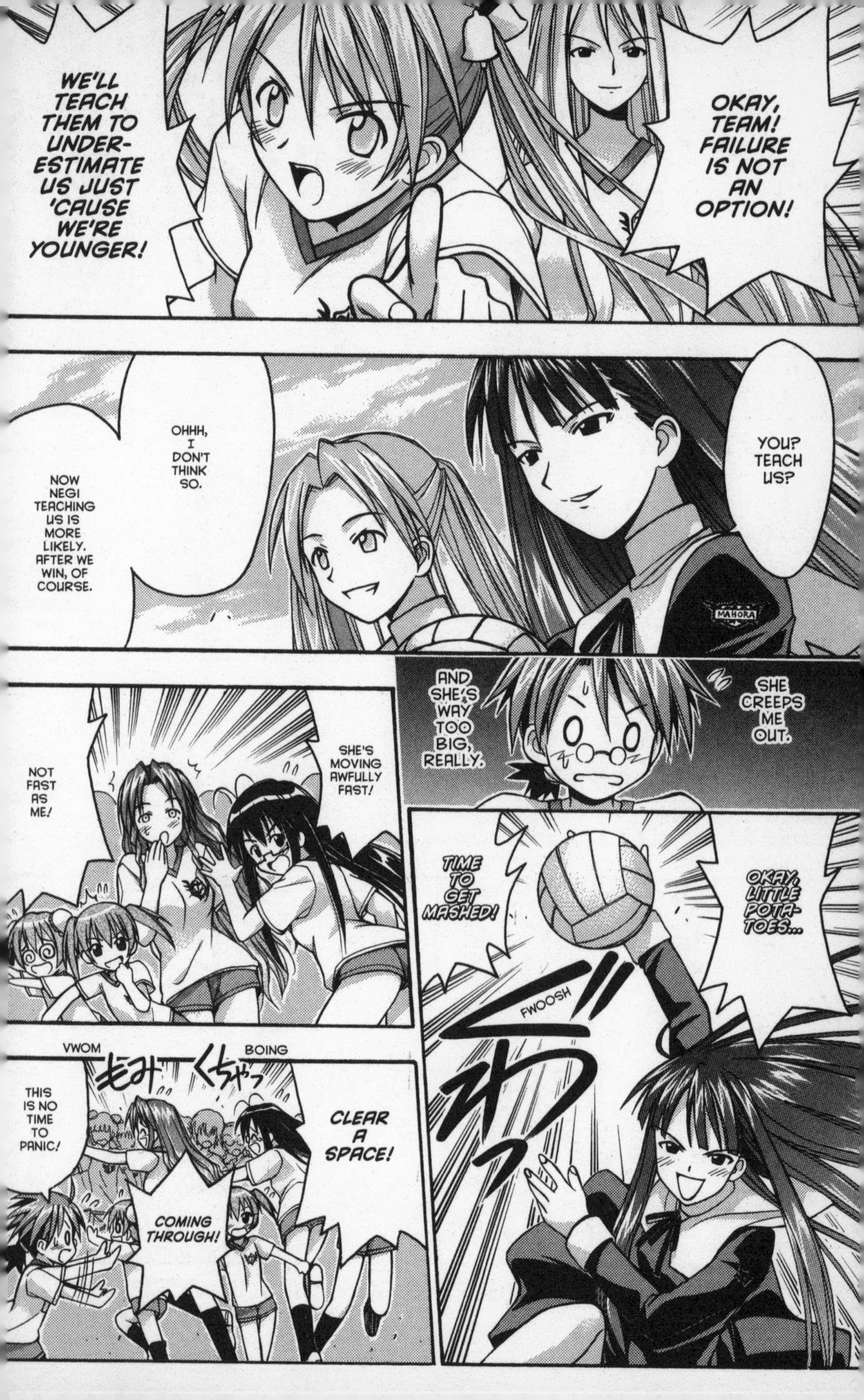

OKAY, TEAM! FAILURE IS NOT AN OPTION!
WE'LL TEACH THEM TO UNDER-ESTIMATE US JUST 'CAUSE WE'RE YOUNGER!
YOU? TEACH US?
MAHORA
OHHH, I DON'T THINK SO.
NOW NEGI TEACHING US IS MORE LIKELY. AFTER WE WIN, OF COURSE.
SHE CREEPS ME OUT.
AND SHE'S WAY TOO BIG, REALLY.
OKAY, LITTLE POTATOES...
TIME TO GET MASHED!
FWOOSH
SHE'S MOVING AWFULLY FAST!
NOT FAST AS ME!
BOING
VWOM
CLEAR A SPACE!
COMING THROUGH!
THIS IS NO TIME TO PANIC!

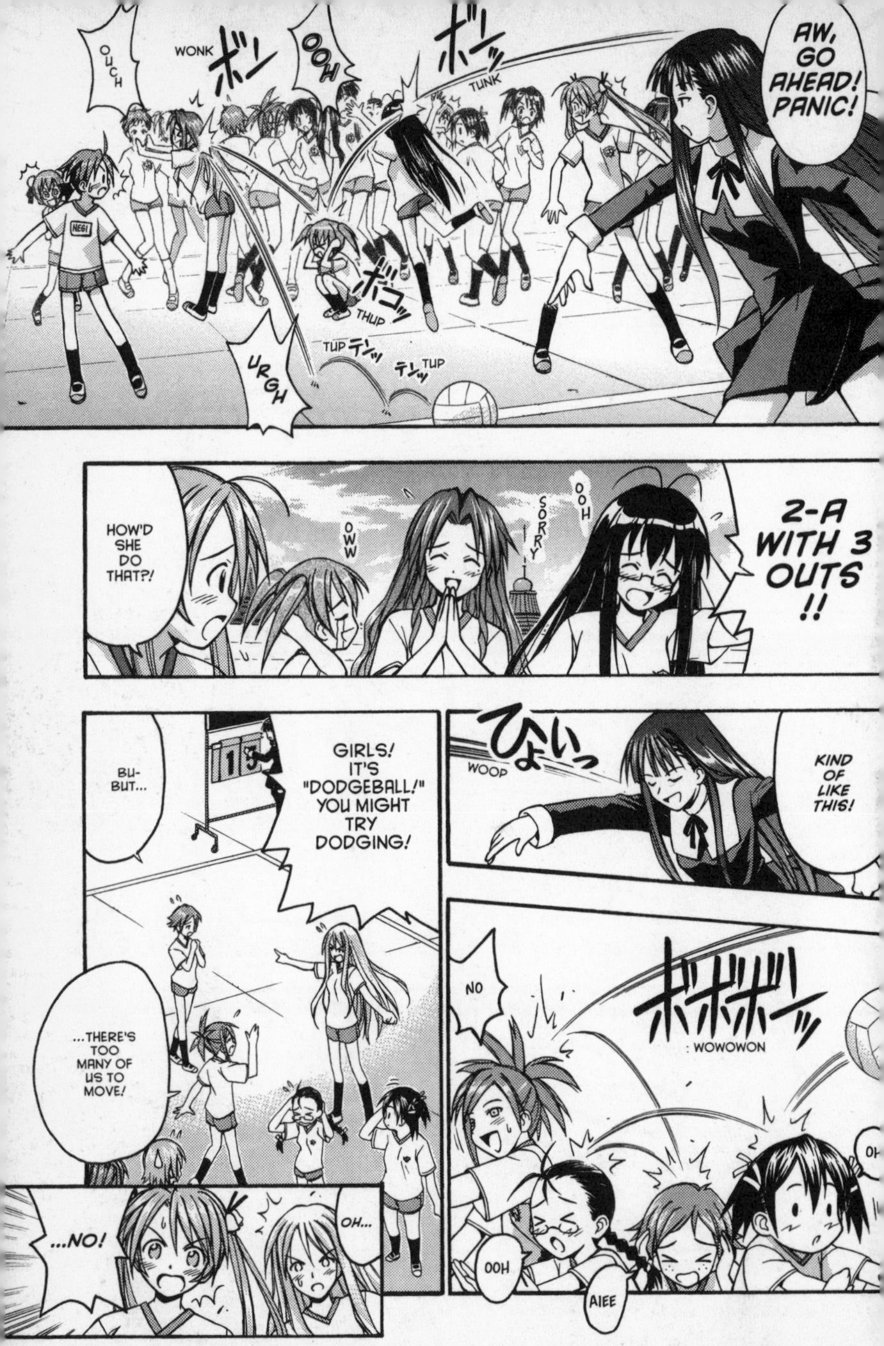
AW, GO AHEAD! PANIC!
ボーッ
TUNK
OOH
ボン
WONK
OUCH
ボゴッ
THUP
URGH
TUP テンッ
TUP テンッ
2-A WITH 3 OUTS !!
OOH
SORRY
OWW
HOW'D SHE DO THAT?!
KIND OF LIKE THIS!
ひょいっ
WOOP
OH
ボボボーッ
: WOWOWON
NO
AIEE
OOH
GIRLS! IT'S "DODGEBALL!" YOU MIGHT TRY DODGING!
BU-BUT...
...THERE'S TOO MANY OF US TO MOVE!
OH...
...NO!

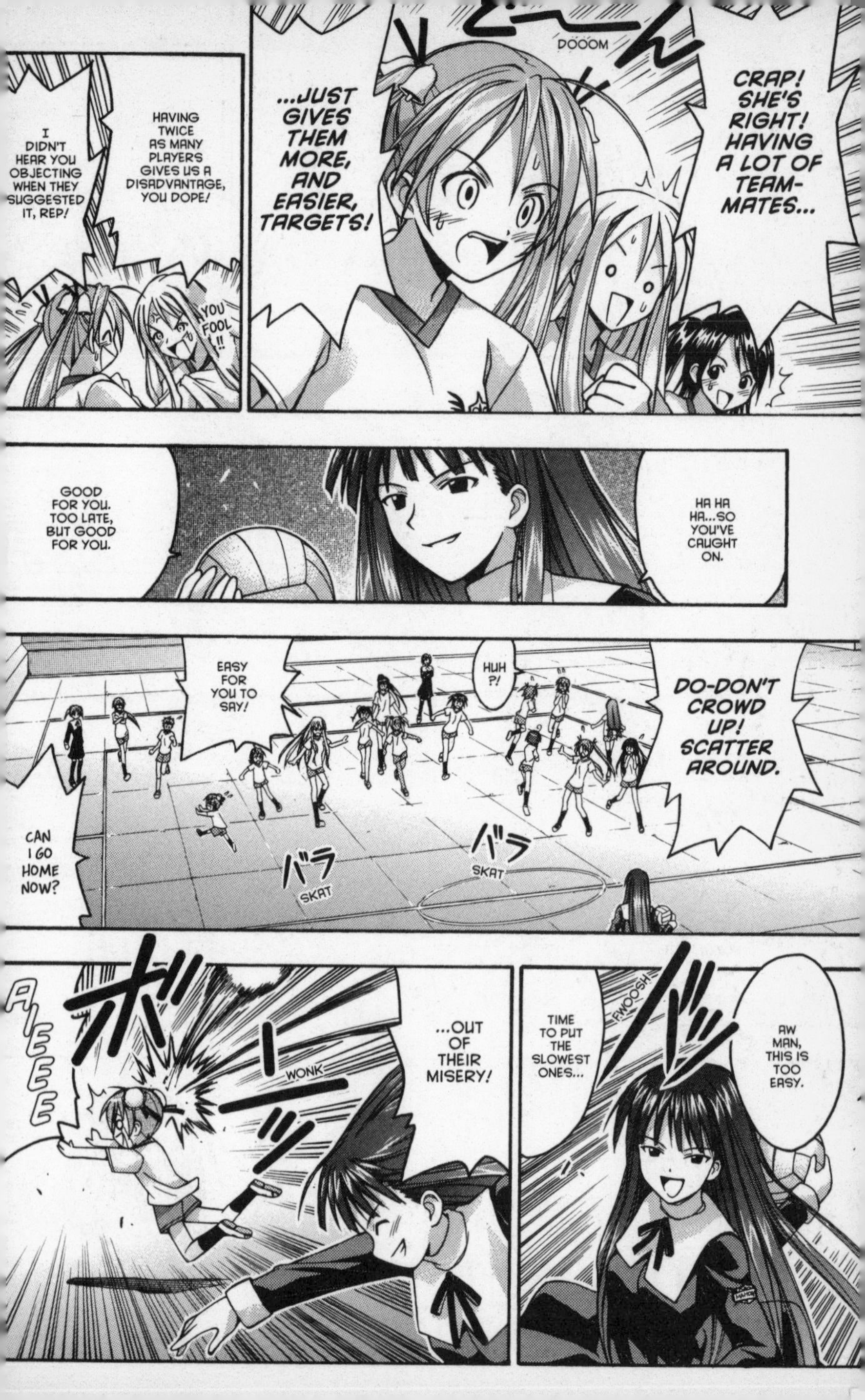
DOOOM
CRAP! SHE'S RIGHT! HAVING A LOT OF TEAM-MATES...
...JUST GIVES THEM MORE, AND EASIER, TARGETS!
HAVING TWICE AS MANY PLAYERS GIVES US A DISADVANTAGE, YOU DOPE!
I DIDN'T HEAR YOU OBJECTING WHEN THEY SUGGESTED IT, REP!
YOU FOOL!!
HA HA HA...SO YOU'VE CAUGHT ON.
GOOD FOR YOU. TOO LATE, BUT GOOD FOR YOU.
DO-DON'T CROWD UP! SCATTER AROUND.
HUH?!
EASY FOR YOU TO SAY!
SKAT
SKAT
CAN I GO HOME NOW?
AW MAN, THIS IS TOO EASY.
FWOOSH
TIME TO PUT THE SLOWEST ONES...
...OUT OF THEIR MISERY!
WONK
AIEEE

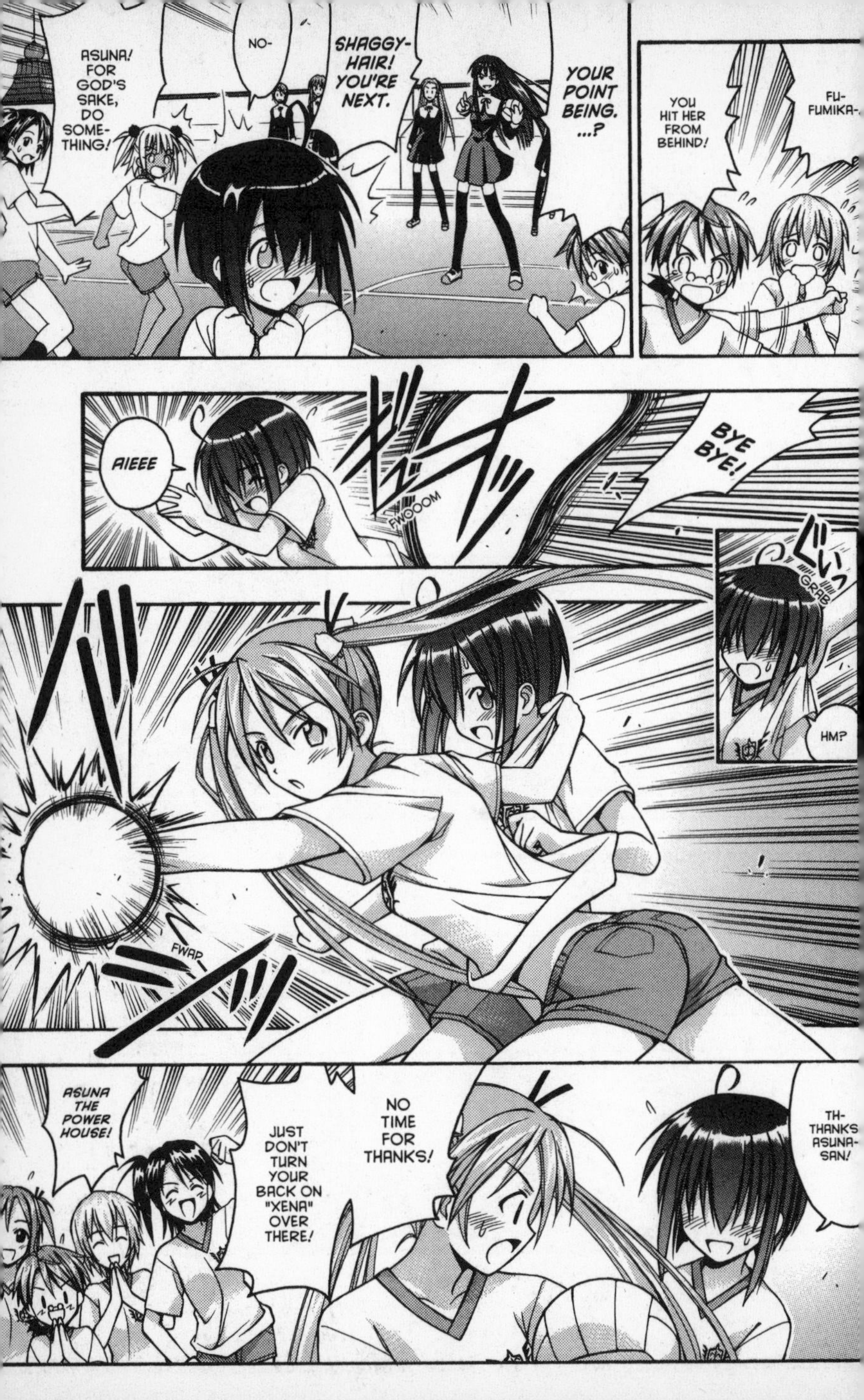
FU-FUMIKA-.
YOU HIT HER FROM BEHIND!
YOUR POINT BEING. ...?
SHAGGY-HAIR! YOU'RE NEXT.
NO-
ASUNA! FOR GOD'S SAKE, DO SOMETHING!
BYE BYE!
FWOOOM
AIEEE
GRAB
HM?
FWAP
TH-THANKS ASUNA-SAN!
NO TIME FOR THANKS!
JUST DON'T TURN YOUR BACK ON "XENA" OVER THERE!
ASUNA THE POWER HOUSE!

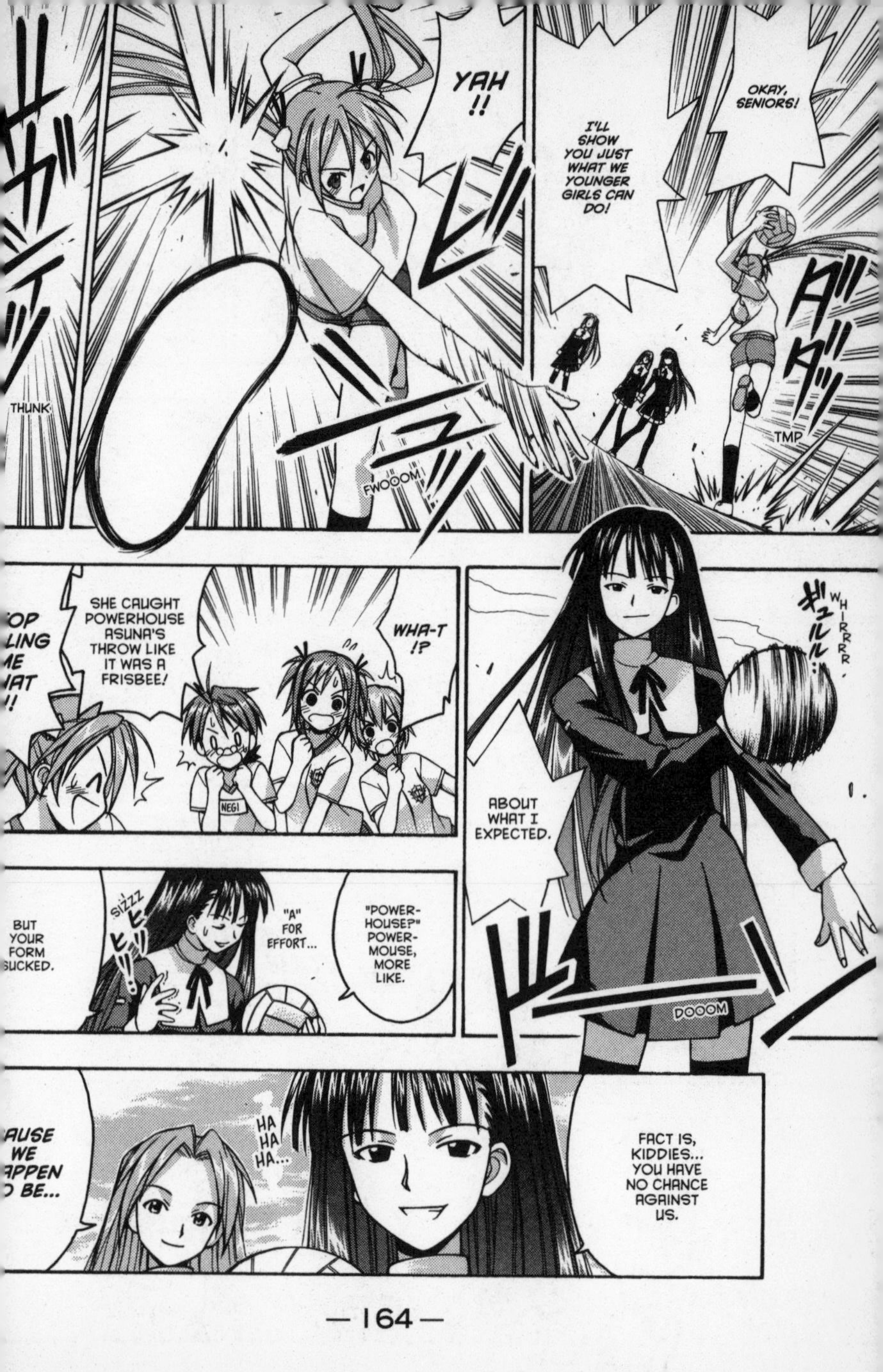
OKAY, SENIORS!
I'LL SHOW YOU JUST WHAT WE YOUNGER GIRLS CAN DO!
TMP
YAH !!
FWOOOM
THUNK
WHIRRRR
ABOUT WHAT I EXPECTED.
DOOOM
WHA-T !?
SHE CAUGHT POWERHOUSE ASUNA'S THROW LIKE IT WAS A FRISBEE!
NEGI
"POWER-HOUSE?" POWER-MOUSE, MORE LIKE.
"A" FOR EFFORT...
SIZZZ
BUT YOUR FORM SUCKED.
FACT IS, KIDDIES... YOU HAVE NO CHANCE AGAINST US.
HA HA HA...

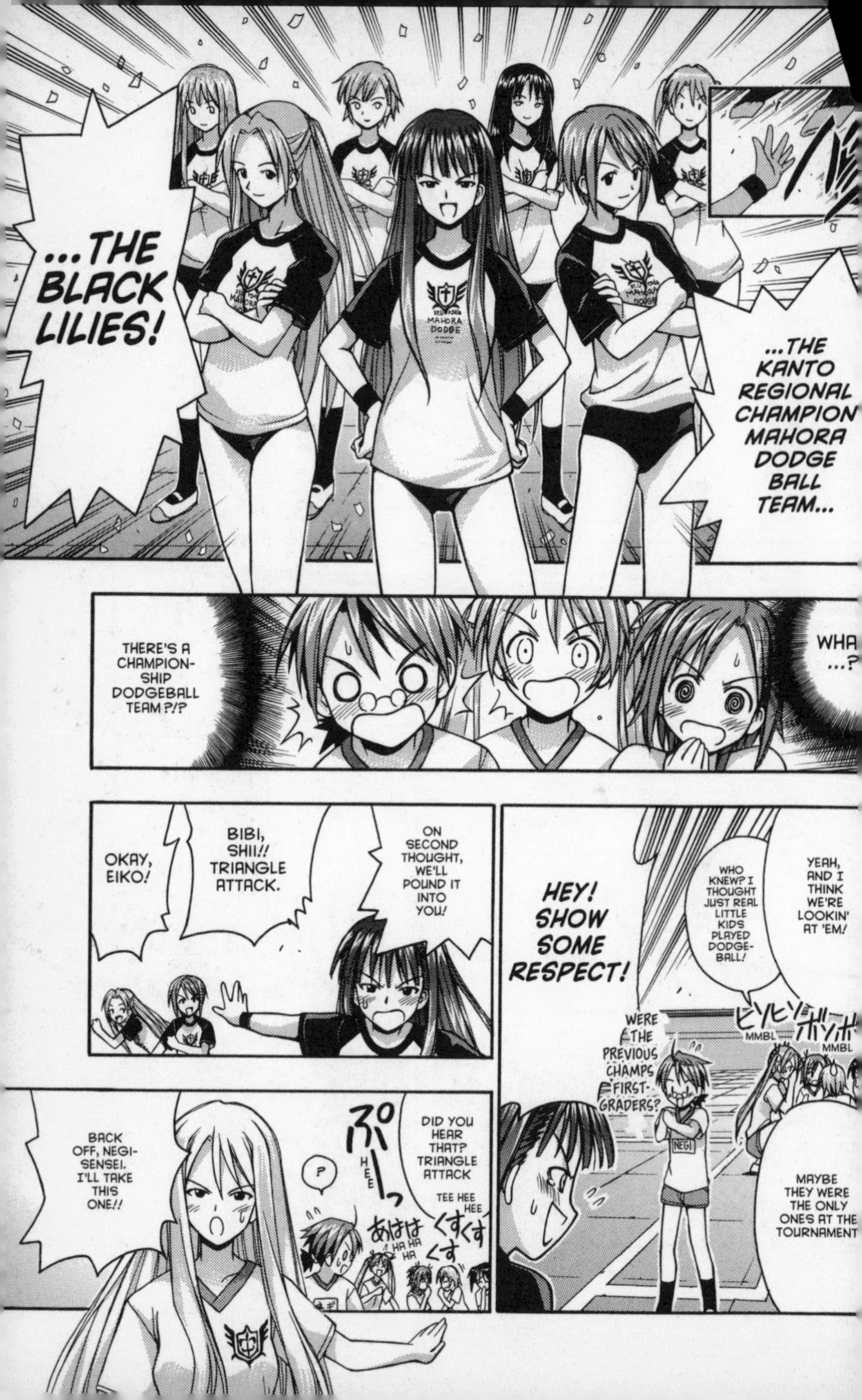
...THE KANTO REGIONAL CHAMPION MAHORA DODGE BALL TEAM...
...THE BLACK LILIES!
WHA ...?
THERE'S A CHAMPIONSHIP DODGEBALL TEAM?!?
YEAH, AND I THINK WE'RE LOOKIN' AT 'EM!
WHO KNEW? I THOUGHT JUST REAL LITTLE KIDS PLAYED DODGE-BALL!
HEY! SHOW SOME RESPECT!
ヒソヒソ MMBL
ボソボ MMBL
WERE THE PREVIOUS CHAMPS FIRST-GRADERS?
MAYBE THEY WERE THE ONLY ONES AT THE TOURNAMENT
ON SECOND THOUGHT, WE'LL POUND IT INTO YOU!
BIBI, SHII!! TRIANGLE ATTACK.
OKAY, EIKO!
DID YOU HEAR THAT? TRIANGLE ATTACK
ぷーっ HEE
?
TEE HEE HEE くすくすくす
あはは HA HA HA
BACK OFF, NEGI-SENSEI. I'LL TAKE THIS ONE!!

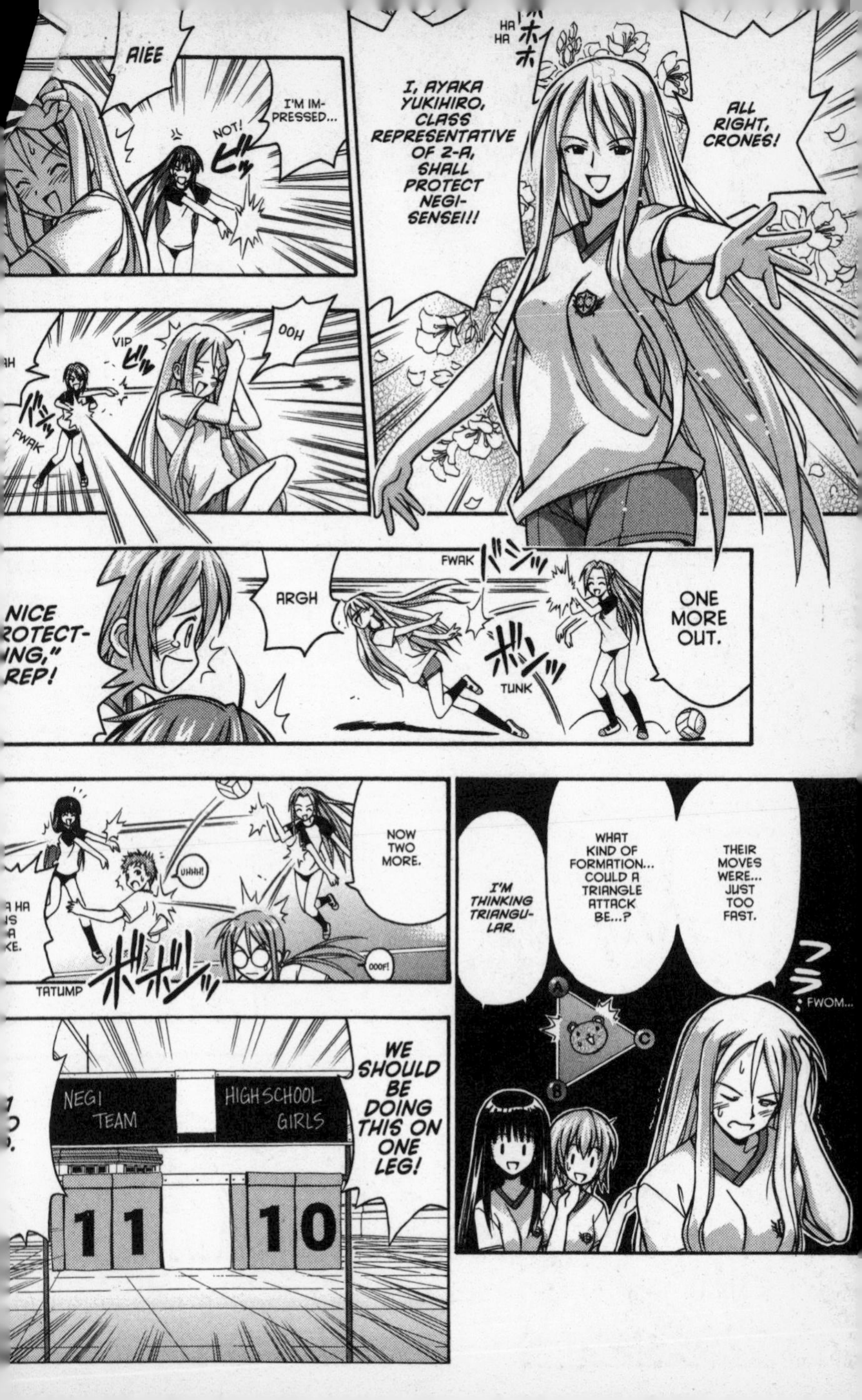
ALL RIGHT, CRONES!
HA HA
I, AYAKA YUKIHIRO, CLASS REPRESENTATIVE OF 2-A, SHALL PROTECT NEGI-SENSEI!!
AIEE
I'M IM-PRESSED...
NOT!
OOH
VIP
FWAK
ONE MORE OUT.
FWAK
TUNK
ARGH
NICE ROTECT-NG," REP!
THEIR MOVES WERE... JUST TOO FAST.
WHAT KIND OF FORMATION... COULD A TRIANGLE ATTACK BE...?
I'M THINKING TRIANGU-LAR.
FWOM...
A
C
B
NOW TWO MORE.
UHHH!
OOOF!
TATUMP
WE SHOULD BE DOING THIS ON ONE LEG!
NEGI TEAM
HIGH SCHOOL GIRLS
11
10

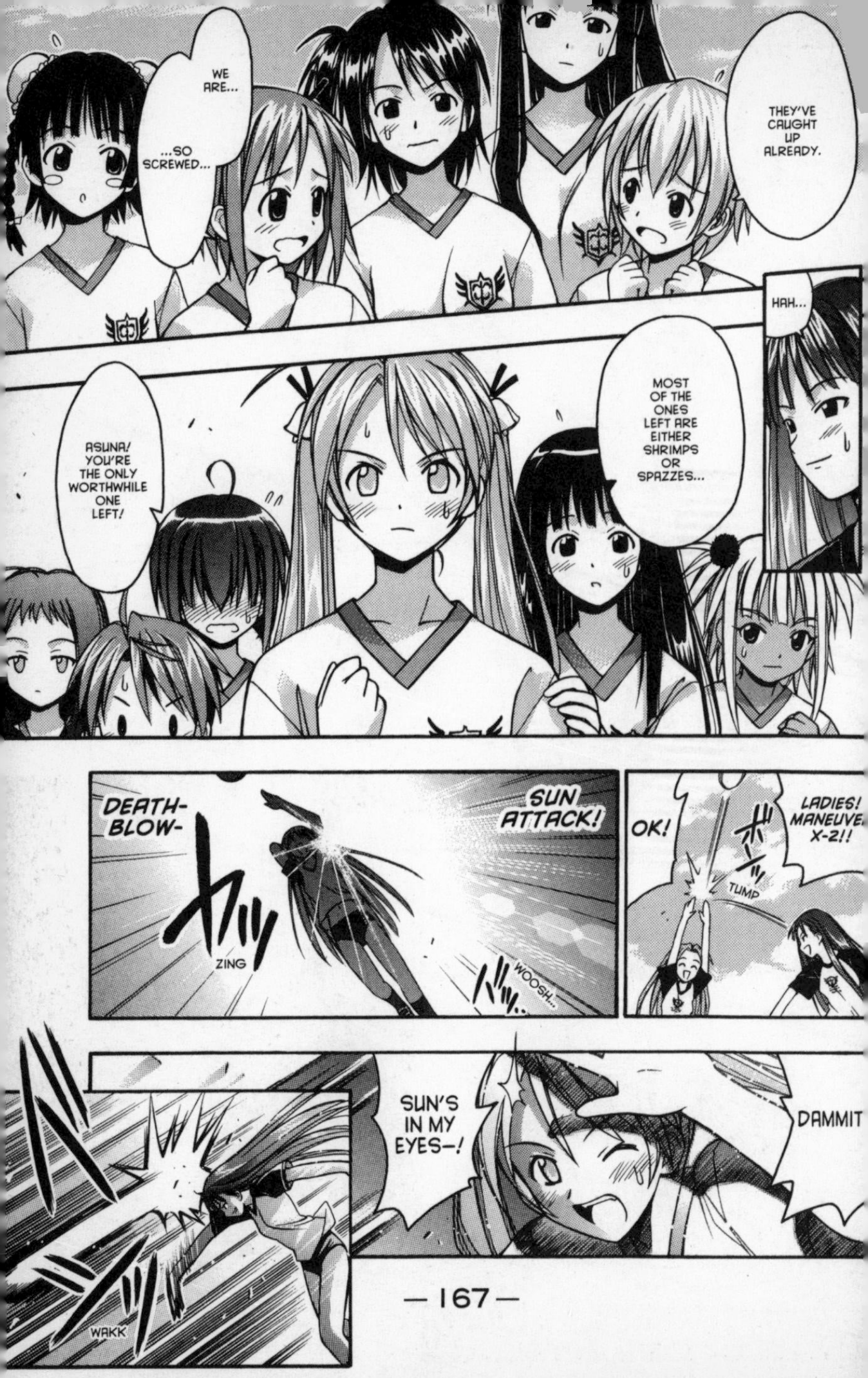
THEY'VE CAUGHT UP ALREADY.
WE ARE...
...SO SCREWED...
HAH...
MOST OF THE ONES LEFT ARE EITHER SHRIMPS OR SPAZZES...
ASUNA! YOU'RE THE ONLY WORTHWHILE ONE LEFT!
LADIES! MANEUVE X-2!!
OK!
TUMP
DEATH-BLOW-
SUN ATTACK!
ZING
WOOSH...
DAMMIT
SUN'S IN MY EYES—!
WAKK

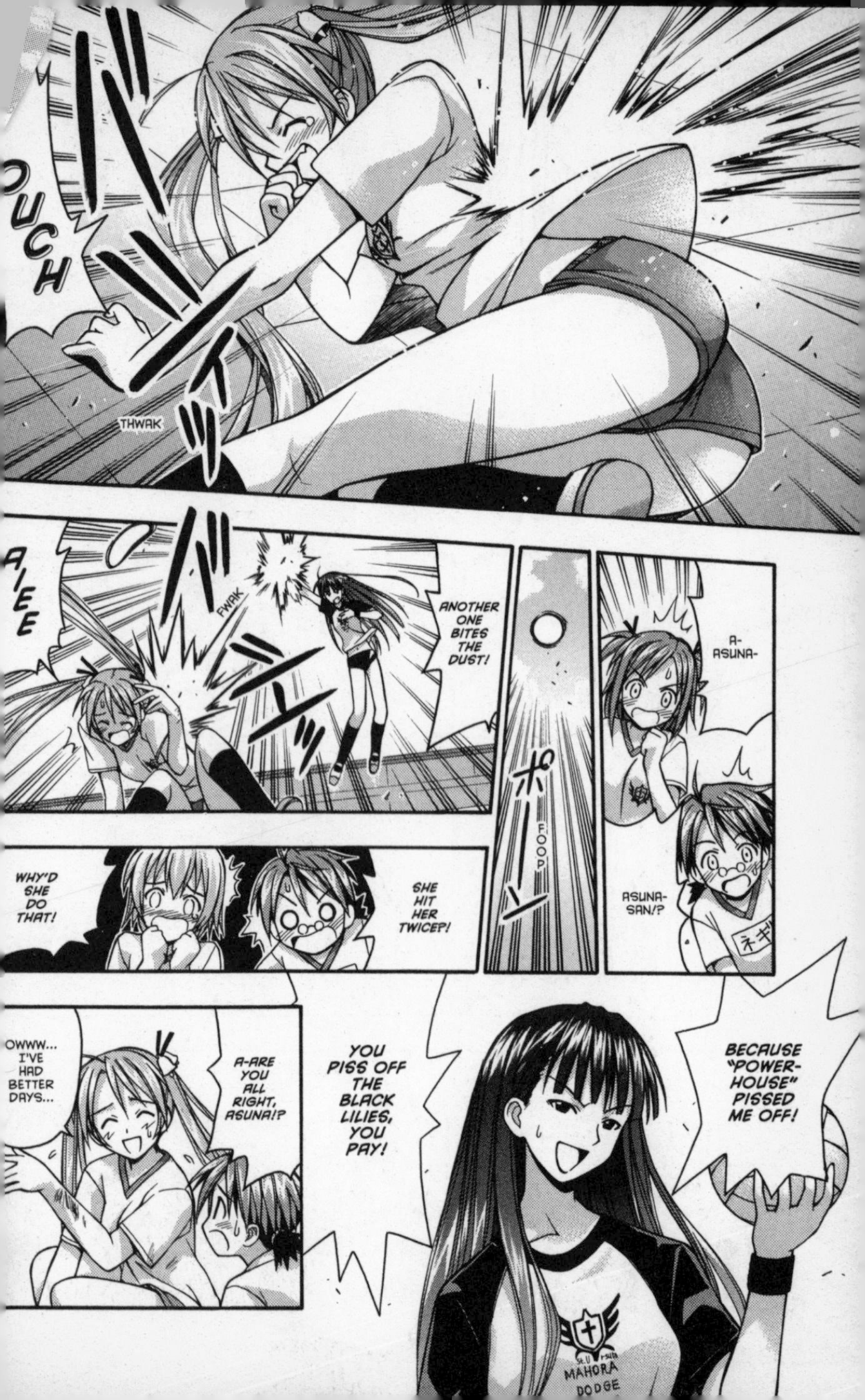
OUCH
THWAK
A-ASUNA-
ASUNA-SAN!?
FOOP
ANOTHER ONE BITES THE DUST!
FWAK
AIEE
SHE HIT HER TWICE!?
WHY'D SHE DO THAT!
BECAUSE "POWER-HOUSE" PISSED ME OFF!
YOU PISS OFF THE BLACK LILIES, YOU PAY!
MAHORA DODGE
A-ARE YOU ALL RIGHT, ASUNA!?
OWWW... I'VE HAD BETTER DAYS...

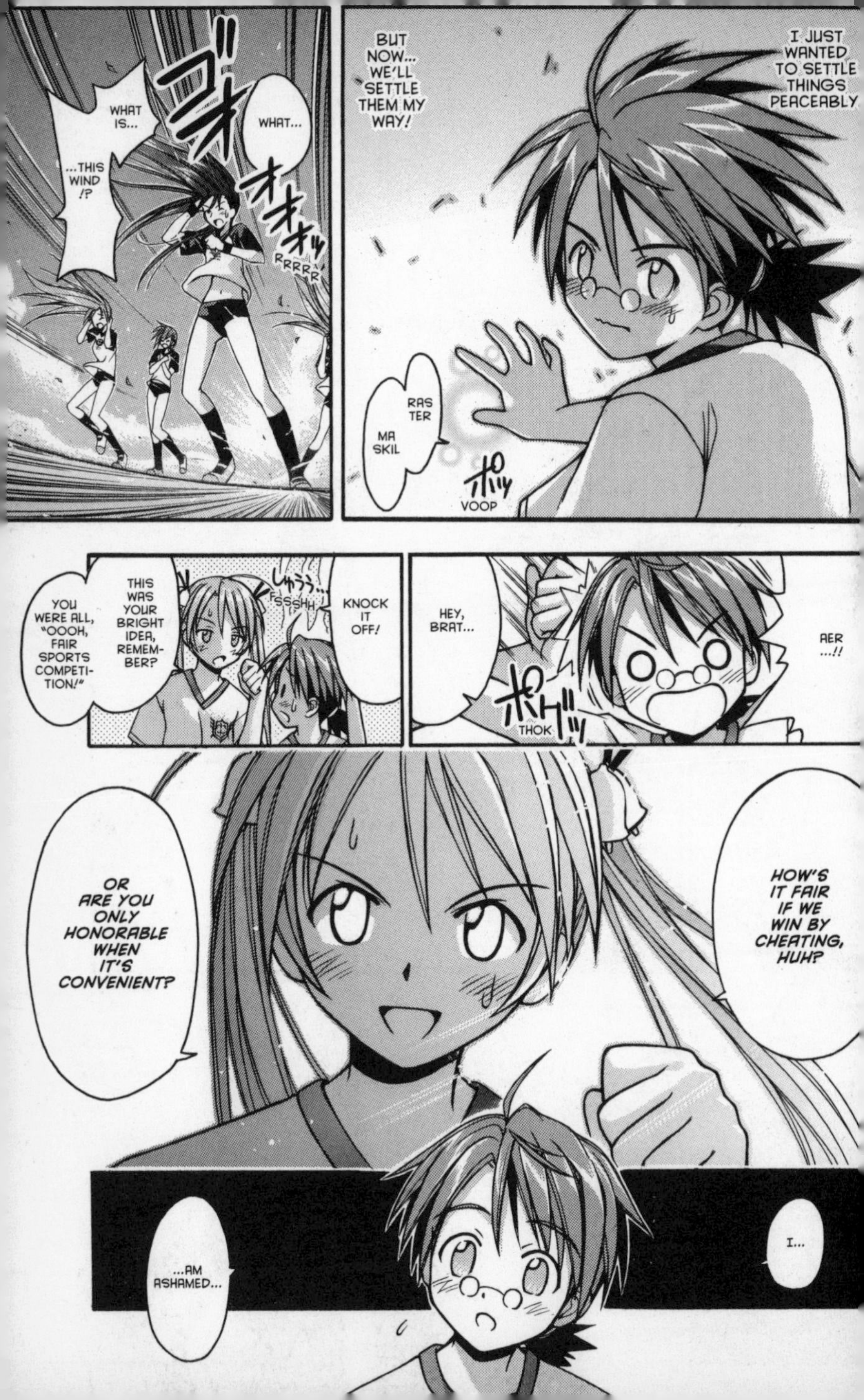
I JUST WANTED TO SETTLE THINGS PEACEABLY
BUT NOW... WE'LL SETTLE THEM MY WAY!
RAS TER MA SKIL
ポッ
VOOP
ゴオオオッ
RRRRRR
WHAT...
WHAT IS...
...THIS WIND!?
AER ...!!
HEY, BRAT...
ポグッ
THOK
KNOCK IT OFF!
しゅううう...
FSSSHH
THIS WAS YOUR BRIGHT IDEA, REMEMBER?
YOU WERE ALL, "OOOH, FAIR SPORTS COMPETITION!"
HOW'S IT FAIR IF WE WIN BY CHEATING, HUH?
OR ARE YOU ONLY HONORABLE WHEN IT'S CONVENIENT?
I...
...AM ASHAMED...

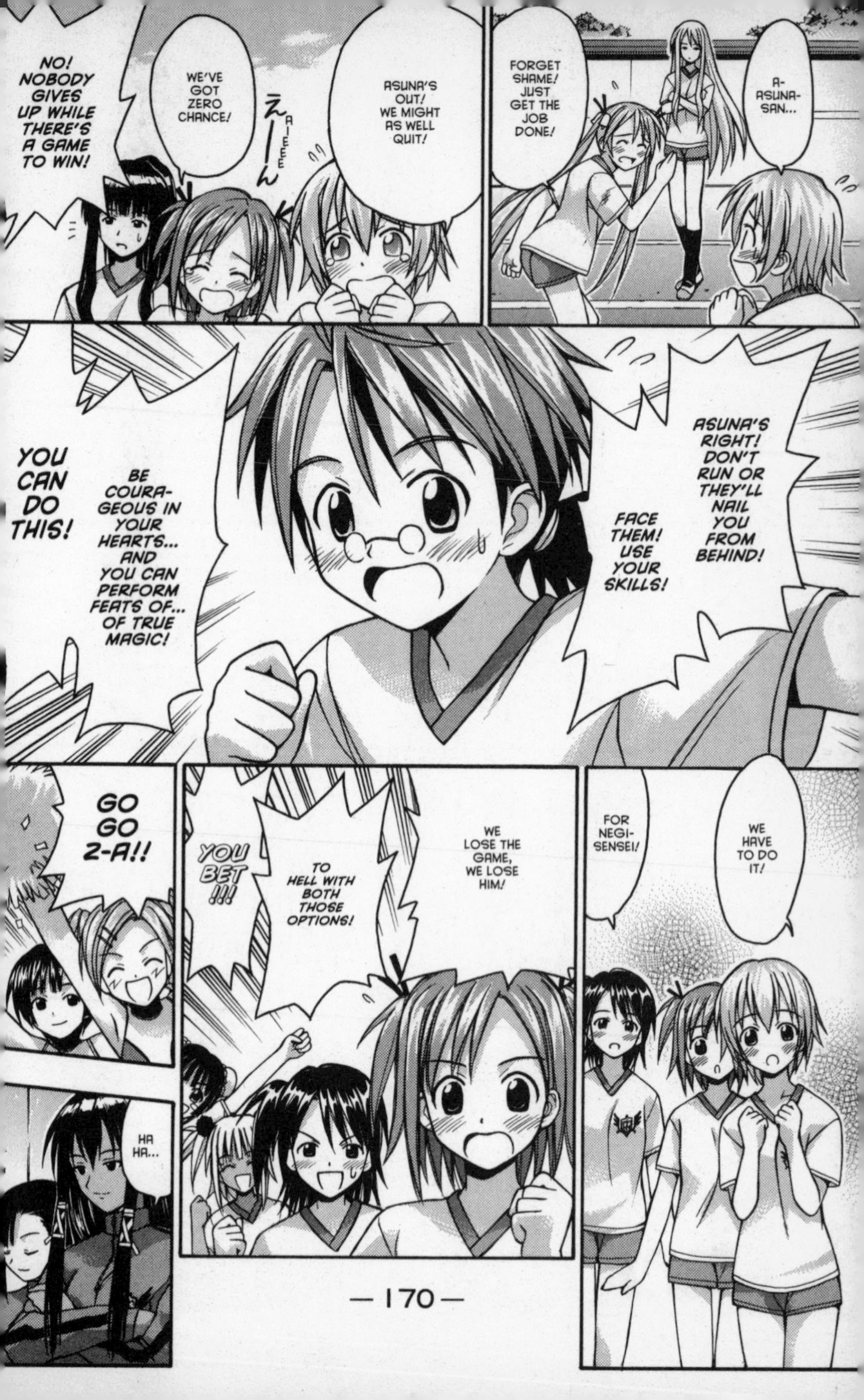
A-ASUNA-SAN...
FORGET SHAME! JUST GET THE JOB DONE!
ASUNA'S OUT! WE MIGHT AS WELL QUIT!
えーん
AIEEE
WE'VE GOT ZERO CHANCE!
NO! NOBODY GIVES UP WHILE THERE'S A GAME TO WIN!
ASUNA'S RIGHT! DON'T RUN OR THEY'LL NAIL YOU FROM BEHIND!
FACE THEM! USE YOUR SKILLS!
BE COURAGEOUS IN YOUR HEARTS... AND YOU CAN PERFORM FEATS OF... OF TRUE MAGIC!
YOU CAN DO THIS!
WE HAVE TO DO IT!
FOR NEGI-SENSEI!
WE LOSE THE GAME, WE LOSE HIM!
TO HELL WITH BOTH THOSE OPTIONS!
YOU BET!!!
GO GO 2-A!!
HA HA...

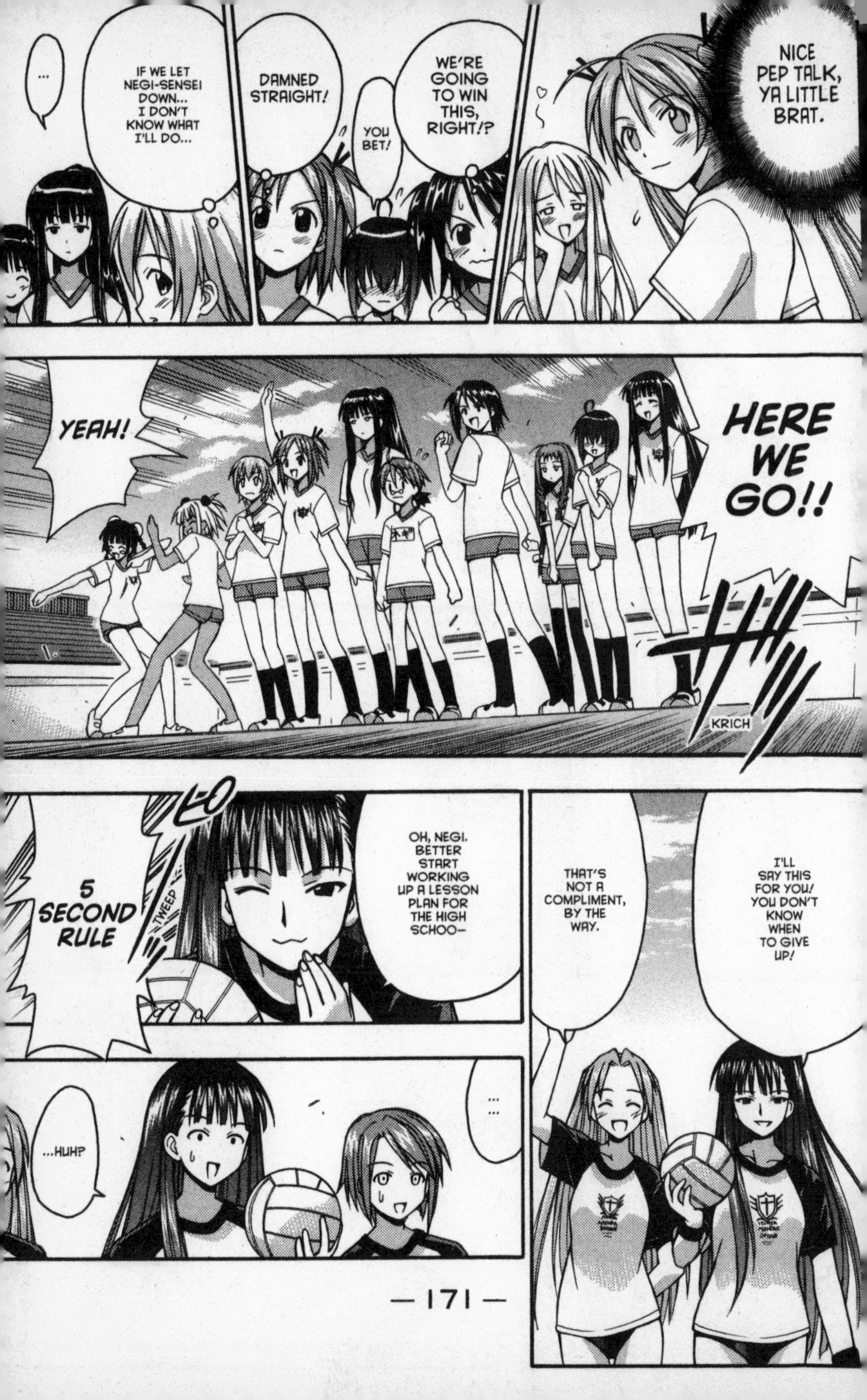
NICE PEP TALK, YA LITTLE BRAT.
WE'RE GOING TO WIN THIS, RIGHT!?
YOU BET!
DAMNED STRAIGHT!
IF WE LET NEGI-SENSEI DOWN... I DON'T KNOW WHAT I'LL DO...
...
HERE WE GO!!
KRICH
YEAH!
I'LL SAY THIS FOR YOU! YOU DON'T KNOW WHEN TO GIVE UP!
THAT'S NOT A COMPLIMENT, BY THE WAY.
OH, NEGI. BETTER START WORKING UP A LESSON PLAN FOR THE HIGH SCHOO—
TWEEP
5 SECOND RULE
......
...HUH?

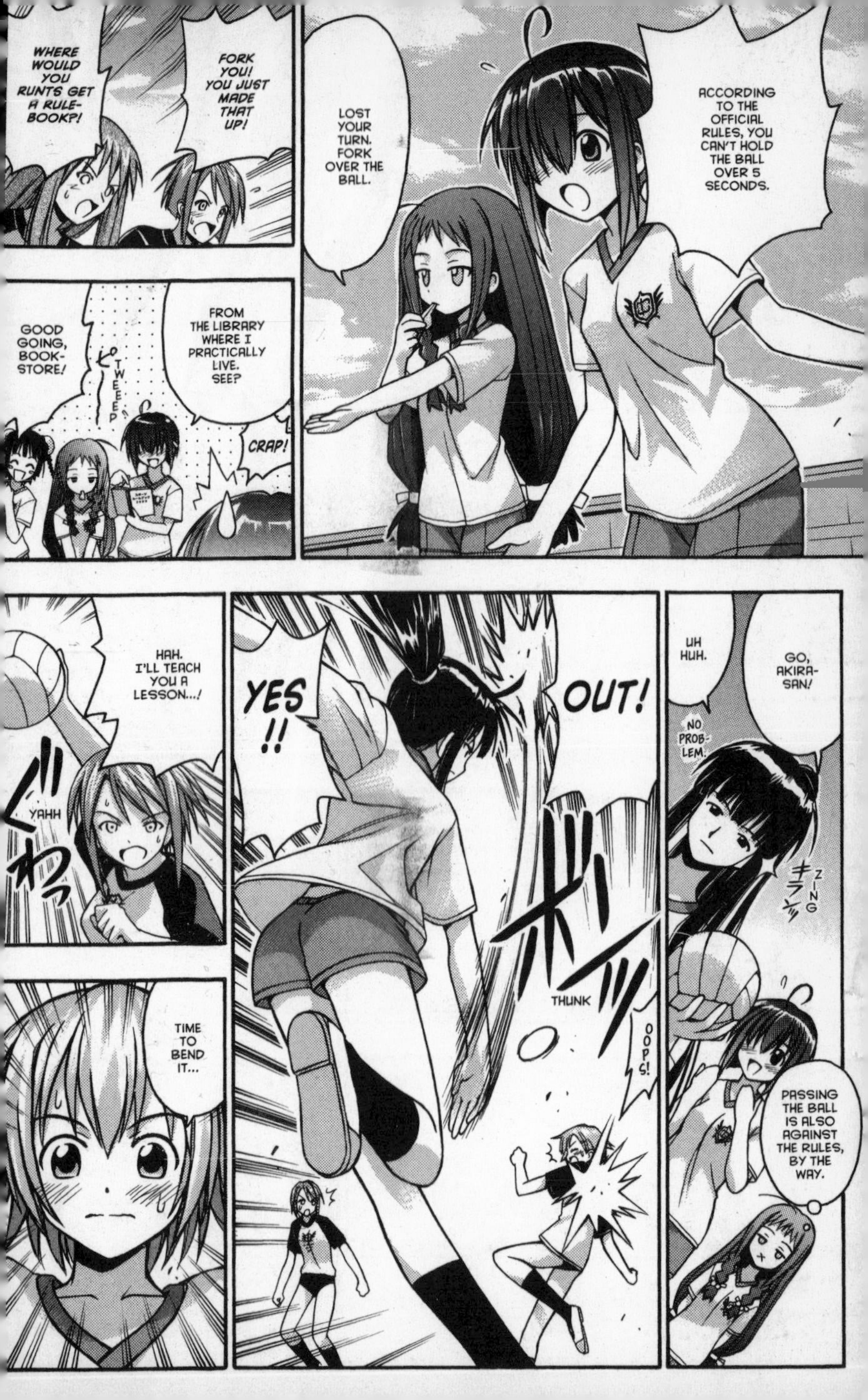
ACCORDING TO THE OFFICIAL RULES, YOU CAN'T HOLD THE BALL OVER 5 SECONDS.
LOST YOUR TURN. FORK OVER THE BALL.
FORK YOU! YOU JUST MADE THAT UP!
WHERE WOULD YOU RUNTS GET A RULE-BOOK?!
FROM THE LIBRARY WHERE I PRACTICALLY LIVE. SEE?
TWEEEP
CRAP!
GOOD GOING, BOOK-STORE!
GO, AKIRA-SAN!
UH HUH.
NO PROB-LEM.
ZING
PASSING THE BALL IS ALSO AGAINST THE RULES, BY THE WAY.
OUT!
YES !!
THUNK
OOPS!
HAH. I'LL TEACH YOU A LESSON...!
YAHH
TIME TO BEND IT...

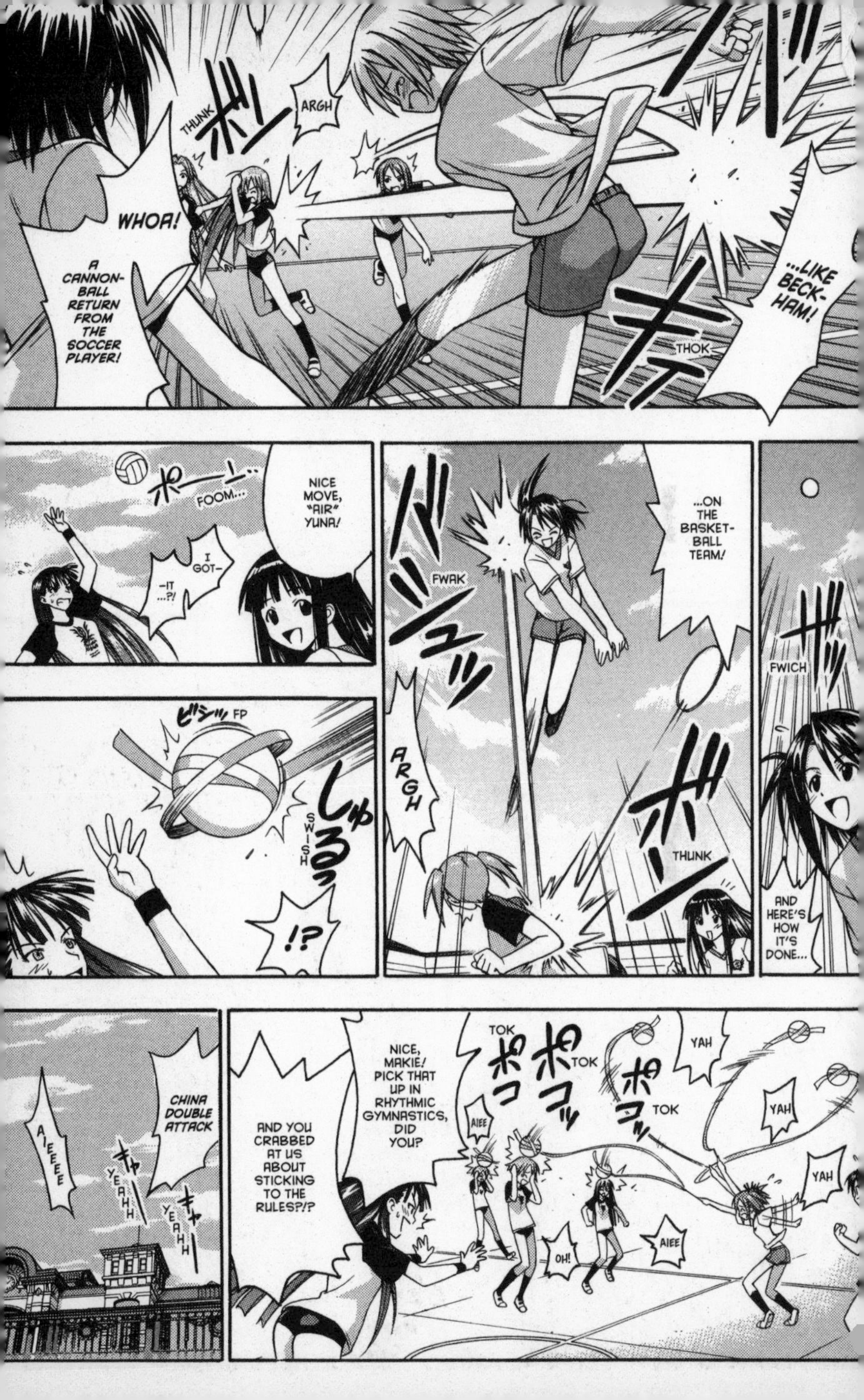
...LIKE BECKHAM!
THOK
ARGH
THUNK
WHOA!
A CANNONBALL RETURN FROM THE SOCCER PLAYER!
FWICH
AND HERE'S HOW IT'S DONE...
...ON THE BASKETBALL TEAM!
FWAK
ARGH
THUNK
NICE MOVE, "AIR" YUNA!
FOOM...
I GOT-
-IT ...?!
FP
SWISH
!?
YAH
YAH
YAH
TOK
TOK
TOK
AIEE
AIEE
OH!
NICE, MAKIE! PICK THAT UP IN RHYTHMIC GYMNASTICS, DID YOU?
AND YOU CRABBED AT US ABOUT STICKING TO THE RULES?!?
CHINA DOUBLE ATTACK
YEAHH
YEAHH
AIEEEE

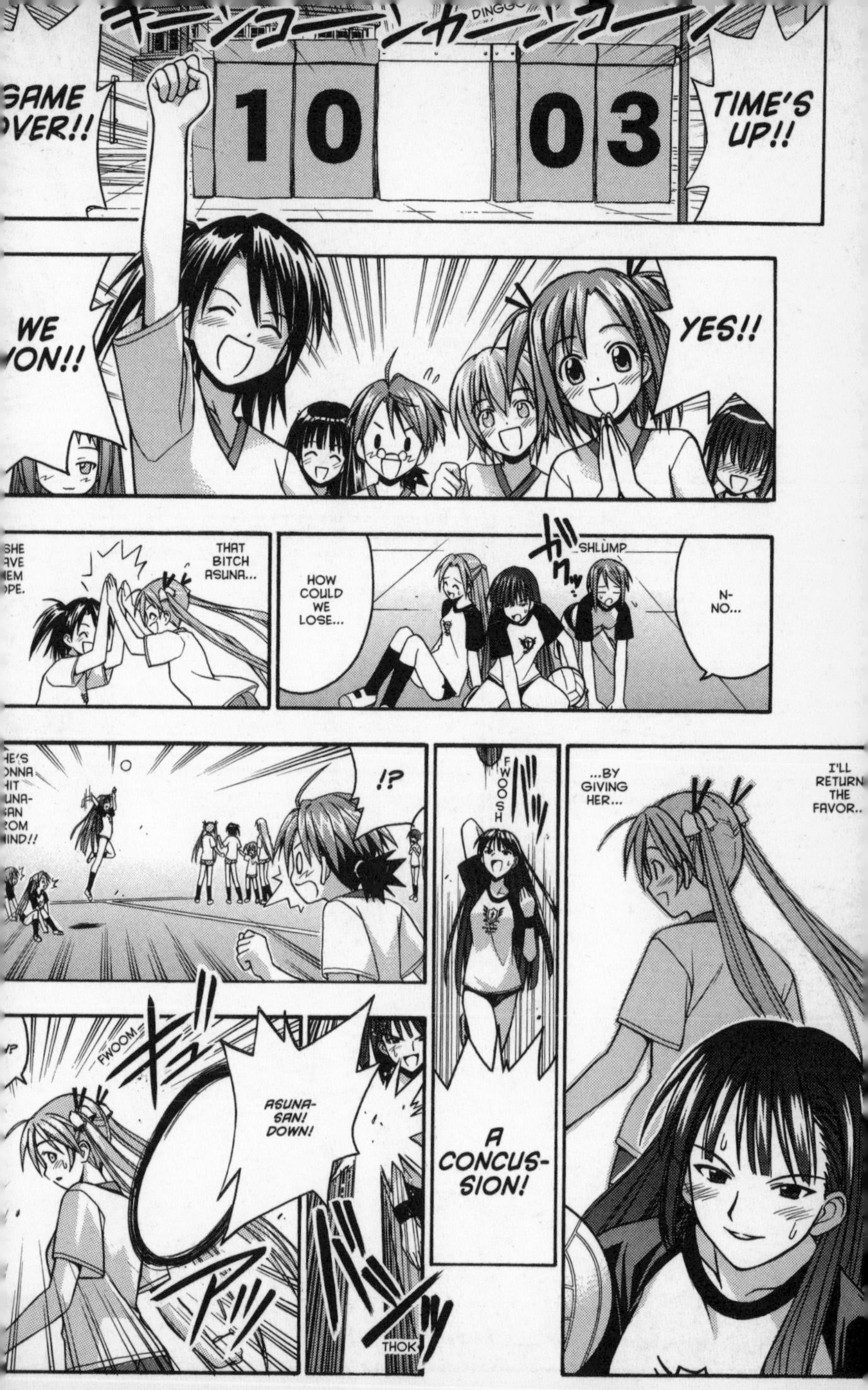
キーンコーンカーンコーン
DINGGO
TIME'S UP!!
GAME VER!!
YES!!
WE ON!!
N- NO...
SHLUMP
HOW COULD WE LOSE...
THAT BITCH ASUNA...
SHE AVE HEM OPE.
I'LL RETURN THE FAVOR..
...BY GIVING HER...
FWOOSH
A CONCUSSION!
!?
HE'S ONNA HIT UNA-SAN ROM IND!!
ASUNA-SAN! DOWN!
FWOOM
THOK

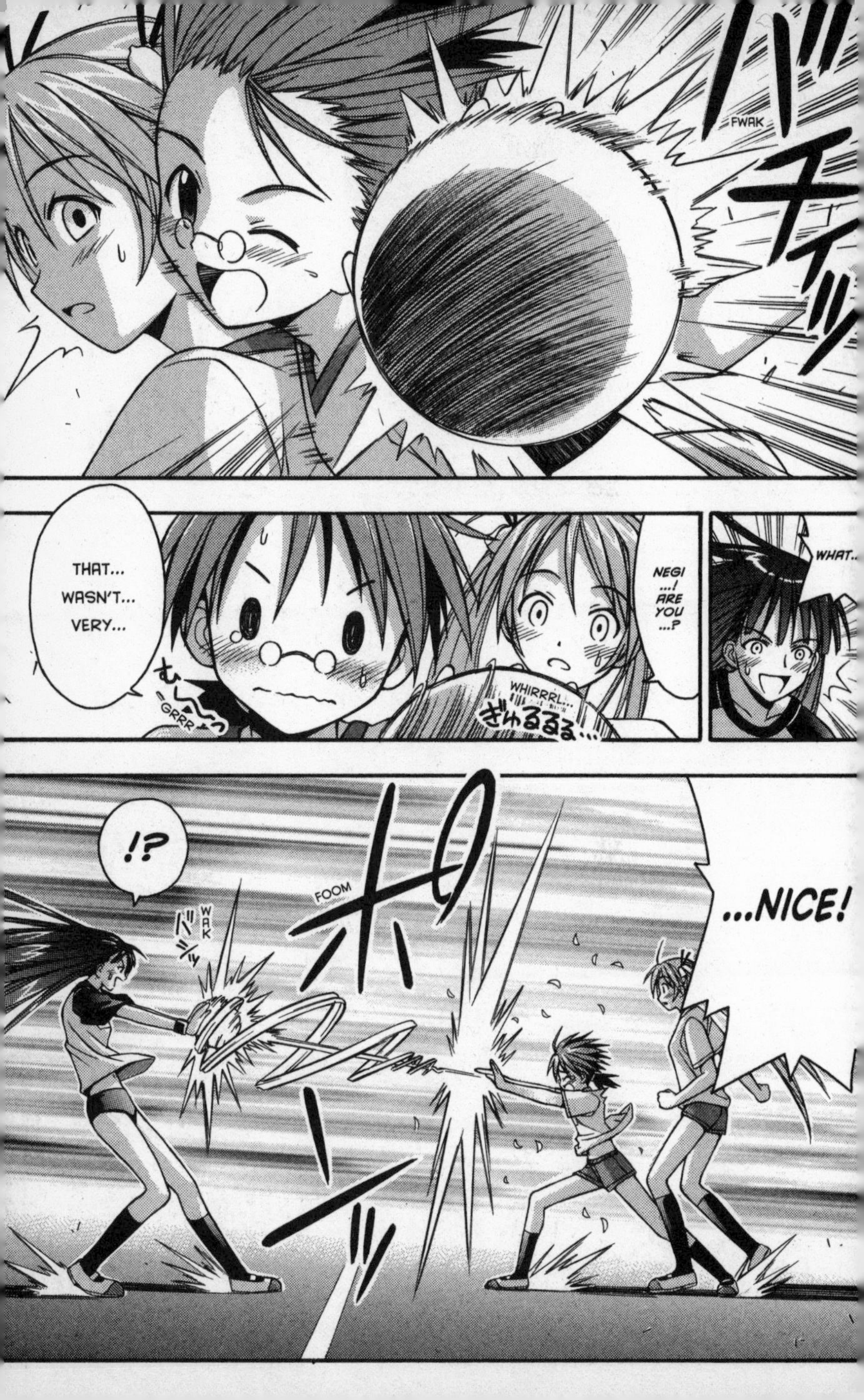

FWAK
WHAT...
NEGI ...! ARE YOU ...?
WHIRRRL...
ぎゅるるる...
THAT... WASN'T... VERY...
GRRR
...NICE!
FOOM
WAK
!?

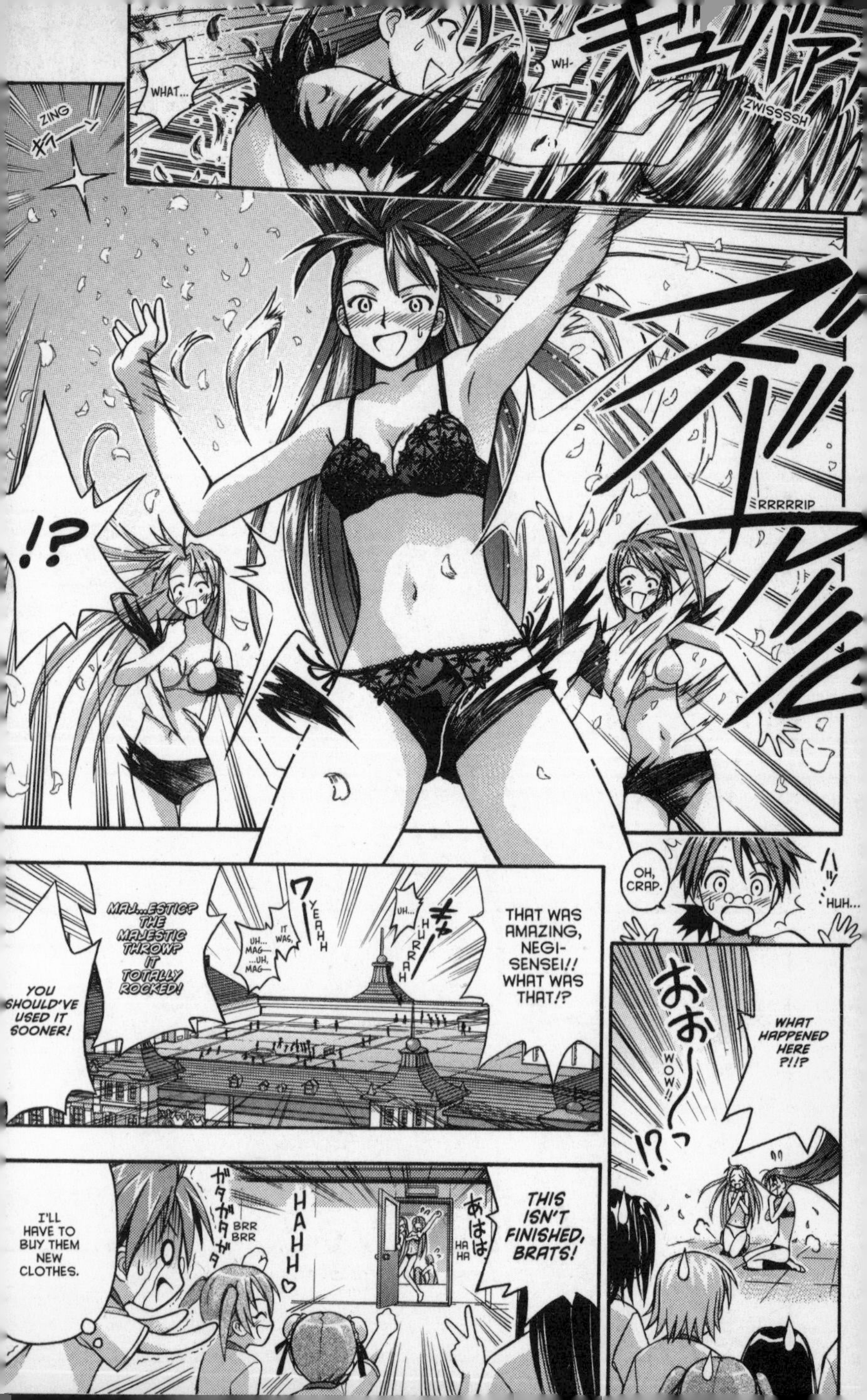
ギュバア
ZWISSSSH
WH-
WHAT...
ZING
ギィーン
ズバァァァ
RRRRRIP
!?
ハッ
HUH...
OH, CRAP.
THAT WAS AMAZING, NEGI-SENSEI!! WHAT WAS THAT!?
HURRAH
UH...
YEAHH
IT WAS, UH... MAG— UH, MAG—
MAJ...ESTIC? THE MAJESTIC THROW? IT TOTALLY ROCKED!
YOU SHOULD'VE USED IT SOONER!
おお〜
WOW!!
WHAT HAPPENED HERE ?!!?
!?っ
THIS ISN'T FINISHED, BRATS!
あはは
HA HA
HAHH♡
ガタガタ
BRR BRR
I'LL HAVE TO BUY THEM NEW CLOTHES.

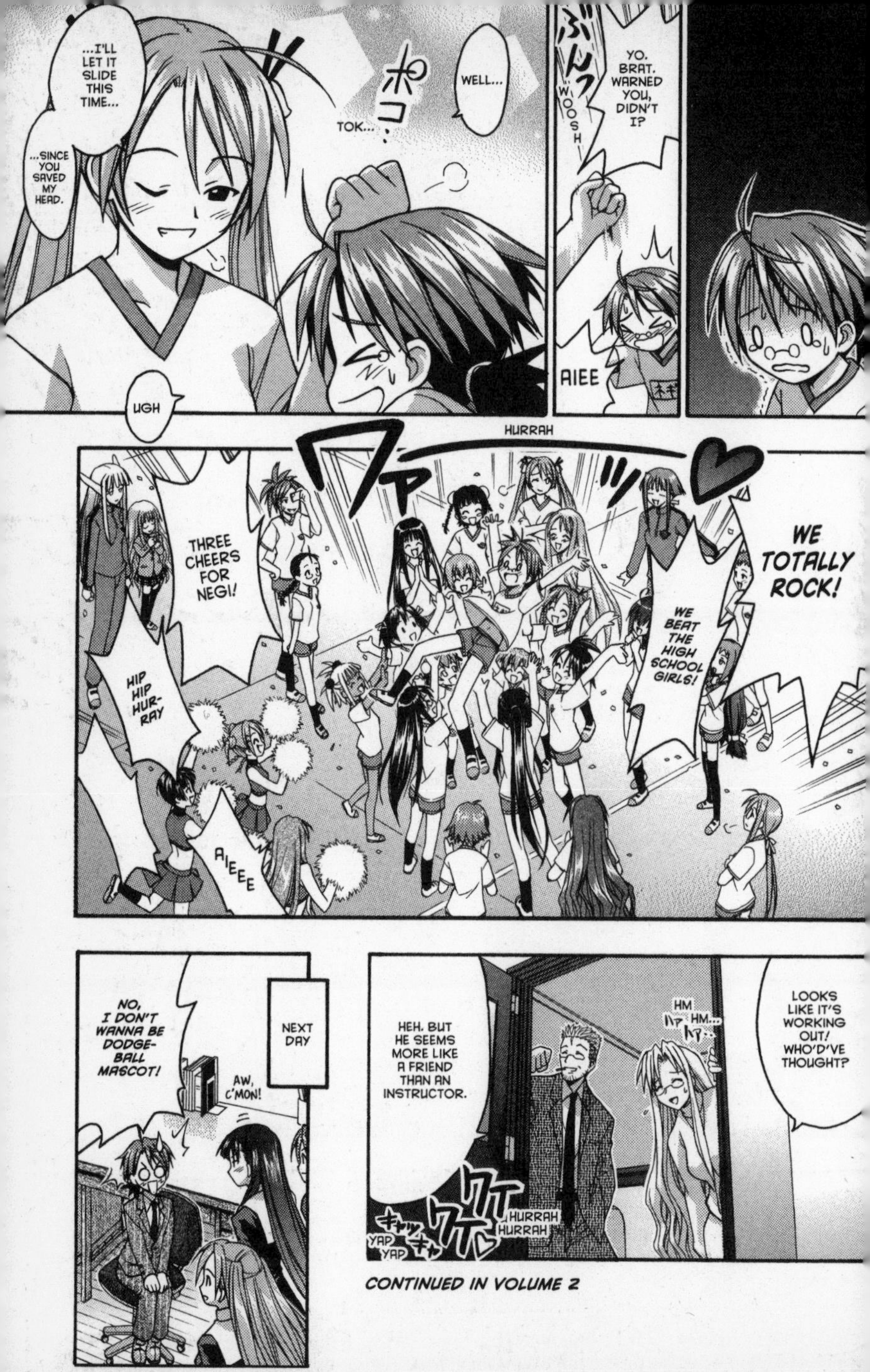
YO. BRAT. WARNED YOU, DIDN'T I?
WOOSH
AIEE
WELL...
TOK...
...I'LL LET IT SLIDE THIS TIME...
...SINCE YOU SAVED MY HEAD.
UGH
HURRAH
WE TOTALLY ROCK!
WE BEAT THE HIGH SCHOOL GIRLS!
THREE CHEERS FOR NEGI!
HIP HIP HUR-RAY
AIEEE
LOOKS LIKE IT'S WORKING OUT! WHO'D'VE THOUGHT?
HM HM...
HEH. BUT HE SEEMS MORE LIKE A FRIEND THAN AN INSTRUCTOR.
HURRAH HURRAH
YAP YAP
NEXT DAY
NO, I DON'T WANNA BE DODGE-BALL MASCOT!
AW, C'MON!

CONTINUED IN VOLUME 2

– STAFF –

Ken Akamatsu
Takashi Takemoto
Kenichi Nakamura
Masaki Ohyama
Keiichi Yamashita
Chigusa Amagasaki
Takaaki Miyahara
Kei Nishikawa

Thanks To

Ran Ayanaga
Toshiko Akamatsu

Welcome. . .

. . . to the launch of the Del Rey Manga line! It all starts here, with four new series from Japan: *Negima!* by Ken Akamatsu! *Gundam SEED* by Masatsuga Iwase! And *Tsubasa: Reservoir Chronicle* and *xxxHOLiC*, both by CLAMP! Together, these four series represent some of the best and most popular manga series published in Japan.

We're dedicated to providing our readers with the most enjoyable, authentic manga experience possible. Our books are printed from right to left, in the Japanese printing format. We strive to keep the translations as true to the original as possible, while giving the English versions the same sense of adventure and fun. We keep Japanese honorifics intact, translate all sound effects, and give you extras at the back of the books to help you understand the context of the stories and keep track of all the characters. It's the next best thing to being able to read Japanese yourself!

For information on upcoming releases, visit www.delreymanga.com, and while you're there be sure to sign up for our newsletter. If you do, you'll be the first to hear all the scoop on Del Rey Manga, and you'll have the opportunity to talk back directly to the editor (that would be me) and say what works for you in our books, and what doesn't. Manga wouldn't be the red-hot phenomenon it is without your support, and we want your feedback.

See you in volume 2!

Dallas Middaugh

Dallas Middaugh
Director of Manga, Del Rey Books

About the Creator

Negima! is only Ken Akamatsu's third manga, although he started working in the field in 1994 with *AI Ga Tomaranai*. Like all of Akamatsu's work to date, it was published in Kodansha's *Shonen Magazine*. *AI Ga Tomaranai* ran for five years before concluding in 1999. In 1998, however, Akamatsu began the work that would make him one of the most popular manga artists in Japan: *Love Hina*. *Love Hina* ran for four years, and before its conclusion in 2002, it would cause Akamatsu to be granted the prestigious Manga of the Year award from Kodansha, as well as going on to become one of the best-selling manga in the United States.

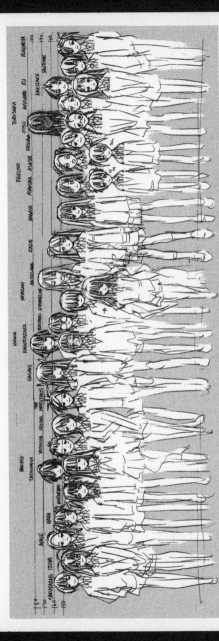

"PROFESSOR" NEGI, MAGUS
PROVISIONAL 3-A HEIGHT CHART

SAKURAZAKI IZUMI AYASE NADA MURAKAMI NAKASE TATSUMIYA YOTSUYA SHIINA THE NARUTAKIS SASAKI KONOE KAGURAZAKA YUKIHIRO EVANGELINE MIYAZAKI HASEGAWA ZAZIE NAGASE RAKUSO ASAKURA ASAHI KASUGA TOBISAKA OTSU AKUSAWA KU KAKIZAKE SAOTOME KUGIMIYA
180
170
160
150

"MAGISTER NEGIMA!" CONCEPT ART COLLECTION

OFFICIAL PROVISIONAL VERSION

COMMENTS BY KEN AKAMATSU

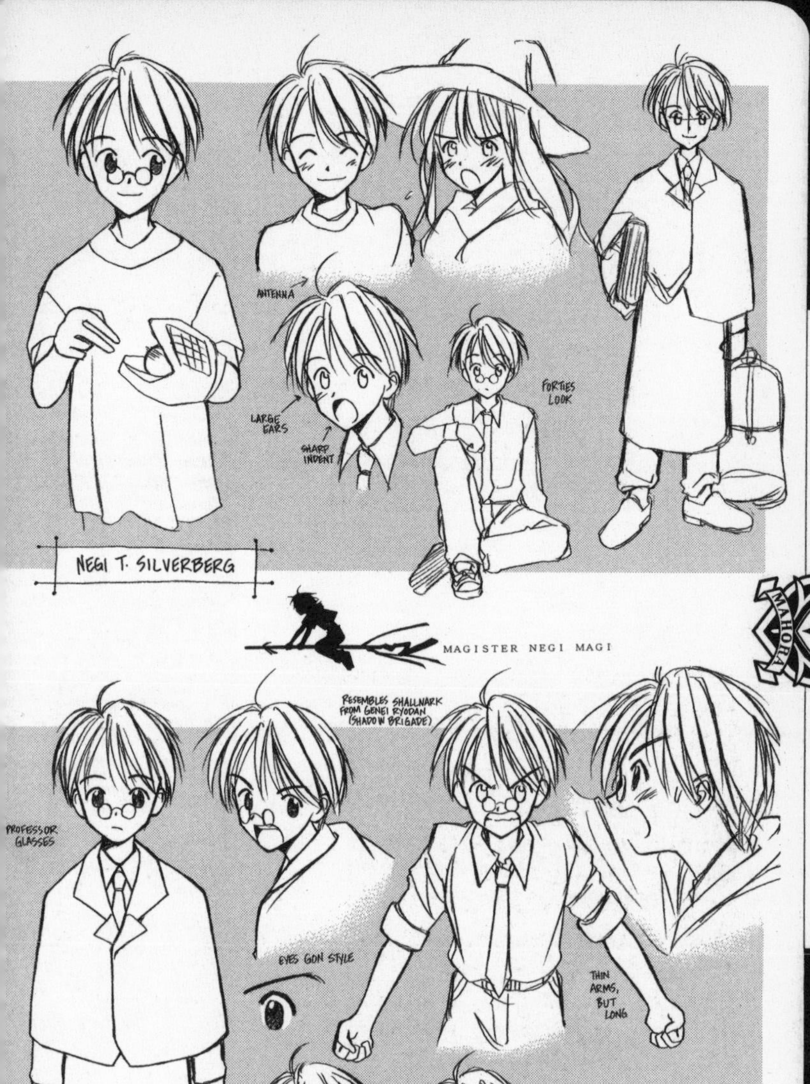
ANTENNA
LARGE EARS
SHARP INDENT
FORTIES LOOK
NEGI T. SILVERBERG
MAGISTER NEGI MAGI
RESEMBLES SHALLNARK FROM GENEI RYODAN (SHADOW BRIGADE)
PROFESSOR GLASSES
EYES GON STYLE
THIN ARMS, BUT LONG
SUPER DEFORMED SHOULD BE MORE LIKE GON STYLE THAN AZUMANGA

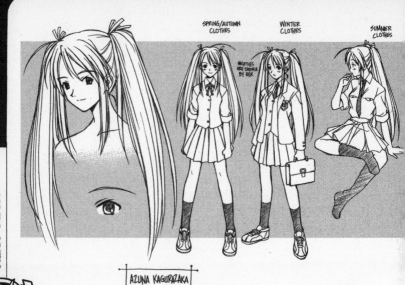

SPRING/AUTUMN CLOTHES

WINTER CLOTHES

SUMMER CLOTHES

HAIRTIES ARE CHOSEN BY HER

AZUNA KAGURAZAKA

THE CONCEPT ART FOR THE MALE AND FEMALE PROTAGONIST. NEGI'S LIKE, "WHAT?" (^^;) WE ENDED UP REJECTING THIS VERSION, OPTING FOR A MORE CHILDISH, ROUND FACED CHARACTER.
HE IS CUTER THAT WAY AFTER ALL~ ♡
THE FEMALE PROTAGONIST IS BASICALLY TAKEN FROM A HEROINE CHARACTER FROM A CANCELLED PROJECT I WAS WORKING ON BEFORE "NEGIMA". THESE TWO ARE LIKE SIBLINGS, SO MAYBE ITS A LITTLE ODD AS A LOVE COMEDY?

MAGISTER NEGI MAGI

140cm

159cm

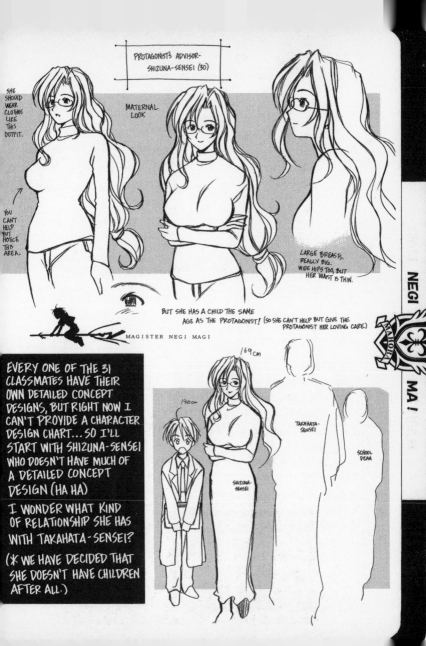

PROTAGONIST'S ADVISOR—
SHIZUNA-SENSEI (30)

SHE SHOULD WEAR CLOTHES LIKE THIS OUTFIT.

MATERNAL LOOK

YOU CAN'T HELP BUT NOTICE THIS AREA.

LARGE BREASTS, REALLY BIG. WIDE HIPS TOO, BUT HER WAIST IS THIN.

BUT SHE HAS A CHILD THE SAME AGE AS THE PROTAGONIST! (SO SHE CAN'T HELP BUT GIVE THE PROTAGONIST HER LOVING CARE.)

MAGISTER NEGI MAGI

169 cm

140 cm

TAKAHATA-SENSEI

SCHOOL DEAN

SHIZUNA-SENSEI

EVERY ONE OF THE 31 CLASSMATES HAVE THEIR OWN DETAILED CONCEPT DESIGNS, BUT RIGHT NOW I CAN'T PROVIDE A CHARACTER DESIGN CHART... SO I'LL START WITH SHIZUNA-SENSEI WHO DOESN'T HAVE MUCH OF A DETAILED CONCEPT DESIGN (HA HA)

I WONDER WHAT KIND OF RELATIONSHIP SHE HAS WITH TAKAHATA-SENSEI?

(* WE HAVE DECIDED THAT SHE DOESN'T HAVE CHILDREN AFTER ALL.)

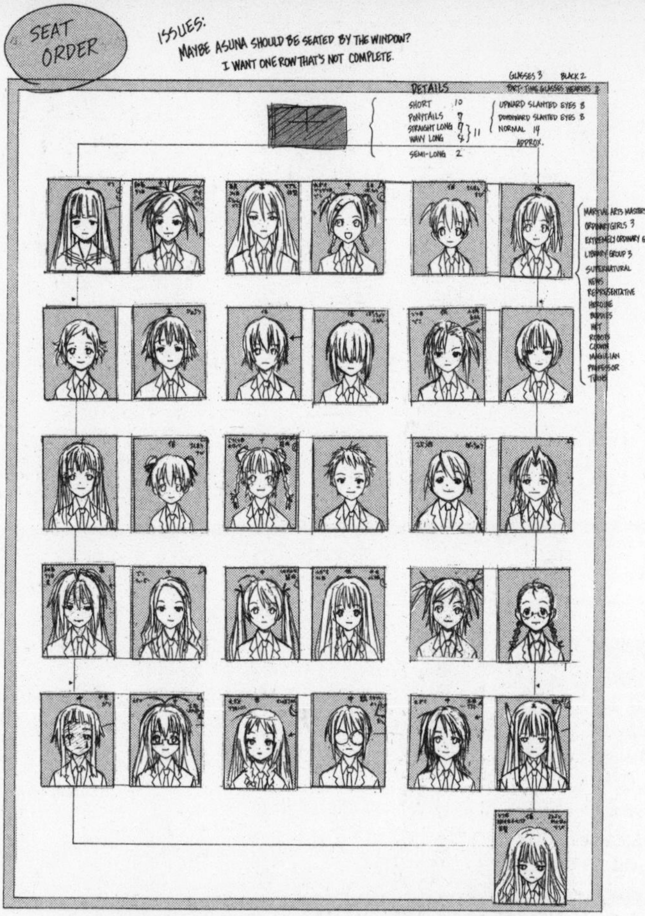
SEAT ORDER
ISSUES:
MAYBE ASUNA SHOULD BE SEATED BY THE WINDOW?
I WANT ONE ROW THAT'S NOT COMPLETE.
GLASSES 3
BLACK 2
DETAILS
PART-TIME GLASSES WEARERS 2
SHORT 10
PONYTAILS 7
STRAIGHT LONG 7
WAVY LONG 4
11
SEMI-LONG 2
UPWARD SLANTED EYES 8
DOWNWARD SLANTED EYES 8
NORMAL 14
APPROX.
MARTIAL ARTS MASTERS 4
ORDINARY GIRLS 3
EXTREMELY ORDINARY GIRLS
LIBRARY GROUP 3
SUPERNATURAL
NEWS
REPRESENTATIVE
HEROINE
BUDDIES
NET
ROBOTS
CLOWN
MAGICIAN
PROFESSOR
TWINS

NEXT, WE'LL BE SHOWING THE CLASSMATE CONCEPT DESIGNS ~ (^^).

MAYBE YOUR FAVORITE GAL WILL SHOW UP. SEE YOU IN VOLUME 2 THEN!

MAGISTER NEGI MAGI MAGISTER NEG

Translation Notes

Japanese is a tricky language for most westerners, and translation is often more art than science. For your edification and reading pleasure, here are notes on some of the places where we could have gone in a different direction in our translation of the work, or where a Japanese cultural reference is used.

If you're reading all of the manga from the launch (and if you're not, go pick up *Gundam SEED*, *xxxHOLiC*, and *Tsubasa* right now!), you'll have seen that we've gone to great effort to keep our translations as authentic as possible. Nowhere did that pose such a challenge, however, as with *Negima!*

Two decisions we made early on in planning the line were to maintain Japanese honorifics as appropriate (for example, if a manga were set in, say, America, there would be little point in keeping them), and to translate all sound effects. We've managed to do both of these things in all of our books, but *Negima!* has been the most—shall we say—troublesome.

To begin with, take a look through the book at all of the sound effects. Akamatsu-sensei sure does like to use them, doesn't he? Where in our other manga we were experiencing 0 to 5 sound effects per page, with several pages lacking effects entirely, *Negima!* has more like 2 to 10 effects and asides per page! As difficult as it was to translate them all (and I'm not certain, but it's possible we managed to miss some along the way), *Negima!* highlights why it is so necessary to do the extra translation work and provide the reader with a more complete, immersive reading experience.

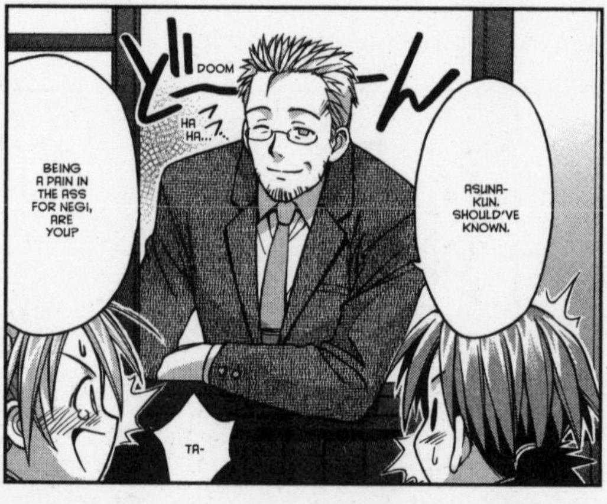
ASUNA-KUN. SHOULD'VE KNOWN.
DOOM
HA HA...
BEING A PAIN IN THE ASS FOR NEGI, ARE YOU?
TA-

While honorifics came up in our other manga, they were definitely a major necessity in *Negima!* because it takes place in a school—a very formal setting in Japan. An understanding of Japanese honorifics drives home the relationships between the characters. Look at when Negi first runs into Takahata—he calls him by his first name with no honorific at all, clearly indicating they are good friends.

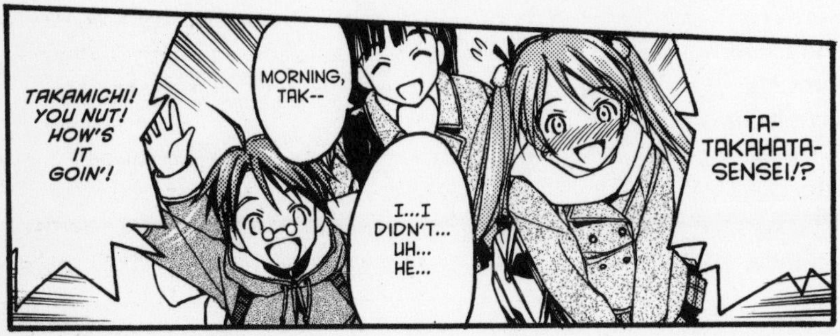
TA-TAKAHATA-SENSEI!?
MORNING, TAK--
I...I DIDN'T... UH... HE...
TAKAMICHI! YOU NUT! HOW'S IT GOIN'!

Likewise, when Takahata interrupts Asuna and Negi after school, he calls them both Asuna-kun and Negi-kun, which to Negi should indicate friendship, while to Asuna it's simply an acknowledgment that she is a student and Takahata is a teacher.

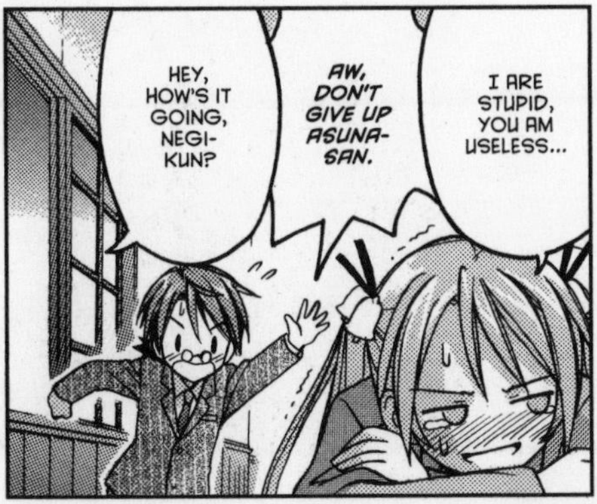
I ARE STUPID, YOU AM USELESS...
AW, DON'T GIVE UP ASUNA-SAN.
HEY, HOW'S IT GOING, NEGI-KUN?

Preview of Volume 2

Here is an excerpt from Volume 2, on sale in English now.

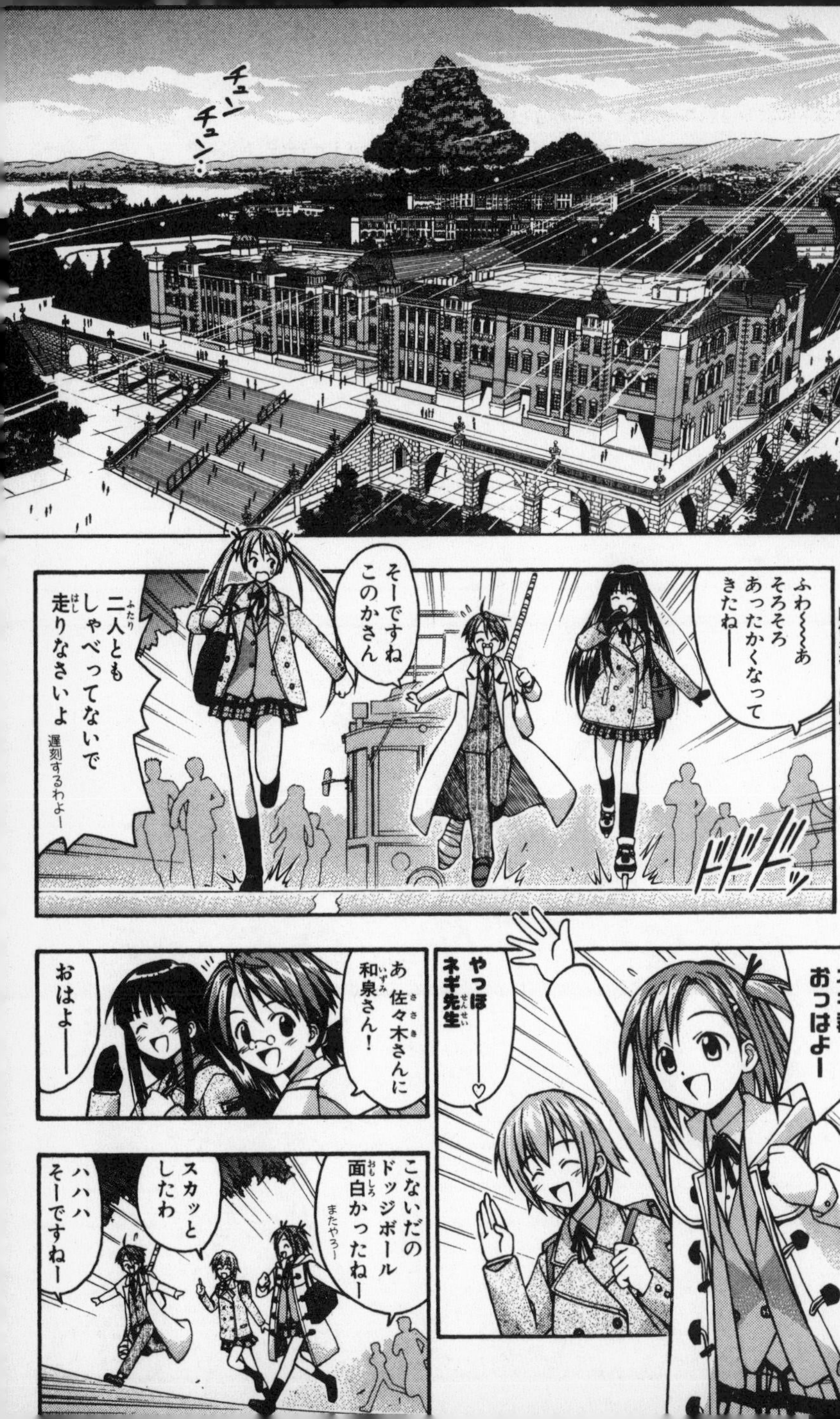
チュンチュン…
ふわ〜〜あ そろそろあったかくなってきたね——
ドドドッ
そーですね このかさん
二人とも しゃべってないで 走りなさいよ
遅刻するわよー
ネギ君 おっはよー
やっほー ネギ先生♡
あ 佐々木さんに 和泉さん!
おはよー——
こないだの ドッジボール 面白かったねー
またやろー
スカッと したわ
ハハハ そーですねー

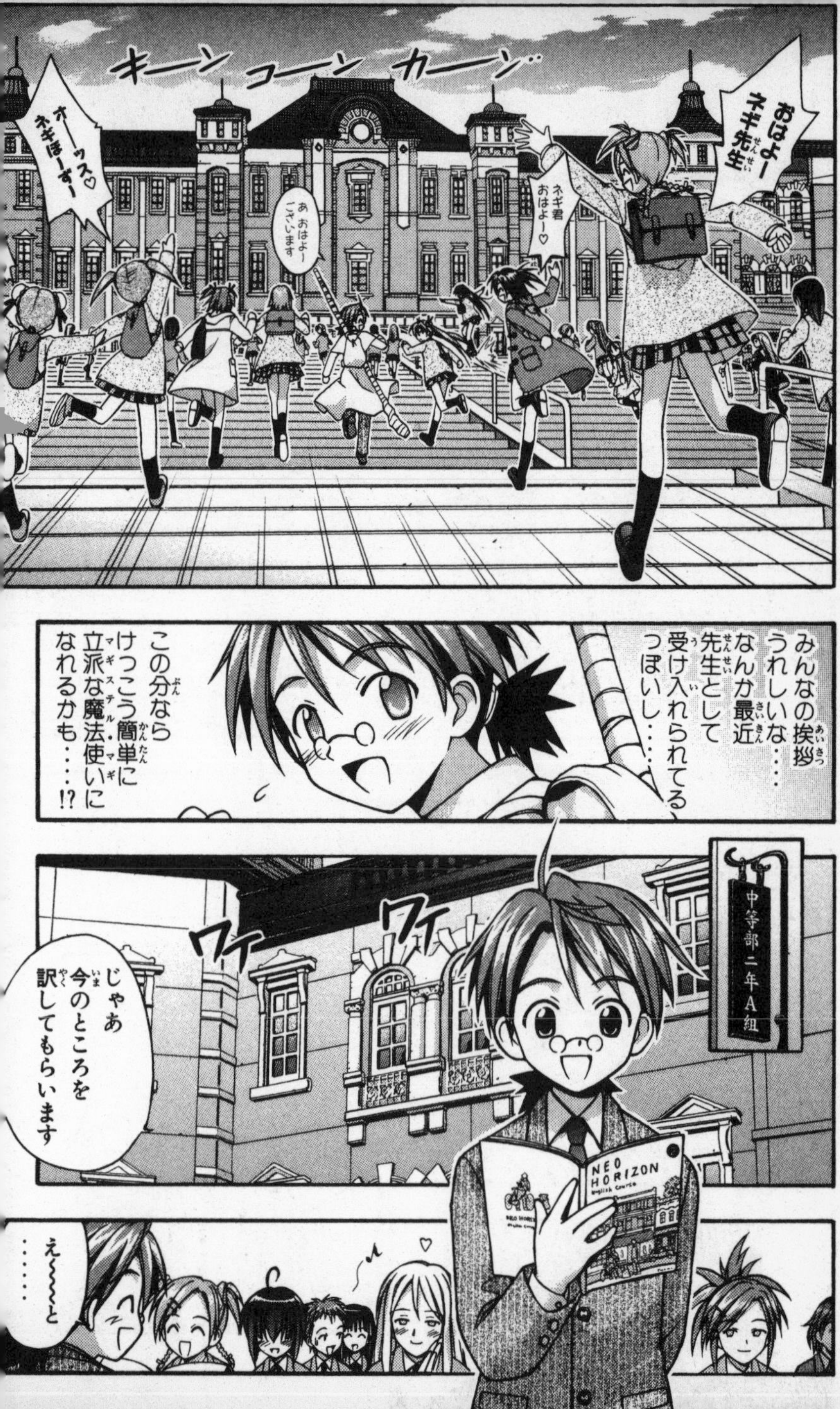
キーン コーン カーン
おはよーネギ先生
ネギ君おはよー♡
あ おはよーございます
オーッスネギぼーずー♡
みんなの挨拶うれしいな……なんか最近先生として受け入れられてるっぽいし……
この分ならけっこう簡単に立派な魔法使いになれるかも……!?
中等部二年A組
ワイ ワイ
NEO HORIZON English Course
じゃあ今のところを訳してもらいます
え〜〜〜と……

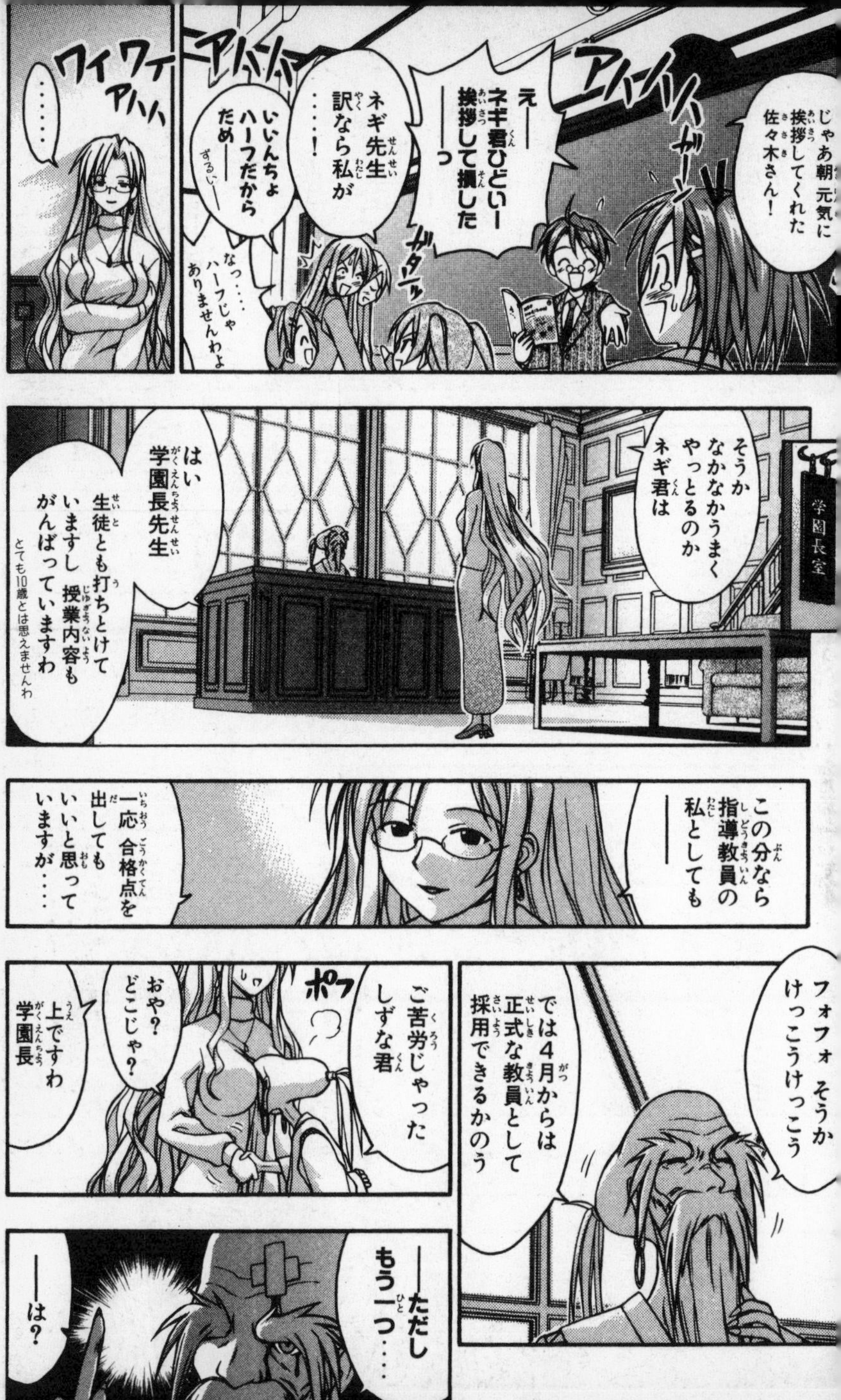

じゃあ朝元気に挨拶してくれた佐々木さん！
ガーン
アハハハ
え――ネギ君ひどいー挨拶して損した――っ
ガタッ
ネギ先生訳なら私が……！
いいんちょハーフだからため――
ずるい――
なっ……ハーフじゃありませんわよ
アハハハ
ワイワイ
アハハ
……
そうかなかなかうまくやっとるのかネギ君は
学園長室
はい学園長先生 生徒とも打ちとけていますし 授業内容もがんばっていますわ
とても10歳とは思えませんわ
この分なら指導教員の私としても――
一応合格点を出してもいいと思っていますが….
フォフォ そうかけっこうけっこう
では4月からは正式な教員として採用できるかのう
ご苦労じゃったしずな君
ポフ
おや？どこじゃ？
上ですわ学園長
――ただしもう一つ….
――は？

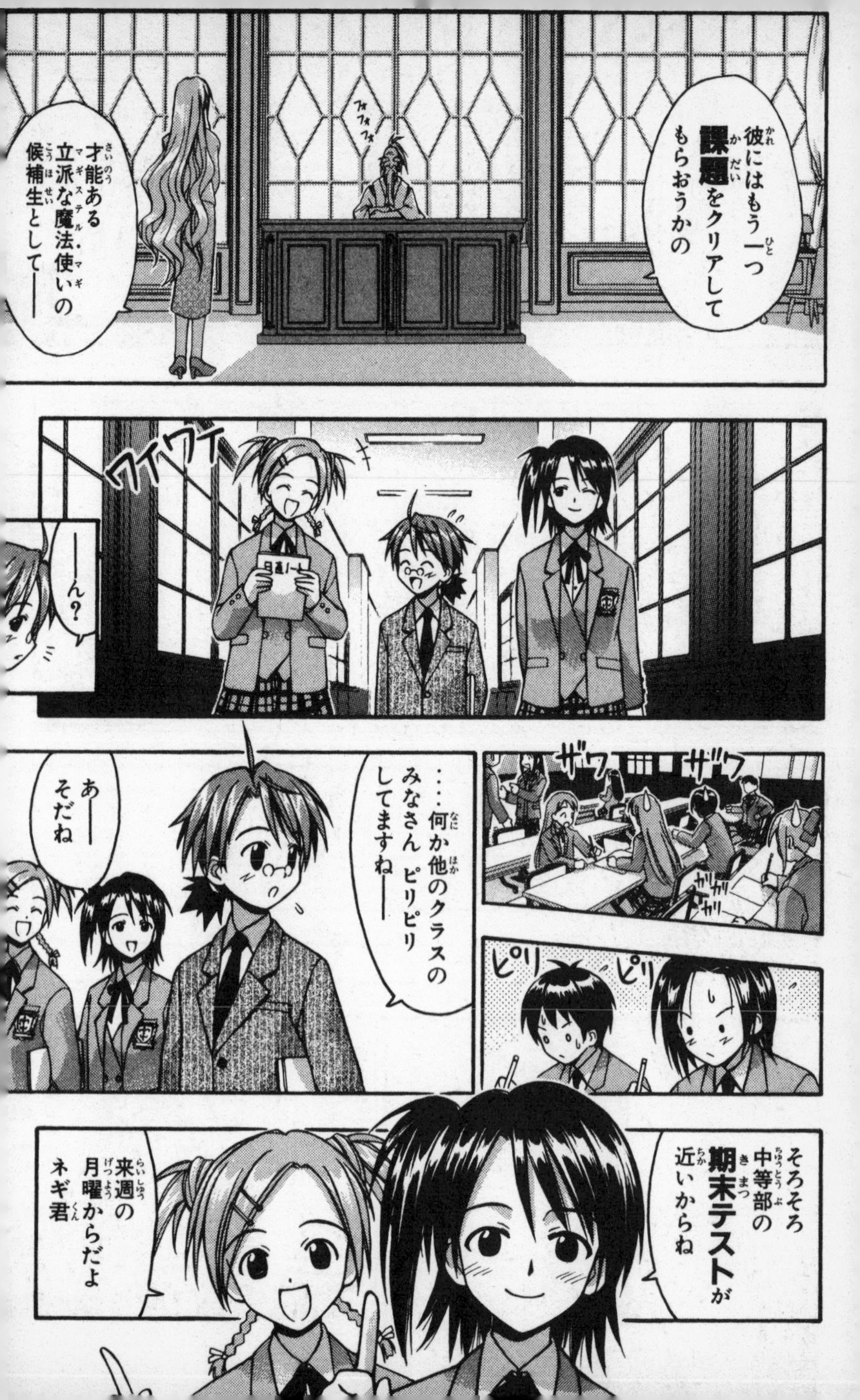
彼にはもう一つ課題をクリアしてもらおうかの
フォフォフォ
才能ある立派な魔法使いの候補生として——
ワイワイ
——ん?
ザワ
ザワ
ガリガリ
ガリ
ピリ
ピリ
…何か他のクラスのみなさんピリピリしてますねー
あ——そだね
そろそろ中等部の期末テストが近いからね
来週の月曜からだよネギ君

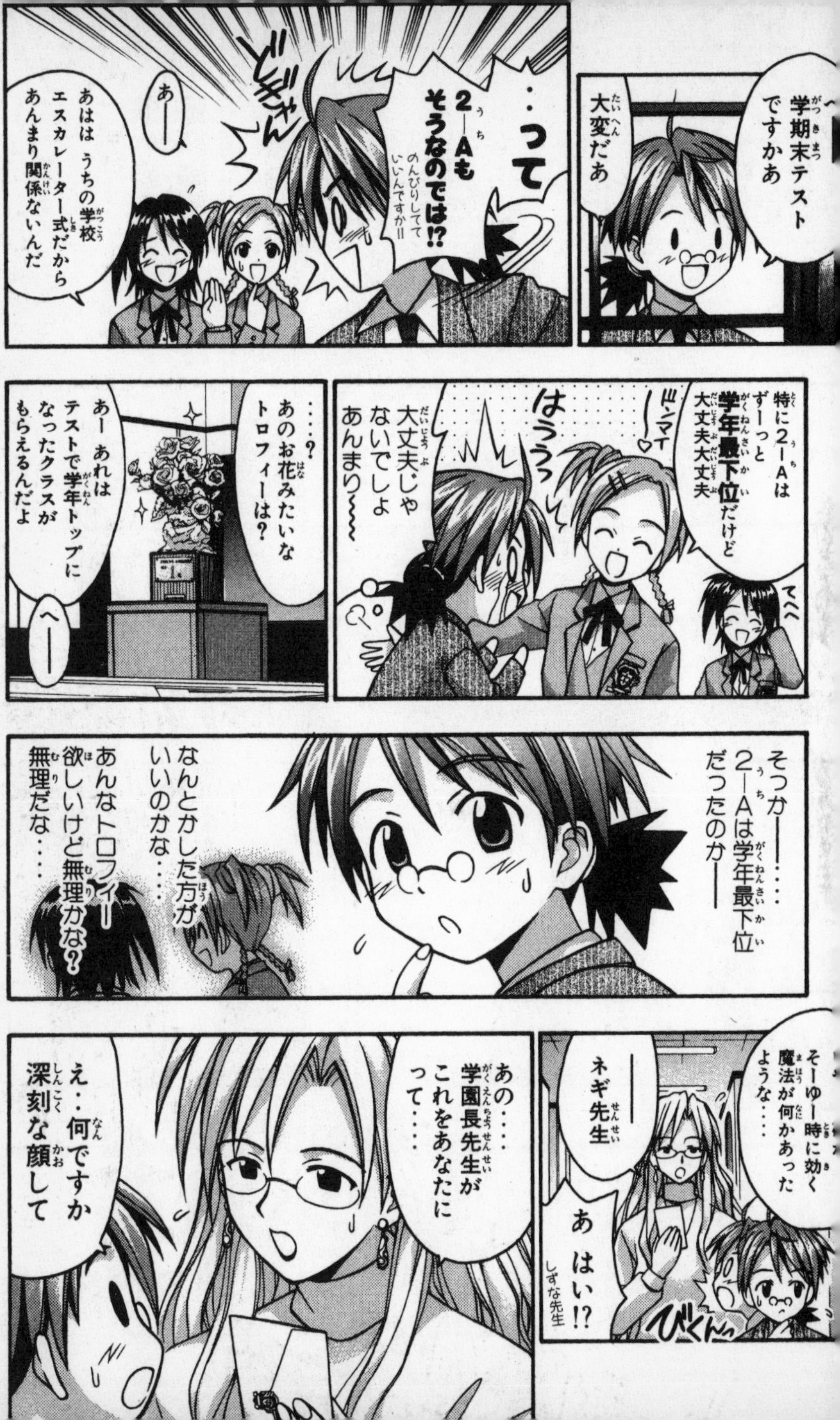
へー 学期末テストですかあ
大変だあ
・・・って 2-Aもそうなのでは!?
のんびりしてていいんですか!!
どぎゃん
あ――
あはは うちの学校エスカレーター式だからあんまり関係ないんだ
特に2-Aはずーっと学年最下位だけど大丈夫大丈夫
ドンマイ～♡
はうぅっ
てへへ
大丈夫じゃないでしょあんまり～～～
・・・? あのお花みたいなトロフィーは?
あー あれはテストで学年トップになったクラスがもらえるんだよ
へ――
そっか――・・・ 2-Aは学年最下位だったのか――
なんとかした方がいいのかな・・・
あんなトロフィー欲しいけど無理かな? 無理だな・・・
そーゆー時に効く魔法が何かあったような・・・
――ネギ先生
あ はい!?
しずな先生
びくんっ
あの・・・学園長先生がこれをあなたにって・・・
え・・何ですか 深刻な顔して

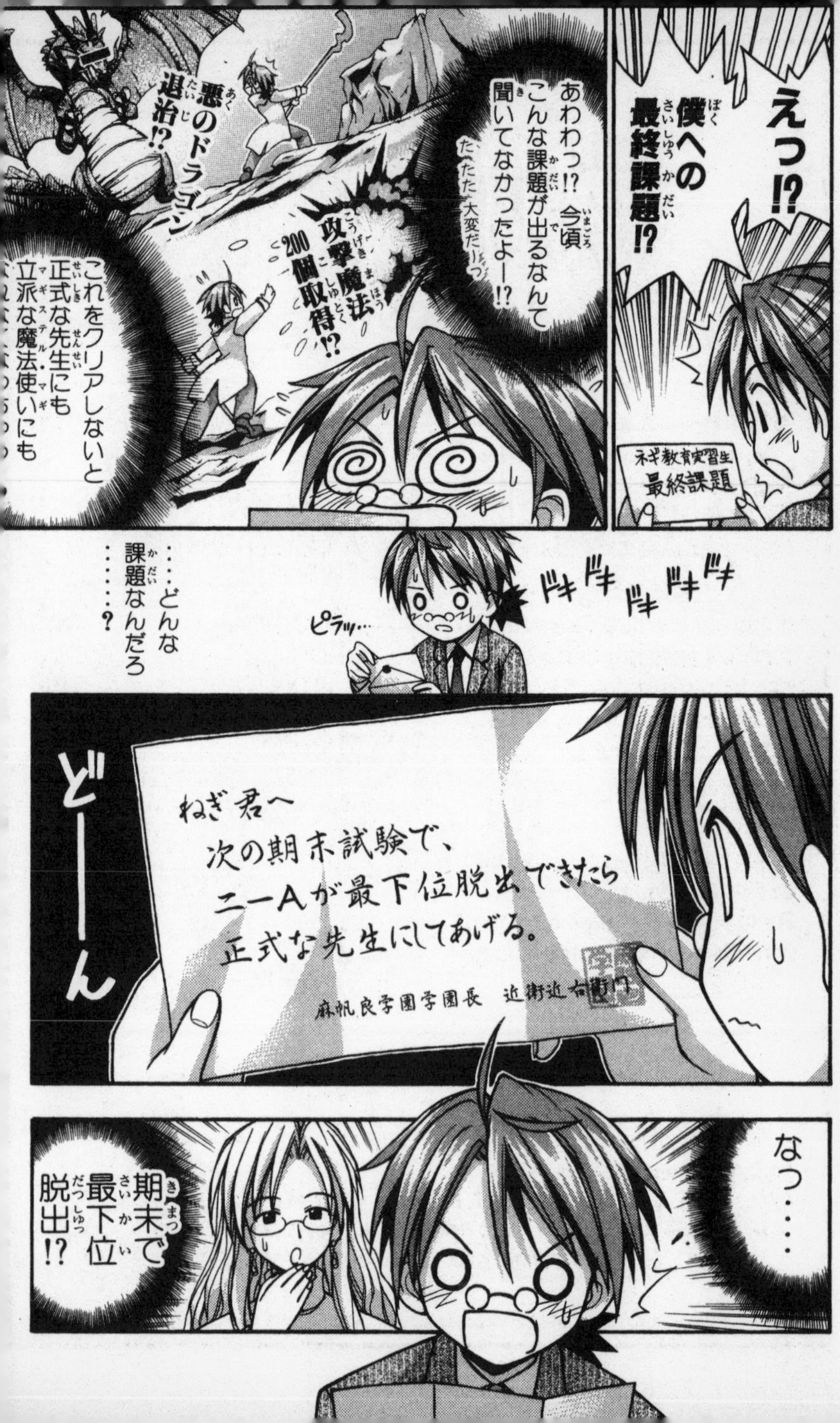
えっ!?
僕への最終課題!?
ネギ教育実習生 最終課題
あわわっ!? 今頃こんな課題が出るなんて聞いてなかったよー!?
たたた大変だーっ
攻撃魔法200個取得!?
悪のドラゴン退治!?
これをクリアしないと正式な先生にも立派な魔法使いにも
ドキドキドキドキドキ
ピラッ…
……どんな課題なんだろ……?
どーーん
ねぎ君へ
次の期末試験で、
ニーAが最下位脱出できたら
正式な先生にしてあげる。
麻帆良学園学園長 近衛近右衛門
なっ……
期末で最下位脱出!?

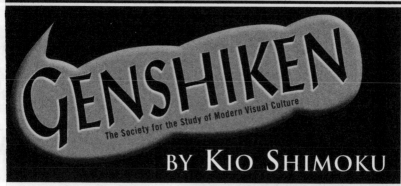
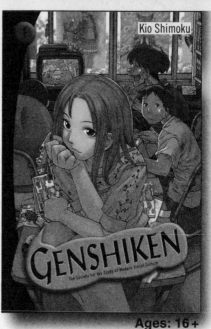

BY MINORU TOYODA

"We have been telling all the people we meet to read this manga!"
—CLAMP, creators of Tsubasa

A fun, romantic comedy, Love Roma is about the simple kind of relationships we all longed for when we were young. It's a story of love at first sight— literally. When Hoshino sees Negishi for the first time, he asks her to be his girlfriend. Shocked, Negishi nevertheless agrees to allow Hoshino to walk her home, while he explains why he is in love with her. Touched, Negishi begins to feel something for this strange young boy from her school.

Ages: 16

Special extras in each volume! Read them all!

BY CLAMP

Watanuki Kimihiro is haunted by visions. When he finds himself irresistibly drawn into a shop owned by Yûko, a mysterious witch, he is offered the chance to rid himself of the spirits that plague him. He accepts, but soon realizes that he's just been tricked into working for the shop to pay off the cost of Yûko's services! But this isn't any ordinary kind of shop . . . In this shop, Yûko grants wishes to those in need. But they must have the strength of will not only to truly understand their need, but to give up something incredibly precious in return.

Ages: 13+

Special extras in each volume! Read them all!

VISIT WWW.DELREYMANGA.COM TO:
• View release date calendars for upcoming volumes
• Sign up for Del Rey's free manga e-newsletter
• Find out the latest about new Del Rey Manga series

TOMARE!

[STOP!]

You're going the wrong way!

Manga is a completely different type of reading experience.

To start at the *beginning*,
go to the *end*!

That's right! Authentic manga is read the traditional Japanese way—from right to left. Exactly the *opposite* of how American books are read. It's easy to follow: Just go to the other end of the book, and read each page—and each panel—from right side to left side, starting at the top right. Now you're experiencing manga as it was meant to be.